'Do you have an Rashad prompt **expectancy on h.... .... .ong face.**

'Not yet,' Polly admitted, matching his honesty.

Polly's brain had flatly rejected marrying him at first. They barely knew each other, and it would be insane. *And yet...* She did want him—in fact she wanted him more than she had ever wanted any man—and she was not an impressionable teenager any longer. In fact, what if she *never* met another man who made her feel the same way Rashad did? That terrible fear held her still and turned her hollow inside, because he made her feel alive and wanton and all sorts of things she had never felt before. And, what was more, she was discovering that she *liked* the way he made her feel.

'Perhaps I can help you to make up your mind,' Rashad murmured with silken softness. 'You will see it as a form of blackmail, but in reality it is the only possible alternative if you do not wish to marry me.'

Polly's head reared up, blue eyes wide and bright. 'Blackmail?' she exclaimed in dismay. 'What are you talking about?'

Brides for the Taking

With this ring...

At their mother's deathbed,
Polly and Ellie Dixon are given a name, a ring—
and news of a half-sister they've never met!

The search for their heritage leads these three sisters
into the paths of three incredible alpha males...and
it's not long before they're walking down the aisle!

Don't miss this fabulous trilogy, starting with...

The Desert King's Blackmailed Bride
February 2017

Continuing with Ellie's story...

The Italian's One-Night Baby
April 2017

And look out for Lucy's story, coming soon!

THE DESERT KING'S BLACKMAILED BRIDE

BY
LYNNE GRAHAM

First Published in Great Britain 2017
By Mills & Boon, an imprint of HarperCollins*Publishers*
1 London Bridge Street, London, SE1 9GF

© 2017 Lynne Graham

ISBN: 978-0-263-92508-1

Our policy is to use papers that are natural, renewable and recyclable
products and made from wood grown in sustainable forests. The logging
and manufacturing processes conform to the legal environmental
regulations of the country of origin.

Printed and bound in Spain
by CPI, Barcelona

Lynne Graham was born in Northern Ireland and has been a keen romance reader since her teens. She is very happily married to an understanding husband, who has learned to cook since she started to write! Her five children keep her on her toes. She has a very large dog who knocks everything over, a very small terrier who barks a lot, and two cats. When time allows, Lynne is a keen gardener.

Visit the Author Profile page at millsandboon.co.uk for more titles.

CHAPTER ONE

KING RASHAD EL-AMIN QUARAISHI studied the photos spread across his office desk. Six feet three inches tall, he dominated most gatherings, having inherited his grandfather's unusual height. Black-haired and possessed of long-lashed dark eyes, he had also inherited the perfect bone structure that had made his mother a renowned beauty in the Middle East. Indeed, his smouldering dark good looks continually inspired admiring comments on social media and he was greatly embarrassed by the fact.

'A cornucopia of feminine perfection,' his chief adviser, Hakim, remarked with fervour. 'A new reign, a new queen and, we trust, a new *dynasty*! Truthfully, fortune will smile now on the fortunes of Dharia.'

Although his royal employer appeared somewhat less enthusiastic, he did not disagree. But then Rashad had always known that it was his duty to marry and father a child. Unfortunately it was not a project that inspired him. After all, he had married before and at a very young age and he knew the pitfalls. Living with a woman with whom he might not have the smallest thing in common would be stressful. Misunderstandings and personality clashes would abound in such a relationship and if the desired conception did not occur in record time the stress would multiply and the unhappiness and dissatisfaction would settle in.

No, marriage held very little appeal for Rashad. The best he could hope for in a future bride was that she would have sufficient sense and practicality to enable them to live their separate lives in relative peace. He did not expect much in the way of support from a wife because his first wife had clung to him like superglue. Nor was he likely to forget his parents' famously stormy marriage. Regardless, he also understood and accepted that the very stability of his country rested on his capacity to act as a respected role model for his people.

Over the past twenty-odd years the population of Dharia had suffered a great deal and change and innovation were no longer welcome because in the desire for peace everybody had rushed to re-embrace the traditional relaxed Dharian outlook and customs. The heady years of his father's extravagance and his blind determination to force Western ways on an extremely traditional country had resulted in a government that became increasingly tyrannical and inevitably clashed with the army, who acted to defend the constitution with the support of the people. The history of that popular revolution was etched in the ruins of the former dictator's palace in the city of Kashan and in the prompt restoration of the monarchy.

Tragically, a car bomb had killed off almost all of

Rashad's family. In the aftermath his uncle had hidden him in the desert to keep him safe. He had only been six years old, a frightened little boy more attached to his English nanny than to the distant parents he rarely saw and in the turmoil following the bomb and the instigation of martial law even his nanny had vanished. The palace had been looted, their loyal staff dispersed and life as Rashad had come to know it had changed out of all recognition.

'Your Majesty, may I make a suggestion?' Hakim asked.

Rashad thought for an instant that his adviser was going to suggest that he flung all the photos of potentially suitable brides into a lucky dip and chose blind. It would be a random form of selection and very disrespectful of the candidates, he acknowledged wryly, but he was cynically convinced that his chances of a happy union would be just as good with that method as with any other. Marriage, after all, was a very risky game of chance.

His wide sensual mouth compressed. 'Please...' he urged.

Hakim smiled and withdrew the file he carried below his arm to open it and extend it to show off a highly detailed picture of an item of jewellery. 'I have taken the liberty of asking the royal jeweller if he could reproduce the Hope of Dharia...'

Rashad stared at him in astonishment. 'But it is lost. How can it be reproduced?'

'What harm would there be in having a replacement ring created? It is a powerful symbol of the monarchy. It was the family's most important heirloom but after this long there is very little likelihood that the original ring will ever be found,' Hakim pointed out seriously. 'I feel that this is the optimum time to do this. Our people feel safer when old traditions are upheld—'

'Our people would prefer a fairy tale to the reality that my late father was a rotten ruler, who put together a corrupt and power-hungry government,' Rashad interposed with the bluntness that was his trademark and which never failed to horrify the more diplomatic Hakim.

While consternation at such frankness froze the older man's bearded face, Rashad walked over to the window, which overlooked the gardens being industriously watered by the palace's army of staff.

He was thinking about the ring superstitiously nicknamed the Hope of Dharia by the Dharian people. The ring had been a gorgeous fire opal of fiery hue, always worn by the King at ceremonial events. Set in gold and inscribed with holy words, the ring had acquired an almost mystical aura after being brought into the family by his saintly great-grandmother, whose devotion to charitable enterprises had ensured that she was adored throughout the kingdom. In other countries a king might wear a crown or wield a sceptre but in Dharia the monarchy's strength and authority had rested historically and emotionally in that ancient ring. It had vanished after the palace had been looted and, in spite of intensive searches, no indication of the opal's whereabouts had ever been established. No, the ring was gone for good and Rashad could see Hakim's point: a well-designed replacement would undeniably be better than nothing.

'Order the ring,' he instructed ruefully.

A fake ring for a fake king, he reflected with innate cynicism. He could never shake off the knowledge that he had not been born to sit on the throne of Dharia. The youngest of three sons, he had been an afterthought until his brothers died along with his parents. He had been left at home that day because he was an excessively energetic and noisy little boy and that reality had saved his life. Rashad's massive popularity with the public still shook him even while it persuaded him to bend his own ideals to become the man his country needed him to be.

Once he had wanted to fall in love and then he had got married. Love had been glorious for all of five minutes and then it had died slowly and painfully. No, he wasn't in the market for that experience again. Yet he had also once believed that lust was wrong until he fell in lust many times over while he was finishing his education at a British university. Whatever, he was still grateful to have enjoyed that fleeting period of sexual freedom before he had to return home to take up his duties. And unfortunately home signified the rigid court protocols that ensured that Rashad was forced to live in a little gilded soap bubble of perceived perfection as a figurehead that inspired the most ridiculous awe. Yes, his people would enjoy the restoration of the ring and all the hoopla of dreams and expectations that went with it…but he would not.

* * *

Polly glanced at her sister, Ellie, and managed a strained smile as a middle-aged blonde woman approached them after their mother's short funeral, which had taken place in an almost empty church.

Both young women had found the ritual a sad and frustrating event. Ellie, who was two years younger than Polly, had no memory of their mother while Polly had vague memories of an occasional perfumed smiling presence while she was still very young. Their grandmother had raised the two girls and the older woman had passed away only a few months earlier. For more than ten years the Dixon sisters had not even known if their mother was still alive. That was why it had been a considerable shock to be contacted out of the blue by a complete stranger to be told of Annabel Dixon's passing.

That stranger, a volunteer at the hospice where their mother had died, Vanessa James, was only marginally more comfortable with the situation than they were, having frankly admitted on the phone that she had tried hard to persuade their long-lost parent to contact her daughters and speak to them *before* her death. At the same time she acknowledged that Annabel had struggled to make herself understood in the later stages of her illness and such a meeting could have been frustrating and upsetting for all of them.

'I've booked us a table at the hotel for lunch,' Vanessa James announced with a determined smile as she shook hands firmly with both young women.

'I am so sorry that we are meeting in such unhappy circumstances.'

Polly had never felt less like eating and she made an awkward attempt to admit that.

'It was your mother's last wish and she set aside the money to cover the meal,' the older woman told her gently. 'It's her treat, not mine.'

Polly's pale skin flushed red with embarrassment, her white-blonde hair acting as a foil to accentuate her discomfiture. 'I didn't mean to be ungracious—'

'Well, even if you didn't you would have every excuse to feel uneasy about this situation,' Vanessa remarked wryly. 'Let me tell you a little about your mother's last years.'

And the sisters listened while the older woman told them about the terminal illness that had begun to deprive their mother of independent life and mobility while she was still only in her forties. She had lived in a nursing home and had died in the hospice where Vanessa had got to know her well.

'That's so very sad,' Ellie lamented, flicking her red hair back off her troubled brow, her green eyes full of compassion. 'We could have done so much to help her...if only we had known—'

'But Annabel didn't *want* you to know. She was aware that you had already spent years nursing your grandmother through her decline and she was determined not to come into your life and become another burden and responsibility. She was very independent.'

The three women sat down at the table in a quiet

corner of the restaurant and rather blankly studied the menus presented to them.

'I understand you're studying to be a doctor,' Vanessa said to Ellie. 'Annabel was so proud when she heard about that.'

'How did she find out?' Ellie pressed. 'It has been years since she last contacted our grandmother.'

'One of your mother's cousins was a nurse and recognised Annabel a couple of years ago when she was hospitalised. She brought her up to date with family developments. Annabel also made her promise not to approach you.'

'But why? We would have understood how she felt!' Ellie burst out in frustration.

'She didn't want you to see her like that or to remember her that way. Having always been a rather beautiful woman she was a little vain about her looks,' Vanessa explained gently.

Polly's mind was wandering. Thinking of her sibling's studies, she was very conscious that she had never achieved anything of note in the academic stakes and had done nothing to inspire a mother with pride. But then one way or another, life had always got in the way of her hopes and dreams. She had stayed home to take care of their ailing grandmother while Ellie had gone off to university to study medicine and she was proud that she had not been selfish. After all, her kid sister had always been very clever and she had a true vocation to help others. She knew just how guilty Ellie had felt about leaving her to cope alone with their grandmother but, really, what would have been the point of *both* of them losing out on their education? At school, Polly had been an average student, only plodding along while Ellie streaked ahead.

'I did so hope that you were in touch with your younger sister and that you would bring her with you today,' Vanessa James remarked, startling both women into looking across the table at her with wide eyes.

'What younger sister?' Polly exclaimed with wide blue eyes the colour of gentian violets.

Vanessa surveyed them in dismay before telling them about how their sibling had gone into foster care when Annabel could no longer look after her. She was four years younger than Polly and apparently their grandmother had refused to take her in.

'We had no idea we had another sister,' Ellie admitted heavily. 'We really know nothing about our mother's life…well, only what Gran told us and that wasn't much and none of it was flattering. She certainly never mentioned that there were *three* of us!'

'When Annabel was young she led quite an exciting life,' Vanessa volunteered ruefully. 'She was a highly qualified nanny and she travelled a great deal and lived abroad for long periods. She worked for some very wealthy families and earned an excellent salary, often with lots of perks thrown in. But obviously when she had children of her own she couldn't take them to work with her, which is why you ended up in your grandmother's care. But when you were both still quite young, Annabel *did* return to London, where she tried to set up a childcare facility. She poured all her savings into it. She was planning to bring the two of you home to live with her. But, sadly, it all went wrong. The business failed, the relationship she was in fell apart and she discovered that she was pregnant again.'

'And she gave birth to another girl? What's our sister called? Why are we only hearing about her now?' Polly gasped, only a little touched by the news that the mother she had never known had actually once planned to raise her own children. Indeed that struck her as a very remote possibility because it had seemed to her as a child that she had a mother who ran away from responsibility. Even worse, her outlook was coloured by the reality that she and Ellie had been brought up by a woman who bitterly resented the responsibility of having to raise her granddaughters at a time in her life when she had expected to take life at an easier pace.

Their sister's name was Penelope Dixon and Vanessa had no further information to offer. 'I did approach social services but as I'm not a blood relative I wasn't in a position to push. One of you would have to make enquiries. Penelope could have been adopted but I understand that if that proves to be the case you could leave a letter on file for her should she ever enquire about her birth family.'

Their meals were brought to the table. Vanessa withdrew three envelopes from her bag. 'Your mother has left each of you a ring and I must ask you to take charge of your youngest sister's ring for her—'

'A...*ring*?' Polly repeated in a renewed daze of astonishment.

'And with each a name. I assume, your fathers''

names…although Annabel was very evasive on that score,' the older woman revealed uncomfortably. 'I should warn you now that I'm not sure that Annabel actually *knew* who your fathers were beyond any shadow of doubt.'

Polly paled. 'Oh…' she said, in a voice that spoke volumes.

'She wasn't specific but I did receive the impression that when she was living the high life, looking after her rich employers' children, she may…er…possibly have been a little free with her favours,' the other woman advanced in a very quiet voice of apology.

'Sorry…? You mean…?' Polly began uncertainly.

'She slept around,' Ellie translated bluntly with a grimace. 'Well, thank you for being honest enough to tell us that before we get excited about those names. But with that particular disease, I know that Annabel may have had problems accessing her memories and she may have become confused when she tried to focus on the past.'

The instant Vanessa handed Polly her envelope, Polly ripped it open, patience never having been one of her virtues. A heavy and ornate gold ring with a large stone fell out and she threaded it on her finger but it was far too large. It was, she finally registered, a man's ring, not a woman's. She peered down at the stone, which flickered with changeable hues of red, orange and yellow.

'It's a fire opal, very unusual but not, I understand, particularly valuable,' Vanessa proffered. 'It's also an antique and foreign made.'

'Right...' Polly muttered blankly, returning to extract the small sheet of paper enclosed in the envelope and frown down at it.

Zahir Basara... Dharia.

'My...my father may be of Arabic descent?' Polly murmured in sheer wonderment, because, in the most obvious terms, she looked as though she had not a drop of more exotic climes in her veins and indeed had been asked several times if she was from Scandinavia. 'I have heard of Dharia—'

'Your mother was a nanny in the royal household there...right up until the royal family died,' Vanessa volunteered.

And Polly immediately wondered if there was a connection to her birth name, which had been Zariyah and which was on her passport. Her grandmother had always called her Polly, having disliked her foreign name.

'I've got an emerald!' Ellie announced as if she had just opened a Christmas cracker, her whole demeanour suggesting that she had no intention of taking either ring or name too seriously.

'And the name?' Polly pressed with rampant curiosity, hoping that it would be the same as her own putative father's because at least that would suggest that the relationship had been more than a passing fling.

'Possibly a name of Italian extraction. I'll keep it to myself for now though.' Ellie dug the envelope into her bag with an air of finality but she was unusually pale. At Vanessa's instigation she also took charge of the envelope intended for their sister, Penelope. 'Maybe our mother *collected* engagement rings—'

'My ring is a man's,' Polly argued.

'Yes, but there could have been an intention to make it smaller,' Ellie pointed out calmly. 'I wish she'd left us a letter telling us about herself. Would it be possible for us to visit the hospice, Vanessa? I'd very much like to see where Annabel spent her last days and speak to the staff.'

And while the two other women became involved in an intense discussion about the hospice, the disease that had taken Annabel's life and the research that Vanessa's charity raised funds to support, Polly drifted off inside her head, something that she did frequently when her imagination was caught.

Just then she was thinking about the fire opal and wondering if it had been a symbol of love. Ellie was of a more practical bent but Polly liked to think she had, at least, been born to parents who had been in love at the time of her conception. Love between two people of different cultures would have been testing, she reflected, and perhaps those differences had become too great to surmount. Even so, that name in the envelope had sparked a mad craving inside her for facts about the country of Dharia.

Did she have Dharian blood running in her veins? Was it even possible that her father could still be alive? And that he might want to get to know her?

Polly had a deep longing to have a real parent. Her mother had virtually abandoned them and while her grandmother had not mistreated Polly and Ellie she certainly hadn't loved them. Polly thought it would be absolutely wonderful to have a parent who actually cared for her as an individual, someone who would celebrate her strengths and overlook and forgive her weaknesses.

'You're not charging off to some foreign country to make enquiries,' Ellie said drily, having perused her sister's ring and the name on the piece of paper and surmised exactly where her sister's fertile imagination was taking her. 'It would be insane.'

And Polly had never ever done anything insane, *never ever…*

No, she had not defied her grandmother when she had won a place at art college and the older woman told her that she couldn't take it up because it was her duty to go out and get a paying job to help support the household. While suitably employed in a lowly but enjoyable position for a charitable enterprise, Polly had contented herself with the outlet of evening art classes shared with other enthusiastic amateurs.

Polly had never been particularly adventurous, so she knew then with a sinking heart that it was very unlikely that she would ever get to visit Dharia. She didn't have the money for air fares or holidays, she wouldn't have the cash to chase up some father armed only with what could well prove to be as common a name in Dharia as John Smith. No, it was a dream and Polly knew dreams didn't come true unless you were willing to take risks and seize the moment…

Polly was aware of being stared at in the passport queue at the airport outside Kashan. It was the blonde hair, she thought ruefully, aware as she looked around her with eager curiosity that her pale colouring seemed rare in Dharia.

She was here in her father's country, she was finally *here* and she still couldn't believe it! Ellie had made it possible, taking on part-time work in spite of her heavy study schedule and insisting that she could get by for one term at least without her sister's financial help. Even so, it had still taken Polly months of saving to acquire sufficient funds for such a trip. Her budget was tiny and she would be staying in a little bed-and-breakfast establishment near the bazaar in Kashan. As long as it was clean, she would be happy, and if it wasn't clean she would clean it for herself.

Encountering another prolonged stare from a dark-eyed male, Polly flushed and wished she had braided her hair. When she went out and about tomorrow, she promised herself, she would put on a sunhat to cover her head. After all, Dharia wasn't a tourist-orientated country and was kind of old-fashioned. She definitely wouldn't be wearing the shorts and vest top she had packed, for while there were no veiled women around those she had seen wore unrevealing clothes with longer hemlines than were fashionable.

Finally she reached the head of the queue and handed over her passport. That seemed to be the signal for another couple of men to approach the booth and a split second later one addressed her. 'Will you come this way, please?'

To her bewilderment she was accompanied to the baggage hall to reclaim her luggage and then her case and her bag were taken from her and she was shown into a bare little room containing several chairs and a table. Her case and bag were then searched in her presence while she wondered why her passport had not been returned. What were they looking for in her luggage? Drugs? A cold shiver of fear ran through Polly even though she had nothing stronger than headache tablets in her possession. She had heard horror stories about people being strip-searched and when a female airport security guard entered, her slight frame stiffened into defensive mode. There was an exclamation as one of the men removed the fire-opal ring from her handbag and held it high where it caught the bare light bulb above and sent a cascade of colour flickering across the drab grey walls. The trio burst out into excited speech in their own language and seconds later the two men slammed out, taking the ring with them. The female officer stared fixedly at her and Polly breathed in slow and deep in an effort to calm herself.

'You are very beautiful,' the woman said, startling her.

A sickly smile pulled at Polly's tense mouth because she didn't know how to respond to that remark in such trying circumstances. 'Thank you,' she said finally, reluctant to be rude.

The minutes ticked by like a hammer slowly beating down on her nerves. Her companion answered her phone. Polly linked her hands together on her lap and wondered why they had all seemed so excited about the ring. Was it a stolen ring? Was that possible? But what sort of ring could possibly attract such immediate recognition when according to Vanessa it was not worth much money?

Another woman entered with a tray of aromatic tea. Polly's companion stood up and offered her a cup. It smelled of mint and her hand shook as she lifted the glass up to her tense mouth to sip the fragrant brew.

'Why am I being kept here?' she dared to ask then.

'We are waiting for instructions,' she was told.

'And the ring?'

Both women exchanged looks and neither made an answer. Polly was angry that her ring had been taken from her because she treasured it as her sole remaining link with the mother she had never known. When would her ring be returned to her? At the same time she was trying to take encouragement from the fact that she had not been strip-searched and that tea had been brought. It was a misunderstanding. What else could it be? She had done nothing wrong. But had her mother done something wrong years back in the past?

How was she supposed to answer that question? In many ways, her mother remained a complete mystery to her eldest daughter. Annabel had travelled the world in luxury to look after other people's children while abandoning her own to the tender mercies of her own mother, who had been a most reluctant guardian. She had, however, dutifully provided financial support for Polly's grandmother and her daughters for many years. When that support came to a sudden unannounced halt, Polly had learned a lot about how to live on a very tight budget.

The sisters had inherited nothing from their grandmother. She had left the contents of her house, all that she possessed, to her son, Polly's uncle, complaining bitterly that her daughter had ruined her retirement by forcing her to raise her illegitimate children. It was a label Polly had always hated, a word the younger generation rarely used because it wasn't fair to tag a child with something that they had played no active part in creating. But it was a word that had meant a great deal to her staunchly conservative and judgemental grandmother, who had been ashamed that her only grandchildren had been born out of wedlock.

While Polly agonised on the other side of Kashan, Hakim, who rarely moved fast, was positively racing down the main corridor of the palace in his haste to reach his King. His rounded face was beaming and flushed, his little goatee beard quivering. Rashad was in his office, working diligently as usual.

'The ring!' Hakim carolled out of breath, holding it high in the air like a trophy before hurrying over to lay it down reverently on the top of the desk. 'It is found.'

Rashad frowned and sprang upright, carrying the ring in one lean brown hand to scrutinise it in the sunlight pouring through the window. 'How was it found? Where was it?'

Hakim explained about the British woman being held at the airport.

Rashad's dark as jet eyes hardened. 'Why is she not in prison?'

'This must be carefully handled,' Hakim urged. 'We would not want to cause a diplomatic incident—'

'A thief is a thief and must be held accountable,' his King assured him without hesitation.

'The woman is young. She could not have been the thief. She has not been questioned yet. The airport police wished to first ascertain with the palace that the ring was the genuine article. There is great excitement in Kashan. Crowds are already forming at the airport.'

Rashad frowned. 'Why? How could word of this discovery already have spread?'

'The airport grapevine was most thoroughly aired on social media,' his adviser told him wryly. 'There will be no keeping a lid on this story—'

'Crowds?' Rashad prompted in bewilderment.

'The woman concerned is not being viewed as a thief but as the woman who has brought the Hope of Dharia home to our King. When I add that she is young and apparently beautiful...well, if you think about how your great-grandmother came to your great-grandfather and brought the Hope with her, you can see why our people are thrilled.'

But Rashad was still frowning. A large gathering of thrilled people could translate all too easily into civil unrest. He could barely comprehend his aide's fervent attitude to what was, after all, only a legend, polished up by the next generation to enhance and romanticise the monarchy and their alliances. 'But that was a century ago in another age and it was a set-up to achieve exactly what it did achieve...a marriage that suited both countries at the time.'

'It is dangerous to have crowds congregating at the airport. I would humbly suggest that you have the woman brought here to be questioned. It will keep the whole matter under wraps without causing undue comment.'

Rashad was thinking with regret of the old dungeons in the palace basement. He didn't think Hakim wanted the British woman put in the basement. He reminded himself that the ring had come home and that the woman was apparently too young to have been responsible for its disappearance. 'Very well. I suppose it will be interesting to hear her story.'

'It is a complete miracle that the Hope of Dharia has been returned to us,' Hakim declared fervently. 'And a wonderful portent of good events yet to come.'

Sadly, there was nothing miraculous about Polly's feelings as she was herded out of the airport by what looked suspiciously like a rear entrance as they emerged into a loading bay surrounded by crates. She was clammy with fright in spite of the presence of the female security guard but her rarely roused temper was also beginning to rise. She was a law-abiding, well-behaved traveller. How dared they force her to endure such treatment?

'You are going to the palace!' the woman told her in a voice that suggested that she expected Polly to turn cartwheels of joy at the news. 'It is a great honour. They have even sent a car and a military escort for you.'

Polly climbed into the rear passenger seat of a shiny white four-wheel drive. She linked her hands tightly together on her lap. Over twenty years ago her mother had been employed at the palace and now she was re-

ceiving an unexpected opportunity to see the place,
she told herself, striving to take a more positive view
of her circumstances. If she got the chance to ask questions she might even meet someone who *remembered*
her mother working at the palace. Of course, that could
only lead to a very awkward exchange, she acknowledged reluctantly. Had her mother slept around? Had
she been involved with more than one man? And how
on earth was she supposed to find *that* out without
seriously embarrassing herself and other people? For
the first time, Ellie's forecast that seeking out her father would be like looking for a needle in a haystack
returned to haunt Polly and she resolved to keep her
personal business strictly private until she was confident of her reception.

A military truck crammed with armed soldiers led
the way out of the airport and Polly's nervous tension increased as a big crowd of people surrounded
the convoy when it slowed down to leave the complex. Faces pressed against the blacked-out windows,
hands thumped noisily on the outside of the car and
there was a great deal of shouting. Something akin to
panic briefly gripped Polly's slender frame and perspiration beaded her brow. She shut her eyes tightly
and prayed while the car pulled away slowly and then
mercifully speeded up.

The car drove down a modern thoroughfare lined
with tall buildings and lots of people standing around,
apparently there to stare at the car she was travelling in.
There were masses of people everywhere and a surprising suggestion of a general holiday mood, she thought

in surprise as people waved in a seemingly friendly and enthusiastic fashion as the convoy passed by.

They left the city of Kashan and the crowds behind to travel into a desert landscape empty of human habitation. Flat plains of sand ornamented with rocky outcrops stretched in every direction and in the distance she could see giant dunes. There was something about that view stretched taut below a bright blue sky and the burning sun that made her want to paint in a medium different from her usual dreamy pastels. Distracted, Polly blinked as the car purred through giant gates into a startlingly green and lush spread of gardens dotted with trees and shrubs and colourful flowers.

Ahead loomed a very old building that was topped by a variety of large and small domes and which spread in all directions in a haphazard design.

The door beside her opened and Polly eased back out into the simmering heat, her lightweight trousers and tee shirt instantly sticking to her dampening skin. It was incredibly hot. A single female figure stood beneath the huge entrance portico and as Polly approached she bowed very low and motioned a hand in silent request that she follow her.

Clearly, she wasn't under arrest, Polly reflected with intense relief, her curiosity flying as high as her imagination as she entered the palace, but her anger at the fearful uncertainty she had endured remained. They padded down a very long and very broad hallway lined with ornately carved stone columns. Her sandals squeaked as she trekked after the woman into the depths of the great sprawling building. They traversed a shallow staircase and crossed a scantily furnished large room towards French windows that stood wide open.

Oh, dear, Polly thought in dismay, back to the horribly hot outdoors and the unforgiving burn of the midday sun.

She walked hesitantly out into a walled courtyard and her companion departed. Water gushed down into a fountain overhung by palm trees. The tiles on the ground formed an elaborate pattern faded by time. Polly moved straight into the shade by the fountain, desperate for the cooler air.

A young woman in a long fashionable dress appeared and dealt her a small tight smile, sweeping a hand helpfully at the table and two chairs sited in full sun. Suppressing a groan, Polly moved closer just as quick steps sounded from behind her. The young woman immediately dropped down onto her knees and bowed her head. Polly blinked in astonishment and slowly turned round.

A very tall man with blue-black hair and eyes as keen as a hawk's surveyed her. The hunting analogy was apt, she conceded, because she felt cornered and intimidated. He emanated authority and danger like a force field. He was also, very probably, the best-looking man she had ever seen outside a modelling advert and she knew who he was, thanks to her Internet research on the country of Dharia. He was the recently crowned ruler of Dharia, King Rashad. She swallowed hard, thoroughly disconcerted and shaken that she was being granted a personal meeting with such an important individual.

Her mouth had run dry and she parted her lips, struggling to think of something to say but he got there before her.

'I am Rashad, Miss Dixon. I would like to hear how the ring came into your possession.'

I am Rashad, she thought, as if there were only one Rashad in the whole world. And looking at him, she thought there might well only be one man quite like him in the Arab world, a remarkable man who had single-handedly united his country's different factions to bring about peace and who was universally and quite slavishly adored for that commendable achievement.

'The truth is…there's not much I *can* explain,' Polly admitted shakily, for the instant she connected with those striking dark brown eyes as luminescent as liquid gold in the sunlight she could barely breathe, never mind think and vocalise.

CHAPTER TWO

'PLEASE SIT DOWN,' Rashad urged in a harshened undertone because he was finding it a challenge to maintain
his normal self-discipline.

An instantaneous lust to possess was flaming
through his lean, powerful frame and the uniqueness
of that experience in a woman's radius thoroughly unsettled him. But then the woman in front of him was,
admittedly, quite exceptional. Polly Dixon was blin-
dingly beautiful with hair of that silvery white-blonde
shade that so rarely survived childhood. Her wealth
of hair fell in a loose tangle of waves halfway to her
waist. Her skin was equally fair, moulded over a heart-
shaped face brought alive by delft blue eyes and a sultry full pink mouth. She wasn't very tall. In fact she
was rather tiny in stature, Rashad acknowledged abstractedly, doubting that she would reach any higher
than his chest, but the ripe curves of her figure at breast
and hip were defiantly female and mature.

Polly gazed back at him, dry-mouthed with nervous tension. He had amazing cheekbones, a perfect
narrow-bridged nose and a full wide sensual mouth en-

hanced by the dark shadow of stubble already visible on his bronzed skin. With difficulty she recollected her thoughts and spoke up. 'I gather all this fuss is about the ring that I had in my bag,' she assumed. 'I'm afraid I know very little about it. It only recently came into my possession after my mother died and I think that she had had it for a long time—'

Rashad's sister-in-law, Hayat, brought tea to the table, acting as a discreet chaperone and stepping back out of view.

'What was your mother's name?' Rashad enquired, watching Polly lick a drop of mint tea off her lower lip and imagining that tiny pink tongue flicking against his own flesh with such driving and colourful immediacy that he was glad of the table that concealed the all too masculine swelling at his groin.

Polly was starting to feel incredibly tired as well as desperately thirsty and she sipped constantly at the tea, wishing that it were cold enough to gulp down. 'Annabel Dixon,' she admitted heavily. 'But I don't see what that—'

Rashad had frozen into position. Lush black lashes swooped down to hide his eyes and then skimmed upward again to frame startled gold chips of enquiry, his surprise unconcealed. 'When I was a child I had a nanny called Annabel Dixon,' he revealed flatly. 'Are you saying that that woman was your mother?'

'Yes…but I know very little about her and nothing at all about her time here in Dharia because I was brought up by my grandmother, not by my mother,' Polly told him grudgingly while marvelling at the idea that her mother had looked after Rashad as a little boy. 'Why is the ring so important?'

'It is the ceremonial ring of the Kings of Dharia, a symbol of their right to rule,' Rashad explained. 'It has great emotional significance for my people. The ring went missing over twenty-five years ago when my family died and the dictator Arak staged a coup to take power here. Who is your father?'

Polly stiffened at his question. A headache was forming behind her brow and she was wishing she had access to the medication in her case while also dimly wondering when she could hope to be reunited with her luggage. 'I don't know but if all this happened twenty-five years ago it must've happened around the time I was conceived, so you see I have no further information to offer. I had no idea the ring was a lost treasure, nor do I know how my mother got hold of it or why she kept it. Surely she would've known how important it was?'

'I would've assumed so,' Rashad conceded. 'I was in her care with my brothers from birth to the age of six and during that period your mother must have learned a great deal about my family.'

'What was she like?' Polly was betrayed into asking.

He looked at her in surprise.

'I don't really remember her...at least I have only the vaguest of recollections. Perhaps you don't remember anything about her,' Polly added hastily, her very pale face flushing as she gave him that escape clause.

'She was always smiling, laughing,' Rashad recounted quietly. 'I was fond of her...as were my brothers. She was not blonde, like you...she had red hair—'

Polly nodded stiffly, thinking about her sister's red hair, which Ellie hated. 'Is there anyone else here who would still remember her?' she asked daringly. 'Naturally I'm very curious about her.'

'Few of the staff from that era remain in the household,' Rashad responded with regret, his lean dark face shadowing because so many of the palace staff had died in the coup.

'So what happens to the ring now?' Polly pressed tautly.

'It must remain here in Dharia,' Rashad pointed out in some surprise, as if she should have grasped that reality immediately. 'This is where it belongs.'

Polly lifted her chin, her blue eyes darkening with annoyance even as a mortifying trickle of sweat ran down between her breasts below her loose tee shirt. She might be feeling hot and bothered and impossibly tired but there was nothing wrong with her wits. 'But it is *my* ring and it's the only token I will ever have from my mother.'

Rashad was taken aback by her statement. 'That is most unfortunate but—'

'For me, *not* for you!' Polly interrupted fierily, her anger sparking at his immense assurance and his assumption that she would simply accept the situation.

Rashad was unaccustomed to being interrupted and even less familiar with the challenge of dealing with an angry woman. An ebony brow lifted at a derisive slant. 'You are more fortunate than you appreciate,' he told her levelly. 'You could have been accused of theft simply for having the ring in your possession—'

Polly rammed back her chair and stood up, bracing her hands down on the table to steady herself because that quick impulsive movement had left her a little dizzy. 'Well, go ahead and have me charged with theft!' she urged furiously. 'How *dare* you treat me like a criminal? My journey has been interrupted. I was marched off by security staff in front of an audience at the airport, held against my will in a nasty little room for hours and had the life threatened out of me when a crowd mobbed the car on the way here—'

'You were selected at random at the airport to be searched in a drug-screening scheme we have recently established,' Rashad interposed smooth as glass. 'I regret that you have been inconvenienced and embarrassed and will ensure that what remains of your holiday compensates you for the experience.'

Backing further away from the table and its support, Polly valiantly straightened her back and squared her shoulders to lift her head high. 'I want my mother's ring back!' she declared stridently.

Rashad rose fluidly upright, shamefully entertained by the sheer fury that had erupted in her face, flushing the skin to a delicious shade of pink, darkening her bright blue eyes to violet and compressing her lips into a surprisingly tough line. 'You must know that that is not true. The ring did not belong either to your mother or your family—'

'It was left to me. Therefore it belongs to me.'

Rashad raised a black brow as he strode towards

her and she warily backed away, her legs feeling oddly weak and unusually clumsy.

'The most basic law is that a stolen item may not be considered the legal possession of the person it is given or sold to because the individual who gave or sold it did not have the right of ownership to do so.'

Polly wasn't listening to him. After all, now he was talking like a lawyer and, even in his light grey designer suit, he looked like a fantasy against the colourful backdrop of the courtyard. He didn't look real, indeed none of what had happened to her since she first set foot on the soil of Dharia felt remotely real, so far did those events lie outside her experience. And all of it, *him*, her surroundings and the whole complex problem of the wretched ring, not to mention the heat, which she was finding unbearable, was becoming too much for her.

'I'm not going to discuss it with you because it's *my* ring, not yours!' Polly flung back at him dizzily while she wondered why her fantasy image of him was turning a little fuzzy round the edges and putting him into a soft focus that did very little to blur the hard cast of his lean, darkly handsome features.

'You are being most unreasonable,' Rashad told her without skipping a beat while he stared at her, fascinated by the firebrand personality hidden beneath that beautiful fragile outer shell. 'You are even being—forgive me for saying it—a little childish.'

Perspiration trickling down her forehead, Polly's small hands balled into fists. 'If you weren't who you are I'd thump you for saying that!'

A harried knock sounded on the French windows that led back into the palace and Hayat rose to answer it, bowing backwards out of his presence in the same way the staff had behaved over a century ago. The old ways were not always the *right* ways, Rashad reflected with a sigh. Polly shouting at him and threatening him with a ludicrous assault had had a wonderfully refreshing effect on his mood. Had she any idea how many Dharian laws she had just broken? No, nor would she care were she to be informed because she was angry with him and felt free to express her anger openly and honestly. Rashad had never enjoyed such freedom of expression or action. All he had learned about from the age of six was duty and the always dire consequences of *not* doing one's duty.

Hakim was framed breathless in the doorway, frantically indicating a need to speak to him.

Rashad suppressed his irritation at the interruption. After all, whatever good or bad thing had happened, it was his job to deal with it, regardless of mood and timing. For one final self-indulgent moment, he focused on Polly, marvelling at her pale perfection in the sunlight. 'I don't think you could hit me even if you tried to do so,' he responded silkily. 'I am highly skilled in almost every form of combat.'

'But you talk like a textbook,' Polly mumbled shakily, moving jerkily forward as if she was struggling to walk back to the table.

But she didn't make it. Her small frame crumpled down on the tiles in a heap. Hayat released a small startled scream but Rashad was a lot more practical.

He bent down and scooped Polly up off the ground, astonished by how little her slight body weighed. Hayat went from screaming to wailing an urgent cry for help indoors so that a squad of guards came running in an unnecessary panic that their King was in danger.

Rashad refused to put Polly down when others offered to release him from his burden. Hakim was already calling the palace doctor. 'I will speak to you when we are alone,' he murmured guardedly.

'What is the matter with her? Bad temper!' Hayat remarked to no one in particular in the lift, which was uncomfortably full of people. 'She shouted at the King. I could not believe my eyes or ears.'

Rashad wondered idly whether Hayat had been a playground sneak, who told tales on her peers. She was very snide about other women and always in his vicinity as if she feared he might not notice female flaws without her drawing them to his attention. He knew that as the sister of his late wife she regarded herself as a superior being. She belonged to a leading Dharian family. And every prominent Dharian family had put forward their daughters as potential brides for the King, a dangerous state of affairs that had convinced Rashad that he had to choose a bride from another country to maintain the peace between the various clans all jockeying for social position.

Rashad laid Polly down on a silk-clad bed. She was starting to recover consciousness, her eyelids flickering, little formless sounds emerging from her full pink lips. But even in that condition she contrived to look remarkably like an idealised image of an angel he had once seen in a book.

'Dr Wasem is here,' Hakim said at his elbow, and Rashad stepped back from the bed, suffering one of those weird 'moment out of time' sensations and momentarily spooked by it.

Being men, they retreated to the corridor while the female contingent of the household took charge.

'I wonder what is wrong with her,' Rashad said tautly.

'I wonder what our excitable crowds will make of this latest development. One of your guards used his phone in the lift. I frowned at him. He should have desisted immediately. What kind of discipline have we here when even the men dedicated to protecting you are taking a part in this media gossip nonsense?' Hakim was steadily working himself up into a rant.

'She was so pale. I should have realised it wasn't natural for her to be that pale,' Rashad breathed as if his adviser hadn't spoken.

Minutes later, Dr Wasem joined them. 'Heatstroke,' he pronounced with a hint of satisfaction at the speed of his diagnosis. 'Normally I would suggest our guest be taken to hospital but I am aware of the current mood in our city. The women will ensure that she is rapidly cooled down and rehydrated. I wonder whose idea it was to take a woman who had already endured a long flight outside during the hottest part of the day? Even our constitutions are taxed in such temperatures as we have in summer.'

A slight flare of colour outlined Rashad's stunning cheekbones. Sunstroke.

'That is serious—'

'Not as serious as what I have to tell you,' Hakim whispered once the doctor turned away to reel off further instructions to the cluster of women at the bedroom door.

With difficulty, Rashad rose above the guilt he was experiencing because sunstroke could be very serious and his guest could have had a fit, convulsions or even a heart attack if her temperature were not speedily reduced. He was appalled by his own thoughtlessness. 'And what is that?'

'Our guest may say she is called Polly but the name on her passport is Zariyah,' Hakim divulged in an even lower-pitched whisper.

'But that is...that is my great-grandmother's name. It is rarely used,' Rashad framed in shock, for the name was not used in Dharia out of respect for his ancestor's memory. 'How can her birth name be Zariyah?'

'My suspicions have taken me in a direction I really do not wish to go,' Hakim admitted heavily. 'But her mother's possession of that ring and her use of that name for her child, added to her unexplained disappearance all those years ago, deeply concerns me...'

'It is not possible that she could be a relative!' Rashad protested with rare vehemence.

'With the timing, added to your father's predilection for dallying with pretty women on the staff, it is sadly...possible,' Hakim spelt out grimly. 'A DNA test must be taken. Our guest could be your half-sister.'

'My…' Half-sister? Reeling with shock, Rashad had frozen into position by the wall as he struggled mightily to handle that shattering possibility while instinctively swallowing back any repetition of that familial designation.

That was not a result he wanted. No, he didn't want that, he definitely *didn't* want to discover that he had been sexually attracted to a long-lost family member. The very idea made him feel sick. But hadn't he once read somewhere about such unnatural attachments forming between adults who had not been raised together as children?

'It must be confirmed one way or another. We must know,' Hakim repeated doggedly. 'Annabel Dixon was a flirtatious woman and your father was—'

The strong bones of Rashad's bronzed face set hard as granite as he spoke. 'I *know* what he was.'

CHAPTER THREE

POLLY SURGED BACK to recovery to find herself naked and being sponged down. In horror at her condition and the strange faces surrounding her she began to struggle to sit up and cover herself.

'I am sorry but this treatment is necessary to bring your temperature down quickly,' a pretty young brunette explained from the head of the bath in which she had been lain. 'I'm Azel and I'm a nurse. You are suffering from heatstroke and although this must be unpleasant for you, it is not as unpleasant as more serious complications would be.'

Heatstroke? Polly recalled the claustrophobic burning heat of that courtyard and suppressed a groan, knowing she should have admitted that she was far too hot out there. She was embarrassed by the fact that she had fainted and caused a whole fuss. Furthermore she had a vague memory of shouting at King Rashad and of threatening to thump him. Her cheeks prickled with mortification and she said nothing until the treatment was complete. The nurse took her temperature and blood pressure and pronounced both satisfactory before she was finally patted dry with a towel. She was then eased into some sort of silky garment and tucked into a very comfortable bed as if she were a young child.

An older man entered and introduced himself as Dr Wasem. He took a sample of her blood and a swab from her mouth before advising her to have a light meal and rest.

As if she were going to just lie there and sleep after all that had happened, Polly thought in disbelief. But once she had drunk as much water as she could manage her eyelids began to slide down as though weights were attached to them, her body sinking into the comfy mattress, and she was asleep before she knew it.

When she wakened, darkness had fallen and she focused in bemusement on the woman seated in a small pool of light near the door. It was Azel, the nurse who had addressed her earlier. Slowly she sat up and voiced her most pressing need. Urged to leave the bed with care in case she felt dizzy, she padded into the bathroom and freshened up with relief. It was after midnight and the silence within the palace walls was unfamiliar to a born and bred Londoner, accustomed to the sound of traffic and the outside glow of street lights.

A knock sounded on the door. 'Do you want anything out of your case?' Azel asked helpfully.

Grateful to finally be reunited with her luggage, Polly retrieved the necessities.

'I've ordered a light meal for you. You must be very hungry.'

'It's the early hours of the morning here,' Polly pointed out in surprise.

'The palace is staffed round the clock. It's a very convenient place to live,' Azel imparted with a smile.

A tray was brought and Polly tucked happily into a chicken salad. She wondered what time it was at home, not having yet got her head around the time difference. She would phone Ellie in the morning, she thought ruefully. In spite of her sleep, she still felt ridiculously tired and tomorrow when she got back to her interrupted holiday she would feel better able to explain how her unexpected inheritance from their late mother had brought her nothing but trouble. Her sister would be unsurprised, she thought fondly, for Ellie had a more cynical outlook on life than her older sister.

The next time she wakened, she could see the brightness of day lightening the wall above the curtains and she was alone. Rising, she dug clean clothes out of her case and she went for a shower. Well, this would be a tale to tell, she reflected with rueful amusement, flying out to Dharia in the hope of exploring her parentage only to end up spending the night in the royal palace.

A maid appeared with a trolley once she had returned to the bedroom and she chose a selection of foods from what was on offer and ate with appetite while she planned what she would say to her sister when she called her. She was reluctant to say anything that would wind up Ellie's fiery temper and more aggressive nature. Placed in the same position, Ellie would have been screaming for the assistance of the

British Embassy before they even got her out of the airport.

But when she dug into her handbag for her phone she couldn't find it even after emptying the bag contents out onto the bed. Her mobile had clearly been stolen. Her money was intact, as was her passport, but her phone was gone. She was furious. It was a cheap phone too, not one she would've believed anyone would think worth stealing. Well, she would take that up with King Rashad when she next saw him. In the meantime, she still needed to ring Ellie, who would be panicking because she hadn't got in touch when she had promised to do so. Honestly, even though Polly was older, Ellie treated her like such an innocent just because she had never been abroad before, Polly mused, shaking her head.

She opened the bedroom door and found a maid and an armed guard standing outside, which took her aback. She was even more disconcerted when the soldier wheeled round and dropped to his knees, bowing his head, muttering something in his own language. Well, good luck with that, whatever it was or meant, Polly decided, politely ignoring his display when it occurred to her that perhaps it was a prayer time of day and he was devout.

'I need a phone,' she told the maid. 'I have to phone my sister.'

The maid beamed and took her back into her bedroom to show her the landline by the bed. Polly suppressed a groan, not wishing to mention that she had wanted a mobile phone to make a free call on an app because she wasn't sure the young woman's English would be up to that explanation. With a sigh, reflecting that Dharia with its oil wealth could surely afford one phone call after the ordeal she had been put through, she lifted the handset.

Ellie answered her call at predictable speed. 'Where are you? Why has it taken you so long to phone me? I've been really worried about you!'

And Polly proceeded to give her sibling the watered-down version of the truth that she had already decided on but she did have to explain that their mother had apparently had no right to even have the fire-opal ring, never mind bequeath it to anyone.

'Well, I think a lawyer would need to decide that, not some jumped-up foreign ruler!' Ellie exclaimed, angrily unimpressed. 'You have to fight this, Polly. Are you sure you're free to leave the palace? Why have they a guard stationed outside your door? Try going for a walk and see what happens. I'm very suspicious about the set-up you've described and I think I may approach the Foreign Office to ascertain what your position is and ask for advice—'

'Do you really think that's necessary?' Polly prompted ruefully. 'Don't you think you're taking this all too seriously?'

'Polly…you don't pick up on warning signals!' Ellie condemned with heartfelt concern. 'You're always making excuses for the bad things people do…I'm not sure I could trust you as a judge of human character!'

Polly completed the call, her face flushed and sheepish. Now Ellie was up in arms and ready to do battle!

Although she believed her sister's concern was ground-less she was willing to test Ellie's suggestion that she try going for a walk. She grabbed her sunhat and sun-glasses and left the room, turning left at random and moving along a stone corridor, pausing to look down at an inner hall covered with the most eye-catching mosaic tiles she had ever seen.

She traversed a wide stone staircase and stilled again to admire a big wide corridor of elaborate arches that stretched away into the distance to frame the far vista of a lush garden at the end. As she set off to ex-plore she noted that the guard was following her but not closely and he was so busy chattering to the maid that had accompanied him that Polly reckoned she could've turned cartwheels without him noticing. She wandered down the corridor and peered out into the gorgeous garden that shaded a pool in the shape of a star. The stone arches surrounding the courtyard were as exquisitely carved and detailed as handmade lace. It was truly beautiful and had she had her phone with its camera she would have loved to take photographs.

Her exploration ranged deeper into the building until she finally recognised the main hall where she had ar-rived the day before, and she was approaching the en-trance when the woman who had served tea to her and the King appeared out of a doorway.

'Miss Dixon?' she called with a very artificial smile. 'The King asks that you join him for lunch.'

'How lovely,' Polly responded with a rather more natural smile, her face heating as she recalled her first meeting with Rashad, the gorgeous talker of textbook English.

Turning to follow the woman, she faltered only slightly when she finally registered that her guard of one had turned into a guard of six while she was wandering and all of them backed away in concert and flattened themselves back against the wall and averted their eyes as she passed by. Weird, *really* weird— maybe it was considered impolite to look too directly at a female, she pondered uncertainly. Certainly, her companion's jaw had tightened so much in response to that display that it might have been carved from stone.

Lunch was mercifully being served indoors, Polly appreciated as she entered a room with a polished marble floor and contemporary furnishings that fitted in surprisingly well with the ancient walls. Rashad appeared without warning, striding in through a connecting door to the left only to stop dead the instant he saw her. Her feet stopped too and without her meaning to still them where she stood. And there he was, she thought rather giddily, jaw-droppingly gorgeous and breathtakingly sexy. Sexy wasn't a word she normally applied to or indeed even *thought* of around men, but it rushed to her brain the minute she saw Rashad and it made her wonder if that was the main drawback of being a virgin and essentially inexperienced. Did sheer curiosity about sex give her a more impressionable response to men? But it had never happened to Polly around any other man, she reasoned, irritated by her wandering thoughts.

'Please sit here,' her companion interposed, tugging out a chair at the table Polly hadn't even noticed ahead of her.

'You look better today,' Rashad commented quietly as he settled down opposite her, his attention locked to the delicate colour in her cheeks and the sparkle in her blue eyes.

'Yes, feeling better too. Sorry about the fuss I caused,' Polly responded dismissively, trying not to look directly at him, utterly unnerved by the effect he had on her usual calm state of mind.

Rashad was disappointed that her hair was braided. He had never seen such beautiful hair before. Simply the novelty of different colouring in a country where most people had black hair, he told himself doggedly. She was wearing trousers again and a loose white top and he would not allow himself to wonder the things that his brain wanted to wonder. He angrily shut that side of himself down and began to make excruciatingly polite conversation of the sort he was accustomed to making at foreign dinner parties.

'My phone wasn't in my bag when it was returned to me,' Polly announced without warning, encountering eyes so dark they glittered like stars in the light filtering through the open doors behind him.

'Enquiries will be made on your behalf,' Rashad fielded smoothly, well aware that the phone had most probably been confiscated as a security precaution at Hakim's order. 'I am sure it will be found and returned to you.'

'Thank you,' Polly said equally politely, wonder-

ing why he seemed so different from the man he had
seemed to be the day before.

He was more controlled, almost stiff and expression-
less, the lean strong bones of his face cool and set, his
jawline hard. Wary? Hostile? Offended? She marvelled
at the extent of her own curiosity and scolded herself
for it. Why should she care? She would soon be taking
up residence in her little bed-and-breakfast place near
the bazaar in Kashan and she could be fairly sure that
she would never meet an actual reigning king again in
her lifetime. He could only be lowering himself to sharing a meal with a foreign commoner to pursue the con-
troversial topic of the fire-opal ring he wanted to retain.

'About the ring,' she began abruptly.

'We will not discuss that now,' Rashad decreed
without hesitation. 'When you have fully recovered
from your illness we will discuss it.'

Off-balance at the flat refusal, Polly studied him
for several tense seconds. He was the most infuriat-
ing man. She could see that he expected the subject to
be dropped simply because he had issued an embargo
and his sheer level of assurance hugely annoyed her. 'I
am fully recovered,' she traded quietly. 'And grateful
as I am for the care I received when I took ill and the
hospitality which has been offered to me here, I would
like to return to my holiday plans as soon as possible.'

'Perhaps we will discuss that tomorrow,' Rashad
fielded without batting a single lush black eyelash.

'You do realise,' Polly whispered, because that hard-
eyed brunette she couldn't quite warm to was seated
only ten feet away, 'that you are making me want to

thump you again? I thought it might be my high temperature that caused my loss of temper yesterday but I can now see that it was merely you being you—'

A brilliant smile unexpectedly stole the grim aspect from his lean, dark, brooding features. 'Me being me?' he queried with perceptible amusement in a clear encouragement for her to expand on her feelings.

'Horribly bossy. And I can see you're used to people doing exactly as you say—'

'Because I am the King,' Rashad filled in helpfully.

'But you're not *my* King.' Polly made that distinction with a slow sweet smile of mingled exasperation and reluctant amusement.

When he saw that smile, Rashad froze and leant back into his chair, squaring his shoulders while he wondered if she was flirting with him. Probably not, his brain told him. The British women he had been intimate with a few years earlier had used methods that were considerably more direct to attract and hold his attention.

'But you are still my guest,' Rashad retorted with lashings of cool. 'And the Dharian rules of hospitality are strict. One should never make a guest uncomfortable—'

'But you're doing exactly that right now!' Polly hissed at him in frustration.

His long brown fingers clenched taut round the cutlery. He tore his gaze from her lovely face, painfully aware that she made him very uncomfortable. With the discipline of years strengthening him, he studied his plate and he ate in complete silence.

'In fact, you're only making me want to stick a fork in you,' Polly whispered across the table.

And that was it—Rashad lost that minor battle. A wholly inappropriate laugh broke from his lips when he failed to stifle his enjoyment. Polly studied him in surprise and then encountered the brunette's chilling appraisal, which suggested that amusing the King could well be a capital offence.

'We will talk again tomorrow,' Rashad informed her quietly as they vacated the table they had shared.

Polly had to forcibly put a lid on her growing frustration with him. She was being too polite, she told herself. He had blocked her questions and refused to discuss the matter of the ring or tell her when she could leave. But did that really matter? After all, she was being treated like an honoured guest. Staying in the lap of luxury in a truly magical royal palace, another little inner voice chipped in gently, was scarcely a penance. It was a gift to be housed in such a gorgeous building, to be waited on hand and foot and to be wonderfully well fed. How could she possibly form a bad opinion of her host? It wasn't as though she had been stashed in some primitive prison cell. Moreover she was being granted an intriguing glimpse of a very different and far more colourful lifestyle.

Satisfied by that more positive take on her unexpected stopover in a royal dwelling, Polly wandered off to enjoy all that the exotic palace had to offer. She ignored the troop of men, armed to the teeth, and the maid following close behind her, and roamed from the magnificent desert views available from the recently built rooftop terrace down through the state rooms, with their superb intricate brass-covered arched doors and elaborate interiors, right down to the kitchen, with its army of busy staff, who fell silent and froze in shock when she first appeared.

With the maid acting as an interpreter, Polly ended up seated in yet another shaded courtyard, being plied with chilled strawberry and honey tea and an array of fantastic little pastries. Somewhere about then she decided that she was having a truly wonderful holiday even if it was not advancing her an inch in her unlikely search to find out more about her father.

Possibly that had always been an unrealistic goal, she thought in disappointment. Too much time had passed. How did she even risk voicing the name she had been given when the poor man might not be her father at all and was probably long since married? She didn't want to upset anyone and the mother she barely remembered had been sufficiently dysfunctional in her relationships even with her own family that she did not feel she could place much faith in Annabel Dixon's judgement.

Later that afternoon a dialogue that would have very much shocked Polly was about to take place. Hakim had collected the DNA results and had received such a shock that he had passed much of the afternoon at prayer, wrestling with his guilt and with sentiments it was too late to express. Having unburdened himself, he had then received a shock almost as great when events that had taken place a quarter of a century earlier were clarified for him by an unexpected source. Sharing that information with his King was almost more than Hakim could bear but he did not have a choice.

'Our guest is *your* granddaughter?' Rashad repeated with incredulity. 'How is that even possible, Hakim?'

The older man sighed heavily. 'At the time my son Zahir died we were estranged. That has been a lifelong source of regret to me. I was aware that he was involved with the nanny but I also suspected her of having other male interests on the staff at the time. I knew that my son wished to marry her and he refused to listen to my objections. I urged him not to marry her—citing the example of my own parents, who married across the cultural divide—and my son took offence.'

Rashad was silent while his trusted adviser unburdened his troubled conscience. Zahir had been Hakim's only child and that much more precious for that reason, and the day after the death of Rashad's family Zahir had died heroically trying to defend the palace and its inhabitants from Arak's squad of hired mercenaries.

'And now you see the consequences of my miscalculation. I spoke to my son from my head instead of from my heart. He loved this woman and she was already pregnant. He would not have told me *that*,' Hakim acknowledged hoarsely, his emotions roughening his usually steady voice. 'When the nanny vanished after his death I never thought about her again…why would I have? But I have only now learnt that Zahir married her privately and secretly only the day before he died. May I humbly request some time off to go home and discuss this astounding discovery with my wife—?'

'Of course,' Rashad breathed tautly, struggling to absorb the apparent truth that Polly, in spite of her misleading colouring, actually carried Dharian blood in her veins. 'But who does she resemble?'

'*My* mother,' Hakim confided tremulously. 'That hair. I should have suspected it the instant I laid eyes on her. I must also ask you to put all matters pertaining to my grandchild and the current unrest in the streets in the hands of my two deputies, because I am no longer a suitably independent and disinterested third party—'

'That I refuse to do,' Rashad responded instantaneously. 'I trust you as I trust no other man close to me.'

'You do me great honour in saying so but I—'

'Go home to your wife, Hakim,' Rashad urged gently. 'For today at least put family first and official duty second.'

Freed from the risk that Polly could be a half-sibling, Rashad smiled thoughtfully. Well, surprisingly, he was *her* King because although she did not know it her paternity granted her dual citizenship. He wished he could tell her that but it was her grandfather's right to break such news, not his.

The following morning other concerns swiftly consumed him when one of Hakim's aides brought the most popular newspaper in Dharia to him. The secret of Polly's true name on her passport was a secret no longer and it was just the kind of nonsense liable to inflame the superstitious with fanciful ideas. A single king, a single woman named Zariyah after his great-grandmother, the return of the Hope of Dharia... Such coincidences were being interpreted as supernatural signposts of heavenly endorsement in the home of his birth.

Rashad heaved a sigh. It was little wonder that Polly's birth name was now being chanted in the streets. He could not possibly let her leave the palace, for there was no chance of her enjoying an anonymous holiday after her passport photograph had been printed in the newspaper. Proving that the hysteria was generalised throughout every strata of Dharian society, the usually sensible editor had totally ignored all safety concerns when he put such information into the public domain.

And Rashad's day only darkened in tenor when he was informed that an official from the British Embassy was currently waiting to be seen. The diplomatic incident that Hakim had feared was beginning to happen...

Polly was watching the local television station as she ate her breakfast and wishing she could speak the language. She had tried and failed to access a European television channel. But she did not need Arabic to recognise that the massed crowds in the streets of the capital city were on the edge of overexcited. She wished she could read the placards some of them carried and waved along with the Dharian national flag.

Having promised to phone Ellie again, she did so. Her sibling startled her by admitting that she had spoken to a man from the Foreign Office and that official enquiries were being made about her so-called arrest and imprisonment at the royal palace.

'Oh, my goodness, Ellie!' Polly fielded in consternation. 'How could you *do* that? I'm having a really interesting time here—'

'This ring business you're involved in stinks to high heaven of some sort of a cover-up. I don't think you have a clue what's happening out there. As usual you're just sailing along and letting people push you around—'

Polly let her sister state her case and finally agreed that it was time she returned to the holiday she had booked and that she would *demand* the right to leave the palace and return to Kashan. Before she could lose her nerve she used the palace switchboard and asked to be put through to the King, wryly amused by her own daring.

'I have to speak to you,' Polly declared boldly as soon as she heard his dark deep drawl. 'And as I may shout, it would be better if we didn't have an audience.'

At his end of the phone, Rashad almost groaned out loud for palace protocol stated that he should never ever be left alone with a member of the female sex. He knew it was to protect him from the slurs and scandals caused by his father's debauchery but it was not easy to escape the tightly linked net of strict procedure.

'Meet me on the roof terrace,' he urged abruptly. 'I hear you were there yesterday and it is shaded. I'll join you as soon as I can.'

The strangest shred of compassion infiltrated Polly. It was clearly a no-no for him to meet up with her alone. When did the Dharian King ever get to be alone? She had seen the security team that followed him everywhere he went and she wondered what it was like to live in such a goldfish bowl where every word and every action was monitored.

Polly left her room and told the maid she wanted to walk alone. The three men guarding her room studied her in wonderment but when she moved off, she was not followed and relief spread through her because she felt really free for the first time within the royal walls with no one watching over her.

The shade on the roof terrace took what she believed to be a rather odd form. A giant tent had been set up at one corner. Within it opulent floor cushions surrounded a fire pit and there was an array of the implements she assumed were required to brew the traditional tea. Walking out of the bright sunshine, Polly sank down with relief on a cushion to enjoy the view. It was fifteen minutes before Rashad appeared through another entrance onto the terrace.

'We are breaking rules,' he told her with a sudden flashing smile of such charisma that her heart jumped inside her. 'This is not allowed.'

'Sometimes it's fun to break rules,' sensible Polly heard herself say dry-mouthed because for the first time Rashad was wearing traditional clothing, a muslin cloth bound by a gold rope hiding his black hair, a pristine white long buttoned robe replacing Western clothing. And that cloth merely accentuated his stunning dark eyes and arresting bone structure, so that breathing was barely an option for her as he sank with fluid animal grace down opposite her.

'And sometimes there is a price to pay for breaking

those rules,' Rashad murmured with wry amusement. 'Why did you want to speak to me?'

'I want to leave the palace and start my holiday,' Polly told him simply, even though she knew that somewhere down deep inside her she really didn't want that at all. It was the rational thing to do, she reminded herself doggedly. She did not belong in a royal palace.

Rashad linked long brown fingers and flexed them. 'I'm afraid I can't agree to that.'

He even had beautiful hands, Polly was thinking abstractedly before she engaged with what he had actually said and it galvanised her into leaping upright in disbelief. 'So, I *am* a prisoner here?' She gasped in horror that her sister could have been correct in her far-fetched suspicions.

'Do not lose your temper,' Rashad urged levelly. 'Allow me first to explain the situation we are all in—'

'The only person in a situation here is *me*!' Polly exclaimed angrily.

'There is great unrest in Kashan. You would not be safe…you would be mobbed. While no one would wish to harm you in any way, excited crowds are very hard to control.'

'I don't know what you are talking about.'

'Sit down, listen and I will explain,' Rashad instructed with quiet strength.

'No, you can explain while I stay standing,' Polly responded, determined not to give way on every point.

'Very well.' Rising as gracefully as he had sat down, Rashad stepped back out of the tent and strode over to the rail bounding the terrace. 'A century ago—'

'A century ago?' Polly practically screeched at him, gripped by incredulity that that could possibly be the starting point of any acceptable explanation for her apparent loss of all freedom.

'Close your mouth and sit down!' Rashad raked back at her in sudden frustration, his dark deep voice startlingly like a whiplash in the silence. 'If you refuse to listen, how can I speak and explain?'

Polly compressed her lips and sat down with a look of scornful reluctance on her heart-shaped face. 'Well, if you're going to shout about it—'

'I must make you aware of the most powerful legend in Dharian history. A hundred years ago, my great-grandmother, Zariyah, came to Dharia with the fire-opal ring and gave it to my great-grandfather, who then married her. My people think it was love at first sight,' Rashad advanced. 'But in actuality it was an arranged marriage, which was very popular and which ushered in a long period of peace and prosperity for Dharia—'

'That name,' Polly whispered with an indeterminate frown. 'Zariyah. That's the name I was given at birth.'

'The ring is also invested with enormous significance in the eyes of my people. The name on your passport was *noticed*. It may even be the reason why you were singled out for the drug screening process we have begun. You also brought the ring back to Dharia—'

'Not to give to you!' Polly objected vehemently.

'You are much given to interruption,' Rashad fired back at her rawly.

'And you are much given to being quietly listened to.'

'My country endured dark times for over twenty years. My people suffered greatly under the dictator, Arak,' Rashad told her in a curt undertone. 'They are very superstitious. Your appearance, your name and your possession of the ring has led to a hysterical out-pouring of sentiment in the streets. At this moment in Kashan, people are waving signs bearing the name Zariyah because my great-grandmother was very much loved. If you left the palace, you would be mobbed and it would be extremely dangerous.'

Polly stared back at him with a dropped jaw. She could barely get her head around what he was trying to tell her. 'You mean, the coincidence of me having that name and the ring is sufficient—?'

'To cause all that excitement? Yes,' Rashad confirmed heavily.

Polly stared numbly into the fire pit, genuinely be-mused by what he had explained. People were dem-onstrating in the city and waving those placards on her behalf? It was beyond her comprehension and her lashes flickered over blue eyes widening in growing amazement.

'But I don't understand. What do they want from me?' she queried numbly.

'In a nutshell, they want you to marry their King,' Rashad replied very drily. 'A single monarch, a single

woman with the name of a famous queen…in their eyes
it's a simple equation.'

'They want me to *marry* you?' Polly cried incred-
ulously.

'And everything about you plays into their fantasy
conclusion,' Rashad imparted with an edge of bitterness because the more he watched those crowds waving flags in the streets, the more his sense of duty
warred with his brain. 'You are very beautiful. What
man would not wish to marry such a beauty? And while
you could have followed some inappropriate career as a
stripper or a lap dancer, which would admittedly have
doused their enthusiasm somewhat—'

'I beg your pardon?' Polly exclaimed furiously,
jumping upright again.

'Instead you work in a homeless shelter helping the
underprivileged,' Rashad completed. 'Yes, our media
are every bit as given to spying as your own. You have
been framed even in the newspapers as the perfect wife
in the eyes of my people.'

Polly bolted out of the shade of the tent to stand by
the rail in the golden sunshine, staring out at the lines
of the shallow sand dunes gradually shifting into larger
ones in the distance. 'I'm mortified—'

'I am trapped,' Rashad traded without sympathy,
raging at the fates that had created such a disturbing
and difficult situation. When he was crowned he had
sworn to do whatever it took to make the people of
Dharia secure and happy and he had never once considered that sacrifice of freedom as a personal con-
straint. Only now when it came to the question of his

marriage was he finally appreciating the true cost of that pledge. But it also gave him a great deal to think over, he acknowledged, studying Polly and wondering what it would be like to go with the flow of popular sentiment rather than sit it out and hope it eventually died a natural death.

'Certainly not by me!' Polly lashed back at him, one small hand lifting in emphasis off the rail.

Without warning Rashad caught her hand in his, studying the slender bones below the skin that was so pale against his bronzed colouring and the intricate tracing of blue veins at her inner wrist. As if under a compulsion, he bent his proud head and pressed his mouth to that soft, smooth, delicate skin.

Polly studied that down-bent head in complete shock while tiny little tendrils of prickling awareness traversed her entire body. That one little contact was so screamingly sensual she couldn't believe it. She had had passionate kisses that left her cold as ice but the brush of Rashad's mouth across her wrist made her nipples tighten almost painfully inside her bra and forced a surge of hot liquid heat to rise between her thighs in a manner that made her rigid with discomfort. She quivered, shaken, aroused, suddenly out of her depth with him in a way she had never been before. When that skilled mouth roved across her palm and shifted to enclose a single fingertip and suck it, her knees trembled and her legs almost gave way beneath her in response.

Mesmerised, Polly looked up into shimmering golden eyes alight with raw sexual hunger.

An urgent burst of Arabic sounded from somewhere

behind them and she flinched in surprise while Rashad immediately dropped her hand.

Hakim was outraged by what he had seen. He had trusted his King. He had overlooked the reality that his King was a young man with all the appetites of a young man in the company of a beautiful young woman.

'This meeting is most improper,' Hakim informed his granddaughter unhappily. 'But I do not blame you for it.'

Further exchanges took place over Polly's head, which was bent because she was seriously embarrassed. After all, she had requested the private meeting and was guilty of disrespecting what appeared to be the cultural norms of Dharia. Rashad had only kissed her hand though, for goodness' sake, she thought angrily, thoroughly disliking the old man who had intervened and who was contriving to behave as though he had interrupted a raw and shocking sex scene.

'I am Hakim, Miss Dixon,' the older man informed her gently as he led her off the terrace. 'May I call you Polly? Or is it Zariyah?'

With difficulty, Polly recalled her manners. 'No, my grandmother wouldn't call me by my birth name. When I was old enough to understand it *was* my true name, she told me it was foreign and outlandish and she refused to use it, so she gave me the name Polly instead.'

'That is a great pity but perhaps in time that could be remedied,' Hakim remarked incomprehensibly above her head. 'Would you be willing to talk to me? I have something of very great importance to tell you...'

CHAPTER FOUR

HAKIM ESCORTED HER to a room that he described as his office but which more closely resembled an old library.

Polly sank down in a comfortable armchair but sat bolt upright again, eyes wide with astonishment, when Hakim informed her that he was her grandfather.

'But how could you possibly know that?' she whispered unevenly.

'My mother…' Hakim handed her a creased old photo of a smiling blonde woman. 'My son, your father…'

Polly peered down in wonder at the photo of the attractive dark-eyed young man in the photograph. 'Is his name Zahir Basara?'

Hakim gently corrected her pronunciation and regretfully informed her of her father's death when the palace had been overrun twenty-odd years earlier. Tears stung Polly's eyes as he broke that news while frankly admitting that he and his only child had been at odds at the time of his demise.

'He wanted to marry your mother,' he explained. 'But I refused to support him. My own parents had a mixed marriage. My mother was the daughter of a

Swedish missionary working here. Although my parents stayed together they were not happy. My prejudice blinded me towards the woman my son loved—'

'I can understand that...but are you really sure that your son was my father? His is the name my mother left me with the ring, but—'

Tears dampened Polly's cheeks as her emotions spilled over because she felt so horribly guilty for doubting that name now. How much had she let her grandmother's bitterness colour her own attitude towards her mother? Annabel Dixon had not been lying, nor had she been unsure of who had fathered her first child. Her late mother had told her the truth.

'There can be no doubt because we did a DNA test. A sample was taken from you by the doctor without your permission,' Hakim confided gravely. 'DNA samples of the dead were conserved after the coup that killed our King's family and many others at the palace. I am very sorry that we ordered the test to be done without your awareness—'

'But why *did* you order it?' Polly murmured in bewilderment, too preoccupied by what he had told her to be angry when it had resulted in her finding an actual blood relative of her late father's. 'Why would you do such a thing?'

With quiet assurance, he explained that her arrival with both the Hope of Dharia ring and the name of a former queen had roused the suspicion that she could be a child of Rashad's late father. 'He was a most unscrupulous man with women. He had many extramarital relationships. We are not aware of any children born from those liaisons but it has always been a possibility. Imagine my astonishment when the computer found a match with my own son...'

Polly was just beginning to adapt to the shattering idea that she was in the company of her actual grandfather, who appeared to be a great deal more warm and pleasant in character than her maternal grandmother had proved to be. 'It must have been a nasty shock—'

'No, it was wonderful,' Hakim contradicted with a wide smile. 'My wife, your grandmother, wept with joy and cannot wait to meet you. We are strangers but we would dearly love to be considered family...'

At that generous statement, Polly's eyes flooded with tears again. 'I think I would like that too. Apart from my sister, I've never really had what people call a family. But doesn't it make a difference to you that Zahir and my mother weren't married?'

'But they *were* married,' her grandfather countered and he explained.

'My mother must've been devastated,' Polly commented sickly, trying to imagine the pure horror of marrying the man you loved and losing him again the next day.

'Dharia was in uproar and naturally Annabel fled home to the UK. There was nothing here for her to stay for. She must also have been aware that Zahir's family were hostile to her,' he completed sadly. 'I was very much in the wrong in the way I dealt with their relationship, Polly.'

A small hand covered his and squeezed comfort-ingly. 'You didn't know. You made a mistake. You wanted the best for your son. You didn't know what the future held...none of us do,' she pointed out quietly.

Hakim beamed at her, his rounded face flushed with pleasure. 'Will you give my wife and myself the opportunity to get to know you?' he asked humbly. 'We would be very grateful.'

Polly mumbled that she would be equally grateful. Tears were tripping her up again and she blinked them back in exasperation but her needle-in-a-haystack search for her father had come to an amazing conclusion. Her father was gone, as was her mother, but she had discovered other relatives to comfort her for that loss. It was more, she felt, than she could have hoped for before she set out on her journey.

'But do not be holding hands with the King again,' Hakim advised in an undertone. 'The fault was his, not yours, but I will not have your reputation soiled.'

'Are relations here in Dharia between single men and women so strict, then?'

'Only when the King is involved,' her grandfather admitted wryly. 'He is a public figure. He must not be seen to resemble his late father by practising any over-familiarity with a female. Once he is safely married, he will not need to be so concerned about appearances.'

Polly's right hand tingled and her face warmed while she distractedly recalled what Rashad had done with her finger. She wondered what an actual kiss would have felt like. With her imagination catching fire at the idea, a wanton charge of heat filtered through her lower limbs and filled her with self-loathing embarrassment. 'Is he planning to get married, then? Has he a wife lined up?'

'Not as yet but he *must* marry,' Hakim told her cheerfully. 'It is a monarch's duty to take a wife and have children to provide stability for the next generation.'

As far as Rashad was concerned, there was definitely a high price to be paid for all that bowing and scraping and luxurious privilege, Polly acknowledged ruefully. She remembered him saying that breaking the rules brought consequences and remembered how quickly Hakim's censure had brought those consequences home. Rashad had known exactly what he was talking about. She had been naïve and thoughtless, she reckoned ruefully, and, if Rashad was never allowed to be alone with a woman, surely it was little wonder that he had got a little carried away with her hand?

Wasn't it even possible that her request to see him alone had given him the wrong impression? Polly winced at the suspicion that he might have believed she was deliberately inviting that kind of attention. But on another level, warmth was still pooling in her pelvis at the recollection. He was a very handsome, very sexy guy and, for Polly, it had been an educational experience to finally realise why other people made such a fuss about the act of sex. If a man just kissing your hand could make you feel that overheated... At that point, she broke off her wandering thoughts and buried them deep.

Her maid wakened her with breakfast at what appeared to be dawn the next morning and told her with eyes that danced with mischief that she was going on a trip. Polly was not told where she was going or why or whose company she would be in and she assumed that that was probably because the young woman's small stock of English wasn't up to that challenge. She wondered if Rashad had managed to contrive some discreet way of returning her to her holiday plans but, when she began packing, the maid's confusion suggested that that was not the explanation. Had her kindly grandfather made some arrangement for her? Regardless, Polly was delighted by the prospect of seeing a little more of her father's country because all she had so far seen were the city streets and the view from the palace rooftop.

The maid led her down a service staircase and through a long tracery of quiet corridors and courtyards that suggested they were taking a more than usually circuitous route through the sprawling palace. They finally emerged into a garage packed with opulent vehicles and with noticeable ceremony she was ushered into an SUV. As they filtered out through the palace gates she noted that another two cars were accompanying them.

She would phone Ellie later, she promised herself guiltily. In truth she didn't want to hear any more of her sister's dire predictions after Rashad had bluntly explained the status quo. She didn't like the situation and neither did he, but there really wasn't very much that could be done about it, was there? It wasn't his fault or hers that his people had chosen to weave her into the legend of his great-grandmother and the fire-opal ring.

While the convoy of vehicles drove out into the desert, Polly settled back in the air-conditioned cool to enjoy her sightseeing. When they began to trundle up and down dunes, she told herself it was exciting although in reality the steep inclines and declines unnerved her. At one stage they passed by a long train of camels laden with goods and there was much hooting of car horns and shouted exchanges. When they descended the last dune she saw the oasis and her breath caught in her throat because that lush spread of green dotted by palm trees and a natural pool was so very beautiful and inviting in such an arid dusty landscape. The car came to a halt and the door was opened.

Without warning, Polly was engulfed in a whooping and chattering crowd of women. It unsettled her but the sociable smiles were a universal language of intent and she smiled as much as she could in response. That tolerance became a little more taxed when she was led into a tent and a long dress was presented to her with the evident hope that she would take off her trousers and tee shirt to put it on. Briefly, Polly froze while she wondered if trousers on a woman were a cultural no-no in such company and she decided to change for the sake of peace. Furthermore the dress, which was covered with blue embroidery, was really very pretty and she surrendered, not even objecting when her hair was unbraided and brushed out because it seemed to give her companions so much pleasure and satisfaction.

Ellie would tell her that she was much too busy being a people-pleaser to do as she liked but Polly loved to make those around her happy, she conceded guiltily as she was escorted between black capacious tents and taken into a very large one overlooking the pool. She sank down in the merciful shade and then Rashad strode in, as informally dressed in jeans and an open shirt as she was formally dressed.

'Rashad...' she murmured in sincere surprise, feeling her entire body heat as hot as the sun outside and her muscles pull taut in reaction to his sudden appearance. 'I suppose I shouldn't call you that. It's too familiar. What do—?'

'You call me Rashad,' he interposed without hesitation. 'How are you feeling after what Hakim told you last night?'

'Still shocked but mainly...' Polly considered thoughtfully '...incredibly happy to have discovered who I am even if I feel very sad that my father is no longer with us. I also like my grandfather.'

'He is a fine man, fiercely loyal and wise.' Rashad tilted his arrogant dark head to one side and lifted a broad shoulder and dropped it again in a sort of fluid fatalistic shrug that was as electrifyingly sexy as all his lithe physical movements. 'When he finds you gone from the palace this morning, however, he will be ready to kill me—'

'You arranged for me to be brought out here?' Polly frowned. 'Why?'

'It was bring you here or jump balconies to visit you in your bedroom. The bedroom would have been the worst option of all,' he told her with derisive amusement lancing through his stunning dark golden eyes.

In truth, very little amused Rashad in the sardonic and cynical mood he was in. He had spent most of the night thinking rather than sleeping, angrily confronting the issue that Polly's arrival with the ring had created and coming to terms with his own position. And the truth of what he should be doing had soon faced him. *There was no choice.* She was the woman his people wished him to marry. No other woman could even hope to fit into a legend. In reality he did not wish to marry at all but that was *his* problem, scarcely the problem of the people he ruled. His sense of duty, moreover, was strong. He would not be a selfish ruler like his father; he would put his people first and foremost in his life. It would be a challenge to remarry even though he could see decided advantages to marrying Polly, whom he, at least, *desired.* He believed that choosing an unknown wife from a photograph, basing the decision on her heritage and what others with a vested interest said about her, would be much more likely to lead to a dissatisfactory marriage. After all, at least he had got to *meet* Polly and draw his own conclusions...

Rashad's eyes were surrounded by the blackest, thickest, longest lashes she had ever seen on a man, Polly was acknowledging giddily, briefly wondering why every cutting edge in his lean dark features was set so hard, from his exotic cheekbones to his aggressive jawline, lending a tough, angry edge to his face. Assuming that that could only be a misapprehension on her part, she savoured the truth that he was still drop-dead beautiful in a way she had never known a man could be.

It was a serious challenge to drag her attention away from either his lean, darkly handsome features or his tall, powerfully muscled body. Indeed the sheer pull of Rashad's erotic allure thoroughly unsettled Polly because she could now feel and recognise the desire he incited in her and it was like nothing she had ever felt in her life before. That physical hunger that she had tried and failed to feel with other men was much more powerful and all-consuming than she had expected.

'I had you brought out here to the oasis so that I could ask you to marry me,' Rashad informed her levelly.

'But we're strangers!' Polly exclaimed in disbelief, totally unable to understand what he had just said and take it seriously.

'No, we are not. I already know much more about you than I would know about a bride I chose from a photograph...which, by the way, is my only other option,' Rashad admitted, choosing to tell her that unattractive truth. 'An arranged marriage would be considered normal for a man in my position although the practice has died out in our society. I've already had one arranged marriage and I don't want another—'

'You've already had *one*? You've been married before?' Polly whispered in wonderment, because she knew he was only thirty-one years old.

'I was married at sixteen—'

'I'm sorry but I think that's...barbaric,' she muttered helplessly. 'You were far too young—'

'We both were but those were more dangerous times and alliances had to be made and marriage was how it was done,' Rashad explained. 'I had no choice and I would very much prefer to have a choice this time.'

'But you said you felt *trapped* by your people's expectations,' Polly reminded him, dancing round the whole topic of his proposal rather than actually getting to grips with it because she just couldn't comprehend the enormity of what he was suggesting. 'Now you say you *want* to meet those expectations—'

'Why not? They chose you but I choose you too,' Rashad murmured huskily, his dark eyes flashing gold over her intent and expressive face. 'I want you.'

And his earthy appraisal left her in no doubt of what he was referring to. That hungry sensation surged and pulsed along her nerve endings and flipped her tummy over to leave her breathless. Her skin flushed, her body coming alive, and she shut her eyes because she could no longer withstand the intensity of his hot gaze.

'And you want me,' Rashad told her with maddening confidence.

Polly's eyes opened and her hands knotted into fists. 'I think you've—'

'No, don't fight me…it turns me on and if you do that I can't promise to keep my hands off you as I should,' Rashad framed in a roughened tone of warning.

'It turns you on…' Polly repeated in wonderment.

'Because nobody *ever* fights or argues with me. You can have no idea how boring that becomes,' Rashad admitted grimly.

In possession of a very sparky and forceful sister, Polly almost disagreed because she could not imagine finding pleasure in the apparently stimulating effect of dissension. Instead she said nothing, she simply shook her head. 'Sexual attraction is not a good basis for marriage—'

'It is for me,' Rashad countered without hesitation. 'I am convinced that you would make me the perfect wife.'

'But nobody's perfect!'

'More perfect than flawed,' Rashad qualified smoothly. 'The discovery that you have Dharian blood in your veins only adds to your appeal. This is your world now as much as it is mine and you have a family who will love and support you here.'

Polly bent her head down to escape the temptation of his glittering dark eyes. It was a powerful argument to know that there was another world and another family for her to explore. Apart from her sister she had never had a caring family to lean on, which was why Hakim's welcome had meant so much to her. She wanted to get to know that family and their culture, she wanted to spend time with them, which, with the cost of travel set against her low salary, would be very difficult once she returned home as scheduled at the end of the week.

'There would be advantages and disadvantages to marrying me,' Rashad outlined with dry practicality. 'I do not believe you would be unduly influenced by my wealth but as my wife you would be very rich. On the other hand, you would lose the freedom to do and say exactly as you wish because royals are expected to behave according to protocol. Sometimes that protocol feels stifling but it is there for our protection.'

Polly flushed very pink because although he had

said he hoped she would not be unduly influenced by his wealth, her mind had immediately flown to the good she could do with more money and she was mortified by that embarrassing moment of unwelcome self-truth. But poor Ellie was steeped in student debt and struggling and would be for many more years to come. Moreover, both sisters were desperately keen to trace their missing youngest sister, Penelope, and get to know her, but the hiring of a private detective was utterly beyond their financial means at present. She swallowed hard, ashamed of her thoughts and deciding that money had to be, in truth, the root of all evil and temptation.

'What happened to your first wife?' she asked him abruptly to escape those shameful thoughts of wealth and what she could do with it.

'Ferah contracted blood poisoning from a snake bite and died five years ago,' Rashad revealed in a harshened undertone. 'She did not receive medical attention quickly enough.'

'I'm sorry,' she murmured automatically because her mind was reeling under the burden of all that he had said and her own desperate confusion.

'Do you have an answer for me?' Rashad prompted with an air of expectancy on his lean, strong face.

'Not yet,' she admitted, matching his honesty.

Her brain had flatly rejected marrying him at first. They barely knew each other and it would be insane... *and yet*? She did want him, in fact she wanted him more than she had ever wanted any man and she was not an impressionable teenager any longer. In fact, what if she *never* met another man who made her feel the same way that Rashad did? That terrible fear held her still and turned her hollow inside because he made her feel alive and wanton and all sorts of things she had never felt before. And what was more, she was discovering that she *liked* the way he made her feel.

'Perhaps I can help you to make up your mind,' Rashad murmured with silken softness. 'You will see it as a form of blackmail but in reality it is the only possible alternative if you do not wish to marry me—'

Polly's head reared up, blue eyes wide and bright. 'Blackmail?' she exclaimed in dismay. 'What are you talking about?'

'If you don't marry me, you will have to leave Dharia immediately. Only your departure will end this madness on the streets and in the media.'

Polly was aghast at that cold-blooded conclusion. 'You're willing to throw me out of the country?'

Hard dark eyes held hers. 'If that is what it takes, yes…and naturally I would not wish you to return in the near future,' he decreed harshly.

Polly was shaken by that solution because she had been planning to get to know her grandparents, her newly discovered Dharian family. She had no doubt that Hakim and his wife would be willing to visit her at least once in London but it would not be the same as staying on in Dharia and having the chance to explore her father's heritage and culture for herself.

'I cannot allow the current security situation to continue,' Rashad informed her grimly and he went to the doorway of the tent to clap his hands. 'We will have tea while you consider your options.'

Polly didn't see how tea was going to be the answer to anything but the sheer amount of entertaining ritual involved in the brewing of tea by two robed men at least gave her something to watch while her brain struggled to deal with a rising tide of anxiety. He was using blackmail even if on one level she could understand his position. It was very unfair from her point of view, though, that she should have to suffer for something that was in no way her fault. In many ways by piling on that extra pressure of an immediate departure, he was taking her right to choose away from her.

'Seriously…' she began furiously, 'you would actually force me to go home?'

'When it comes to what is best for my country I will always do it,' Rashad countered with a roughened edge to his dark deep drawl. 'That is my duty.'

Polly compressed her taut lips, her hand clenching angrily round her cup. She knew he meant it. It was stamped in the resolve that had hardened his lean, darkly handsome face. Either she stayed on in Dharia and agreed to marry him or she went home again and stayed there. She didn't need to be pregnant to be offered a shotgun marriage, she reflected angrily. That was what he was offering her with the crowds providing the firepower of pressure.

Yet when it came to marriage all that went with Rashad in terms of baggage and culture and his people's expectations was simply huge. Even so, she quite understood why he was willing when his next-best option was a marriage to a complete stranger about whom he would essentially know nothing.

'Of course, you'd get the ring back if you married me,' she said with a flat lack of humour.

'And gain a gorgeous blonde wife,' Rashad traded with a sudden charismatic smile that lit up his bronzed face, illuminating the hard cheekbones and hollows that gave his features such strong definition.

Polly glanced across the fire pit at him and the knowledge that if she said no she would never see him again sliced into her like the sudden slash of a knife blade. That prospect, she registered in mortification, was not something she wanted to think about. No more easily could she imagine being forced to walk away from the new family she had found. Perspiration beaded her upper lip as she fretted.

Marrying Rashad would be like taking a huge blind leap in the dark and she wasn't the sort of woman who took risks of that nature, was she? But if it worked, there would be much to gain, she reasoned ruefully. She would have her grandparents for support. She was already powerfully attracted by Rashad.

'The answer is…yes. It's insane but…*yes*,' Polly muttered almost feverishly before she could lose her nerve.

Although relief slivered through Rashad at her agreement that relief was threaded with undeniable resentment over his predicament. After all, he had been backed into a corner and forced to marry again. This was *his* choice, he reminded himself sternly. *She* was his choice and far superior to a bride who would have been a complete stranger, but the stubborn streak of volatility Rashad always kept suppressed had flickered from a spark into a sudden burning flame, for it was impossible for him to forget how very much he had hated being married.

CHAPTER FIVE

'IT'S NOT TOO late to change your mind,' Ellie said with
a hint of desperation while she watched the television
to see the partying taking place in the streets of Kashan
to celebrate Rashad and Polly's wedding day. 'Well,
they probably do have you on the tea towels and you
would need to be smuggled out of the country in disguise if you *jilted* him!'

'Obviously, I'm not going to jilt him,' Polly said
quietly, wishing her sister would stop winding up her
nerves with her dire forecasts.

Ellie had landed in Dharia forty-eight hours earlier
and she had given her elder sister every conceivable
lecture against marriage since her arrival.

*Marry in haste, repent at leisure. Do you realise
what you're getting into? Are you even sure you will be
his only wife? What if everything Rashad shows you on
the surface is simply a front to persuade you to marry
him? Look at those people partying at the announcement! He needs you more than you need him. That
should make you suspicious. What if he has another
woman hidden somewhere? A woman he really loves?*

Polly had dutifully listened to every possible argument but she had absorbed few of her sibling's warnings for the simple reason that she suspected that she was falling in love with Rashad. Yes, she had finally worked that out all on her own. How else had she contrived to overlook his threat to throw her out of the country if she didn't agree to marry him?

On her side of the fence, her reasons for marrying Rashad had become resolutely practical over the two short weeks that had passed since his proposal. One, her grandfather spoke very highly of his ruler, and she trusted Hakim and his wife Dursa because she was genuinely convinced that they would rate her need for happiness higher than any desire to see their grandchild wed their King. Two, Rashad had been honest with her. He had paid her no extravagant compliments and had made no mention of love and she had accepted that latter handicap with the strength of a patient, optimistic woman because she hoped that in time his feelings for her would change. Three, there was just something very powerful about Rashad that called to Polly on a very deep level and she couldn't put it into words or explain it, so she had come to think of it as the start of love. She simply knew that she wasn't capable of walking away from him.

And how did she know that? she asked herself as the cluster of chattering maids surrounding her twitched at the skirts of her elaborate wedding outfit and attached more jewellery to her, although she was already laden down with gold and precious gems because Rashad's uncle had saved the family jewel collection along with his youngest nephew. How the fire-opal ring had become detached from that collection would probably never be known but Hakim believed that his son had very possibly taken it and given it to Polly's mother, Annabel, for safekeeping during the chaos following the explosion that had claimed the lives of Rashad's family. Her father, Zahir, had after all been the most senior soldier in the palace that awful day and had died himself within twenty-four hours.

She could never walk away from Rashad when her own family was so deeply involved with the country of Dharia. No, she knew that even if her marriage turned out to be a bad marriage she was very likely stuck with it until the day she died because her grandfather had spelt out to her that she had to think in terms of for ever when it came to marrying a ruling king. Rashad's father had divorced twice before wedding Rashad's mother and those matrimonial breakdowns had been interpreted as signs of his general instability and his lack of staying power and sense of duty as a monarch.

'And even worse, you've hardly seen Rashad since you agreed to marry him,' Ellie reminded her with anxious green eyes.

'He's had so many people to meet and so many arrangements to make,' Polly responded quietly, for Rashad had spent the last fortnight travelling around Dharia. 'He has to consult with others about everything he does to come up with a consensus. It's the way he operates to keep everybody happy that they've had their say and Grandad says it works beautifully.'

Ellie stood back a step to examine her sister's gor-

geous appearance. Traditional red and gold embroidery
and rich blues had been laid down on the finest cream
silk fabric that flowed like liquid and screamed designer just like the matching shoes. Her head was bare,
her hair loose, as was the norm in Dharia for a bride. A
magnificent set of sapphires glittered at her ears, her
throat, her neck and her wrists. Delicate henna swirls
decorated her hands and her feet and beneath the dress
she wore a chemise with a hundred buttons for her
groom to undo on the wedding night. Ellie was more
intimidated than she wanted to admit by the pomp and
ceremony of Rashad and Polly's wedding and the deep
fear that she was losing her sister to another world and
another family. She knew that Polly's affections ran
loyal and true but how could she possibly compete?

As for Rashad? Well, it went without saying that he
was very, very nice to look at, very well spoken as well
as educated and civilised but, like the buttons waiting
to be undone beneath Polly's dress, what was her future
brother-in-law *really* like below the smooth polished
façade? That was the main source of Ellie's concern
because in her one brief meeting with Rashad she had
reckoned that a great deal more went on below that
smooth surface than trusting, caring Polly was probably willing to recognise. A man traumatised as a boy
by the loss of his entire family, forced into marriage
at sixteen, widowed ten years later and then raised to
a throne over a population who worshipped him like a
god because he had rescued them from a dictator's tyr-
anny? That was quite a challenging life curve to have

survived. How much did her sister genuinely know about the man she had agreed to marry?

'Would you *please* stop worrying about me?' Polly urged Ellie with troubled blue eyes. 'I want this to be a happy day.'

'I'm always happy if you're happy,' Ellie declared, giving her a gentle but fond hug of apology.

But Polly knew different. Ellie had always been a worrier, expecting the worst outcome in most situations. She refused to borrow that outlook, wanting to look forward with all the hope and optimism that her wonderful discovery of her loving grandparents had already fanned into enthusiasm. Why shouldn't their marriage work out? She wasn't expecting an easy ride. Of course there would be obstacles and surprises and disappointments but surely there would also be joys and unexpected benefits along the way?

She refused to admit even to her sister how isolated and rejected she had felt at having barely spent even a moment with Rashad since agreeing to marry him. And worse still and far too private for her to share, how very apprehensive she actually felt at the prospect of having sex for the first time with a man she had yet to even kiss...

The wedding was to be very much a public event and screened on television. Refusing to give way to nerves, Polly went downstairs with her sister and her bevy of chattering companions to be ushered into the throne room that had been set up to stage the ceremony.

A sharp pang of regret pierced her that she should still have an unknown sister who could not be part of her day and she wondered how soon after their marriage it would be acceptable for her to ask Rashad for his financial help with that problem. How else was she to locate their missing sister, Penelope?

As she strove to ignore the camera lenses while at the same time studiously trying not to do anything unsightly with her face, her nervous tension surged to an all-time high. And then she saw Rashad, exotically garbed in magnificent red and gold ceremonial robes, and all her anxiety was swallowed alive by a sense of awe and wonder that she was on the very brink of marrying such a divinely handsome male. She felt ridiculously schoolgirlish when she looked at him but, on another, much more intimate level, she also felt surprisingly wanton.

Rashad made her wonder about stuff that she had truly never wasted time thinking about before because for so long sex had been part of other people's lives but never hers. That was just how it had been while her freedom was restricted by her grandmother's long illness. Her gaze locked onto the wide sensual curve of Rashad's mouth and she simply tingled as she wondered what he would taste like, what that glorious long bronzed muscular physique of his would look like naked and, inevitably, what it would be like to be in bed with him. As her colour fluctuated wildly, a tide of heat claimed her innermost depths to encourage an embarrassing dampness at the heart of her and she pressed her thighs together and stood rigid as a rod to discourage her colourful imagination. It embarrassed her to be so very impressionable.

'Wow...' Ellie mumbled at her elbow, overpowered by the sheer medieval splendour of their surroundings. 'Who's that guy with the bridegroom?'

'Some Italian Rashad went to uni with. I haven't met him but I think his name is Rio,' Polly whispered, unable to focus on anyone but Rashad because she was now wondering why her future husband looked so impossibly moody and tense. Didn't he realise that he should be smiling for the cameras? Or was any show of human emotion forbidden to him as a ruler? Or was it even possible that he genuinely loathed figuring as a leading light in such a public event?

The ceremony was short and sweet, translated into both their languages. Polly's hand trembled in the firm hold of Rashad's when he slid the ring onto her slender ring finger. His slightest touch invoked a storm of churning, rippling awareness throughout her entire body and she was embarrassed by it, questioning that it could be normal to be so susceptible to a man. But that anxiety was squashed by her astonishment when she belatedly registered that her wedding ring was a feminised miniature of the famous fire-opal ring that Rashad wore on his hand. It seemed deeply symbolic to Polly that he had deliberately made a feature of the ring that had first brought them together and a brilliantly warm and happy smile softened her previously tense mouth as she looked up at him with starry eyes of appreciation.

His wide sensual lips almost made it into an answering smile of acknowledgement but his shimmering dark eyes remained cool and evasive and a faint pang of disappointment touched Polly. Yet somehow she sensed that his self-discipline was so inflexible and so intrinsic to his character that he would not allow any relaxation of his innate reserve to betray his true feelings. Simultaneously and for the very first time she wondered what those feelings actually were...

Of course she knew and accepted that he wasn't in love with her, even respected his essentially honest nature because he had not tried to deceive her with any false show or foolish promises. But there was something so distinct about his obvious emotional withdrawal that she felt guiltily unnerved by it.

At least Polly was pleased about the ring, Rashad was thinking wryly. It was very probably the first *positive* thought he had had in the two frantic weeks of meetings and reorganisation required before it was possible for him to free up the time to become a husband. And future father, he reflected joylessly. Back to the life of being a sperm donor and praying that the seed took root this time around, he reflected with a pang of distaste. That was, after all, he believed, the *only* reason for him to even get married: to father a child and create the generational continuity for the throne that his people needed to feel safe in the future. He recalled Ferah's heartbreak when she had learned that she had a medical condition that made conception a virtual impossibility and guilt engulfed him over his derisive musings. The ability to have a child would have meant the world to his first wife.

Did Polly have any idea what she had got herself into? And why hadn't he made the effort to warn her?

Why hadn't he? he asked himself afresh, disconcerted by that truth and belatedly recognising that he could have told Polly many things that would have put her off marrying him but that, inexplicably, he had shared not a single one of them. He breathed in slow and deep, more than a little disturbed by the worrying nature of his failure to discuss something so very crucial to the likely success of their marriage. His conscience was suddenly laden down by that awareness.

Admittedly it was a sore subject from his point of view and he saw no good reason to dangerously overshadow the present with the tragic clouds of the past. In truth he had never shared his feelings about marriage with any living person and loyalty and honour demanded that he protect his first wife's memory. After all, Ferah had suffered horribly from the stigma of a ten-year childless marriage and in death she deserved his respect at the very least.

'You need to smile,' Polly whispered under her breath as Rashad guided her out of the throne room in front of an audience of clapping and cheering well-wishers.

'Why?' he whispered back, long-lashed dark golden eyes narrowed. 'It is a solemn occasion.'

'But you're behaving as though you're at a funeral,' Polly muttered in instinctive complaint while they took their seats at a massive long top table in a giant banqueting room already filled with tables.

No, not a funeral but possibly the bonfire of his most

unrealistic hopes, Rashad labelled cynically, his facial muscles tightening so that his bronzed skin traced his sculpted features even more closely. He had hoped to stave off marriage for at least another few months but Polly's explosive effect on the Dharian population had killed that possibility in its tracks. But now that he had fallen dutifully into line, hopefully everybody would be happy for a while and he could relax again. With another person beside him though, with a *wife*... His lean, darkly handsome face tensed again, his dark eyes flashing gold with disquiet until he looked at her afresh. His very beautiful wife, who had shivered with excitement when he'd kissed her hand. He almost groaned at how hard that tantalising memory made him.

As the reception wore on Polly became increasingly troubled by Rashad's grave demeanour. For a split second she glimpsed Ellie laughing uproariously at the side of Rashad's friend, Rio, and that stark contrast sobered her even more. Surely the bride and groom should appear even happier? But Rashad wasn't talking, he wasn't smiling, he was the very antithesis of happy and she was shocked and unnerved by it. Most particularly, Ellie's warnings were haunting her again.

How much do you really know about Rashad?

And all of a sudden Polly was in the deeply unenviable position of admitting that she knew virtually nothing about the man she had just married. As soon as the meal was done she submersed herself in her grandparents' sincere happiness on her behalf and their evident conviction that she had married a man who would move heaven and earth to make her happy. Seemingly they saw nothing amiss with Rashad's behaviour.

Was he one of those very moody men one heard about? Oh, dear…oh, no, she thought in dismay at the prospect of being wed to a man who switched from sun to shade at the roll of a dice. Or was it only her that was noticing—or *imagining*—that something was wrong? Was she seeing Rashad from a different perspective now? After all, Hakim was very much a man who served his King and as long as Rashad was courteous her grandfather would be content with the surface show and question no deeper. But it was a little more complicated for a wife, Polly reasoned anxiously, particularly a wife, who suddenly felt as though she had married a stranger…or a Jekyll and Hyde character.

A white open-topped limousine, accompanied by a heavy escort, drove them slowly through the streets of the capital city to the airport. Hundreds of soldiers and police held the excited crowds back behind barriers. Polly waved and smiled as her grandfather had told her she must while marvelling that Rashad's marriage could ignite such demonstrations of sheer joy. She could only hope that she would somehow manage to live up to the people's no doubt high expectations of her and in an undertone, above the loud clamour, she shared that thought with Rashad.

'Get pregnant. That's probably the only thing they really want,' Rashad pronounced very drily.

Polly's blue eyes widened to their fullest extent as her head whipped round to stare at his lean, darkly handsome face in shock. 'Are you serious?' she framed, shrinking not just from his blunt words but from the harshness with which he voiced them.

'You can't be that naïve,' Rashad responded drily. 'It's not as though either of us have a choice in that department and that cliché about honeymoon babies would be a real feat to pull off.'

Polly had paled, the delicate lines of her face freezing as she carefully turned her head away again to dutifully continue waving and smiling. But neither the wave nor the smile came as freely or as easily as earlier because her heart had frozen inside her and her tummy had turned over sickly at his response.

When Rashad had said, 'I want you' was that why? He simply needed a wife to impregnate as quickly as possible? And why, oh, why was she only now thinking about something that should have been obvious to her from the outset? Obviously a king wanted and needed an heir. She hadn't even thought about birth control and now she could see that even the mention of it would go down like a lead balloon. Was she ready to get immediately pregnant? Were they to have no time to become accustomed to living together as a couple before they became a family?

Rashad noticed that Polly had transformed into a still little statue by his side and faint dark colour flared along his cheekbones because he was discomfited by the reality that he had taken his bitterness out on her. 'I'm sorry,' he said instantly. 'I didn't mean that quite the way it sounded.'

As if from a distance, Polly looked down at the lean brown hand suddenly resting warmly on hers but it was too little, too late from a bridegroom who had avoided all physical contact throughout the long and exhausting day they had shared.

Freeing her hand without making a drama of doing so, she said flatly, for the sake of peace, 'I'm sure you didn't.'

I'm sure you didn't mean to be that blunt and insensitive.

I'm sure you didn't mean to make me feel like a rent-a-womb.

I'm sure you didn't mean to pile so much pressure on me when conception is not something I can control.

I'm sure you didn't mean me to see just how ruthlessly pragmatic you are about conception.

But you did.

She kept up her valiant smile but her eyes stung with tears and her heart felt as if he had taken it in his hand and crushed it. What remained of her determination to have a happy wedding day drained away as well.

If he wasn't prepared to make any effort, why should she?

CHAPTER SIX

POLLY DROPPED OFF into a nap on the helicopter flight. The noise of the engine combined with her fatigue to simply knock her out. She surfaced when Rashad shook her shoulder. Flushed and bewildered, briefly not even aware of *where* she was, she stumbled stiffly upright to move to the exit, only to be scooped out and carried away from the craft like a bundle. But the natural heat of Rashad's body penetrated even through their clothing and she stiffened in dismay, engulfed by the glorious scent of him. It was a typical Eastern layered fragrance and the already familiar hints of sandalwood, saffron and spice were outrageously exotic and she breathed him in dizzily, all her senses firing as he settled her firmly into the vehicle awaiting them.

'Where are we?' she framed slightly unsteadily when Rashad climbed in after her.

'By the sea. My grandfather used to come here to fish,' Rashad proffered, sounding rather more animated than he had earlier.

And in reality, he was feeling much more relaxed than he had been at the outset of the day. Haunted as he was by destructive memories, the wedding had been like a long dark tunnel of recollection he'd had to fight his way through without betraying himself. But then he would feast his gaze on his bride and the wild seething hunger she incited would claim his brain like an intoxicating drug that made rational thought impossible.

In the midst of recalling their last conversation, Polly stiffened and glanced at him from beneath her eyelashes in a quick sidewise foray, noting the classic purity of his strong profile and the more relaxed line of his beautiful mouth. Evidently escaping the wedding fervour at the palace and the street celebrations in Kashan had revitalised him.

'When I was a little boy, my grandfather brought me here to stay with him several times,' he told her.

'So, you're into fishing?' Polly gathered, forcing herself to speak, to make the effort, although it was hard when she herself was in a remarkably tough and unforgiving mood. He had spoiled her day. He had ridden roughshod over her feelings. But then maybe Rashad didn't have much in the way of feelings, she reflected, feeling downright nasty because he had hurt her. Get knocked up on the honeymoon and please everyone? He had very much picked the wrong bride for that little project. And yet that brief instant when he had carried her out of the helicopter had enveloped her in a cascade of erotic anticipation that made her want to lock herself away because she wasn't quite sure she could trust herself to maintain restraint around him.

'No, I'm not,' Rashad admitted. 'Fishing is too slow a pastime for me. I only have such good memories of those trips because it was rare for me to receive any male attention in those days. I literally never saw my father…and for that matter, I seldom saw my mother. I was my father's third son by his third marriage and of very little importance in the royal household.'

'So, there was a sort of hierarchy in your family?' she remarked, her curiosity engaged in spite of her mood. She was taken aback to learn that he had had little contact with his royal parents even before their death. Yes, she had grasped that her mother had been his nanny but she had still possibly naively assumed that he had continued to enjoy regular interaction with his mother and father.

'Of course. Nobody ever said no to my eldest half-brother because they believed that one day he would be King. Naturally as third in line behind two healthy siblings it was not considered possible that I would ever inherit the Dharian throne.'

Polly watched his lips part and then close again, his strong jaw clenching. She knew that he was remembering the two half-brothers who had died with his parents and her soft heart was pierced on his behalf. 'I'm sorry that you had to lose your family to become what you are today.'

'As God wills,' he murmured with husky finality.

Night was folding in fast around them. The sun was going down in scarlet splendour over the dark shimmering sea while against that backdrop and raised on a rocky outcrop above the beach she could see the silhouette of a battlemented stone building. 'A…castle…?' Polly mumbled. 'We're going to stay in a castle?'

'My grandfather and his friends once used it as a fishing lodge. Don't worry,' Rashad told her, misinterpreting her reaction. 'It's not as medieval as it looks. Our private apartments were renovated soon after I became King. The castle is one of our national treasures—'

'You mean it's open to the public?' she prompted in surprise.

'Only when we're not using it—which means it's open most of the year. It's a Crusader castle and if we want to attract tourists we must offer historic sites. The royal family owns all the sites but from now on we will share them with our people.'

Minutes later, Polly slid out of the car in a stone courtyard while staff rushed around them bowing and grabbing up luggage and smiling endlessly to display their pleasure at their arrival. And Polly thought in wonderment, Rashad's *talking* again. Was that because it was their wedding night with all the expectations that that signified? What else could it be? Her chin lifted and her mouth compressed.

They were ushered into a giant stone room furnished like a very opulent historical set piece. She gazed in awe at the huge scarlet and gold fabric-draped four-poster bed and the matching silver and mother-of-pearl-inlaid furniture. 'Please tell me there are modern washing facilities somewhere,' she whispered.

With a husky laugh, Rashad opened a small arched door in one corner and spread it wide to display the marble-tiled bathroom, presumably custom built to fit the circular turret room.

His laugh and that spontaneous smile brought her head up again, silvery blonde hair spilling across her shoulders, and she connected with black-lashed golden eyes so heated in their steady regard that something in her pelvis burned, liquefied and positively ached. Her heart raced and her face hurt with the effort it took not to smile back but how could she smile and forgive and forget when all her husband wanted her for was to provide him with an heir? He had pretty much ignored her throughout their wedding day, she reminded herself stubbornly, and if his outlook had improved it could only be because he now expected to have sex with her.

Momentarily, as she freshened up at the vanity unit, she paused when she caught a glimpse of her hectically flushed face in the mirror. She couldn't do it— she *couldn't* do the sex thing coldly, on demand, not the way she felt now!

She had always wanted that first experience to be special and she had expected it to be special with Rashad right up until he had made her feel like an anonymous female body to be impregnated. Was she being unfair? Even unreasonable? She knew he needed an heir but following on from his behaviour throughout their wedding that had been a step too far into the dark for her to accept.

Her body was hers alone to share or deny. She had always been the least likely woman to be coaxed into doing anything she didn't want to do because for all her eagerness to please she had always had a very strong sense of self. But until she met Rashad she hadn't actually *wanted* to have sex with anyone, not that acting as her grandmother's carer for years had given her many opportunities in that department, she conceded ruefully. But right now, this night, *this* moment felt very wrong to her because she needed more from Rashad than he had so far given her to feel safe with him…and yet?

Deep down inside she wanted him, *craved* him as much as her next breath of air, she acknowledged in driven discomfiture. Her brain might say one thing but her body was singing an entirely different tune. Her breasts were full and tight and there was something like a little flame burning low in her pelvis that had made her all tender and damp and aching in a place she had literally never thought about before. But it wasn't right, she reminded herself doggedly. Where was her self-respect? Her courage?

Well, what are you waiting for? she asked her now wildly flushed reflection in the mirror. She had to tell him before expectations got out of control.

Rashad watched Polly emerge from the turret room and he strode forward, involuntarily drawn by the sheer effect of her delicate ethereal looks and all that beautiful trailing white-blonde hair. He stretched out a hand to clasp her smaller one, tugging her to him with an impatience he couldn't control even though his brain was warning him to go slow. There was so much hunger inside him for the bubbling warmth of her smile and the as yet undiscovered delights of her slender body and he wrapped his arms round her to capture her.

'Rashad…' Polly gasped, disconcerted by that sudden advance.

'You're my wife now. In some ways, I don't really believe it yet,' he confided in a thickened undertone, slowly winding a brown hand into the fall of her silky hair, long brown fingers gently caressing her pale-skinned throat. 'I can't believe you're mine—'

'Yes, b-but...' Polly stammered, struggling to hold onto her wits that close to Rashad when she could feel the thump of his heartbeat through their clothing and the heat and strength of his big muscular body against hers. He was fully aroused and she could feel the hard thrust of him against her. In receipt of that very sexual message the kind of brutal need she had never had cause to feel before held her rigid with momentary indecision. In that instant she wanted *so* badly to let him touch her just as she urgently wished to touch him. She ached to smooth explorative fingers over that long bronzed muscular body and learn everything that had until now been denied her.

'And there is no fancy protocol that can keep us apart now,' Rashad continued with a raw-edged smile of satisfaction, his gorgeous black-lashed, dark golden eyes locked to her wide blue gaze as he lowered his head.

His sensual mouth came down on hers with a devastating hunger that travelled through her slight length as violently as a lightning bolt. His tongue plunged deep, electrifying her with sexual desire. He tasted so good she moaned into his mouth, helpless in the grip of her desire to deny herself, never mind him. Rashad pushed up the long trailing length of her dress and found her, fingers flirting with the silky panties she wore and then sliding beneath the elastic to find her feminine core. Something similar to spontaneous combustion detonated at the heart of Polly's quivering body. She was so eager to be touched, she felt scarily out of control and that shocked her, reminding her that she *had* to pull back if she was to have any hope of defusing a difficult situation with honesty. Feeling as she did, it was wrong to be submerging herself in wholly physical sensation, she reminded herself fiercely, and she yanked herself back out of his arms with so much force that she stumbled back against the footboard of the huge bed, her hair tumbling across her face.

Taken aback by that vehement withdrawal, Rashad stayed where he was, a bemused frown forming between his black brows, dark yet bright as stars eyes glittering and narrowing. He had never looked more beautiful to her disconcerted gaze. 'What's wrong?' he asked levelly.

'I can't do this with you tonight,' Polly muttered hoarsely, still struggling to control the inner quaking of need that had momentarily burned right through her defences. Even as she stood there she was alarmingly aware of the pained ache between her thighs, the high of her excitement abating with painful slowness. 'I'm sorry, I can't. I'm not ready to go to bed with you… er…yet…'

'We are married.' Rashad framed the words with pronounced care, without inflexion, without expression. 'We are man and wife. What possible objection could you have?'

'Probably nothing that you will really understand,'

Polly countered in a discomfited tone. 'I hardly know you, Rashad. I haven't really even seen you since I agreed to marry you and today you were weird—'

His extreme stillness remained eerily unchanged. 'Weird?' he repeated darkly. 'In what way?'

'How can you ask me that when you wouldn't speak to me or look at me or even touch me if you could avoid it throughout the wedding festivities?' Polly demanded emotionally. 'I would have settled for friendliness if that was the best you could do.'

'Polly…it was a state wedding with television cameras and an army of onlookers. *Friendly?*' An ebony brow elevated in apparent wonderment and his entire attitude made her feel small and stupid and childish. 'I don't have the acting ability to relax to that extent in that kind of public display—'

Polly had turned very pale. 'It was more than that. You acted like…like you were *hating* having to marry me!'

Rashad lost colour below his bronzed skin, his strong facial bones tightening, because in truth he was in deep shock at what was unfolding. He was a very private man. Even as a child he had been forced by circumstance to keep his thoughts and feelings absolutely to himself. And in all his life nobody had ever been able to read him as accurately as *she* just had and it made him feel exposed as the fraud he sometimes feared that he was. He had done his duty, he conceded bitterly, but clearly he had not done it well enough to convince his bride. 'Why would you think such a thing of me?'

'If you lie to me now, it will be the last straw!' Polly warned him shakily. 'I deserve the truth.'

Rashad angled his proud dark head back in the smouldering silence that had engulfed them. Somewhere in the background Polly could hear the timeless surge of the sea hitting the shore outside and, inside her own body, she could feel the quickened apprehensive beat of her heart.

'For me, the last straw would be that you have married me today and now, quite independent of any reason or discussion, have decided that you will *refuse* to consummate our marriage!' he bit out rawly. 'That, by any standards, is unacceptable.'

His roughened intonation made Polly flinch at the standoff she had hoped to avoid by explaining her feelings. 'Trust a man to bring it all down to sex!' she shot back bitterly. 'Of course you can't get me pregnant if we don't have sex, so I suppose that has to be your main grounds for complaint—'

'I've had enough of this,' Rashad ground out abruptly, too many damaging memories tearing at him to allow him the calm and patience required to deal with an emotionally distraught bride. 'I'm going out.'

Polly was stunned by the idea that he would simply walk out on a row. 'You can't just walk out... Where are you going to go, for goodness' sake? We're on a beach surrounded by desert in the middle of nowhere! And what will people *think*?' she exclaimed in sudden consternation.

'Let me see...' Rashad inclined his handsome dark head to one side in a way that made her want to slap him, the slashing derision in his gaze unhidden. 'They will think that a honeymoon baby is unlikely,' he breathed curtly. 'But thankfully they will not know that my bride refused me!'

He strode through a connecting door she hadn't noticed until that precise moment and the door thudded shut in his wake. The silence that spread around Polly then felt claustrophobic and, her throat tight and dry, she collapsed down on the side of the bed, her lower limbs limp as noodles. What had she done? she asked herself in belated consternation. What on earth had she done? The right thing? Or the *wrong* thing?

In the room next door, Rashad paced the floor, smouldering with a rage so emotionally powerful it disturbed even him. But he never ever lost his temper with anyone because the need to regulate any potentially dangerous outburst had been beaten into him at an early age. He had taught himself to master his volatile nature, he had taught himself to quell the passion that fired him and...and walk away. But the look on his bride's face when he'd walked away had been frankly incredulous. Too late he was discovering the downside to marrying a woman unafraid to fight and argue with him.

As he paced, on several occasions he strode back towards the door that separated their rooms, eager to defend himself, but each time he stopped himself and backed off again. What, after all, *could* he say to her? That the knowledge he was on show in front of cameras invariably paralysed him with unease? That such intense attention had never been welcome to him and that her ability to behave with cool normality had astounded him? A man, particularly a king, was supposed to be stronger than that, more disciplined, more able to perform the essential duty of public appearances. A king was not supposed to be introspective or emotional, he was supposed to be a powerful figurehead, a flawless role model and a very strong leader. While Rashad reiterated his stringent uncle's most frequent directives inside his own head, he continued to pace in raging frustration.

He had married a foreigner with a different set of values. A foreigner who had fired an erotic hunger in him that was stronger than anything he had ever expected or even *wanted* to feel. In such a situation, it was downright unnerving and absolutely outrageous to positively *crave* another opportunity to argue with her. Tearing his attention from the door between them, he ripped off his ceremonial robes and donned more comfortable clothing. He had stayed long enough out of view not to rouse household comment at his abandonment of his new bride, he reasoned grimly as he left the room and strode down to the stables.

At least his horse wasn't going to ask him unanswerable questions and pick up on his deficiencies, he reflected with bitter humour. He wasn't sure of his ground with Polly, he acknowledged, furious at that demeaning reality. In truth his previous experience with Western women had been purely sexual and casual and nothing more than that. But he did have considerable experience of being denied sex. That Polly should do that to him when he recognised that she felt

the same chemistry he did had enraged and frustrated
him beyond bearing.

What did she want from him? What the hell did she
expect from him? So, he had acted *weird*?

Possibly a bit stiff and silent, he interpreted as he
directed his stallion, Raza, across the desert sands at a
pace that his guards were stretched to match. But then
Rashad had been born to the saddle and raised from the
age of six within a nomadic tribe, who ranged freely
across the vast desert landscape that spanned several
countries and recognised no boundaries. That same
innate yearning for complete freedom had been bred
into his bones but the sleeker, more sophisticated man
he had inevitably become wished he had paused to
take a cold, invigorating shower before his departure.

He didn't get women, he reflected, recalling Rio
once admitting the very same thing. And if Rio, an in-
curable playboy with vast experience of the opposite
sex, didn't understand women, how was Rashad ever
to understand the woman he had married?

Ironically he had been brought up to believe that
he would own his wife's body and soul much as he
owned his horse. Maybe he should've thrown that at
her to show how far he had travelled from the narrow-
minded indoctrination of his youth. So backward had
his ancestors been that they would have taken such a
refusal as a justification for forcing the issue. He was
fairly certain Polly would not have been impressed by
that admission and he could not imagine ever wanting
to physically hurt a woman. But there were other ways
of harming and hurting a wife. Even by the tender age

of six he had heard and seen enough in the palace of his childhood to grasp that his mother was pitied by some and blamed by others for his father's relentless debauchery. That was why when Polly had banished him from the marital bed he had wanted to protect her reputation by waiting in the room next door.

But, in spite of that concession, Rashad remained blazingly, scorchingly angry with his bride. What a way to embark on a new marriage! This was not what *he* had wanted. Separation was not a way forward and sex was not a reward for good behaviour. And what was Polly's idea of good behaviour? Rashad hadn't a clue. He was right back to where he had started out, utterly in the dark as to what way he had somehow contrived to fall short…

Eventually, and only once Polly had surrendered all hope that Rashad would reappear and discuss their quarrel, she removed her jewellery and undressed and got into the giant bed. She felt curiously overwhelmed and deflated by the reality that she was *alone* on her wedding night. She couldn't even understand her own reaction, because she had *asked* him to leave her alone and now to feel dissatisfied on that score seemed perverse.

In truth, she recognised ruefully, on some level inside herself she had expected Rashad to reason, persuade or even seduce her into changing her mind. But Rashad hadn't done anything so predictable. Instead he had walked out on her. Angry? Bemused? Hurt? She discovered that she didn't like to think that he was either hurt or confused by her behaviour. But she *must* have hurt his pride, she finally acknowledged unhappily, wondering why she had not foreseen that very obvious consequence.

The next morning, she came awake with the sunlight. At some stage while she still slept her luggage had been unpacked. Her grandparents had insisted on equipping her with a new and more appropriate wardrobe to wear after the wedding. She had picked out styles she liked with a trio of Dharian designers and had been concerned by the likely cost of such exclusivity even after Hakim assured her that he was well able to afford such a generous gesture.

Polly extracted a comfortable dress and smilingly dismissed the maid kneeling at the door ready to assist her into her clothing. The blue sundress was light and airy and, with canvas shoes on her feet, she sat down to breakfast on the terrace on the floor below, to enjoy the view of the sea while telling herself repeatedly that she was not one whit bothered by Rashad's vanishing act. At some stage of the night that had passed, however, she *had* reached new conclusions about what she had done.

When she had been getting so wound up before the wedding, Rashad had been completely absent and unable to answer or soothe any of her concerns. Her sister's dire fear that she was making a mistake had encouraged her own insecurities, which in turn had exploded when Rashad had appeared to act differently throughout their wedding day. Had she imagined that he was different? Had she been looking for trouble, seeking a fatal flaw that would give her the excuse to step back and take stock of her new marriage? After all, what did she want from Rashad when she already knew that he didn't love her?

Honesty, respect, trust, caring, affection, she listed anxiously, her lovely face clouding as she acknowledged the unrealistic level of desired perfection inherent in making such a list about a man, particularly on the very first day of a brand-new marriage.

When Rashad in person appeared out of seemingly nowhere and joined her without fanfare and with a seemingly relaxed smile to bid her a good morning, Polly was so disconcerted she almost fell off her chair in shock.

'My goodness, I was wondering where you were!' she exclaimed helplessly.

Her attention involuntarily welded to the impressive physique outlined by a white tee shirt that hugged his muscular chest and biceps and faded jeans that outlined his narrow waist and long powerful thighs. In fact, although the sun hadn't at so early an hour been bothering her, she heated up so much she began to perspire. 'Last night—'

'We will not discuss last night,' Rashad broke in decisively. 'We were both overtired after the wedding.'

'Seriously…we're sweeping the dust under the carpet?' Polly muttered in astonishment.

Rashad answered her in Arabic, and then with an affirmative yes, the sculpted full line of his eloquent mouth firming, his devastating dark eyes cloaked by his lashes.

A fair brow lifted in growing disbelief. 'And you think that's *all right*?'

'I think it is better than the alternative,' Rashad told her truthfully, heaping sugar into his mint tea.

Polly stared down blindly at her own tea. 'What happened to the man who said dissension could be stimulating?'

'He learned that that brand of stimulation can be treacherous,' Rashad countered with level cool.

And that fast, Polly wanted to scream at him again and so powerful was that urge that her teeth chattered together behind her murderously compressed lips. He could set off a seething emotional chain reaction inside her and make her madder than anyone else had ever done and it seriously unsettled her. She sipped at her tea with a stiff-fingered hold on the tiny glass cup and looked out to sea in angry silence, her mouth tightly compressed.

'You see now we have nothing to talk about because you can't gloss over a major row and simply pretend it never happened,' she then pointed out, not feeling the smallest bit generous, especially not after having lain awake for half of the night wondering where he was, how he felt and what he was doing. Evidently if he simply moved on past the dissension without requiring any contribution from her, he had done no such wondering.

'We did not have a row, we had different opinions.' Rashad persisted in his peace-keeping mission much as he persisted against all odds to direct challenging meetings staged between enemies and rivals.

Polly almost lunged across the table as she leant abruptly forward, silvery blonde hair rolling across her slim shoulders like a swathe of heavy silk. 'I *want* a row!'

Rashad levelled resolute dark eyes on her, raw tension gripping him because he only had to look at that rosy soft mouth of hers to want to back her down on the nearest horizontal surface. Hell, it didn't even have to be horizontal, he acknowledged, his inventive mind rushing to supply every erotic possibility imaginable. His jeans uncomfortably tight around the groin, he flexed his broad shoulders. 'You're not getting one.'

'Even if I say please?' Polly pressed helplessly, because she genuinely believed that they had to discuss what had happened to move beyond it.

'With regret…not even if you beg,' Rashad spelt out a tinge more harshly. 'Rows are divisive and risky and we will not have them—'

'Says the King. But we still need to clear the air,' she muttered, shaken by an increasing fear that he really did believe such an approach could work.

'As far as I am concerned the air is already clear and further discussion would be overkill,' Rashad concluded in a tone of finality as he began to peel a piece of fruit, waving away the manservant who immediately approached him in a keen attempt to save him from the labour of such a petty task.

'Well, then you can *listen*,' Polly told him in desperation.

Rashad tensed at that seemingly new threat, dark eyes flashing gold below lush black velvet lashes as

he focused on her. Why was she trying to destroy his
calm and enrage him again? He had behaved honour-
ably the night before. He had not argued. He had not
threatened. He had walked away. This morning he had
not uttered one word of reproach. If he had told her
how he *really* felt about what she had done his anger
would've blown the roof of the castle off and scared
her. Whether he liked it or not, he was what he was, the
heir to a ruthless lineage, and his belief that his wife
belonged to him ran like a thread of steel through his
every reaction even while his intelligence told him that
life didn't work like that any more.

She looked so innocent and so very beautiful and
yet she was totally off-the-wall crazy in Rio's parlance,
Rashad acknowledged ruefully. Yet why did he continue to find that strange trait so incredibly attractive?
Why, when he was in the worst possible mood, did
that trait make him want to smile? He concentrated
on his tea, which was less likely to unnerve him than
the odd thoughts assailing him without warning. He
told himself that he didn't want to listen, didn't want
further criticism or a greater burden of guilt. After all,
he knew who was ultimately at fault. Somehow he had
screwed up. If his brand-new bride wasn't happy, he
had to be to blame.

'And perhaps now that you've eaten you could dis-
miss the staff?' she added in a disturbing indication
that she was likely to become loudly vocal once again.

Rashad signalled the two hovering servants to dis-
miss them before springing upright with fluid agility

and sitting back down on the low wall bounding the castle ramparts.

Polly immediately froze in her seat. 'No, don't do that,' she said anxiously, blue eyes fixed to him in dismay.

'Don't do...*what*?'

'Don't sit there with your back turned to a dangerous drop,' Polly urged.

Rashad studied her in disbelief and then glanced round in a sudden movement that made her gasp to scrutinise the dangerous drop she had complained about. A couple of hundred feet of scrub and rocks sloped gently down towards the beach and he had climbed it many times with a blindfold as a little boy on a dare.

'Please get up and move away from it,' Polly whispered unsteadily.

Rashad studied her again, noticing how pale and stiff she had become. 'It's *not* a dangerous drop—'

'Well, it is to me because I'm terrified of heights and just looking at you sitting there is making me feel sick!' Polly launched at him at vastly raised volume with only a hint of a frightened squeak, her annoyance at his obstinacy having risen higher still.

Rashad raised calming hands as though he were dealing with a fractious child and rose with exaggerated care to move to the castle wall. OK...point taken.'

Polly flushed to the roots of her hair and slowly breathed again. 'I just don't like heights—'

'I think I've got that,' Rashad confided straight-faced.

'So, you're planning to listen now to me?' Polly enquired stiffly.

Impatience flashed through Rashad and no small amount of frustration at her persistence. Water dripping on stone had a lot in common with his new wife. But he was clever enough to know that listening was an important skill in negotiation and experienced enough to know that marriage encompassed an endless string of compromises and negotiations. 'I'll listen but not here. I'll show you round the castle and you can talk... quietly,' he added softly, but the dark-eyed imperious appraisal that accompanied it was a visual demand for that audible level. 'No shouting, no crying, no dramatic gestures.'

'I don't do crying and dramatic gestures,' Polly told him in exasperation.

By nature, Rashad recognised the ironic fact that, of the two of them, *he* was more volatile and more likely to be dramatic and his handsome mouth quirked at that sardonic acknowledgement. The night before, Polly had been very understated but a rejection was a rejection, no matter how it was delivered, and not a pattern Rashad wanted to find in his wife. He looked at her; in truth he never tired of looking at her and the plea in her shadowed blue eyes would have softened the heart of a killer.

'OK,' he agreed grudgingly. 'But if you embark on another argument—'

'You'll lock me up and throw away the key,' Polly joked.

'Considering that that is exactly what my ancestors

did with their wives, you could be walking a dangerous line with that invitation,' Rashad murmured, teasing on the surface but fleetingly appalled by how much that concept attracted him when it came to the woman smiling back at him.

CHAPTER SEVEN

'EVERYTHING HERE IS unfamiliar to me. Your lifestyle, the customs, the language,' Polly murmured quietly as they walked along the battlements past stationed guards to take advantage of the aerial views. 'When you add you and a new marriage into that, it can occasionally be overwhelming.'

That made remarkably good sense to Rashad, who had been braced to receive a quiet emotional outpouring of regrets and accusations. Relief rising uppermost, he squared his broad shoulders and breathed in deep. 'I can understand that.'

'And I've barely seen you since the day I agreed to marry you. I realise that with your schedule you had no choice but it made me feel insecure.'

Rashad was downright impressed by what he was hearing, it never having occurred to him that a woman in a relationship with him could speak her mind so plainly and unemotionally. In silence he jerked his chin in acknowledgement of the second point.

'Yesterday was a very challenging day for both of us.' Polly's voice shook a little when Rashad settled an arm to her back to steady her on the uneven stones beneath their feet, long fingers spreading against her spine to send a ridiculous little frisson of physical awareness travelling through her all too susceptible body.

'It was...'

'I've never been in a serious relationship before...'

Rashad stopped dead. *'Never?'* he questioned in disbelief. 'But you are twenty-five years old.'

Polly explained about her grandmother's long, slow decline into full-blown dementia and the heavy cost that had extracted from her freedom while her sister was away at university. 'So, if I'm a little inexperienced in relationships, you'll have to make allowances on that score,' she told him tautly.

A frown line was slowly building between Rashad's ebony brows. His fingers smoothed lightly up and down her spine as if to encourage her to keep on talking as he stared down at the top of her pale blonde head, far more engaged in what she was telling him than she would have believed.

Polly could feel the heat of embarrassment rising into her cheeks in a wave. Gooseflesh was forming on her arms, the hairs at the back of her neck prickling while the warm hand at her spine had tensed and stilled. 'And I think that may be why I sort of freaked out last night because I was a bit nervous...*of course* I was...and you hadn't made me feel safe or special or anything really!' Conscious her voice was rising in spite of her efforts to control it, Polly looked up at Rashad in dismay and discomfiture.

And for the very first time, Rashad understood his bride without words and he felt like the biggest idiot ever born because he had been guilty of making sweeping assumptions without any grounds on which to do so. It had not once crossed his mind that Polly might be less experienced than he was. Indeed he had even worried just a little that he might not be adventurous enough or sophisticated enough to please her. With a sidewise glance at the guards studiously staring out at the desert and the beach, Rashad bent down, scooped his surprised bride up into his arms and carried her indoors. Doors were helpfully wrenched open ahead of him by the staff as he strode back to their bedroom.

'What on earth are you doing?' Polly exclaimed when he had finally tumbled her down in a heap on the giant bed in which she had slept alone the night before.

'Giving us privacy,' Rashad advanced with a sudden smile of amusement that sent her heart racing. 'I don't wish to offend you but I had made the assumption that you would have enjoyed at least a few lovers before me—'

'And why the heck would you assume that?' Polly demanded with spirit.

'Your values are more liberal. Here, although young adults now tend to choose their own partners, it is still the norm for women to be virgins when they marry. That would be more unusual in your society.'

'I suppose so,' Polly conceded reluctantly because she knew her sister fell into the same 'unusual' category, Ellie having admitted that she had yet to meet a man who could tempt her into wanting to cross that sexual boundary. 'But my sister and I were both brought up in a very strict home. My grandmother believed that both I and Ellie were illegitimate and until she fell ill she policed our every move because she was afraid that we would repeat what she saw as our mother's mistakes and come home pregnant and unmarried.'

'I know very little about your background.' Rashad settled fluidly down on the edge of the bed in a relaxed movement. 'Even your grandfather warned me against having unrealistic expectations of you—'

Polly flushed scarlet. 'My...*grandfather*? Please tell me you're joking—'

'There was no discussion, Polly, but I guessed what he meant. He merely wished to protect you from the risk of me being naïve in that line. I am *not* naïve,' Rashad completed with wry emphasis. 'But Hakim and I have naturally never discussed anything that intimate, so he could have formed no idea of my attitude in advance.'

In receipt of that explanation, her mortification ebbed. It was evident that her grandparents had made the same assumption and she couldn't find it in her heart to fault her grandfather for trying to shield her from the threat of Rashad's disappointment.

'You're not that old-fashioned,' she commented with a helpless little giggle. 'But obviously Grandad is.'

'I spent several years studying at Oxford University and that was an enlightening experience being a mature student,' he told her wryly.

'Must've been,' Polly conceded, picturing Rashad with his film-star good looks and wealth let loose to enjoy a student's freedom. 'Was that after your wife passed away?'

His lean, strong face tensed. 'Of course. I could not have left her behind here to be oppressed by her father.'

Polly frowned. 'How...*oppressed*?'

'In essence my late uncle was a good man but he was also a bully. I say that with respect because without his intervention I would not be alive,' Rashad admitted levelly. 'On several occasions during Arak's dictatorship rumours of my continuing existence put a price on my head. I could have been hunted down and killed like an animal but the tribe took me in as one of their own and protected me because my uncle was their sheikh.'

It was the first time he had given her a little window into the sheer turmoil of his formative years and it sobered Polly as nothing else could have done. Certainly it could not have been all rainbows and roses being brought up by a bully, most particularly not if he owed his very life to that same bully, who had coolly married the putative future King of Dharia off to his own daughter at the age of sixteen. Her heart was touched and she pressed her hand briefly against a lean masculine thigh in silent empathy.

'It seems we do, in spite of all that has happened, have something in common,' Rashad remarked with a flashing smile of such intense charisma that she couldn't drag her attention from his lean, darkly handsome features. 'We were both raised by strict guardians.'

'Yes,' Polly conceded feverishly, encountering the dark golden depths of his eyes with a mouth that was running dry and a stomach awash with butterflies as awareness of their proximity kicked in with electrifying effect.

'I do not want you to be nervous of me, *habibti*,' Rashad confided huskily. 'I promise you that I will never do anything that you do not want.'

'I...I pretty much want everything!' Polly confided with a strangled little laugh of self-consciousness because she didn't feel it was fair to go on acting as if she were a terrified virgin because she was not.

'Everything...' Rashad savoured the word and she flushed. 'I love your honesty.'

And he kissed her, slowly, carefully, nibbling at her lower lip, then tracing it with the tip of his tongue. In fact he turned up the temperature so gradually she was barely aware that one of her hands had crept up to spear into his thick black hair and the other to tighten on a strong shoulder. She wanted more, much more, she acknowledged, her whole body turning warm and languorous in response while the little prickles and tingles of desire were already pinching at her nipples and warming her pelvis.

'I will make it special,' Rashad intoned into the scented depths of her tumbling hair, his dark deep drawl roughened by the knowledge that she was giving him her trust.

'You can't promise that,' Polly felt forced to tell him prosaically. 'If it hurts, it's not your fault. I'm not *that* ignorant—'

'Hush...' Rashad groaned.

'No, you stop setting standards,' Polly warned him

playfully, tracing his hard jawline with a gentle fore-finger, marvelling at how much closer she felt to him as he pressed her back against the pillows and leant back to flip off her shoes, letting them fall to the tiled floor.

'I've done that all my life—'

'But not here, *now*...when it's only the two of us,' Polly persisted helplessly.

And for a split second, Rashad contemplated the strangeness of not seeing everything in the light of passing or failing and shouldering the blame, but it was too engrained a habit for him to even imagine. He shook off that alien concept and homed in on his bride instead, studying that ripe rosebud mouth with an amount of hunger that threatened his control.

He kissed her again and the passion he couldn't con-ceal burned in that kiss and it thrilled her as much as the hungry thrust of his tongue melding with her own. He was *so* intense, she thought tenderly, no mat-ter how hard he tried to hide it. He took far too many things far too seriously. Maybe she would be able to make him lighten up a little and relax more. But that solemn thought was quickly engulfed by the intoxi-cating delight of his demanding mouth crushing hers beneath his own. Little noises she didn't recognise es-caped her throat.

He slid her out of her dress with admirable ease, so deft at the challenge that she was a little surprised to find herself lying there clad only in her lace underwear. All of a sudden she was worried about what he would think of her body, which she knew was kind of aver-age. Breasts neither large nor small but somewhere in between. Hips a little larger than she would have liked, legs and ankles reasonably shapely, she reflected ruefully, shutting her eyes, just lying there, not wanting to beat herself up with such foolish thoughts.

'*Ant jamilat jiddaan*… You are so beautiful,' Rashad told her with fervour, and she dared to open her eyes again.

And yes, it *was* her body he was scrutinising much as if she were the seventh wonder of the world. Emboldened, Polly arched her spine to make the most of her assets, relishing his admiration while thinking no more about her physical imperfections. Her blue eyes settled on him and she murmured shyly but with determination, 'You're still wearing too many clothes.'

His dark golden eyes gleamed with appreciation and he pulled off his tee shirt to reveal a bronzed and indented muscular torso worthy of a centrefold. The tip of her tongue crept out to moisten her dry lips as her gaze crept inexorably down to the revealing bulge at his groin. Apprehension was the last thing on her mind as he unzipped his jeans, showing her the intriguing little dark furrow of hair snaking down over his taut flat stomach. She stopped breathing altogether as he came back to her and fastened his mouth hungrily to hers again, the warmth of his big body against her an unexpected source of pleasure.

He unclasped her bra and cupped a pale pouting breast, long fingers toying with the taut pink tip, rolling it, gently squeezing the distended bud before sucking it into his mouth and teaching her that that part of her body was much more sensitive than she would ever have believed. The tug of his lips on the straining tips of her breasts sent a pulling sensation arrowing down into the heat rising between her thighs. Lying still became a challenge while her hips dug into the mattress beneath her. The hollowed ache at the heart of her increased, making her restless and stoking her craving for more.

'You're not letting me touch you,' Polly muttered in a rush, gripped by the fear that she wasn't being much of an equal partner. 'Isn't this supposed to be a two-way thing?'

'It is but it would please me most if this first time between us is for you, not for me,' Rashad countered with assurance.

A little red in the cheeks, Polly abandoned her objections, particularly when he made a point of pinning her flat with another passionate driving kiss and her temperature rocketed up the scale. He tugged off her panties and finally touched her where she most longed to be touched, tracing the delicate skin at the apex of her thighs and concentrating on the tiny nub that seemed to control her every nerve ending.

The pleasure was the most irresistible sensation she had ever known. In an impatient movement Rashad disposed of his jeans and glided down the bed to part her trembling legs. She felt like a sacrifice spread out before him and it heightened her arousal. Before very long he contrived to teach her that what she had deemed to be irresistible pleasure could grow exponentially to an almost unbearable level. And she had never felt her body rage out of her control before until those frantic feverish moments when Rashad thoroughly controlled her with his carnal mouth and skilful fingers. Almost immediately he transformed her keen curiosity into an overpowering demanding need. Her spine arched, her hips rose and jerked and her heart thumped as madly as though she were sprinting. And then stars detonated behind her eyelids and the whole world went into free fall along with her body.

He slid over her and ran his mouth down the sensitive slope of her neck to her shoulder. A compulsive little shiver racked her languorous length. Her lashes lifted on his lean, darkly handsome features and she smiled, a little giddily, a little shyly, recalling how much noise she had made in climax and the way she had clawed at his hair and his shoulders. He brought out the bad girl hiding inside her and she rather thought she liked that, and the shimmering gold satisfaction in his eyes suggested that he did as well.

He nudged against her tender cleft and she tensed, feeling him there, hard and ready. He pushed into her with greater ease than she had expected but then he had prepared her well. Her delicate inner walls stretched to accommodate him and then he shifted his hips and sank deeper, sending a sharp little pang of pain through her that made her grit her teeth.

'Do you want me to stop?' Rashad asked thickly.

'No…' she wailed in shocked protest as in answer to his movement an exquisite little shimmy of internal friction eddied through her pelvis.

Rashad was fighting to stay in control, struggling to think about anything other than what he was doing. He shifted again, gathering her legs up over his arms, and drove into her hard and fast, rewarded by the gasp of pleasure she emitted. She was very vocal and he loved her lack of inhibition. He gripped her hips and pounded into the hot, wet grip of her glorious body with a growl of savage pleasure.

Polly could only compare the experience to a wild and thrilling roller-coaster ride. A tightening band of tension formed low in her body and the crazy rush of intense sensation heightened as he quickened his pace, changing angle, hammering into her receptive body with delicious confident force. Excitement flooded her as another climax beckoned and she could feel her body surging up to reach it, gloriously out of her control. She hit that peak with a wondering cry and then dropped her head back against the pillows, drained but wonderfully relaxed. Rashad groaned and shuddered and buried his face in her tangled hair.

'That was amazing,' she told him cheerfully as soon as she had enough breath to speak, one hand smoothing possessively over his long, sweat-dampened back.

Rashad's dark head reared up, a startled look in his dark eyes as he searched her flushed and smiling face. And then he threw back his head and laughed. 'Polly... only you would tell me that!' he said appreciatively, dropping a kiss on her brow. 'I thank you. It was even more amazing for me, *aziz*.'

'Do you think it would have been like this for us last night?' she asked, suffering a belated attack of regret.

'No, we were both too tired and irritable and I had no idea I would be your first lover,' Rashad replied, letting her off that hook with newly learned generosity as he freed her from his weight and rolled over.

Her hand sought and found his below the sheet. Had she had the energy she would have turned cartwheels because she felt happy and too laid-back to guard her words. Succumbing to her curiosity, she said lightly, 'Your first marriage was arranged, wasn't it?'

His fingers flexed and tensed beneath the light cover of hers. 'Yes.'

'Did you love her?' Polly pressed helplessly, desperate to know even though she didn't understand why she should have such a craving to know that information.

'Yes,' Rashad replied, stifling his unease at being forced to think back to his miserably unhappy first marriage. 'How could I not? We were childhood playmates.'

And somewhere within Polly a little hurt sensation sprang up like a claw that had the power to scratch her deep where it didn't show. She didn't understand it because it was surely good news that he had contrived to love Ferah, regardless of the reality that it had been an arranged marriage. But perhaps she had not been quite prepared to hear that he had known Ferah so well, a young woman who would have understood so much more about Rashad than Polly probably ever would. Her predecessor, she acknowledged unhappily, would be a tough act to follow.

CHAPTER EIGHT

'YOU'RE DOING VERY WELL,' Rashad assured Polly seven weeks later. 'Your posture is much improved.'

With the ease of practice, Polly ignored the audience of grooms and guards gathered round the palace horse paddock. When Rashad had first informed her that he planned to teach her to ride she had laughed out loud in disbelief and outright denial of the idea because Polly had never been into anything even remotely athletic. Unfortunately, Rashad considered the ability to ride a horse an essential skill and from the instant she was put aboard a four-legged monster and then panicked at the height she was from the ground, the lessons had begun. If you had a weakness, you worked hard to conquer it: that was how Rashad expected her to operate. And backsliding and excuses weren't allowed.

If Rashad knew the actual meaning of the word 'honeymoon' he was hiding the fact very well, Polly conceded with rueful amusement while her mount trotted obediently round the paddock, her own body moving easily now in the saddle as Rashad had taught her to move. When she had pleaded her fear of falling as an excuse to avoid the activity, Rashad had borrowed a mechanical horse from somewhere and set it up with crash mats in the basement gym and she had spent two ghastly days learning how to fall as safely as possible. At no stage had she required Dr Wasem's attention but she had certainly picked up a few bruises before she'd learned the technique of tucking in her arms and her head and rolling to lessen the impact of a fall. When the doctor had cautiously suggested to Rashad that learning to ride could be considered a rather risky activity for a woman hoping to conceive, Rashad had scoffed.

'That will probably take at least a year to achieve!' Rashad had remarked dismissively to Polly, releasing her from the fear that her ability to conceive would be under constant scrutiny.

In fact, on that score, she had worried unnecessarily, she conceded with relief. Rashad appeared to have neither a sense of urgency nor indeed any level of expectation when it came to the question of his bride falling pregnant. Of course they weren't taking any precautions either, so she supposed that over time the odds of conception would naturally increase. It could hardly have escaped her notice that his first marriage had been childless but, when taxed on that question, Rashad had quietly admitted that Ferah had had a medical condition that made her infertile.

Rashad lifted Polly down off the mare and stared down at her with brilliant dark eyes of satisfaction. 'I'm really proud of you,' he admitted huskily. 'You've conquered your fear.'

Polly grinned. 'I'm going for a shower,' she told him cheerfully.

Their audience had vanished back to their duties when she trudged into the building at the rear of the stables that housed luxury changing and washing facilities. They had stayed at the castle by the sea for only two weeks before Rashad's necessary attendance at an important meeting of his council had interrupted their seclusion. They had returned to the palace, where it was much easier for Rashad to oversee the progress of various projects and still take time off.

But Polly still retained tantalising memories of the sea and the castle. They had picnicked on the beach and gone swimming, for both of them were proficient in the water. They had talked late into the night on the terrace and rumpled the bed sheets until dawn lit the skies. By the end of that stay at the castle Polly had admitted to herself that she had fallen head over heels in love with her husband. He could charm her with a smile and seduce her with the smallest touch but his greatest skill was that he made her feel wonderfully happy and content.

Rashad had reached the shower block ahead of her. She started in surprise when she saw him: a lithe, dark, electrifyingly sexy figure sheathed in a polo shirt, tight riding breeches and riding boots. As soon as she appeared he shut the door and locked it behind her, towering over her as she relaxed languorously back against the stone wall. He ran a calloused fingertip lightly over her pouting pink lips and breathed thickly. 'I can't keep my hands off you when I think of you getting naked in the shower, *aziz*.'

A shiver of excitement as stimulating as a storm warning snaked through Polly's slender body. While formal in so many other ways, Rashad was wonderfully earthy about sex. Over the past weeks they had probably had sex virtually everywhere they were left alone together in the palace. In his office, in the stables, in unoccupied rooms he showed her round and once, thrillingly, over the dining-room table. Polly was equally challenged to keep her hands off Rashad's gloriously masculine body. And as many of their unplanned encounters had proved to be the most sensational she literally stopped breathing when a certain smouldering look appeared in Rashad's dark golden eyes. It made her feel like the most seductive and beautiful woman in the world. And it was a level of intimacy with a man that she had never dreamt of experiencing.

Polly leant back against the wall, almost boneless with anticipation of his touch, her blue eyes starry. She was intensely aware of her own body, already screaming a welcome as her gaze slid down his body to the desire outlined by his breeches and impossible to hide.

'Getting naked, Your Highness,' she murmured playfully, 'would appear to be a sensible idea.'

Rashad planted his hands beside her head and pushed his lean strong body into hers, letting her feel the urgency of his need. 'Sensible is the very last thing you make me feel—'

Polly gazed up at him, loving every proud line and hollow of his lean, hard face and the stunning black-

fringed dark eyes that often made her breath hitch in
her dry throat. 'Well, if I have to suffer, why shouldn't
you?' she teased.

Challenged, Rashad dug his hands into the silky
swathe of hair she had unbraided and brought his
mouth crashing down in hungry demand on hers. The
very taste of her was an aphrodisiac. He was wound up
tight as a spring and Polly was the only woman who
had ever had that much power over him. He craved
her body like a drug and revelled unashamedly in her
responsiveness. At first, his extreme need for her had
disturbed him and he had tried to restrain that need,
but a willing Polly in his bed every night, and most
unforgettably a Polly wantonly bending over the dining-room table while offering him a cheeky smile of
challenge, had demolished his resistance entirely. They
had a scorchingly sexual and satisfying connection he
had never thought to find in marriage.

Polly's clothes came off long before they made it
into the shower. He tormented her swollen nipples with
his mouth while his lean fingers probed the receptive
wetness between her thighs and expertly fuelled her
hunger. He hauled her up to him and brought her down
on him, bracing her hips against the wall to take her
with hard, forceful thrusts that made her cry out in excitement and blissful pleasure. Barely able to stand in
the aftermath, she rested up against him for support
and let him carry her into the shower.

'How useful are you finding Hayat?' he asked curiously as he switched on the multi-jets of water.

'She's indispensable,' Polly admitted, for she was

making her first official appearance as Rashad's wife that evening at a diplomatic dinner in the capital, Kashan. 'She's explaining everything I need to know. She's like a walking book on faces, etiquette, clothes. I couldn't do without her.'

'That's good,' Rashad responded, hiding his surprise at the news. Polly's grandfather had suggested Hayat for the role of supporting Polly and it seemed the older man must also have seen a side to the waspish brunette that Rashad had failed to appreciate. At the same time, however, as his sister-in-law, he acknowledged that Hayat deserved superior status and recognition.

Having shampooed her hair, Polly surveyed Rashad as he lounged back against the tiled wall, slumberous and relaxed and all male to her appreciative gaze. She padded forward and rested her hands down on his wide shoulders before slowly tracing them down over his washboard abs, watching his lush black lashes shift upward, his dark golden eyes shimmer tawny with renewed desire.

'You are so predictable,' she scolded. 'Do you ever say no?'

At that sally, Rashad grinned with unabashed enjoyment, slashing cheekbones taut below his bronzed skin. 'Do you want me to?'

And no, she didn't, she acknowledged as her hands went travelling down over his lean, powerful physique in confident reacquaintance. She turned him on and she liked that power very much, adored the way he closed his eyes and simply let her do as she liked with him, the evidence of his arousal hard and smooth and pulsing between her fingers. She stroked, cupped, knelt at his bare brown feet and used her mouth on him until he groaned and shuddered and lifted her up to him with impatient hands and brought her down on him again with all the explosive demanding passion he couldn't control. Afterwards she was limp with satiation and drowsy as he washed her down, showering away the proof of their intimacy and roughly rubbing her dry with fleecy towels. Having to get dressed again was a trial, she reflected.

'I'm so sleepy,' she complained as he walked her back through the palace, his hand engulfing hers and maintaining a physical link with her that she appreciated.

'Take a nap before this evening. You'll be standing around a lot meeting people before the meal,' he warned.

'Do you need a nap?' his bride asked him winsomely.

'We will neither of us sleep if I join you in our bed, *habibti*,' Rashad parried with highly amused dark eyes and a flashing smile of acknowledgement. 'I'll catch up on some work in my office until it's time to get ready for the dinner.'

Screening a yawn and wondering why she was so very tired when she slept like a log most nights, Polly stripped in their bedroom. She pulled on a nightie rather than shock her maid, who seemed to think that sleeping in the nude was scandalous, and she slid into bed. Her sore breasts ached beneath the fabric and she put her hands over them, momentarily questioning why she was getting all the usual symptoms of her period arriving but nothing was actually happening.

She was wakened with a light snack and tea and warned that Hayat was waiting to see her. Hayat was in charge of her wardrobe and her itinerary. Reluctant to keep the other woman waiting, Polly ate and dressed in haste to join her. As she pulled on her jeans and teetered on one leg a wave of giddiness attacked her and she lurched and fell back against the bed. Her maid started forward in dismay while Polly waved her back and breathed in slow and deep, remaining where she was until the sensation ebbed. Maybe she should've eaten a little more after so much physical activity, she thought ruefully.

'Nabila said you were unwell,' Hayat commented, moving forward. 'Should I call Dr Wasem?'

'A spot of dizziness, nothing more,' Polly dismissed, knowing that the smallest hint of illness was sufficient to send the whole household into a state of either panic or premature celebration on her behalf and, as she was well aware that it was simply 'that time of the month' when she never felt that great, she didn't want to cause a fuss. Hayat had educated her about the Dharian attitude to her health and Rashad's, admitting that concern on their behalf was easily awakened by rumour and speculation and generally overexcitable in nature. Rashad's bout of tonsillitis the year before had had the leading newspaper questioning why their King had not been hospitalised and had accused the royal household of risking his health with an old-fashioned hands-off approach to medicine. Dr Wasem had been mortally offended.

'You are sure you are feeling all right?' Hayat prompted. 'Your devoted husband would never forgive me if anything happened to you.'

'I'm fine,' Polly said, wondering why that word, 'devoted', had seemed to acquire a sarcastic edge on Hayat's lips. 'It's just that time of the month, that's all. I always feel a little run-down.'

The brunette gave her a tiny smile. 'I am sorry your hopes have been disappointed...'

Polly bent her head and rolled her eyes. Hayat and the rest of the household might be eagerly awaiting the announcement that she was pregnant but neither Polly nor Rashad were concerned, both of them believing that at the very least actually conceiving would take several months. Moreover such close scrutiny on such a score was seriously embarrassing. 'I'm not disappointed, Hayat. We're only newly married.'

'I watched my sister break her heart over her inability to conceive,' Hayat told her. 'It is very hard for a woman to be in that situation—'

'But I'm not in *that* situation,' Polly broke in, hoping to shut down the too personal conversation for, while she found Hayat very efficient, she maintained careful boundaries with her and never quite relaxed in her company. The brunette was unpopular with the other staff and Polly had taken heed of that warning to stay on her guard.

'Soon enough, as time goes on, you will be,' Hayat

forecast with a look of exaggerated sympathy on her pretty face. 'How could you not be concerned?'

Polly shrugged a stiff shoulder in dismissal of the topic. 'You wanted to see me?' she prompted, keen to push the conversation in a less personal direction.

'Oh, yes. I brought the royal jewellery for you to choose from,' Hayat pointed out, indicating the large wooden box on the table. 'But I left the amber set out for you because it will exactly match the dress you're wearing.'

Polly studied the very ornate gold and amber collaret and suspected her neck might break under the sheer weight of it. 'It looks very heavy—'

'It's a favourite of Rashad's. The set first belonged to his mother,' Hayat told her quietly.

Hayat was a fund of such information about Rashad and the royal family and Polly invariably took the brunette's advice. Well, if Rashad liked it... she thought ruefully, although she was challenged to imagine him even noticing what she was wearing. He wasn't that kind of man. He didn't notice much in the way of feminine detail, having once tried to describe a dress she'd worn and he'd admired as 'that blue drapey thing'.

When it came to more practical matters, however, Rashad was a roaring success, she thought fondly. She loved Rashad so much more than she had ever thought she could love any man and, while as yet he might not love her, he was definitely attached to her. In a crowded room, his attention continually sought her out. Her favourite British foods now magically made regular appearances at mealtimes. Flowers arrived for her every day. Furthermore, he had insisted that they should settle Ellie's student loans, Polly thought with pleasure as she went into the bedroom to phone her sister in privacy.

'Ellie is part of *our* family now,' Rashad had pointed out. 'In the same way as your other sister will be when we eventually find her.'

Rashad had hired a London investigation agency to search for her missing sister the very day after she told him about her existence. Indeed Rashad took on Polly's deepest concerns as if they were his own and she loved that trait because for the first time ever she felt cared for and looked after without being made to feel like a burden or a nuisance. In the dark of the night she wakened to find him wrapped round her and, even though she got far too hot sleeping that close to him, she rejoiced in their closeness and kicked off the bedding instead of pushing him away.

'Polly!' Ellie exclaimed with satisfaction. 'I've got news about Penelope.'

'Oh, my goodness,' Polly muttered in shock, dropping down on the edge of the bed.

'Don't get too excited,' Ellie warned her. 'We haven't found our sibling yet but that investigation agency Rashad's London lawyer suggested certainly seem to know what they're doing—'

'Money talks,' Polly said wryly.

'Don't I just know it.' Ellie sighed guiltily. 'Here I am free of all my student debt thanks to the two of you.

I can't ever thank you enough for that. I've got all sorts of choices now that I didn't have before—'

'Penelope?' Polly prompted, uncomfortable with her sister's gratitude.

'Well, for a start, our sister doesn't go by that name. She is called Gemma Foster now. You'll be getting the agency report as well,' Ellie pointed out. 'Gemma was adopted but her parents, the Fosters, died and that landed her back into the foster system. She's twenty now and we just have to track her down.'

'Right.' Polly swallowed her disappointment that that was as far as the agency had got in their search for their sister and returned to an issue that was currently more on her mind. 'Remember you said that it usually takes at least six months to conceive—'

'That is *not* what I said!' Ellie sliced in, sounding infuriatingly like the newly qualified doctor she now was, having recently passed her finals. 'I said that was the average but obviously a woman *could* get pregnant the very first time she has sex without precautions. Nothing about conception is etched in stone. Why are you asking me about this again?'

'Just curious, that's all.'

'Don't be putting pressure on yourself in that department,' Ellie advised sagely. 'You're both young and healthy and you'll likely conceive sooner rather than later.'

The evening dress Polly was planning to wear was in autumnal shades of brown and gold with muted hints of tangerine. Her maid brought the amber set to her and she donned it with a frown because the necklace was every bit as weighty as she had feared and the exotic earrings were almost as bad. Fully dressed, her maid having bundled up her hair into an elaborate updo that gave her the height she lacked, she scrutinised her appearance, ready to admit that once again Hayat's advice had proved indispensable. The amber jewellery and the more mature hairstyle lent an impressive note of glamorous dignity to what might otherwise have been a rather plain outfit.

She did not see Rashad until she climbed into the limousine in which he awaited her and quite predictably, because he was never ever anything other than punctual to the minute, he was complaining that she had cut her timing too fine. As she turned towards him with a mischievous smile his attention settled on the collaret encircling her white throat and his lean, strong face snapped taut, sudden pallor accentuating his superb bone structure.

'You look stunning,' he murmured almost woodenly, turning his handsome face away, his jawline rigid.

'Is there something wrong?' Polly pressed uncertainly.

'No,' he asserted but not very convincingly.

The dinner was Polly's first public appearance at Rashad's side since the wedding and she was keen to get everything right. Hayat had prepared her well with a key sheet of useful information, listing names and faces and functions to ease her into the social evening.

Rashad, holding himself in rigid check, was temporarily drowning in his own memories. He could not see that amber necklace without also seeing Ferah wearing it. It had been her favourite, the colour of the semi-precious stones reflecting her brown eyes. During the drive to the embassy, he was steeped in the memories he had locked into a little box at the back of his head. He saw Ferah, laughing and smiling, full of energy and happiness at the outset of their marriage. Ferah before life had scarred her and fatally wounded her and *he* had let her down. Fierce discomfiture and guilt gripped him.

'Why did you choose that jewellery?' he asked with as much nonchalance as he could contrive.

'The amber gems match the dress perfectly,' Polly replied in some surprise.

'I prefer you in brighter colours,' Rashad imparted flatly, making a nonsense of the compliment he had initially paid her.

Polly squared her slim shoulders and gave a very slight shrug. 'I can't wear blue all the time. I have to ring the changes.'

Her soft mouth had settled into a surprisingly defiant line because she was annoyed with him. Didn't he realise how nervous she was at attending her first official function as the new Queen of Dharia? Didn't he appreciate that she needed support and encouragement rather than criticism? All right, he didn't like the dress, but he should have kept his opinion to himself, she reflected angrily.

Instead of clinging to his side as Rashad had expected, Polly vanished into the crush. It was obvious that she did not feel a need for his presence. Once or twice he heard her musical laughter and wondered what she was laughing at and, indeed, *who* she was laughing with. He told himself that he was grateful that she had found her own feet but, as a man whose first wife had never strayed more than a foot from him at such occasions and at all times followed his lead, he was perplexed and a shade threatened by Polly's independence.

'You've made a real find in the wife stakes with Polly,' a familiar voice drawled and Rashad's dark head spun.

'Rio?' he said in surprise. 'What are you doing back in Dharia?'

Rio Benedetti dealt him an amused smile. 'The Italian Ambassador knows we're friends and, as I had to check out a location for one of our hotels here, I volunteered to do my patriotic best to oil the wheels of diplomacy for him—'

'You mentioned Polly,' Rashad reminded him, unsettled to hear his wife's name on Rio's lips and at the same time to recognise Rio's admiration for her, because Rio was a notorious womaniser.

'Yes. She's lively and intelligent, a positive asset rather than the encumbrance you once feared a wife would be,' his old friend pointed out.

The faintest tinge of colour highlighted Rashad's hard cheekbones, for when he had been studying at Oxford with the younger man he had confided in him in a manner which, now that he was older and wiser, he would not risk repeating. 'I no longer fear that prospect,' he parried. 'In fact I am discovering that marriage suits me surprisingly well—'

Boldly impervious to hints, Rio laughed. 'Why are you surprised? She's gorgeous!'

'You seemed to be finding her sister equally attractive at our wedding,' Rashad commented, firmly moving the exchange away from his wife, whom he refused to discuss even with a close friend.

Rio grimaced. 'No, that went to hell in a handbasket for reasons I won't share. I'm afraid I landed the sister with the temperament of a shrew. By the looks of it, you got the sweet-natured one so be grateful for that reality,' he advised.

Rashad glanced across heads to where Polly stood engaged in animated dialogue with the British Ambassador. 'I'm very grateful,' he said grimly.

'Then why do you look anything but grateful?' Rio asked very drily.

Rashad truly didn't know how to answer that direct question. He shrugged a broad shoulder in smouldering silence. His brilliant dark eyes were hooded, his teeming thoughts full of conflict. He was well aware that he was being unreasonable. He had wanted a confident, independent woman as a wife and he had got one. Why was he now wishing that she would cling just a little? Seek him out for advice and guidance? Flash her eyes restively round the room, looking anxiously for him as if she needed and missed him? Why was he being so perverse? So illogical?

He invited Rio to dine with him at the palace and without hesitation chose the same evening that Polly invariably spent with her grandparents, Hakim and his wife. The less Polly was exposed to Rio, the better, he decided with pious resolve.

* * *

'You did incredibly well tonight,' Rashad told Polly on the drive back to the palace. 'You didn't once look to me for backup either.'

A sensation of unease niggled at the base of Polly's skull. Why did he make that sound more like a negative than a plus? Why had he kept his distance throughout the evening? Was she ever going to understand the man she had married? The minute she believed she had solved the mystery of Rashad he would do something she wasn't expecting and confuse her again.

'I thought you wanted me to be independent—'

'I do,' Rashad confirmed. 'I can't always be by your side and sometimes you will have to attend such events alone.'

'So why am I *still* getting a mixed message here?' Polly queried a shade tartly.

Rashad shrugged a broad shoulder as he sprang out of the limo, relieved to be back on palace ground. He knew he was being difficult, he knew he was being too emotional but he was a seething tangle of conflicting feelings inside himself and struggling to hide the fact. In truth, Polly had shone like the brightest of stars at the dinner and without the smallest help from him. He had been very impressed by the natural warmth she exuded. Yet she had still somehow managed to maintain a certain amount of royal distance and formality, a formality which in no way came naturally to her for she was one of the most unstudied personalities he had ever met. In short she had contrived to be the public success that Ferah had always longed to be but had never managed to be. That cruel comparison stopped Rashad in his tracks and yet another surge of guilt and regret bit into him.

Polly sped after Rashad into the palace, wondering what the heck was wrong with him. By the time she actually caught up with him he was poised by the window in their bedroom. He flashed night-dark brooding eyes over her lovely face as she entered. Brilliant dark golden eyes screened by ridiculously long black lashes. Her heart skipped a sudden beat, her breath catching in her throat. Her hand flew up to her constricted throat and rested on the weight of the amber necklace. With a sigh she stretched her fingers round to the clasp at her nape to undo it.

'Let me,' Rashad urged, taking her by surprise as he strode forward.

The ornate collaret lifted and he settled it down in a careless heap on a tall dresser. 'Don't wear it again,' he urged her in a roughened voice.

'Wear what?' Polly queried as she reached up and unhooked each earring in swift succession before looking at him in the mirror for further clarification.

'The ambers. I'll buy you another set,' he promised curtly, his lean dark face shuttered.

Her violet eyes kindled with curiosity. 'What's wrong with this set?' she asked bluntly.

Rashad tensed, dark lashes sweeping down to screen his expression. 'It was Ferah's favourite.'

'Oh...' Polly gasped as if he had punched her and deprived her lungs of breath, and in a way that was exactly what he had done. He didn't like seeing her wearing his first wife's much-loved jewellery? What was she supposed to take from that admission?

'It awakens unfortunate memories,' Rashad declared abruptly.

He had loved his first wife and clearly he couldn't bear any reminder of her, Polly assumed, thoroughly discomfited by that awareness. 'I'm your wife now,' she reminded him flatly, wishing that that timely reminder didn't sound quite so childish.

'I'm well aware of that,' Rashad said drily.

'And maybe I don't brush up as nicely as Ferah did in the ambers but you've just made me want to wear them every darned day!' Polly admitted in a helplessly aggressive tone. 'After all, she is gone and I'm here and I have feelings too!'

'This is a crazy conversation.' A questioning black brow elevated, doubtless urging her to think more carefully about what she was saying.

But Polly had had enough and she didn't feel like pretending or indeed lying to save face. 'No, I'm a possessive woman. Either you're mine or you're *still* hers!' Polly fired at him in angry challenge.

'Ferah is my past as you are my present and my future,' Rashad countered in exasperation.

Polly's violet eyes widened and glittered and she planted her hand truculently on one slender jutting hip. 'But your past is raining on my present so I'm not getting a fair deal,' she told him accusingly.

Rashad groaned out loud, frustration gripping him. 'What am I supposed to do about that? I cannot help my past. I cannot forget my memories—'

'No...' Polly conceded. 'But you could share them.'

'*Share* them?' Rashad exclaimed, an expression of appalled fascination stamping his lean, darkly handsome face. 'What man would do that?'

'A man who wants a normal relationship with his wife. If your memories are coming between us, you need to share them,' Polly told him abruptly, for in actuality she was none too sure of the worth of what she was proposing. After all, she didn't really *want* to think about Ferah. She preferred to forget that his first wife had ever existed, which was probably distinctly mean and ungenerous of her. Would it be worse for her to have Ferah fleshed out as a person? Ferah, the woman he had loved who must have loved him too?

'My memories are *not* coming between us,' Rashad assured her with brooding ferocity. 'And I prefer to keep my memories to myself—'

'Oh, tell me something I don't already know,' Polly scoffed in a helpless rush of bitterness. 'It's like when you were made someone locked you up internally and threw away the key!'

'I am what I am—'

'Too set in your ways to change?' Polly skimmed back thinly.

'We have only been married for a couple of months. What sort of miraculous transformation were you expecting this soon?' Rashad derided.

Polly paled at that sardonic recap and intonation and turned away. 'I'm going to bed.'

'I'm going for a ride,' Rashad told her between gritted teeth.

'No, you're walking out on me again because I've said things you don't want to deal with!' Polly condemned angrily.

Rashad settled stormy dark golden eyes on her and froze. 'Very well. I will stay.'

To talk? To share? Or to prove her wrong in her contention that he'd walk away sooner than deal with difficult issues? With a determined little wriggle, Polly unzipped her dress while watching Rashad shed his clothing. Watching him made her mouth run dry, all that sleek bronzed flesh overlying lean, hard muscle being exposed. Flushing at her thoughts, she pulled on a robe and went into the bathroom to remove her makeup.

Now he was furious with her, she ruminated wryly. Golden fury had blazed like the heat of the sun in his beautiful eyes. But he wouldn't admit that he was angry. Nor would he raise his voice or lose his temper. His absolute control of his emotions mocked her trembling hands because she was so wound up she felt as though she might explode with the powerful anxious feelings racing round inside her.

Seeing her in his first wife's jewellery roused 'unfortunate memories'. It made him angry too. Had he watched her tonight in that wretched amber necklace and wished she were Ferah? What else was she supposed to think?

Rashad studied Polly's slender figure. The silk of the robe outlined the rounded curve of her derriere and delicately shaped her pouting breasts, hinting at her prominent nipples. His reaction was instantaneous and it infuriated him but there it was: the lust to take, the lust to possess gripped him almost every time he looked at his wife. The strength of that craving disturbed him as much as his loss of self-discipline. Hard as a rock, he stepped into the shower and put the jets on cold but it didn't help because all that out-of-control emotion washing about inside him like a dangerous rip tide threatening to drag him down only heightened his arousal, exacerbating his need to be close to Polly in the only way he knew.

Share his memories? Was Polly crazy to suggest such a thing? He did not want to relive his unhappy marriage to Ferah. The two women could not have been more different, he conceded heavily. Polly wanted to talk about sensitive issues but Ferah had refused to talk and had brooded on her disappointments until she was overflowing with the bitterness and self-pity that had eventually plunged her into long depressive episodes. How could he even consider sharing that unlovely truth with Polly?

Polly undid the robe and wondered if it would be a little ridiculous for her to put on a nightdress because they had had a disagreement. When she normally wore nothing to bed but her own skin a nightdress would be like making a statement, wouldn't it be? Ultra-sensitive and on edge, she glanced uncertainly at Rashad as he strode out of the bathroom. The air positively crackled when she collided with burning dark golden eyes and she noticed, really couldn't help noticing, his condition.

'Yes, I want you,' Rashad intoned thickly. 'But then…I *always* want you.'

'Don't say it like you wish you didn't!' Polly exclaimed, her mouth running dry, her heartbeat speeding up.

'It can be inconvenient—'

'What's a little inconvenience?' she whispered, achingly aware of him, struggling to remind herself that he hadn't dealt with her demand for more information and that she should be light on understanding while playing it cool and offended.

'I couldn't be gentle in the mood I'm in—'

Polly tried and failed to swallow. There was a wildness in his eyes, a gritty roughened edge to his dark deep drawl and, in the strangest way imaginable, she welcomed that hint that he was not as much in control as he usually was. It was almost as though a barrier had come down inside him, one of several barriers that kept her at a determined distance. 'I might not necessarily *need* gentle right now...'

Without the smallest hesitation, Rashad crossed the space between them in one stride, both arms snaking round her to bring her crashing up against his hot, muscular body. His sensual mouth feasted on hers with a ferocity that suggested she could be the only thing standing between him and insanity and she gloried in a fervour that empowered her at a moment when her self-esteem had taken a battering. After all, it was hard to be proud of being Rashad's consolation prize in the bride stakes, the replacement wife virtually forced on him by the Dharian people.

'I *burn* to be with you,' Rashad growled, erotic energy radiating from him as he brought her down on the bed, his hunger unleashed and sizzling with un-ashamed intensity. 'Every minute of the day. My appetite for you consumes me.'

She would have told him that that cut both ways but his mouth crushed hers again and the taste of him was like an aphrodisiac, the plunge of his tongue making her body arch up in a wave of shivering delight that shot a fire storm of response through her veins. There was a ripping sound as he extracted her impatiently from the entangling folds of the silk robe. Long, knowing fingers zeroed straight in on the slick pink flesh at the heart of her and she jerked and moaned out loud, on the edge of spontaneously combusting with excitement.

Rashad flipped her over and drew her up on her knees. With a heartfelt growl of satisfaction he sank into her in a single compelling thrust. She was stretched almost to the point of pain but simultaneously the raw pleasure stormed through her nerve endings like a healing drug. He took her hard and fast and that sense of being on an edge flung her up onto an endless high of breathless excitement. Carnal pleasure gripped her bone and sinew. His lack of control thrilled her because she knew that she wasn't in control either. In any case, this was Rashad and she loved him, trusted him, *needed* him, and that his savage hunger for her should be even stronger when he was angry and troubled comforted her. After all that same primal need to connect with him at such times was just as powerful and driving for her.

She was riding a ravishing surge of excitement when a skilled hand rubbed against her throbbing bud of

pleasure and the world burst into Technicolor fireworks
behind her eyelids. She jerked and cried out, caught up
in a rolling climax that detonated deep in her pelvis
and totally wiped her out. When she collapsed back
down on the bed, Rashad rolled her into his arms and
lay there with her, struggling for breath, his heart still
thundering against her.

'I'm sorry,' Rashad gritted unevenly. 'I was rough,
selfish. I am truly sorry—'

'No…I liked it…'

Long fingers pushed up her chin to force her eyes
to meet his, his concern evaporating to be replaced by
the beginnings of sheer masculine awe. 'You *liked* it?'
he whispered wonderingly.

'Uh-huh,' Polly confirmed, her colour rising inexorably beneath that stunned appraisal.

'Sometimes I feel as though there's a crazy storm
rising inside me—'

'Tension, emotion…'

'That I've failed to get under control,' Rashad pronounced, his beautiful mouth tightening with dissatisfaction.

'But you don't need to control it, not with me. With
me, you don't have to put up a front, you don't have to
impress.' Polly wrapped a possessive arm round his
lean, damp body, small fingers smoothing down sooth-
ingly over his ribcage. 'I want you to be yourself.'

'Be careful what you wish for.' Rashad turned his
tousled dark head away from her. 'Ferah chose to die
sooner than remain with me,' he said flatly, no emotion whatsoever in the statement.

Completely taken aback by that shockingly sudden change of topic, Polly tensed. *'Chose?'* she queried with a frown.

'A few weeks before she was bitten by the snake she took an overdose. Fortunately she was found in time and I arranged for her to have treatment and therapy but sadly it wasn't enough. When she was bitten she concealed the bite until it was too late for the antidote to work,' Rashad revealed. 'She died in my arms. She told me that she was setting me free…'

Polly was appalled, belatedly grasping why any memory of Ferah was liable to upset him. She almost spoke her mind to say that she thought that that was a dreadfully cruel and martyred thing to have said to him in such circumstances but common sense made her bite her lip rather than speak in insensitive haste. 'Setting you free?' she whispered instead.

'Free to marry another woman, one who could give me a child as she could not,' Rashad extended curtly. 'She knew her father had been trying to persuade me to divorce her and take another wife and that I had refused—'

'Her own *father* was willing to do that to her?' Polly pressed in disgust.

'All my uncle saw was the end game and that was the restoration of the monarchy. He saw a king with an heir in tow as a safer bet than one with a barren wife,' Rashad advanced bitterly. 'Ferah knew how he felt because he told her that it was her duty to let me go. She was already depressed. All she ever wanted was to be a mother and when that was denied her she felt worthless. Being made to feel like a burden as well was too much for her. She wasn't a strong person.'

'I'm so sorry,' Polly muttered, feeling inadequate because he had told her a much more unhappy story than she had expected and for the first time she understood that Rashad had been as much wounded by his first marriage as he had been by the traumatic changes and injuries inflicted on him by his dysfunctional childhood. The sheer extent of the losses he had endured turned her stomach over sickly, making her feel outrageously naïve.

'I should've given her more support. It's my fault that she died,' Rashad murmured with grave simplicity.

'It *wasn't* your fault!' Polly argued vehemently. 'She was depressed. You got her professional help. What more could you have done? By the sound of it, her own family did nothing to help her recover!'

Rashad stretched out with a heavy sigh. 'It's in the past and can't be changed, *aziz*. Let us leave it there.'

But although Polly sealed her lips on further comment she couldn't leave it there because she felt ashamed that she had come over all jealous and possessive about his attachment to Ferah and his memories of his first marriage. Her sister had tried to warn her that Rashad had been through the emotional grinder in the past and she hadn't really listened. He had also trained himself to control his emotions and keep his secrets and in his position that was hardly surprising. That he had let the barriers down just for a few minutes with her was a promising sign, she told herself with determined positivity.

CHAPTER NINE

POLLY SHIFTED IN the early hours, partially wakening to the sound of Rashad having a terse conversation with someone on the phone. Blinking, she turned over, eyes drowsy in the half-light before dawn as he put the phone down again and sat up.

'There was an incident on the border during the night.' He sighed, raking long brown fingers through his sleep-tousled jet-black hair. 'A man was shot but mercifully *not* killed. I'll be in meetings all day trying to calm this down, but first I have to fly out there and get the facts.'

He dropped a kiss on her brow and urged her to go back to sleep. A few hours later, Polly rolled out of bed with her usual energy and then stopped dead as a roiling wave of sick dizziness assailed her. There was nothing she could do but rush for the bathroom where she knelt on the cold tiled floor to be ignominiously sick. In the aftermath, she felt weak and shaky and it was a few minutes before she took the risk of standing up again.

She couldn't have fallen pregnant so quickly, she reasoned with herself as she stepped into the shower, needing to feel clean from head to toe. Ellie had said the average conception took around six months but that it could just as easily take longer. No, it was much more likely that she had caught some bug or eaten something at dinner that had disagreed with her digestion. Even so, she thought that it would be sensible to consult the palace doctor.

She dried her hair and got dressed, wondering if Rashad would be gone as long as he had feared. No matter what was on his agenda he generally managed to share breakfast with her and she had learned to cherish their quiet moments together. Her period was a week overdue, she recalled with sudden reluctance, but she hadn't paid any heed to that because she'd suspected that the radical change of diet and climate was playing havoc with her system. After all, last month she had been early so possibly this month her cycle would be late to compensate for that.

Hayat awaited her in the reception room next door with a list of Polly's phone calls and her emails, each starred in terms of what Hayat deemed important. That her sister, Ellie's call only rated the bottom of the list was telling. She learned that she had received an invitation to open the new wing of the hospital in Kashan and asked Hayat if she would arrange an appointment for her with Dr Wasem.

'You are unwell?' Hayat questioned, studying her with a frown.

'No. I simply wish to consult the doctor,' Polly replied.

After a busy half-hour of tests and an examination

with Dr Wasem Polly discovered that she *was* pregnant. Her idle musings to that effect were proven when she had least expected it. In truth she was stunned because Rashad's admission about Ferah's sterility and his laid-back assumption allied to her own that it would take months for her to conceive had all combined to make her look on motherhood as a distinctly distant possibility. Instead it had suddenly become her new reality.

'I am honoured beyond words to break this news to you,' Dr Wasem informed her, his huge smile warm with genuine pleasure on her behalf.

'I'll tell Rashad tonight so I would be grateful if this remains confidential,' Polly responded tactfully, well aware that in the claustrophobic gossip mill of the royal household the good doctor probably wanted to shout her announcement from the rooftops.

'Of course.'

Polly positively floated out of his ultra-modern surgery on the ground floor of the palace. A baby, Rashad's baby. He would be so happy, so *relieved*, she reflected ruefully. He had lived through the pressure of a childless first marriage and all the fertility testing that had gone with it, and she knew that he considered the entire process stressful and potentially disastrous. Now he would be able to relax and forget about worrying, she thought tenderly.

A radiant smile lit Polly's face as she began to formulate plans for the rest of the day. She phoned her sister first and beamed at Ellie's shout of delighted anticipation. Afterwards she called her grandfather's home to speak to her grandmother and ask if she could visit them on another evening. She held back her pregnancy news, wanting to share that with Rashad first.

'That would be best,' Dursa told her granddaughter in her halting English. 'Hakim is travelling with the King and will be away until late and your grandfather would not like to miss your visit.'

Her single social engagement cancelled, Polly decided to spend the rest of the day painting. She had her regular language lesson first, of course, and then spent another hour studying Dharian history and culture. The more she learned about every aspect of Dharian life, the easier she found it to understand Rashad's concerns and share them. It was particularly interesting to learn about the heroine of the legend, the saintly Queen Zariyah. Why *had* her mother named her Zariyah at birth? Her grandfather, Hakim, thought it might have been because the name was revered in Dharia and her mother had wanted to give her that link to her father's heritage, but Polly thought it was just as likely that her mother had simply thought the name was pretty. Evidently she had not appreciated or had possibly not cared that the name was almost never used out of respect for the original Zariyah. Now the world had turned full circle, Polly acknowledged, for while it was known that she was called Polly the media routinely referred to her as Queen Zariyah.

'You're going to paint,' Hayat said unnecessarily when Polly appeared in the loose sundress she usually wore for her sessions.

Polly nodded, wondering why Hayat was staring at

her, her dark eyes cool, her face stiff. Had she offended the other woman in some way? Polly pushed the concern to the back of her mind because she was not in the mood to tackle what would be a difficult conversation. In fact she kept on wanting to smile in the most stupid inane way because she was so happy about the baby she carried. As she relaxed into that startling concept she was finally allowing herself to think about what it would mean to have a child and become a parent.

Certainly, she hoped that she would manage to be a better parent than her own mother had contrived to be. Although she felt guilty feeling judgemental like that, she had had a great deal more compassion for her late mother since she had learned the tragic circumstances of her own birth. Yet Annabel Dixon had moved on from the loss of her husband by very quickly conceiving another child and once again landing the responsibility for that child onto her own mother's shoulders. Polly sighed with regret. It seemed that her mother had led a tumultuous, lonely and unhappy life, for she had never managed to sustain a lasting relationship with any one of her daughters' fathers. She wanted something very different for her own life and her own child, she conceded ruefully. She wanted love and stability and two parents for her baby, so that her child could feel safe and supported as he or she grew up.

The air-conditioned cool of the room set aside for her to use as a studio was welcome. There were two unfinished canvases on easels, one a painstaking watercolour in Polly's signature dreamy pastels of the star-shaped pool on the ground floor, the second a sunset in oils of the desert landscape. The second painting was a new departure for Polly. The colours were more adventurous, the brush strokes bolder, possibly expressing the many changes that had engulfed her since she first came to Dharia, she acknowledged thoughtfully.

And yet had she had a choice there was nothing she would change, she reflected while she painted. Rashad had transformed her life. Her gaze flickered to the ring on her wedding finger, the miniaturised fire-opal ring, and she smiled giddily, marvelling that her mother's legacy, inapt as it might have been, had nonetheless reunited her with her grandparents and allowed her to meet Rashad. Gorgeous but often unfathomable Rashad. He was passionate, clever and driven, sexy beyond words, everything she had not even known she wanted in a man until she met him. But he was also a multifaceted challenge with hidden and dangerous depths and that worried her, for she herself was not introspective and pretty much wore her feelings on the surface.

As the heat of day began to fade Polly went off to shower and change into the blue dress Rashad particularly admired. If he made it back in time she would tell him about the baby over dinner, otherwise over a late supper. In fact it didn't matter how late he got back, she would wait up.

When she reappeared, Hayat was waiting for her again. 'I'm afraid there has been an oversight. The King's friend, Mr Benedetti, is about to arrive to join him for dinner and the King is not here—'

Polly frowned, knowing how important the art of

hospitality was to Rashad and how very rude a last-minute cancellation would be. 'I'll dine with him and explain.'

Hayat gave her a bright admiring smile. 'You are daring—'

Polly raised a brow. 'How?'

'To dine alone with a man who is not your husband.'

Polly laughed. 'Neither my husband nor I are that old-fashioned,' she asserted with confidence.

Rio Benedetti was charm personified, soothing her concern that he might be offended by Rashad's absence with an easy flow of entertaining conversation stamped with an occasional subtle query about Ellie, which made Polly's sisterly antenna prickle with curiosity. After all, Ellie had evinced no similar desire to discuss Rio with Polly, claiming that she had only appeared to enjoy Rio's company at the wedding out of politeness and hadn't actually liked him at all. In fact she had dismissed him as a player with sleazy chat-up lines. Somehow, Rio had got entirely on the wrong side of her spirited sister.

The Italian billionaire did not keep her late and Polly was curled up in a corner couch on her own with a book by the time Rashad strode through the door after eleven that evening. The instant that she saw his stormy dark face, she knew that he was in a temper and concern indented her brow.

'What's happened?' she exclaimed, coming upright in her bare feet, noting that lines of strain bracketed his mouth.

Rashad regarded her in astonishment. She had spent

an entire evening alone with an infamous womaniser, utterly disregarding Hayat's advice. The minute Rashad had received that news he had assumed that his wife found Rio so compellingly attractive that she had decided to throw away the rule book and that thought, that *fear* had simply spawned an ungovernable rage that far outran any emotion Rashad had ever felt. Exhausted as he already was by an endless day of repetitive diplomacy and incessant meetings, Hayat's phone call had incensed him.

'Why didn't you listen to Hayat when she advised you not to dine alone with Rio?'

Polly tilted her chin. 'She didn't advise me *not* to do it, she just said it was daring. I thought that was nonsense when I was only trying to be polite and considerate. Telling him you were unavailable when he was literally on the way here would have been very rude and as he is a close friend of yours I thought you wouldn't want that—'

'Or perhaps the temptation of having Rio all to yourself was too great!' Rashad flung at her rawly. 'He is notoriously sought after by women.'

'Not by my sister,' Polly remarked abstractedly, suddenly recognising that Rashad, whether he knew it or not, was consumed by jealousy. 'You really don't have to be jealous—'

'*Jealous?*' The word hit Rashad like a brick thrown on glass, shattering what little control he retained. 'I have never been jealous over a woman in my life!'

'Sleep on it and then think about it,' Polly advised, losing patience and angry with him because she had been eager to tell him about their baby and now he had wrecked the mood with his temper. He was so volatile, so possessive. On what planet did he live that he believed she could be so eager to make love with him while planning to betray him with his closest friend? Had she been too eager? Was that the problem? Did he think she was some sort of natural-born wanton who could not be trusted in the radius of any attractive man? A dark flush of fuming humiliation reddened Polly's face and chest and she turned her head away from him to walk past him.

Long, lean fingers closed round her wrist to intercept her. 'Where are you going?'

'I've got nothing more to say to you.' Polly yanked her arm free and, feeling the prickle of angry, hurt tears stinging her eyes, she fled past him into the corridor. How could Rashad talk to her like that? How could he even see her in such a light? Was this her reward for matching that dark, passionate intensity of his?

'Polly…'

'I *hate* you!' Polly flung over her shoulder as she started down the stairs that led to their bedroom.

And it was that twisting round to make that final response that unbalanced her. She missed a step and lurched. Her feverish grab at the stone bannister failed and she fell, instinctively turning her body into herself as she had been taught to fall from a horse. Her hip hit stone and she cried out in pain and then the back of her head struck a step and she knew no more…

CHAPTER TEN

A FAINT MOAN parted Polly's lips because her head was aching and she came awake with a sense of frightened confusion. Her eyes opened on an unfamiliar room. She saw a bewildering number of faces, blinked and registered that she was in a hospital bed with the side bars raised.

'Polly?' Rashad breathed tautly, springing out of the chair beside her.

'What?' she mumbled because moving her lips felt like too much effort. 'My head's sore…my hip.'

As she focused blearily on him he stepped back to allow the medical staff to attend to her and she wondered why he looked so tired and why the sun was shining into the room when only minutes ago it had been dark. A nurse checked her blood pressure and gave her a drink while a doctor asked her a series of questions. Her attention, however, stayed squarely on Rashad while she struggled to recall what had happened to her. Black stubble accentuated his stubborn passionate mouth, his luxuriant hair was dishevelled, his eyes shadowed, his powerful anxiety unconcealed.

Recalling her fall on the stairs and the argument that had preceded it taxed her concentration and then, with a sudden whoosh of awareness, all that fell away on the shocking surge of apprehension that shot through her. She pressed a stricken hand against her stomach.

'My baby?' she gasped fearfully.

Rashad strode forward and rested a hand over hers in a soothing gesture. 'Our baby is fine—'

'For the moment. There has been no bleeding but you must rest. The next twenty-four hours are crucial to your recovery,' the grey-haired doctor told her firmly as he urged her to lie still.

Rashad's hand was trembling over hers and just as she noticed that he withdrew it in a sudden gesture and dug it into the pocket of his trousers. He *knew* that she was pregnant; he knew about the baby. She assumed that Dr Wasem had told him after she fell and knocked herself out. Polly closed her eyes, guessing just how guilty Rashad would be feeling. She was still furious with him but she knew his habit of blaming himself for everything bad that happened around him. If she lost their baby he would never forgive himself for upsetting her. How could she be furious with him and yet aching inside herself for what he was feeling at the same time? It was that crazy conundrum called love, she decided ruefully.

While the doctor talked to her about the concussion she had sustained, Polly tried to think clearly and focus but it was no use, she simply *couldn't*. Both her head and her body ached. The mental confusion and the extreme fatigue the doctor had warned her about were steadily closing in on her because there was far too much to think about and it was infinitely easier to close it all out just then and drift. She still had her baby, she reflected with passionate relief, and that was the last clear thought she had.

Rashad paced the silent room. He had tidied himself up in response to Hakim's pleas but he had not eaten, he had not slept. How could he? His temper, that wild surging rage he couldn't always control, could have killed Polly. He looked at her, lying so still in the bed, white-blonde hair tumbling across the pillow, her face showing a little colour now, no longer that wan grey that had terrified him. She was so fragile, so precious…

And the baby? Rashad was still stunned by that development, that incredulous realisation that, if there was nothing medically amiss to prevent it, a pregnancy could happen so quickly, so easily, so…so *normally*, he recognised. He hadn't expected that, hadn't prepared for it either. In fact he had pessimistically assumed that although they might conceive a child eventually it would undoubtedly take a long time. Once again he had made the mistake of allowing past disappointment and disillusionment to influence his expectations in the present. And how could she ever forgive him for that?

He was fatally flawed, almost programmed to disappoint Polly. He had even failed to protect her from Hayat's malice. *'Either you're mine or you're still hers,'* Polly had flung at him, referring to Ferah, and he could see that now—could see that he had failed to make peace with the past and move on to embrace a wife far superior in every way to his first. And if it was wrong and disrespectful to think that then it was better to be wrong but at least rational enough to recognise that truth. Fate had rained gold on him when he least deserved it and he had virtually thrown away the opportunity he had been given, he conceded grimly.

'You *must* eat and rest, Your Majesty,' Hakim whispered fiercely from the doorway. 'How can you support your wife if you are exhausted?'

'As always, the voice of reason,' Rashad conceded wearily, but his every instinct still warred against leaving Polly alone. At least while he watched over her he could actually feel as though he was *doing* something to help, but in reality, while she was under medical supervision, he could only be an onlooker.

Polly wakened and slowly savoured the strength returning to her body. She pushed down the bedding and tugged up her gown to squint at the horrid blue-black bruising covering her hip and stretching down her thigh. Better her hip than her stomach, she decided as a nurse came in and gently scolded her for sitting up in bed without help. Suddenly she was surrounded by staff again and she was changed and the bed was changed and then breakfast was ushered in.

An hour later, Rashad arrived, sleek and shaven in a beautifully cut dark suit. He looked fantastically handsome and considerably more groomed and calm than he had the day before. His stunning dark golden eyes immediately sought hers and instinctively she evaded his gaze, too full of conflict to meet it. He had revealed his lack of trust in her. He had believed that even though they were married she could still be tempted by another man and that she could be unfaithful. How could she overlook or forgive that?

'I have a lot to say to you,' Rashad murmured tautly. 'But first your grandparents are waiting to see you and you should see them now to reassure them.'

'Of course,' she muttered uncertainly, wondering what he had to say to her, wondering what she would say to him.

'If your medical team agree, I can take you home later.'

Polly compressed her lips in silence.

'Hayat has now gone home to her mother. She won't be returning to the palace staff,' he told her in a harsh clipped undertone. 'I was foolish to trust her near you—'

Polly studied him directly for the first time. 'What on earth are you talking about?'

His lean, strong face went rigid. 'Apparently Hayat was angry and jealous that I had married you and she decided to cause trouble between us…and in that she succeeded,' he divulged grudgingly. 'I told her to cancel that dinner with Rio before I left the palace the day before yesterday. But she didn't cancel it. She set you up instead, set us *both* up…challenging you to dine alone with him, knowing that I am *not*—at heart— the liberated male I must strive to be for your sake…'

Polly was shaken by that explanation. 'But why would Hayat be angry and jealous? Were you involved with her before I came into your life?'

Rashad frowned. 'Of course not…she is Ferah's kid sister. I found it hard to warm to her personality, though—'

'Hayat's your sister-in-law?' Polly exclaimed in disbelief. 'Why did nobody tell *me* that?'

'It wasn't a secret. I didn't think it was important. I didn't want to discriminate against her either because she is, or *was*, very efficient.' Rashad lifted his handsome dark head high and expelled his breath in an audible rush, frustration and regret tensing his lean dark face. 'I made a mistake in allowing her access to you and I'm afraid you paid for my lack of judgement.'

Long lashes fluttering down, Polly cloaked her eyes to conceal her incredulity. How could he not have warned her about his familial relationship with the other woman? She remembered Hayat admitting that she had watched her sister break her heart over her inability to conceive and, remembering her own unease around the attractive brunette, she swallowed back angry words of condemnation. His first wife's little sister, someone who would be challenged to wish Rashad's second wife a long and happy life after Ferah's tragic fate.

'Hayat admitted that she resented my remarriage and our happiness,' Rashad volunteered tautly. 'I should have foreseen that likelihood and her spite.'

'Well, it's done and dusted now,' Polly pointed out curtly, because she was annoyed at what she had learnt. 'She's left the staff and as it happens I'm all right—'

'*Inshallah,*' Rashad breathed, rising to leave as her grandparents bustled in, all smiles and concern, to present her with a very large basket of fruit. Their caring and affectionate presence was exactly what she needed to soothe her ruffled feelings at that moment. She received a hail of anxious words and a hug from her grandmother and a quiet squeeze on the shoulder from Hakim, who wasn't given to drama.

Rashad came to collect her from the hospital. He explained that there were crowds waiting for a glimpse of her outside the hospital and they left by a rear entrance.

'Why won't you look at me?' Rashad pressed on the drive back to the palace.

'I'm angry with you,' Polly admitted curtly.

Rashad released his breath on a slow hiss. 'Of course you are. I spoiled what should have been a special moment—'

She assumed he meant that she had missed the chance to tell him privately about their baby.

'Not only that,' she broke in jaggedly. 'You behaved as if I was some kind of harlot who couldn't be trusted alone in a room with a man!'

'I deeply regret the way in which I behaved,' Rashad admitted levelly. 'If I could go back and eradicate what I said I would...but I cannot.'

Colour scoring her cheekbones, Polly chewed the soft underside of her lower lip and made no response. What could she say? She *knew* he regretted it.

'I didn't like being confronted with the reality that you could think of me like that.'

'We will talk when we get home. I don't want to be interrupted,' Rashad murmured tautly.

A tense silence fell and Polly did nothing to break

it. In truth she was as annoyed with herself as she was with him. Wasn't she usually a forgiving person? But what Rashad had said had struck at the very heart of their relationship and had deeply wounded her because she loved him. He didn't know that she loved him. He hadn't asked her to love him. And she wouldn't tell him because he would assume that she craved some kind of matching response from him when she did not. She didn't want Rashad to feel that he had to pretend to feel more for her than he actually did. It would make him uncomfortable and he would be hopeless at faking it. Over the long term, honesty and common sense would be safer than emotional outpourings that would only muddy the water between them.

Tearful staff greeted her on their knees in the entrance hall. She was deeply touched by that demonstration of affection. Rashad's people were very emotional and unafraid to show it. She marvelled that they had a king who worked so hard at concealing every emotion he experienced as if emotion were something to be ashamed of.

'The doctors advised that you rest now,' Rashad reminded her as they entered the private wing of the palace.

Flowers were everywhere in the airy drawing room and piles of gifts cluttered every surface. 'What on earth…?' Polly began to ask.

'As soon as it was known that you had suffered an accident the flowers and the presents came flooding in,' Rashad explained. 'There has been no official announcement of your pregnancy, nor will there be for some time, but I suspect rumours are already on the streets. There were too many servants and guards hovering after your accident and Dr Wasem's anxiety on your behalf was unmistakeable.'

'And what about you?' Polly whispered. 'How did you react?'

'It was the worst moment of my life,' Rashad declared without hesitation, his strong jaw clenching hard. 'Until I realised you were still breathing I was afraid you were dead—'

'Or that I would lose the baby,' she slotted in wryly.

'I could have borne that better than the loss of you,' Rashad parried harshly. 'There could always be another baby...but there is only one *you*. And you are irreplaceable.'

There was a little red devil in Polly's brain because somehow she was not in the mood to listen while he made such comforting complimentary statements. 'No, I'm not,' she disagreed, turning her violet eyes onto his lean, perfect profile. 'You would still have women queuing up to marry you and become your Queen and the mother of your children.'

'Two dead predecessors in the role would limit my appeal somewhat. I would seem like a regular Bluebeard.'

A startled laugh was wrenched from Polly. 'There is that,' she conceded, turning away to hesitantly finger a tiny velvet soft frog toy that had been unwrapped.

It was undeniably a toy intended for their unborn child. Her eyes prickled with tears. Her most private secret had become public and she had been deprived of the right to share the news of her first pregnancy with her husband. She dashed the tears away with an angry hand, scolding herself for getting upset by gifts intended to express heartfelt good wishes.

'I wanted to tell you myself,' she framed gruffly.

'I know...I screwed it up,' Rashad bit out jerkily.

'Maybe we both did,' Polly muttered heavily. 'In a marriage it takes two to screw up. Whatever way you look at it, it's a partnership.'

'No,' Rashad disagreed. 'I didn't allow us to be a partnership. I have no experience of a marriage of equals. I have no experience of sharing feelings or memories. I have always had to keep such things to myself but with you...' He hesitated, shooting a look at her from shimmering dark golden eyes. 'With you, my control breaks down and things escape.'

Polly studied him and her heart felt as though he were crushing it because she bled for him at that moment, seeing him boy and man, rigorously disciplined to hold every feeling in, never allowed to be natural. 'That's not necessarily a bad thing,' she whispered shakily.

'It *was* a bad thing when I confronted you about your dinner with Rio,' Rashad pointed out heavily. 'I was...irrational. Rage engulfed me. I could not bear to think of you enjoying his company or admiring him. You do not need to tell me that I'm too possessive of you...I *know* it. I have never known such jealousy before and it ate me alive—'

'Well,' Polly murmured, inching a little closer because his sheer emotional intensity drew her like a flame on an icy day, 'I understand a little better now. But it upset me a lot that you seemed to distrust me—'

Rashad swung back to her, his stunning eyes bright with regret. 'But that is what is so illogical about it. I *do* trust you and Rio is my best friend and I know he would not betray me but *still* those feelings overwhelmed me!'

Polly brushed his arm with hesitant fingers. 'Because you're not used to dealing with that kind of stuff. You're on a learning curve.'

'I *hurt* you. If it hurts you I do not want to be on that curve,' he breathed rawly.

'But not expressing what you feel makes you a powder keg, which is more dangerous,' Polly argued.

'It won't ever happen again,' Rashad intoned. 'I will be on my guard now.'

'But that's not what I want,' Polly admitted ruefully.

'I have kept too many secrets from you,' Rashad confessed, striding over to the window, deeply troubled by his sense of disloyalty to his first wife's memory but accepting that such honesty was necessary. 'My first marriage was very unhappy—'

'But you said you loved her,' Polly reminded him in complete surprise.

'At the outset when we were teenagers trying to behave like grown-ups, we clung to each other for that was all we had. She was my first love even though we had very little in common. I made the best of it that I could but I did not love Ferah as she loved me,' Rashad declared with strong regret etched in his lean, darkly handsome features. 'And she *knew* it. Her inability to conceive was a constant source of stress for both of us and she became a deeply troubled woman. Nothing I said or did comforted her. I tried many times to get through to her and I failed. What love there was died until by the end we were like two strangers forced to live together.'

Polly stared at him in shock, utterly unprepared for that revelation.

'Now you know the *real* truth,' Rashad completed grimly.

'But…' she began uncertainly, frowning in bewilderment.

'For the last five years of our marriage I was celibate. That side of our marriage ended the day Ferah learned that she could not have a child. She turned away from me,' he revealed curtly, his difficulty in making that admission etched in the strained lines of his lean dark features. 'I felt unwanted, rejected…'

'Of course you did,' Polly framed, still in shock from what he had just told her, her every belief about his first marriage violently turned on its head and her heart going out to him.

'And that is why you were right to accuse me of a lack of enthusiasm on the day we married.' Rashad surveyed her with anguished dark eyes, full of guilt and regret. 'You said you wanted it all so I am telling you everything. I knew it was my duty to remarry but I *dreaded* the thought of being a husband again. I had nothing but bad memories of the first experience and my expectations were very low—'

Polly unfroze with difficulty and sat down on legs

that felt weak, not quite sure she was strong enough to take the honesty she had asked him to give her because what he was now telling her was beginning to hurt. 'I can understand that,' she said limply.

'I was completely selfish in my behaviour. I was bitter and angry. I felt trapped. And then you *saved* me,' he framed harshly. 'I did nothing to deserve you, Polly. I am not worthy of the happiness you have brought into my life.'

Reeling from that 'trapped' word that had pierced her like a knife, Polly studied him in confusion. 'You're talking about the baby?' she pressed. 'That's made you happy?'

His black brows drew together. 'No, I'm talking about you. Our baby is a wonderful gift and I am very grateful to be so blessed but my happiness is entirely based on having you in my life...'

'Oh,' Polly mumbled in surprise.

Rashad crossed the rug between them and dropped down on his knees at her feet to look levelly at her with insistent dark golden eyes. 'I think I probably fell in love with you the first time I saw you. It was like an electric shock. I had never felt anything like it before and of course I didn't recognise it for what it was. It was love but I thought it was lust because I didn't know any better...'

'Love?' Polly almost whispered. 'You *love* me?'

'Madly, insanely,' Rashad extended raggedly. 'I can't bear to have you out of my sight. I think about you all the time. The thought of losing you terrifies me.

And yet I have made mistake after mistake with you and done nothing to earn your regard—'

Polly grinned at him, the happiness he insisted she had brought him bubbling up through her in receipt of such an impassioned declaration. She definitely loved him and loved him all the more for abandoning his reserve and his formality and his pride to convince her of the sincerity of his feelings for her. 'I felt that electric shock thing too,' she told him teasingly. 'Every time I laid eyes on you, I felt like an infatuated schoolgirl. Why do you think I married you? I married you because I fell in love with you...'

'Truly?' Rashad exclaimed in ego-boosting amazement as he sprang upright and stepped back for an instant simply to savour her beautiful glowing face.

'Truly,' Polly confirmed with a helpless beaming smile of encouragement.

Rashad scooped her up very, very gently, being mindful of her sore hip, and carried her into their bedroom to lay her down on the bed. He shed his jacket and tie and settled down beside her to ease her fully into his arms. 'I love you so much, *habibti*. But I am forbidden to do anything more than hold you close for a few days,' he admitted in a roughened voice. 'Yet it is enough to still have that right, believe me.'

Ignoring the hint of soreness from her stiff hip, Polly squirmed round in the circle of his arms to face him. She ran wondering fingers across a high masculine cheekbone and marvelled at the silky black lashes semi-veiling his adoring eyes. 'I think a kiss is in order…and I'm expecting a real award winner of a kiss,' she warned him cheekily.

'I will try to deliver,' Rashad groaned, gazing down at her clear blue eyes with fervent appreciation. 'I always try to deliver—'

'Well, you were pretty nifty in the baby stakes,' she conceded.

'Nifty together…' He nibbled at her full lower lip and she closed her eyes, literally so happy she felt that she should be floating on high, but then she wouldn't have let go of Rashad for anything because his lean, powerful body felt so very good against hers. And they might be different and he might be much more old-fashioned than he was willing to admit, but she knew that they complemented each other beautifully.

EPILOGUE

'I CAN'T BELIEVE that after all this time we still haven't found Gemma.' Polly sighed and shot a pained glance at her sister, Ellie. 'I mean, it's been months and we still know next to nothing about our long-lost sibling!'

'Well, we know that she had a tough childhood and she has no roots to cling to,' Ellie argued in a more measured tone. 'We can also assume that she moves around a lot because we never seem to catch up with her and we know she works in *really* dead-end jobs. That's a lot more than we knew about Gemma starting out.'

Polly nodded reluctantly. 'True…but what if she doesn't *want* to know about us?' she asked worriedly. 'We've advertised in the papers, notified social services that we're looking, informed everyone who has known her in the past that we want to find her—'

'We have to be patient,' Ellie cut in firmly. 'And that's not a trait you possess although, heaven knows, you possess everything else.'

'What's that supposed to mean?' Polly prompted.

Ellie rolled her eyes. 'Movie-star-handsome King as

husband—check. An adoring population who think you can walk on water—check. Constant sunshine overhead, royal palace—check. Loving grandparents—check. An adorable baby son… Yes, I'm talking about you, you little darling!' She stopped to speak to Karim, who crawled across the rug to his aunt to grab the toy she was extending. 'I suppose you're already planning on extending the family?'

Polly flushed. 'Not just yet. I'd like Karim to be a little older before we try again. I'm not a baby machine, Ellie. I mean, look at you, you don't even date—'

'I'm too busy working. Between my shifts and the hospital and the exams I don't have time for a man. Anyway, most of them are a waste of space,' her redheaded sister contended. 'No, I like my life just the way it is. I eat what I like, go where I like, do as I like and that's important to me. The minute a man enters the equation, all your choices start disappearing—'

'And you still have no plans to look into your background?' Polly pressed.

Ellie sighed. 'Actually I'm taking a couple of months off once I complete my residency and I'm planning on heading to Italy and doing a little discreet detective work—'

'Oh, that's great!' Polly gushed approvingly. 'Will you tell me your father's name now?'

Ellie groaned. 'The reason I didn't tell you the name before is that I got given two names—'

Polly's eyes widened. *Two?'*

'Yes,' Ellie confirmed drily. 'Two names. Obviously our mother didn't know which man fathered me and, sleaziest of all, the men were *brothers*. I've done some research. One of the men is alive, the other dead. The living one is a wealthy retired art collector who lives in a *palazzo* outside Florence—his brother passed away years ago.'

Polly stared at her sister in consternation, belatedly grasping why the younger woman had been so silent on the topic of her own unknown father and background. 'Oh, dear...I'm so sorry—'

'No, you got the fairy tale...the military hero father who married our mother...and I got a pair of deadbeat dads,' Ellie mocked with wry humour. 'I'm glad it worked out that way. I can handle messy reality better than you can.'

'I could come to Italy with you!' Polly proffered in dismay. 'Be your support.'

'No, you'd wilt like a flower out of water deprived of Rashad and Karim,' Ellie forecast drily. 'And that's if your husband would even *let* you go—'

'Rashad doesn't tell me what to do—'

'No, but he hates it when you're away even for a couple of days,' Ellie reminded her wryly. 'You came over to see me at Christmas and Rashad was on the phone every five minutes. You actually fell asleep talking to him one night. Having you to stay was like separating a pair of lovelorn teenagers. It's unhealthy to be so attached to each other...'

Polly simply laughed, knowing that Ellie had never been in love. Nothing came between Ellie and the medical career she adored. But Polly had never had that burning ambition for a career and her wants and needs were satisfied by her family circle and her public role as the Queen of Dharia. She was always very busy, particularly since the birth of their son a year earlier. They had a nanny to help with Karim's care but both Polly and Rashad spent a great deal of time with their son. Polly wanted Karim to know how much he was loved and Rashad was determined to play a daily part in his child's routine.

'It's so beautiful here,' Ellie remarked dreamily, contemplating the star-shaped pool into which water flowed endlessly. Lush trees and luxuriant foliage softened the carved stone arches and pillars of the palace walls that surrounded the courtyard. 'You saw this place first, didn't you? Maybe that's why you fell for Rashad.'

'You are such a cynic, Ellie,' Rashad declared with amusement as he joined them.

Karim loosed a yell and crawled at speed across the tiles to greet his father. Rashad chuckled and bent down to scoop up the little boy and kiss him with an unashamed love that touched Polly's heart. The man she had married had slowly learned to loosen up and show his true colours. His passion in bed was now equally matched by the depth of his affection. He said that she had changed him but Polly believed he had changed himself. He was happy now and it showed in the ease of his brilliant smile and the burnished glow of his dark eyes.

'Well, was it the palace that cast a spell over you… or me?' Rashad teased, gazing down at his wife as she moved to his side.

'If you two are going to turn all lovey-dovey, I'm going upstairs for a shower,' Ellie announced in a deflating tone.

'Lovey-dovey?' Rashad queried, walking Polly out of the courtyard with an arm draped round her shoulder and Karim tucked below the other.

'Drippy...mushy,' she translated. 'Ellie hates that stuff.'

'Are we...drippy?' Rashad enquired with a pained look.

'Probably sometimes,' she said fondly. 'Who cares as long as we're happy?'

'I am not drippy,' Rashad proclaimed with distaste as Polly removed Karim from his arms and settled their son in his cot for his nap.

Karim howled as if he had been abandoned in the street and Rashad hovered worriedly.

'He's fine. He always does that. He's just like you, very resilient and he tries it on sometimes. Don't let him think you're going to lift him again,' Polly warned as she dragged Rashad out of the nursery again.

'Tough love...right?' Rashad guessed, wincing as Karim kept on crying.

'Wait,' Polly instructed in the corridor.

When he was deprived of an audience, the crying stopped and their son began to talk to himself quite happily.

Rashad smiled, much relieved by the development.

'Yeah, you're really drippy!' Polly teased with satisfaction, walking into their bedroom.

'I'm not. I'm a concerned parent who doesn't like to hear my child cry,' Rashad argued.

'And I'm what? The evil mother who left him to cry?'

'No, you're the wonderful wife who is giving me an hour of alone time with you before dinner,' Rashad said with a wicked grin as he began stripping off his clothes with alacrity. 'This is yet another reason why I love you so much.'

Polly ran appreciative fingers up over his rock-hard abdomen and watched his muscles ripple, dry-mouthed with admiration. 'I'm greedy... I always make time for you.'

He crushed her lips beneath his with a heady moan of pleasure. 'You taste so good, *habibti*.'

Her body was sparking like a fizzing firework, eager for the ignition point of his. No, they hadn't lost their passion for each other. Admittedly her pregnancy had slowed them down a bit in the final months but she had rediscovered her energy after Karim's birth and the nanny had helped by doing the night feeds. They rolled across the bed kissing and exchanging sounds of mutual love and longing and, as always, it was amazing. They lay together afterwards, wrapped in each other and temporary satiety.

Rashad ran his fingers through her hair, stared down at her peaceful face with true devotion in his gaze. 'You really are the best thing that ever happened to me,' he told her gruffly. 'When I wake up in the morning and see you beside me, my heart lifts and I feel that I can cope with anything.'

'I love you too,' Polly whispered with shining eyes.

And he kissed her again and dinner was served late and Ellie gave her sister a withering glance.

'And you looked at me when I said you were like teenagers?' she quipped.

'Wait until you fall in love,' Polly urged.

'Not going to happen. I'm too sensible,' her sister assured her confidently.

* * * * *

If you enjoyed this story,
don't miss Lynne Graham's other great reads!
THE GREEK'S CHRISTMAS BRIDE
THE ITALIAN'S CHRISTMAS CHILD
BOUGHT FOR THE GREEK'S REVENGE
THE SICILIAN'S STOLEN SON
LEONETTI'S HOUSEKEEPER BRIDE
Available now!

Also look out for the second book in
Lynne's BRIDES FOR THE TAKING trilogy,
coming in April 2017!

'Would you not prefer me to make love to you?'

Darcy gasped. 'You shouldn't say such things to me. You—you know you shouldn't.'

'Are you telling me you don't want me, Darcy?'

She was suddenly quite faint. The things that Zafir's deep bass voice *alone* could do—never mind his looks... Where on earth was she supposed to go with such a question?

'All I'm saying is that I—I need to be sensible, and you're making it impossible for me.'

'Once…not so very long ago…you were my woman. Now we have a child together. That confirms you are *still* my woman.'

'I am no such thing. And nor am I some chattel to do exactly as you tell me just because you think it's some inalienable right you have.'

'Is that really how you view me? As someone who wouldn't even *consider* another person's rights if they happen to conflict with my own? That is a shame. But, that aside, if you're saying that you no longer have any feelings for me other than hatred then I have to remind you that I am still the father of your son and I fully intend to claim my paternal rights—with or *without* your approval—because my people need an heir.'

Secret Heirs of Billionaires

There are some things money can't buy…

Living life at lightning pace, these magnates are no strangers to stakes at their highest. It seems they've got it all… That is until they find out that there's an unplanned item to add to their list of accomplishments!

Achieved:

1. Successful business empire

2. Beautiful women in their bed

3. *An heir to bear their name…?*

Though every billionaire needs to leave his legacy in safe hands, discovering a secret heir shakes up his carefully orchestrated plan in more ways than one!

Uncover their secrets in:

Unwrapping the Castelli Secret by Caitlin Crews

Brunetti's Secret Son by Maya Blake

The Secret to Marrying Marchesi by Amanda Cinelli

Demetriou Demands His Child by Kate Hewitt

The Desert King's Secret Heir by Annie West

Look out for more stories in the
Secret Heirs of Billionaires series coming soon!

THE SHEIKH'S
SECRET SON

BY
MAGGIE COX

First Published in Great Britain 2017
By Mills & Boon, an imprint of HarperCollins*Publishers*
1 London Bridge Street, London, SE1 9GF

© 2017 Maggie Cox

ISBN: 978-0-263-92508-1

Maggie Cox is passionate about stories that can uplift and transport people out of their daily worries to a more magical place, be they romance novels or fairy tales. What people want most, she believes, is true connection. She feels blessed to be married to a lovely man who never fails to make her laugh, and has two beautiful sons and two much loved grandchildren.

Books by Maggie Cox

Mills & Boon Modern Romance

Required to Wear the Tycoon's Ring
A Rule Worth Breaking
The Man She Can't Forget
The Tycoon's Delicious Distraction
In Petrakis's Power
What His Money Can't Hide
The Lost Wife
A Devilishly Dark Deal
The Brooding Stranger
Mistress, Mother...Wife?
Surrender to Her Spanish Husband

Seven Sexy Sins

A Taste of Sin

The Powerful and the Pure

Distracted by Her Virtue

One Night In...

One Desert Night

British Bachelors

Secretary by Day, Mistress by Night

Visit the Author Profile page at
millsandboon.co.uk for more titles.

To Alicia Barber
A unique young woman who has become a very dear friend x

CHAPTER ONE

THE FALL FROM the granite wall happened in an instant, yet strangely time seemed to slow down as Darcy saw herself plunge downwards. It was like an uncanny out-of-body experience. Her mind flashed—happening but *not* happening—just like in a dream. Trouble was, she'd lost concentration due to her mind being dominated by the nerve-racking task at hand—which was hopefully to see the charismatic owner of the regal manor and to tell him at last that their passionate affair had produced a son…

Now, the searing knife-like pain that shot through her ankle as she hit the ground gave her something even more pertinent to worry about. Issuing a string of unladylike curses, she rubbed at the offending bone, wincing as the pain intensified excruciatingly. *How on earth was she going to stand?* The flesh was already reddening and swelling—too fast for her liking. No chance of presenting the poised unruffled appearance she'd had in mind, then…

Even as the realisation descended a heavy-set man in a slightly snug black suit started running towards her from the other side of the splendid gardens. It didn't take much guessing to deduce that he was a security guard. She reminded herself of her intention to stay as calm as possible, no matter what occurred. Then she made herself breathe deeply to try to control the waves of pain that washed over her.

When the man got to her, his breath hitting the frigid October air in tangible puffs of steam, she saw that his fleshy olive complexion was coated with a fine sheen of perspiration.

Despite her dilemma, Darcy quipped, 'You could have saved yourself the effort. I'm clearly not going anywhere any time soon. I think I've twisted my ankle.'

'You are a very silly young woman to risk such a foolish thing. I can tell you now that the Sheikh is not going to be very happy.'

Her realisation that he was referring to the man she'd desperately hoped to see made her feel as though she'd slammed *into* the wall rather than merely falling off it.

'His Highness is the owner of this property and you are trespassing. I have to warn you that he will not take the intrusion lightly.'

'No…I don't suppose he will.'

However her ex-lover reacted when he saw her, it surely couldn't make her feel any worse than she felt already. *Yes, it could.* Darcy had been on edge *before* the accident, never mind now, with the looming possibility of being confronted by him and accused of breaking and entering.

'Look, what's happened has happened, and as much as I need to explain my motives for being here to His Highness, first I'm going to need your help in getting to my feet.'

'That is not a good idea. You need to be checked over by a doctor first. Trying to stand might make the injury worse.'

Staring up at the guard, she witnessed an unexpected glimpse of concern in his chocolate-brown eyes. Then he withdrew a phone from his jacket and spoke to someone at the other end in a language that she was only too familiar with from her days of working at the bank. To make matters worse, the recognition brought with it a vividly searing memory that she expressly didn't welcome right then—especially when she'd stupidly put herself in the mother of all awkward situations.

And all because she'd been driven to scale a wall she never should have attempted in the first place, resulting in a highly inconvenient injury.

But what else was she supposed to do when the necessity of seeing her former lover was becoming ever more urgent? Her worst fears had come true. *He was engaged to be married.* No matter how many times she reminded herself of the fact, her heart vehemently rejected the idea as though it was poison.

At the same time Darcy realised the guard really *wasn't* going to help her to her feet, he abruptly ended his call. Then he withdrew a voluminous handkerchief from his pocket and proceeded to mop his brow.

'The doctor is coming. I have also arranged for you to have some water.'

'I don't need water. I just need some help to get to my feet.'

Suddenly aware that any further attempts to ask for his assistance were futile, Darcy let her head drop with a grimace and the silken wheat-coloured hair that had escaped from her loosely arranged topknot glided down over her cheekbones. She could only pray it was helping to disguise the shock and fear that were pulsating through her. Surrendering to weakness for even the shortest time was anathema to her. The last time she had done such a thing it had cost her dear.

'Who is this doctor, anyway, and will he call an ambulance?'

'You do not need an ambulance. The doctor who is coming is the Sheikh's very own physician. He is highly qualified and has an apartment here.'

'Then I don't suppose I have much choice but to wait for him. I hope he's got some strong painkillers.'

'If you need to take painkillers then you also need water. Do you want me to call someone to inform them that you have had an accident?'

Darcy's heartbeat rapidly quickened. Her mother would hardly take the news calmly. Not when she was apt to turn the slightest mishap into a drama worthy of a soap opera. The last thing she wanted was for her parent's anxiety to spill over to her little boy and worry him.

'No. I don't... Thanks all the same.' Her smile at the guard was tentatively hopeful, but she suspected he didn't believe a word she said.

Because of the dwindling daylight, she hadn't noticed the two figures hurriedly heading towards them from the manor house. But she noticed them *now*. There was definitely the suggestion of urgency in their quickened steps as they started to run.

Deliberately glancing away, Darcy winced as she rubbed at her swollen ankle.

Would the next people to arrive on the scene be the police, to charge her with breaking and entering?

As if intuiting her distress, her companion dropped down in front of her and consolingly patted her arm. Her blue eyes widened in surprise. His behaviour was hardly typical of any security official she knew of. But just then, when she was feeling alone and frightened, despite her fake bravado, the man's kindness was appreciated.

'The doctor will soon tend to your ankle. Do not distress yourself unduly.'

'I'm not distressed. I'm just angry that I climbed the wall. I meant no harm by it. I just wanted to take a peek at the house in the hope that...in the hope that if I saw the Sheikh I might speak with him.'

Her teeth clamped down on her lip as the man's perusal suddenly grew more interested, and she found herself hostage to an uncharacteristic wave of self-pity.

With her voice quavering, she said, 'I read in the newspaper that he had moved here. I used to work for him, you know?'

'Then if you wanted to see him again, you should have rung his office and made an appointment.'

'I've tried doing that, many times, but I was told by his secretary that he had to agree to it first. She never got back to me, no matter how many times I tried. In truth, I don't think he even got my messages.'

'I am sure he did. Perhaps His Highness has his reasons for not contacting you?'

'Rashid.'

The deep bass voice behind them had them both immediately turning their heads. The impressive Arabian attire of the owner of the voice added to Darcy's profound sense of shock when her gaze fell upon his features. His sublimely carved face was etched deep into her memory, but the last time she'd seen it their time together had culminated in a deed that had devastatingly broken her heart. Yet, despite that, her instinct was to greet him with familiarity.

Zafir...

Thankfully she checked the impulse just in time. His haunting black eyes were staring at her hard, she saw, piercing her like the glowing points of a dagger. Although she shuddered, she still drank him in, realising that although he looked a little older he was still as handsome as sin and must still set women's hearts fluttering from here to Kathmandu.

He had also grown his hair.

It fell way past his magnificent shoulders in glossy black waves. The disturbing recollection that the dark strands were like the finest silk to touch made her guiltily yearn to experience running her fingers through the new length...

'The young lady fell off the wall, Your Highness,' the guard interjected, sounding inexplicably protective, 'and she is hurt.'

'Hurting is what she is good at.'

Stung by the bitterly voiced statement, Darcy opened her mouth to protest. *He* was the one who was good at hurting...not her. Or had he so quickly erased *that* little fact from his memory?

'What are you doing here, and why are you trespassing on my property?'

'I'll tell you why—because you wouldn't take my calls or return my messages. You wouldn't even let me make an appointment to see you. God knows how many times I've tried. This was a last resort. In all honesty I would have preferred to have left you alone...but I *had* to see you.'

His glance suspicious, the autocratic man in front of her responded grimly, 'I have never, to my knowledge, received any such messages.'

Darcy's mouth turned sickeningly dry. 'You're joking? Why wouldn't you have received them? I always told your secretary that it was urgent and confidential. Why didn't she believe me?'

'Never mind that right now... If what you say is true then I will be making my investigations. More to the point, what is the reason you want to see me, Darcy? Did you not believe me when I said I never wanted to set eyes on you again? You could hardly have expected any good to come out of our meeting.'

He leaned down to her, and even as she breathed in the exotic scent of agar that highlighted his cologne she saw the expression on his carved face was disturbingly accusing.

'How long have you known that I was here?'

Her eyes widened nervously. 'I only recently found out. There was an article in the newspaper.'

'And you saw the opportunity to get back at me for what happened in the past?'

Her blood ran cold for a moment. 'No! That wasn't the reason I wanted to find you, Zafir. Did you imagine my aim was to try and blackmail you in some way? If you think that then you couldn't be more wrong.' Tears stung the backs of her eyelids like hot springs. Swallowing hard, she continued, 'The article said that you are engaged to be married.'

'And no doubt you want to congratulate me?'

'Don't make light of my pain like that.'

As was her habit, when she was fuming at some injustice or another, she indignantly folded her arms. The movement was a little sharp, and it somehow ricocheted down to her injured ankle. She wasn't able to suppress the groan of pain that rose up inside her.

His ebony eyes darkening in concern, Zafir turned to his immaculately suited companion. 'Dr Eden. Please give the young lady some water and take a look at her ankle...*now*. It might be broken.'

Appalled that that might be the case, with a tremulous sweep of her hand Darcy pushed back her hair and stared. 'I'm sure you'd relish that, wouldn't you?' She all but grabbed at the silver flask that was proffered and imbibed a deep gulp of icy liquid before she said anything else.

As he rose to his full height, the Sheikh's expression was clearly perturbed. 'While you deserve to be punished for what you did to me, I do not take any pleasure in the fact that you have been injured. And just one more thing'

As the slim, middle-aged doctor lithely dropped down to his haunches to examine her foot, the Arabian's black eyes glinted a warning.

'Do not call me Zafir. The use of that name is permitted only to a select circle of family and friends and clearly, Miss Carrick, you should speak in deference to the hierarchy of my position...*you* are my subordinate.'

It jolted her that he'd used her surname, and it gave her little satisfaction that he'd so strongly emphasised the 'subordinate' part. The suggestion of fury in his voice made her heart contract even more. She hadn't immediately succumbed to tears at this latest encounter with him but Darcy felt like crying now.

Once upon a time she'd loved this man more than life itself. Now he sounded as though he hated her. And all because he'd believed his brother's vindictive lies...

'Although I can't say for certain until it's X-rayed, I think what we have here is a severe sprain, Miss Carrick.'

The doctor's slim, cool fingers were gently checking her bones for breakage and prodding the puffy skin around her ankle to inspect it. Straight away his calm assertion along with his professional expertise reinstated her hope that things weren't as disastrous as she'd feared.

A relieved sigh escaped her but then she quickly frowned. *Just who did she think she was kidding?* Things were about as disastrous as they could get. And, having intuited the mood he was in, she suspected that Zafir didn't intend to let her get off lightly for shinning up his garden wall in order to force a meeting. He was the eldest son of the ruling family in the kingdom of Zachariah, and consequently not just important but powerful too, and she knew that if her motivation hadn't been solely to tell him that he had a son and heir she would never have attempted to see him at all.

How many times did a person's self-esteem have to be stamped into the ground before they were forced to admit defeat and walk away?

'We should take you into the house so that we can make some arrangements for your care,' Dr Eden added, his grey eyes flicking towards his impressive employer for confirmation.

The first man to help her reacted first, quickly assuming what must be his esteemed position as the Sheikh's chief security guard. 'I will go and get a stretcher, Your Highness.'

'That won't be necessary, Rashid,' Zafir flashed, his icy gaze irritably scanning Darcy as she sat hunched on the new-mown lawn, massaging her ankle. 'I will carry Miss Carrick over to the house myself.'

Her immediate declaration of indignation at being treated like some extraneous piece of baggage died on her lips. In her more forgiving moments, when she'd flirted with the unlikely idea of somehow meeting up with Zafir again and having a frank conversation with him about what had *really* happened back then, it hadn't been like this. No, *never* like this... The warm, funny, erudite man she'd once worked for and fallen in love with was a very different person from the cold, embittered stranger she was faced with now.

Biting her lip, she murmured, 'I think I'd rather crawl.'

She didn't know if he'd heard her, but to add insult to injury he easily dropped down to lift her into his arms.

'I hope you don't have an accomplice in this little escapade of yours? If you do, no doubt he is long gone. Perhaps he found out that you were not so bewitching after all, and sensibly took the opportunity to flee when he had the chance?'

Swallowing down her hurt that he so naturally assumed she'd been with another man and up to no good, Darcy schooled herself to stay silent instead of reacting. But her senses were awash with pain, and a regret that thundered like a raging river in her blood.

Could he not see beyond his own prejudiced beliefs and realise the truth? Clearly not…

Without further preamble, he swept her up and marched towards the house, with the effete doctor in front and Rashid following behind—no doubt his gaze diligently sweeping the area in case anything else untoward threatened. She didn't dwell on that for long, because now her senses had to contend with the unexpected intimacy of being pressed firmly against the Arabian's chest, knowing that he took no pleasure in the sensation and that all he must feel for her was contempt.

Zafir's heart was beating double time as he carried Darcy over to the sumptuous couch in the drawing room. In his wildest dreams he'd never thought to have the opportunity to hold her again like this. When he'd banished her from his sight over four years ago he'd sworn he wouldn't even *think* of her. But something had told him even then that he was lying. The beautiful face that he'd always likened to his vision of an angel was etched on his heart, whether he wanted it to be or not.

As he helped lower her gently onto the sofa's plumped-up cushions it was no easy task, when her bewitching perfume kept infiltrating his senses and he noted that her extraordinary blue eyes still had the ability to dazzle him more than ever.

But he would be a fool if he forgot for even an instant that this woman had cruelly betrayed him.

If their relationship had progressed he would have given her everything—not least his undying love and devotion—but she had thoughtlessly ruined it all by fooling around behind his back and making a play for his own brother.

Her behaviour was beyond belief. Pretending devotion was clearly just a game to her. With her angelic face and no doubt practised feminine wiles, likely she could twist any man who took her fancy round her little finger and have her way. His brother Xavier had warned him more than once what she was capable of—although Zafir knew his notoriously charming sibling was apt to bend the truth from time to time.

But blood was thicker than water, he told himself and how could he not believe what he'd seen with his very own eyes?

In the aftermath of that shocking incident Xavier had wasted no time in giving him further details of what Darcy was *really* like, saying he'd seen the way she operated at the bank the family owned long before Zafir had appeared to run the head office in London.

The cruel scene he'd witnessed had brought an end to all his hopes. He'd found Darcy in a heated embrace with Xavier.

Her features had radiated her shock and dismay when he'd suddenly surprised them by coming into the room, and immediately she'd denied any wrong-doing. Instead she'd insisted that she'd been trying to get *away* from Xavier, *not* willingly embracing him! That in truth Zafir's brother had been harassing her—had been doing so for months. It was *he* who should be penalised, not *her*…

'Tell the housekeeper to get a drink for my unexpected visitor.' After addressing Rashid, Zafir turned back immediately, to keep Darcy in his sight—although under the circumstances it would take nothing less than a miracle for her to be able to run away. 'What is your preference, Miss Carrick? Tea or coffee?'

The glance he gave her was neither friendly nor particularly polite. He wasn't going to grant the woman any dispensation—that was for sure. Aside from her previous misdemeanours, she had now made an unbelievable attempt to break into his house.

'Neither.'

It was hard not to be moved by the look of anxiety he saw reflected in the blonde's vivid blue eyes and, strangely, it bothered Zafir more than it should have. Was she honestly not concerned that he might call the police and prosecute her for trespass? There was no reason why he *shouldn't*, he told himself. No matter what had gone on between them in the past, he certainly didn't owe her any allegiance.

'I—I just want to know what you intend to do about all this,' she said nervously.

'Forgive me for interrupting, Your Highness,' Dr Eden interjected firmly as he came and stood by the sofa where Darcy was lying. 'But, whatever you decide to do, I'd advise that we get Miss Carrick to the hospital first, so that her injury can be X-rayed.'

Coming out of the stupor he'd fallen into while gazing at Darcy, Zafir nodded abruptly. Retrieving his mobile phone from the inside pocket of the Arabian *khandoura* he wore, he accessed the number of one of London's most exclusive private hospitals to which he had a direct line. Glancing back at his visi-

tor as he requested an ambulance, he had a sudden
notion that she might be going into shock. She was
definitely looking a little flushed, and her eyelids had
fluttered closed as though she barely had the strength
to keep them open.

'Dr Eden.' He authoritatively addressed the medic.
'I must ask you to take Miss Carrick's temperature. It
is my opinion that she looks more than a little unwell.'

'Do not be too concerned, Your Highness,' the
doctor reassured him. 'It is quite a natural reaction
for a person to feel faint after an accident, but I will
gladly do as you ask.'

'Good.'

A short time later, satisfied with the doctor's assurance that Darcy's rise in temperature was not significant enough to be worried about, Zafir waited
impatiently for the ambulance to arrive. In turn, their
patient had become particularly quiet. She was clearly
lost in a mysterious landscape of her own.

He had no idea what she might be thinking. Once
upon a time he wouldn't have had to speculate. He
had been as intimately attuned to her thoughts and
feelings as any man in love could be, and he still carried the grief of her betrayal like a suppurating wound
that would never heal.

The sound of an ambulance siren pierced the
room's growing preternatural stillness, and it had
the same impact as a lightning bolt flashing outside.

As Zafir hurried across the oak floor, with Rashid
behind him, he called out over his shoulder to the
doctor. 'Keep a watch on Miss Carrick. Don't let her
out of your sight!'

'What do you think I'm going to do? Perform some

kind of magic trick and make myself disappear? *I wish*,' Darcy grumbled sarcastically.

Zafir didn't waste time with a response. He was already at the door, throwing it wide in order to hurry out into the hallway. Addressing the man at the front door, who introduced himself as the chief paramedic, he guided him and the two other crew members into the drawing room. Darcy was resting her back against the curve of the elegant couch, as though it had taken the strain off of the accident, but in spite of her little outburst just now she wasn't able to hide the fact that she was worried.

So was Zafir. Right then, he honestly didn't know what he was going to do about the consequences of her fall from his garden wall *or* her startling reappearance into his life. In truth, he was still knocked sideways at seeing her again. And as yet he hadn't decided whether to prosecute her or not. Most people in his privileged circle wouldn't hesitate to throw the book at her.

Hadn't he learned that she wasn't to be trusted? people would say. That she was nothing but a sly opportunist...a *Jezebel*.

He could almost hear the condemning words echo round his brain. Wasting no more time in deliberating—that would have to wait until they had the X-ray results—he instructed the paramedics to do what they had to do and transport her into the ambulance.

She was wearing jeans, a deep blue woollen sweater and a short mustard-coloured jacket. And as the paramedics expertly lifted her slender frame onto a stretcher Zafir observed that she'd grown a little thinner since he'd seen her last. *Had she been eating properly?*

He remembered that she'd often lose her appetite when she was stressed, and even though he knew he shouldn't give a jot if something was troubling her, knew that Darcy was *nothing* to him any more, he gruffly declared, 'I will accompany my guest to the hospital.'

'Of course, Your Highness,' the paramedic responded. 'Just to reassure you, I think it's going to be a very straightforward procedure. The young lady will soon be as right as rain again—you'll see.'

He was a slightly overweight, cheerful-looking man of forty-plus, with a receding hairline—one of those dependable sorts that the great British public would probably describe as 'the salt of the earth'. And, oddly, Zafir was reassured—at least for a minute or two.

When the attentive medical staff at the hospital stretchered Darcy into an examination room, Zafir came with her. Before they'd entered Dr Eden had given them his own efficient assessment and, in deference to his colleagues, told his employer that he would wait for him outside.

All of these events hardly reassured Darcy. The familiar scent associated with anything medical, along with the forbidding-looking examination couch, made her feel queasy, and Zafir's daunting aristocratic presence even more so. But the most pressing thing of all on her mind was her son. At present Sami was in the care of her mother, because she was babysitting him, but what if she had to tell her that she needed to stay in hospital for the night?

Darcy had never told her mother who Sami's father was, and she contemplated how she would couch her words in order to cause the least anxiety. She knew her mother would think she'd lost her mind—climbing the walls of the Sheikh's home in an attempt to speak to him. Especially when she'd ended up spraining her ankle.

Was it worth it? She could hear her mother ask. *You should have gone down the proper route of arranging a meeting with him, no matter how long it took. Look at what you've risked!*

Darcy's heart suddenly felt as heavy as a boulder inside her chest.

And that would be *before* she conveyed to her mother the fact that her ex-employer had been furious at her finding him even *before* she'd told him that he'd left her pregnant and that he now had a son.

Seeing as he was now engaged to be married, the news would hardly be the best he could receive. But, at the same time, what would the repercussions be for *her*? What if he immediately demanded custody of Sami? Or…worse still…wanted to take him back to Zachariah, away from her and all he had known for the past four years? That didn't bear thinking about.

CHAPTER TWO

DARCY HAD A splint and a crepe bandage fitted round her injured ankle. Thankfully, the X-ray had revealed no broken bones, but Darcy had badly torn the ligaments and would need at least three weeks' complete rest to help them start to heal—beginning with one full night at the hospital so that the medical staff could keep an eye on her.

That was the part that alarmed her the most. The swish, luxurious medical facility was clearly private, and there was no way on earth she could afford to spend any of her hard-earned cash on a stay here. It was essential she get home.

Zafir had gone to consult with the doctor and her need to talk to him was growing ever more urgent. The tension she was feeling was near unbearable. But just then he returned, and his arresting presence stirred the air. There was no sign of Rashid or Dr Eden.

The impact Zafir made in his impressive garb hit her anew. With his chiselled, strong-boned features and flowing dark hair his commanding appearance was enough to render anyone speechless. He was simply *magnificent*.

Propped up by a couple of plump pillows in the hospital bed, with her ankle elevated, Darcy felt her heart bump nervously against her ribs. She couldn't help feeling a little intimidated. Instinct told her that with all the drama of her fall perhaps now *wasn't* the right time to tell him about Sami, even though it was the sole reason she'd gone to his house.

Perhaps her confession should take place under more conducive circumstances? If she could arrange such a scenario, might he view her sudden unsettling appearance in his life more favourably?

Impulsively, she reached for his hand. Having not told her mother that she'd be back late, she felt her fears about spending the night away from her young son escalating.

'I can't possibly stay the night here, Zafir. I need to get home. There—there's something important I have to do.'

Mesmerised, he stared down at the slender hand clasping his as if he couldn't quite believe it was hers. Then he lifted his head, and where previously his dark eyes had been entranced, they were now hard with suspicion. Obviously he wasn't going to be extending an olive branch to her any time soon.

'What do you have to do that's so important?' he demanded. 'Is it that you want to tell your accomplice you were unsuccessful in breaking into my house? Is that what you need to do, Darcy? Will there be repercussions for you if you don't get home tonight?'

Wrenching back her hand, she flushed indignantly. 'For goodness' sake—once and for all, I *wasn't* trying to break in and I *don't* have an accomplice. Do you think I've become so desperate and vengeful since you fired me that I'd resort to breaking in to your house when I learnt you were there?'

'I cannot attest to knowing *what* you'd resort to, Darcy. Once upon a time I thought I knew who you were,' he said soberly, 'but clearly I didn't. As for your reasons for turning up at my residence in such a dramatic way—I am his Royal Highness Sheikh Zafir el-Kalil of Zachariah, and naturally my wealth and position draws attention...not all of it innocent.'

Distraught that he clearly still thought she was a liar, when all she'd ever done was stay loyal to him and give him her devotion, she found his words hard to bear. But suddenly part of his statement registered more emphatically.

'I've just realised... That was your father's title, wasn't it? I mean...*he* was the Sheikh of Zachariah, wasn't he? Are you saying that he's passed away and now you're the...?'

'Sheikh of the kingdom... Yes, I am.'

It was as though a shutter had slammed down over his enigmatic gaze and rendered his feelings impossible to read. Was he still grieving? *He must be.* Darcy knew that father and son had been close.

As she twisted her hands together she felt genuine sympathy, unsullied by the turbulent waters that flowed between them. She knew only too well what it meant to lose a devoted father. And once upon a time Zafir had told her how much he loved and admired his esteemed parent, and one day hoped to display some of the wisdom and knowledge he was revered for himself.

'I'm sorry...I mean I'm sorry for your loss,' she added softly.

For a brief moment it looked as if the mistrust and suspicion in his eyes had lessened. But very quickly his expression was stony again, and it brought her firmly back to the present.

Raising his chin, he remarked, 'As I was saying, my position inevitably draws attention and not all of it is welcome. I am fully aware that those who are unscrupulous might try and steal from me from time to time.'

'Well, I'm not one of those.' Her brilliant blue eyes didn't hide her dismay. 'And there's nothing I want that I would be prepared to steal from *anyone*…certainly not anything material. If I couldn't buy it for myself then I'd just as soon forget it.'

'Then what is this urgent need you have to see me? The reason for all the messages you say you left at my office…messages that I never received?'

'I wanted to tell you about that in private. Somewhere we can speak freely.'

The expression on his face told Darcy that she was sorely testing him. His glance impatiently swept the room before returning to rest on her. 'This is private enough. You might not get another chance.'

'Why? Do you despise me so much that you can't bear the thought of seeing me again?'

Hearing the disturbing catch in her voice, Zafir was alarmed. Could *any* man despise a woman who looked like she did?

He remembered the day she'd walked into his office, having been assigned to him as his PA. He had arranged that the bank's administrative manager would select someone for him, as it would be one less thing for him to do on his arrival from Zachariah, and the man who had selected Darcy from the pool of highly qualified secretaries the bank employed had assured him that she was one of the best. Having read her credentials, Zafir had agreed.

When he'd finally met her, his heart had stalled in surprise and pleasure. Her beauty had been the ethereal kind that romantic poets wrote the most exquisite accolades to...

All thoughts of work and the demanding schedule he'd had ahead of him had been instantly forgotten. Being a red-blooded, virile male, all he'd been able to think about was what it would be like to seduce her.

He'd never before experienced wanting a woman as much as he'd wanted Darcy. Her shapely body and golden hair had captivated him from the very first. And it hadn't been only that. As he'd begun to get to know her he'd realised she had so many more attributes for him to admire. Kindness, generosity, and a ready smile no matter what she might be feeling. All came to her as easily as breathing, it had seemed.

A mere week later, having developed the habit of calling her in to his office more regularly than was strictly necessary—either on the pretext of taking dictation or to look over some 'important correspondence' with him—he had known he was falling in love...

Now, pushing his long hair back from his face, he immediately honed his gaze in on her tearful eyes. 'I don't despise you,' he said throatily. 'What is it you want to say? You may as well tell me now.'

Breathing out a sigh, he dropped down beside her on the bed, taking care not to jolt her elevated ankle.

She immediately looked startled, then she quickly collected herself.

'All right, then. After you dismissed me...I—I found out that I was pregnant.'

There was a sudden deafening silence inside Zafir's head. The intensity of it, along with his racing heartbeat, tuned out any other sound. He likened it to standing in the vicinity of an explosion. When he finally composed himself, he considered the possibility that he might be dreaming. She had been *pregnant?* How could that be? He'd always made sure to protect her.

He was suddenly furious. 'Is this some kind of twisted joke you're playing on me, Darcy? I always took care to protect you from such an event. If you were pregnant, then the baby couldn't have been mine. Are you telling me that it was my *brother's*?'

The very idea made him feel sick to his stomach.

'I know you don't regard me very highly, but that's a vile accusation. The baby I had is *yours*, Zafir... your *son*. That first time we were together neither of us were as careful as we should have been. I'd started taking the pill, but I hadn't been taking it long enough before we...before we spent the night together. Even though we'd planned it, everything happened so fast—don't you remember? We could barely contain our feelings.'

She meant that they hadn't been able to keep their hands off each other.

Even now the memory made him feel weak with longing. But at the back of his mind it suddenly nagged at him that in the throes of a desire as powerful and urgent as theirs had been he probably *hadn't* been as diligent with protection as he should have.

The evening they'd first become intimate had been when he'd taken her to one of the newest and most exclusive hotels in London. They had only stayed one night, but Zafir had made sure it was a night she would remember. He'd arranged for the lavish bed to be strewn with rose petals and the luxurious suite to be scented with a rare perfume that he'd had flown in from Zachariah. There had been nothing he wouldn't have done to help Darcy feel as if she was the centre of his universe…to show her that he was devoted to her happiness.

But later, when he'd learnt that she'd been cheating on him, his hopes that they would share the most joyous future together, that he would even go against tradition and make her his Queen, had shatteringly blown up in his face. And now she was telling him that he'd left her pregnant…

Zafir was glad he was sitting down. He felt as if he was in the middle of a storm whose power threatened to unbalance him no matter how hard he fought to stay upright. It wasn't the first time he'd reflected that he might have made the most terrible mistake when he'd let her go. But now, faced with the damning consequences of that decision—as well as wanting to somehow put things right—he needed to absorb the real possibility that he was a *father*. And if he was, he now had an heir.

His dearest wish had seemingly come to pass and he hadn't even known it. But the cruelty of doubt, of not being able to receive the news with any real confidence, still tormented him. Could he *really* have been such an utter fool back then when he'd fired her? Was he *really* the father of her son?

But as he examined her more closely he couldn't help but warm to the idea. 'Was I honestly so irresponsible as not to use protection the first time we made love?'

Darcy flushed. 'We were so crazy for each other that I don't think either of us had time to think about anything much…let alone be sensible.'

Remembering, Zafir was suffused by heat similar to that of a hot air current that swept across the desert sands. *No one could turn him on as she had.*

But he quickly returned to her story. 'Do you have *any* idea of what it means for someone in my position to have a son? It means that the ancient dynastic line of my forebears will continue. Nothing can bring greater satisfaction and purpose than that.'

His mind was racing with the implications of the news and how it was going to affect not just his life and his family's, but the people of Zachariah too.

'I'm glad that it's important to you. So, am I right in thinking that you want to be involved in our son's life?'

'If he *is* my son, then of course I want to be involved in his life. Did you not hear what I just said?'

'But…' Again, Darcy turned pink. 'What about your fiancée? Won't *she* want to have a say in any decision you make about that? It's surely going to come as a great shock to her that you have a son by someone else?'

Realising that he'd barely given his bride-to-be a thought since setting eyes on Darcy again, Zafir knew that he had to get out of marrying a woman he didn't love and had no chance of ever loving. He actually *welcomed* the idea of extricating himself from the arrangement.

Farrida came from a powerful Arabian family that was as wealthy and privileged as his own, and they'd known each other for years, but in truth she was a cold fish. She might be one of the most beautiful women in the kingdom, with an impeccable pedigree, but she had grown up utterly spoilt. Consequently she thought only of herself.

Zafir had only agreed to the marriage because—as his mother regularly reminded him—at some time or other he would have to produce an heir. He needed to put his duty first, and his union with Farrida would be considered highly advantageous by both families.

'Why don't you let *me* deal with that,' he replied tersely, 'and focus on getting your ankle better?'

'You must *know* I'm concerned about the fact you're getting married? It will have implications for me—and my son too. It's been a long, hard road with just my mum to help me with the childcare, so I can work and earn the money we need, and though I won't deny it would be helpful to have your support I don't want to risk losing Sami if you decide to sue for joint custody. Will you agree to his still living with *me*? When you talk about "dynastic lines", it worries me. I've wanted to tell you about our child for so long... but, as I said, I could never get through to you. When I read that you were getting married I knew it was more important than ever that you had the news.'

'And the boy... Sami...he is four now?'

'Yes.'

Darcy saw his glance soften for a moment as he seemed to take the time to reacquaint himself with her features. He followed it up with a lingering examination of her wheaten hair. He had always been fascinated by it... But she brought an abrupt halt to the memory when she started to remember how he'd loved to run his fingers through it.

It was perhaps fortunate when he quickly reverted to his previous less than friendly stance.

'I confess I am still having trouble believing all this, Darcy. I have plenty of reasons *not* to believe you...remember?'

His statement sent cold shivers scudding down her backbone. She saw that she still had to deal with his suspicion and mistrust.

'I never lied to you. I know you don't believe me, but it's true. You weren't the only one who was hurt by what happened. Not only did you think I was a liar and a cheat, but I also had to suffer the humiliation of being fired from my job as though...as though I was *worthless*. What happened wounded me more than you can possibly imagine. Let me go home, Zafir. *Please*,' she implored. 'I really do have to get back tonight. I give you my word that I'll be there should you want to discuss any plans concerning our son.'

He seemed to stare into her eyes for a very long time before he spoke, but she found no reassurance in his gaze...anything *but*. In those endless few seconds Darcy felt as if she was standing in front of a pitiless magistrate who was just about to condemn her to a prison cell for life. Was there *nothing* she could say that would move him?

'No matter how I feel personally about your predicament,' he remarked, 'in all conscience I cannot allow the hospital to discharge you tonight. You will have to stay here until tomorrow, when the doctor will re-examine you. After that, if I am satisfied they have done all that they can to aid your recovery, you can, of course, go home. But you can be sure I will be taking your details.'

'Why? Because you want to see Sami or because you still intend to prosecute me for trespass?'

Now her eyes *did* fill with tears.

His returning glance was unperturbed, and cool as iced water. 'To see my son, of course. I don't intend prosecution now I've learned the reason for your trying to break into the house.'

Sniffing, Darcy blotted her tears with the back of her hand. She bit her lip at his reference to her trying to break in. 'Good. But as to staying here for the night—I couldn't afford to, even if I was at death's door. Not *all* of us have money to burn like...'

'Like *me*? Is that what you were going to say?'

Shrugging his shoulders, as though it didn't disturb him one iota what she thought, Zafir started to walk away. But then he suddenly stopped dead and turned towards her.

Piercing her with eyes as black and mysterious as a moonless night, he breathed, 'You will not have to pay this particular bill, Darcy, *I* will. But do not doubt you will have to recompense me...one way or another.'

As the door of the room swung closed behind him she dropped her head back onto the pillows and stared wildly up at the ceiling. Her physical discomfort had eased, thanks to the pain medication kicking in, but she didn't know how she was going to relay the extraordinary events that had happened to her mother.

And all because she'd finally taken matters into her own hands and recklessly sought Zafir out at his resplendent home...

Coming face to face with Darcy again did not help Zafir to sleep easily in his bed that night. The magic the woman weaved around him was like a drugging opiate that was impossible to resist, and when he was near her he felt like an addict on a recovery programme.

It was well over four years since he had seen her and at last he'd thought he'd got used to the idea that he would never see her again. But fate, it seemed, had had other plans. If it turned out to be the truth that he'd left her pregnant, then his whole life would change now that he had a son and heir.

Just as he was about to drift off to sleep he recalled the memory of her telling him how much she'd been hurt too—*more than he would ever know.* Now he knew what she'd meant—knew that she'd been pregnant by him when he'd fired her from her post—he felt like the cruellest tyrant imaginable for misjudging and abandoning her. But he still couldn't be sure she hadn't cheated on him with his brother, and until he was the idea would hang over him like Damocles' sword.

Waking early, Zafir hastily showered and dressed, then immediately instructed his chauffeur to drive him to the hospital. Half expecting Darcy to have somehow found a way of escaping, despite the fact that he had left Rashid guarding her door and she couldn't presently so much as put her foot to the floor, he couldn't suppress his relief when he saw her sitting on top of the hospital bed, fully dressed. She looked a little peaky, and she didn't seem best pleased to see him.

'Oh, it's you.'

Wanting to smile, he didn't. The situation was far too serious for any levity. 'Yes, it's me. Did you manage to get any sleep last night?'

'What do you care if I did or I didn't?'

'Don't be such a child.'

'I just want to get out of here and go home.'

She impatiently smoothed back a stray corn-gold strand of hair from her face, and her stare was defiant.

Zafir shook his head. 'You are going nowhere until I speak with the doctor—and even then not until you give me your phone number and address.'

That had sounded like a veiled threat, not something even *remotely* reassuring. Inside, Darcy's emotions clamoured. Wasn't it enough that he'd already stamped her heart into the ground and caused irreversible damage?

A mournful sigh escaped her. The reason she'd been so determined to confront him was because they had a son together...she should never forget that.

'I already *told* you I'd give them to you. I *want* to give you the chance to step up to your responsibilities—at the very least I thought you'd want that. And, more importantly, I want my son to know his father and likewise for you to get to know him and be proud of him.'

His tanned brow furrowed. Did she imagine she saw the shadow of pain and regret in his glance?

'I would want all those things too,' he agreed soberly, '*if* he is indeed my son.'

Her stomach lurched at the idea he still didn't believe her.

'In any case, I intend to maintain contact with you. But right now I will go and tell the nurse we'd like to see the doctor.'

Darcy had no choice but to stay put. But when the time came she hoped she would be able to ring for a cab to take her home. She didn't want to resume relations with Zafir by feeling obligated. It was one thing having his support for Sami—if he gave it—and quite another having him lay down the law about what *she* did.

The question was would she be allowed to leave the hospital without any further intervention from him? It was hard to guess. The way her luck was going probably not.

When Zafir returned, she asked hopefully, 'Will I be discharged after I've seen the doctor?'

'We will soon find out. A nurse is coming to transport you to the examination room as we speak.'

A short while later Darcy nervously submitted to the doctor's examination of her swollen ankle. As Zafir watched the proceedings she saw his gaze was steely-eyed and serious.

Faint with worry, she mulled over the possible outcomes. What if they wanted to keep her here for another night? If that happened, what would she do? She was hardly in a position just to walk out. It went without saying that her mother would insist on visiting her, and if that happened by necessity she would have to bring Sami with her. It was a Saturday and the school week was over. But if Sami saw her in hospital she knew he would be distressed, seeing her incapacitated like this…

'Well, Ms Carrick, the outcome of your injury is presenting just as I expected. While it is very sore now, the ankle should heal beautifully if you take the proper care and rest. No doubt you must be relieved you didn't break any bones although you will still have to take some time off work.'

'Thank you. I *am* relieved that it's not as bad as I feared. All I want to do now is go home.'

'That is completely understandable, but first you must see our physiotherapist to be given some walking aids. When you have those, you may leave. The final thing I want to do is to tell you that you're a very fortunate young woman to have been aided by such a personage as the Sheikh of Zachariah himself.'

The doctor was hardly adept at concealing his curiosity as he peered at her more closely.

For his part, Zafir detected the man's too interested examination of Darcy's features straight away. Was he imagining that the delicate blonde with the angelic visage was his mistress? He didn't know why right then, but it seriously aggravated him.

'It won't be necessary for you to guide us to the physiotherapist, Dr Khan. A nurse can just as easily escort us.'

'As you wish, Your Highness.'

The doctor beamed and smiled, but Zafir didn't miss the brief flash of anxiety that flickered across the heavily lidded eyes. He could tell the man wasn't quite sure whether his services had pleased him or not, and no matter how admired he was in his field he wouldn't want to risk losing the Sheikh's patronage under any circumstances.

'I don't know *why* you thought I needed a wheelchair, Zaf—Your Highness.' Colouring in embarrassment beneath the too astute scrutiny of Rashid, as he parked her chair by the side of his boss's gleaming black car, she privately cursed Zafir's insistence that she refrain from using his name because she was supposedly his *subordinate*.

The devastation she'd endured that day when he'd cruelly told her he didn't want anything to do with her any more was still able to wound her grievously. It wasn't unlike the symptoms of post-traumatic stress in that it was ever-present—it never went away. That being the case, she couldn't—*wouldn't* pretend that their association had been a casual one, no matter how high he'd risen in the meantime.

'It's not *that* difficult to manoeuvre a couple of walking sticks.'

The Sheikh's velvety dark brows came together in a forbidding frown. 'Why am I not surprised you would say that? I shouldn't have forgotten how stubborn you can be. Stop making a fuss and I will help you get into the car.'

All of a sudden he clicked opened the strap that secured her and, as Rashid held open the door, lifted her bodily into the car. Carefully arranging her bandaged ankle in the footwell, he briskly fastened her seatbelt and ordered his guard to take care of the crutches. Then, without even sparing her so much as a cursory glance, he sat down next to her. Rashid climbed in next to the driver.

Once more the sensual scent of exotic agar drifted beneath Darcy's nose, whilst the heat from her companion's body seemed to reach out to meld with her own. Pursing her lips, she wondered forlornly if anyone had recorded how fast a woman's heart beat when the love of her life acted as if it was a penance even to be in the same vicinity as her. Was there, in fact, a record for such a thing?

To stave off her distress, she blurted out, 'When I get home you don't have to come in with me. I can manage perfectly well using my walking aids.'

The man beside her turned slowly to survey her. 'Save your breath, Darcy, and listen to me. No matter how much you try to reassure me, I make no apologies for insisting that I accompany you. It would be remiss of me to take you home after your accident and then not come in with you to ensure you have everything you need and are safe.'

Now her heart beat hard for a different reason. He was going to meet their son for the very first time. What would he say? What would he do?

Sami was a sensitive little boy and was likely to be overwhelmed by the intimidating sight of Zafir unless she prepared him first. For all her quick thinking and bravado, how on earth was she going to deal with *that*?

CHAPTER THREE

DARCY HAD BOTH feared and longed for Zafir to meet his son, and it was hard to believe that at long last it was going to happen. Yet when the car pulled up outside the modest townhouse in the leafy London suburb where she lived, her fear about their meeting felt as if it might *choke* her.

She couldn't attest to being sure of him at all. What if he demanded custody of Sami in order to punish her because she hadn't told him about the pregnancy straight away? He was a powerful man with access to the best lawyers in the world. What was to stop him from suing her?

Moistening her dried lips, she nervously met his inscrutable dark gaze. 'You don't have to carry me into the house,' she said quickly. 'I'm happy to go in the wheelchair.'

'Good.'

For a few seconds he seemed amused, but she knew she shouldn't be fooled by some imagined sense of his warmth towards her. Not when he was so sure she'd wronged him.

The faithful Rashid remained waiting outside the car at a signal from his boss, and he watched and waited as His Highness helped her into the wheelchair. Steering her towards the front door, Zafir reached up to ring the bell.

Darcy felt sick to her stomach. It was only natural that she should anticipate the worst, she reasoned. This man was no longer her employer and one-time lover…he was now an unknown entity and a serious threat to all she held dear.

Quickly delving into her jacket pocket, she produced her key just in time. 'You don't need to ring the bell. I have my key.'

'Then give it to me and I'll let us in. Will there be anybody here to help you while your ankle heals?' His tanned brow furrowed, as if the notion that there might not be perturbed him.

Dropping the key into his palm, she scarcely felt able to reply. But in the next instant he'd wheeled her into the carpeted hallway and the only sound that greeted her was the ticking of the grandfather clock… the clock that had once been her dad's pride and joy. Other than that, the house was quiet.

'Sami and I live with my mum, but I think she must have gone out.'

Shutting the door behind them, he commented, 'I take it that means you don't have a husband?'

Planting himself firmly in front of her, the handsome Arabian folded his arms across his chest, leaving her in no doubt that he meant business and was going to find out the truth of her situation by whatever means necessary.

Gulping down an uneasy breath, she answered, 'No.' How could she tell him that she'd only ever wanted one man for her husband and that was him? 'There's no one in my life but Sami and my mother.'

'I can't pretend that I'm unhappy about that.' His long-lashed black eyes focused on her intently. 'It could potentially complicate things if you were in a relationship.'

Knowing what he meant, she tightened her pale hands on the arms of the wheelchair. 'As it no doubt will when you marry this woman you're engaged to,' she said pointedly, unconsciously lifting her chin. 'If Sami goes to stay with you in the future I have to confess I'll be uncomfortable with the idea when I don't even know her. What's she like?'

'Her name is Farrida. She is from an important Zachariah family and her beauty and her intellect are much admired. We have known each other since we were children.'

The aloof manner in which he described his bride-to-be didn't tell Darcy very much about her at all—certainly not about the important things she wanted to know, such as her character and her values.

'Is she a warm and friendly person?' she pressed. 'I suppose what I'm asking is, does she like children?'

His giving his intended a name, as well as listing attributes she definitely couldn't match, made the woman even more threatening to Darcy.

'And do...?' She hardly dared ask the next question. 'Do you love her?'

The glance Zafir returned to her was undeniably weary, as if the subject both bored and irritated him. 'As to whether she likes children or not—she knows that she's expected to produce heirs. This is not a love match. Arranged marriages are common practice amongst those with political power and wealth in my country. My family and hers typify that. Our destiny has always been to marry someone from a similar background.'

'So what you're saying is that you don't have a choice about who you marry?'

The smile he quirked was wry. 'My mother, the Dowager Queen, would not insist if the woman did not please me.'

'What do you mean by that?'

Unfolding his arms, he sighed, and his sigh was tinged with impatience. 'Surely *you*, of all women, must know what I mean? Have you so quickly forgotten how it was between us?'

The startling reminder was like a scythe slashing through her innards, because it was clear he was setting his sights on someone far above *her* background. Whether he would marry the well-connected beauty he spoke of or not, the woman surely had to be a much better bet than she had ever been.

She coughed to ease the tension that was cramping her throat. 'Do you think you could get me some water? The kitchen's just through that door.'

With a concerned expression, her companion briefly exited the room. He reappeared a few moments later with her drink. Once again the beguiling cologne he wore stirred the air, conjuring up potent imagery of a very different land whose history stretched back to the dawn of time.

'Do you need your medication?' he asked gruffly. 'I have it here.'

He gave her the painkillers, along with the glass of water.

'Thanks.' Pressing the foil packet with trembling fingers, Darcy emptied a couple of capsules into her hand. Then she hurriedly swallowed them down with the drink, all the while aware that her one-time lover watched her avariciously, almost like a hawk about to bear down on his prey.

'That's better,' she remarked, for no other reason than that it was something to break the silence that had fallen.

'Even though we are no longer lovers,' Zafir suddenly declared, 'if I choose not to marry Farrida, and it can be proved that Sami is indeed my son, there *is* a way you can repay me for not telling me sooner that you were carrying my child when you left the bank.'

Darcy bristled. 'When I was *forced* to leave the bank, do you mean?'

Unperturbed, the steady black eyes held her gaze. 'That is a conversation for later...not now. Concerning your repayment—I have a solution. I want you to replace Farrida by agreeing to become my wife.'

'*What?* You can't be serious.'

Relieving her of the glass of water, he put it down on a nearby bookshelf. When he turned back, a muscle flinched tellingly at the side of a breathtakingly carved cheekbone.

'One convenient bride is much the same as another. Except that *you* have one important thing in your favour, Darcy. It seems that you have already given me the requisite heir.'

She flinched as though struck, but knew he wouldn't be displaying any remorse for stating things so bluntly. And she was right. All she saw in the silken black orbs was an intimidating mockery that told her it was utterly pointless to argue.

Praying she could remain calm, even though her heart already felt as if it might burst, she said, 'Do you *really* think that I'd marry you after what happened between us? Our relationship didn't work out because you didn't trust me, Zafir. Instead, you believed the despicable lies your brother told you, and didn't see that the sickening incident in that office was nothing but a set-up, engineered to discredit me. You never even gave me a chance to tell you how difficult he was making things for me at work. Straight away you thought me faithless!'

Taking a deep breath in to compose herself, she continued.

'Xavier had been harassing me for months leading up to the day it happened. He was getting more and more frustrated by my lack of interest in him and he wanted to pay me back for it.'

At that moment the sense of abandonment and grief that she'd carried for all these years dramatically reached its peak and spilled over. The feeling was akin to being caught in a wild, untamed storm that had drenched her and now it was too late to escape from being drowned... All she could do was pray it would end soon and that her life would return to some sense of normality.

'Then you heartlessly fired me.'

'And you expect me to believe that?'

'I don't tell lies—especially when it concerns something as important as this. Sami is your son, Zafir. Do you intend to punish me even more than you've done already for telling you the truth about it?'

She was already aware that the knowledge he had a son would change *everything* for him. He had often told her the importance of having a male heir in his culture.

'We made love in the heat of the moment that first time and I'd only just started taking the pill. I didn't have time to properly protect myself, and...if you remember...nor did you.'

'And you didn't consider having an abortion?'

His voice sounded like a husk of its former self, and his glistening brow attested to the tumult of emotion he must be feeling.

'I wouldn't ever have done such a thing.'

'Why not, isn't it common practice in the West the acceptable cost of having your fun and not paying for it?'

She grimaced. 'Whether it is or it isn't, in my experience no woman makes that decision lightly. And, personally, I believe that life is too precious to destroy.'

Frowning, he said tersely, 'So do I—but yet again you have probably told me a duplicitous story. More likely than not, I am not the *only* man you have been intimate with. You forget that there were rumours about the way you conducted yourself around men at the bank. Not least of all my own brother.'

'And did you bother to check out any of these claims? Instead of automatically believing them to be true? And just because your brother is who he is, it doesn't mean that you can trust him. Xavier lies as easily as he breathes, and you don't do yourself any favours being so ready to believe him.'

'Enough!'

Stepping towards her in a moment of white-hot fury, Zafir clenched his fist. His expression was fierce, and Darcy could tell she'd really upset him.

In those electrifying few seconds she wanted to die. No woman could endure what she had in a relationship and then expect things to somehow magically turn around for the better...could they?

But thankfully in the next instant, as if realising he had come perilously close to losing control, he seemed to gather himself.

'Whatever the outcome of this meeting, you can be certain of one thing—' he vowed ominously.

He wasn't able to finish whatever it was he'd been about to say, but she sensed it wasn't good. The very second he was about to break her heart again she heard the sound of a key in the door, along with the sound of childish laughter.

Her family had returned.

'It's my mum and Sami.'

'What?'

Now it was her turn to leave *him* hanging. Eagerly she steered her wheelchair towards the living room door. Just as she reached it, her family did too.

'Mummy, you're back! Are you feeling better now?'

'Much better, my darling, all the more for seeing *you.*'

Affectionately gathering the little boy with dusty blond curls and big brown eyes into her arms, Darcy pressed her lips into his hair, inhaled his familiar musky small-boy scent and forgot that Zafir was even there. All was right with her world because her son was safely home.

'Nanny bought me a new football, Mummy. It's a Chelsea one.' He held up the shiny carrier bag he was clutching for her to see.

Full of excitement, he glanced across his mother's shoulder just then and saw Zafir. His slim little body went rigid. The man's impressive physique and attire might be seen as intimidating by *anyone*, but to a small boy with a head full of adventures—mostly featuring bloodthirsty pirates and sword-wielding warriors—Zafir looked nothing less than *awesome*.

Stepping back a little, Sami croaked, 'Who are *you*?'

Darcy manoeuvred the wheelchair around so that she could catch the expression on her ex-lover's face when he answered. She hardly dared breathe.

At the same time, understandably anxious to know what was going on, her mother, Patricia, leant down to her and whispered, 'Are you all right, love? I didn't see an ambulance outside. How did you get home?'

Having not yet related to her the full story about her accident, Darcy murmured softly, 'This gentleman brought me. I used to work for him. We—we recently met up again and he kindly brought me back from the hospital.'

She hoped that would suffice for now. But as her gaze lit on Zafir she couldn't help but be anxious about what he would say next.

Taking her by surprise, he dropped down to his haunches, his gaze growing noticeably warmer as he addressed the small boy. 'Your name is Sami?'

It wasn't hard to see that Sami was fascinated by him.

'Yes.'

'It is a fine name and it suits you well.'

'It's my dad's middle name, and my granddad's too, but I've never met them.'

'I'm sure you would make them both very proud if they were to meet you.'

With his beloved father now dead, it wasn't possible that such a meeting could ever take place, and Zafir sensed a renewed sting of grief for the man who hadn't just been a wise father and friend, but his mentor too. 'A king amongst kings,' his mother often declared when talking about him.

Zafir's limbs felt like lead. Suddenly mute, he had the disturbing sense of being in a most fantastical dream, where nothing was quite real any more. He looked at the boy. Could he really be his son? A wave of feeling gripped him. Hot on the heels of his initial doubt, a fierce hope was kindling. It was a feeling of the most incredible *joy*…the kind of joy that perhaps visited a person once in a lifetime, and then only if they were lucky.

As he studied the boy more closely his stomach must have flipped half a dozen times. Was it true? Zafir couldn't deny that he saw distinct similarities to himself. Even though the child's hair was almost as fair as freshly churned butter, and a million miles away from being dark, the deep brown almond-shaped eyes, the budding aquiline nose and full lips might have been sculpted by the same divine hand that had created his own. Add to that the ethereal loveliness of his mother, the boy was exceptionally beautiful…eye-catching, in fact.

That brought him back to the woman in question. Seeing Darcy again was a shock that nothing on this earth could have prepared him for, and he was still feeling a kind of dizziness around her—similar to that of a man whose drink had been spiked with some kind of opiate. To contemplate the revelation that their brief, passionate affair had created a child was astounding. The implications were enormous if it turned out to be true.

Even so, at the forefront of his mind burned the question *why* hadn't she found some way to get the news to him when she'd discovered she was pregnant? She'd said that she'd left messages. But he'd never received any of them.

Zafir's chest grew uncomfortably tight. He might be reflecting that Darcy could have got the news to him if she'd *wanted* to…but after being coldly rejected by him and dismissed from her job she had no longer trusted him. Why should she have when he had believed his brother's telling of events over hers?

In her defence, at the time she'd insisted that Xavier had deliberately engineered the compromising scene in which Zafir found them because—as she'd said—he'd wanted to pay her back for holding out on him. He'd been pestering her with his unwanted attentions for weeks, she'd told him, but she hadn't had the courage to report him. Not because she was a coward, but because the situation was clearly a sensitive one. How could she accuse Xavier of sexually harassing her and expect to be believed when his family was as eminent and powerful as theirs was? she'd asked him. Not only that, they were her employers too…

Zafir had found himself presented with one of the worst dilemmas of his life.

Now, not for the first time, he felt sick at the thought that he might have made a terrible mistake in wrongly accusing Darcy. But no sooner had the notion entered his head than he knew it wouldn't be wise to jump to conclusions.

This time he would force himself to take a more measured approach in finding out the truth. And to that end he would insist on taking a paternity test. If it turned out that he *was* the father of her child, then and *only* then would he make the knowledge official and assume his full responsibilities. But for now he wouldn't allow his personal feelings to take precedence—even though his heart had joyously leapt at the idea he might at long last have a son and heir.

Like a moth that on some level must know it would get burned by the flame it couldn't resist, once again he found himself drawn to the blonde sitting quietly in her wheelchair. He got slowly to his feet. Even though she was understandably under par after her accident, her beauty was still radiant. The colour of her eyes was akin to a rare blue topaz, and they dazzled him like diamonds, whilst her pretty mouth made him remember with longing what it had felt like to touch his lips to hers. He had never known a pleasure like it.

The first time Zafir had met her he'd instantly thought her the most beguiling creature he'd ever seen, and had likened her to the stunning flaxen-haired princess from one of the old Arabian tales he'd heard from his nursemaid as a child. The legend went that whenever this princess caught a man in her gaze his heart and soul would be pledged to her for ever.

As if suddenly aware that the silence between them had stretched on too long, Darcy turned to the attractive older woman by her side and addressed her. Zafir had already assumed she must be her mother. Her tinted blonde hair must have once had the same golden hue as her daughter's, he guessed.

In a determined tone, Darcy announced, 'By the way, Mum, I didn't introduce you. This is His Royal Highness Sheikh Zafir el-Kalil of Zachariah.' She flicked him a glance that left him in no doubt that she was on her guard.

His abdomen clenched as though he'd been sucker-punched as Zafir chillingly recalled his instinctive urge to lash out when she'd accused his brother of being a liar. Whether blood was thicker than water or not, he'd broken his own strict code of conduct in reacting like that. As Allah was his judge, he would rather cut off his hand than hurt a single hair on her head...

'And this is my mother, Patricia Carrick, Your Highness.'

'I am honoured to make your acquaintance, Mrs Carrick.' Having been raised always to respect his elders, in the midst of his turmoil he somehow found a smile.

'And this is a privilege *I* never expected, Your Highness.' Her mother couldn't help giving an awkward little curtsey that made her daughter flush.

Her mother was transfixed by the man's attention.

Then, what female *wouldn't* be, no matter how old she was? Darcy mused.

'I know that Darcy once worked for an Arabian bank whose owners had a royal bloodline, but that was quite some time ago now...in fact a few months before she had Sami.'

It was as if Patricia had just pulled the pin on a hand grenade, and the room fell preternaturally quiet. Reminding herself of the reason that Zafir had brought her home from the hospital in the first place, Darcy found herself staring at the neat white bandage taped round her ankle.

Had her mother not yet put two and two together? If not, then surely it was only a matter of time before she did.

Knowing that the last thing she felt like facing was confrontation, Darcy sought to steer her away from the subject. Lifting her hand to conceal a fake yawn, she made her voice apologetic. 'I'm sorry, Mum, but I'm really feeling quite tired, and I'm sure His Highness has to get on. It's been quite an ordeal. I think I'll go and have a lie-down in a minute, if you could watch Sami?'

'Of course, dear. Why don't you let me take him upstairs while you say goodbye to His Highness? Then you can take a nap.'

'Thanks.'

His glance temporarily alighting on the older woman, Zafir made a polite bow. 'It has been an honour meeting you, Mrs Carrick.'

'And you, Your Highness.'

Putting out his hand, he briefly laid it on the child's small shoulder and bestowed upon him a warmly unguarded smile that made his mother's heart stall.

'It has been a delight and a pleasure to meet you too, Sami,' he told him. 'I hope we shall be able to see each other again soon.'

'Cool!' he replied, with the happy grin that he generally reserved for his best friend, Ben, at school.

Darcy mused that her son didn't easily give his trust to anyone. Had some deep inner instinct already made him bond with the man who was his father?

Her teeth grazing at her lip, she watched him run out to the hall staircase, followed more slowly by his grandmother. In just a few short moments she heard his footsteps race excitedly into his room. No doubt he would be playing eagerly with his toys.

CHAPTER FOUR

THE AIR STIRRED behind her and Darcy realised that Zafir had moved to stare out at the postage-stamp-sized garden beyond the French doors. He must think it ridiculously small compared to his own generous acreage. If it weren't for the injury she'd sustained, she would hardly believe that she'd dared to climb his garden wall. But 'needs must as the Devil drives', she thought. Facing the very *worst* of demons wouldn't faze her if it helped ensure her son's well-being and security.

'You don't have to stay any longer,' she told him, her voice sounding strained even to her own ears.

'Oh, but I do,' he insisted, turning to look at her. There was a flash of steel in his eyes. 'There are still a few things we need to discuss.'

'I thought we'd covered most things.'

'Don't play games with me. I want a straight answer from you. Was I really your *only* lover at the time, Darcy?'

Her skin prickled with indignant heat. 'You accused me once before of sleeping with other men because you listened to office gossip. It was a contemptible lie then and it's still a lie now. Do you imagine I'd ever want to see you again if it wasn't for a very good reason? You hurt me so badly, Zafir, that's it's a wonder I could ever hold my head up again. The only reason I wanted to make contact with you is because of Sami.'

'You say you tried to reach me, but how *hard* did you try?'

Once again he rubbed salt into her wounds with the disbelief that sounded in his voice. Had the faith and trust he'd used to have in his ability to make good judgements been *so* diminished by his brother's lies?

Disconsolately, she shook her head. 'Only the person who took my calls and deals with your post can tell you that.'

'Are you saying it was my personal secretary?'

She flinched, because that had used to be *her* role. 'I can only presume that's who it was—or maybe someone who obeyed her instructions?'

Darcy saw him swallow hard.

'Make no mistake. I will be making my own investigations into the matter'

'I shouldn't have let our association become more personal when I came to work for you, however strong my feelings were at the time. But I can't regret it because it gave me my son. He's the only good thing that's come out of that whole sorry episode. Now all I want is for us to have some peace and for our lives to return to normal.'

'Then let me tell you *this*.'

He moved across to her in a flash and, with a rustle of the luxuriant robes he wore over black jeans and cut-off leather boots, dropped down in front of her, one hand possessively trapping hers as it rested on the wheelchair arm. His touch was like being exquisitely burned, and Darcy gasped.

'The first thing that's going to happen tomorrow is that I'm going to take a paternity test with Sami. If it turns out that I am indeed his father, then wheels will very quickly be put into motion to do what is right by him.'

'What do you mean?'

A muscle in the side of his sculpted cheek flinched. 'I mean I will let my family know that I have sired a son and heir and, to that end, I will be returning home to Zachariah to present him.'

'Now, wait just a minute. Do you honestly think I'm going to let you leave the country with him? Let me remind you that he's *my* son too, Zafir. I'm the one who's raised him all these years, not you.'

'And whose fault is that, *habibi*?' His hand firming more tightly round hers, he tugged her towards him. 'You tell me that you tried to reach me—but until I find out if that's true the fact is that I had no idea you'd had a child. If the paternity test turns out to prove without a doubt that he is my flesh and blood, you should understand that there are going to be some serious consequences.'

'Are you *threatening* me?' Shocked by his vehemence, Darcy turned cold. 'There are laws in this country that—'

But she never got the chance to say anything else because suddenly his hands were firmly gripping her waist and he was impelling her towards him. In the next instant he possessively crushed her lips under his. It was a passionate, bruising kiss that was full of fury as well as blistering desire.

Back when she'd first known him the combustible fusion that had driven them into bed that very first time had been white-hot and charged, but even then she'd only succumbed to being intimate with him because she'd been falling in love with him.

Their lovemaking had culminated in her falling pregnant. But never at any time had she considered aborting her baby because their relationship had ended so disastrously. Right from the start Darcy had had an incontrovertible sense that it was her *destiny* to have his child.

But she'd never experienced the taste of punishing anger on his lips until now. It was clear she had to suppress the need and desire that was feverishly charging through her and somehow find the strength to push him away. She should never forget that this man had betrayed her when he'd chosen to believe his brother's lies about her, and that it had cost her much more than just the loss of her job. How could she ever trust him again?

With her eyes brimming with tears and her breath tight, Darcy stared back into the Arabian's stunningly carved visage and for a moment was reassured in her decision to hold back. There wasn't the least bit of remorse in his expression. In fact he seemed infuriated that she'd curtailed the embrace. His own breath was coming in short sharp gasps and he raised the back of his hand to wipe his mouth, as if to wipe away her taste. Then, with noticeably less care than he'd previously exhibited, Zafir pushed her back down into the wheelchair.

'You are no longer going to have everything your way, Darcy. Now that I am back in your life things are very definitely going to change. I will pick you and the child up tomorrow morning, to go to the clinic. In the meantime you should rest as much as possible and get some of your strength back. Don't lock the front door when I'm gone—I'm going to get your walking aids from the car.'

'You're behaving as if you already know the outcome of the test. You surely wouldn't go to all this trouble if you suspected for even a second that you *aren't* Sami's father...that he's someone else's.'

'When it comes to women I am as liable as the next man to being prey to feminine wiles, and in this particular case I want to be absolutely sure I am not being led astray. In my country, do you know how vital it is for its rulers to father sons? We are a rich but small kingdom, and if we don't procreate we run the risk of being taken over by larger tribes in neighbouring kingdoms. I can't emphasise more strongly than that how vital it is that I make certain that your claims are true.'

On that note he left the house, and she heard his deep bass tones carry on the air as he talked to his bodyguard, Rashid. The enormity of the situation washed over Darcy like encroaching floodwater and her body shivered convulsively.

If someone had predicted to her that one day Zafir would come back into her life and want to claim his son, she'd honestly have thought them deluded. Astonishingly, he'd proved her wrong. Her lips were still tingling where his had so passionately left their imprint and she knew they were likely to be contused.

Tentatively touching her fingertips to the softly swollen flesh, she sighed. Even though she knew his visit was no imagined fantasy—that it was electrifyingly *real*—it still felt as though she was in a dream when he appeared in the room again, her walking aids tucked carefully under his arm. He set them down by the sofa.

Every time she was confronted by the sight of him—in spite of his obvious mistrust and the grief he'd left her with—her hopes soared that even if he couldn't bring himself to love her again, as he once had, perhaps he would genuinely want to be a proper father to his son? Right then, she refused to think about his engagement.

'I will leave them here, at the end of the couch, so you can reach them when you need to get up.'

'Thanks.'

'You will not be able to manage to do things on your own for a while, until your injury heals. I'm thinking of hiring a nurse for you.'

A sense that events were taking on a distinct life of their own and running away with her gave Darcy the shivers. She needed to impress upon him the fact that she still had a mind of her own.

Imbuing firmness into her tone, she replied, 'That won't be necessary. My mum is with me, remember?'

Zafir frowned, 'Ah, yes, she lives with you.'

'Yes. She looks after Sami for me when I'm at work, and she'll take care of things until I'm up and about again.'

'And where, may I ask, do you work these days?'

'I work for a temping agency rather than a single employer. The jobs are quite varied and I like that.

It also gives me the flexibility I need to be at home whenever Sami is ill.'

'Resourceful as ever, I see.' The coal-black eyes glimmered thoughtfully.

'I've had to be. Obviously I need to earn money to keep us and pay my rent.'

'You do not own this property?'

'You're joking! Mum and I rent it together. Have you *any* idea how much I'd need to put down as a deposit in order to get a mortgage?' A warm flush swept across her cheeks and she knew she sounded defensive. 'Anyway, I'm really tired now and I need to rest. I'll see you in the morning.'

Zafir nodded. 'I will be here for you at nine-fifteen, to ensure we get to the clinic on time. I advise you to rest that ankle and get to bed early. Where will you sleep tonight? Here on the couch?'

'Yes, probably.'

'Whatever you do, do not attempt the stairs. Have you a downstairs cloakroom?'

She shouldn't be surprised that although he came from a world of privilege he was automatically considering the practicalities of her situation, but she was. 'Yes, I do.'

'Good. Then I'll see you and the child tomorrow.'

Making one last sweeping examination of her, as if to satisfy himself that she could be trusted to keep her word, he turned round and left.

Even though the situation was nowhere near to being conclusive yet, Zafir's first thought when he got home was to ring Farrida and let her know that their marriage was off...that she should no longer consider herself engaged to him.

She wouldn't take the news at all calmly, and would probably rant and rail at him, listing all the reasons why he was a fool to break his pledge—not least of all because their families had wanted their union since they were children and he would never find another woman more suitable than her.

However, he sensibly decided to postpone the call until he'd had the results of the test from the clinic. Farrida could wait...

That night, to while away the inevitably tense hours that ensued, Zafir played cards with Rashid. The man was a lousy card-player, but couldn't be faulted for his enthusiasm. However, it was hard to concentrate on the game when his fertile mind kept taking him down paths he was wary of following.

There were too many as yet unresolved issues for his liking—too many for him to be confident of specific outcomes. But the following day might present the most important revelation of his life so far—that he was the father of the handsome boy whom he'd only discovered existed yesterday.

Although the mere idea of his having a son was unquestionably wonderful, the fact that he hadn't even known of his existence for over four years grievously wounded him. Had the prospect of seeing him again been so unpalatable to her that Darcy had delayed letting him know she was pregnant? Or had she feared what he might do?

He had fired her because he'd found her in his brother's arms at the office, for goodness' sake! The evidence against her could hardly have been more damning.

Yet it still nagged at him that he'd made the most terrible mistake. Why? Because it had become increasingly clear that Xavier had a worrying predilection for indulging in indiscriminate liaisons, and a year after Darcy had gone he'd discovered that he was conducting an intimate relationship with one of the bank's married secretaries—even after being warned that any more compromising behaviour would absolutely not be tolerated.

Zafir had ordered him straight back to Zachariah as punishment, telling him not to return until he could prove he had changed for the better. He would not allow the family's good name to be dragged through the mud. In his opinion Xavier had been far too indulged growing up and this was the result. Consequently he was going to have to demonstrate much more exemplary behaviour and become a man the family was truly proud of before he could even *think* about claiming the generous inheritance left to him by their father...

It was a quarter past nine on the dot the next morning when his chic and luxurious car arrived to collect Darcy and her son. She was clearly insistent on using her crutches, and Sami walked protectively beside her to the car.

Zafir owned to a warm burst of pride that the boy was behaving like a real gentleman at such a tender age. *Some might say that royal blood will out*, he thought, smiling. But although he was charmed by him, his gaze kept gravitating to Darcy.

Today she was wearing a simple navy blue skirt with a fitted matching jacket. The mid-length skirt displayed her shapely knees and calves to perfection, but it was her heart-stopping features and the pretty flaxen hair resting against her nape in a neat pony-tail that inevitably drew his attention.

He could hardly look away, even though he immediately sensed that she wasn't feeling remotely sociable. She was wearing make-up, but the light application couldn't disguise the fact that she was por-celain-pale. Was she nervous about the outcome of the test this morning, in case it proved that he *wasn't* Sami's father?

He deliberately stopped the thought dead in its tracks. One step at a time, he told himself.

When they arrived, a trim uniformed nurse with chestnut hair met them at the entrance of the clinic and led them inside to the suite where the tests would be conducted. As the automatic glass doors swished open Zafir situated himself protectively between Darcy and the boy, as if he had already acknowl-edged that he was head of the family.

'Do you think this will take very long?' she asked him, stopping for a moment as if to take a breather from the effort of using the crutches.

There was a slight sheen of sweat on her brow. Concerned, he gently pressed her shoulder. 'Why? Is it too much for you to stand? I can carry you into the examination room, if you like?'

'No. I'll be all right.'

Her lips formed a tight, reluctant little smile that told him she was far from being 'all right' and he frowned. 'Are you nervous about the outcome of the test?'

'What have I to be nervous about? I've always known the truth—right from day one. It's *you* who suspects I might be lying.'

As if he'd been stung, his hand dropped away. He glanced across at Sami. The last thing he wanted to do was make the child fear him, should he sense there was tension between him and his mother. If the test revealed what his heart willed it to then his greatest desire was that he and Sami would start to build a good relationship—the kind of loving, mutually respectful relationship that Zafir had enjoyed with his own father.

'Your Highness... Ms Carrick and Master Carrick...please follow me and we'll get the paternity test underway.'

The trim nurse who had met them at Reception smiled warmly and led them into a room that, with its ecru couches and colourful cushions, clearly aimed to be as inviting as possible in order to put clients at their ease. But the indelible aroma of antiseptic pervaded the atmosphere and it was impossible to disguise its purpose.

The three of them took their seats and straight away Zafir noticed that Darcy avoided meeting his eyes. Instead she concentrated her gaze on her son. As he privately acknowledged his fear of the test's outcome the capacity for speech seemed to desert him. Never had so much depended on the results of what was a fairly routine test these days, and he found his gut clenching as if to ward off a blow.

For a couple of minutes he fiddled with the band of his thick gold signet ring, just for something to do. Thankfully, they didn't have to wait long before a clinician arrived. The young twenty-something man, who was already losing his hair, took the requisite cell samples by swabbing the insides of their cheeks with cotton buds which were then put into a container, sealed and labelled with their names.

'All done,' he said brightly, surveying them closely with his keen-eyed glance, but being careful not to seem intrusive. 'In twelve hours' time I'll be able to give you the results. You can ring me on this number at about ten tonight, Your Highness.'

Taking a small white card out of his pocket, he handed it to Zafir.

'Are there any further questions?'

Zafir wanted to reply *yes*. How were they supposed to while away twelve hours and not succumb to the most unbearable tension?

As if reading his mind, the clinician—his voice still indomitably cheerful—said, 'I'll take that as a no, then. As you probably know, Hyde Park isn't very far from here, if you feel like taking a walk. There's a good café there, where you can get drinks and food. You can also feed the ducks that swim on the lake. Do you have a wheelchair with you, Ms Carrick?'

Clearing her throat, as if her voice had gone rusty after several minutes' lack of use, Darcy glanced at Zafir then quickly looked away again. 'His—His Highness has one in the car for me.'

'Good. Then I suggest that you go and enjoy the day and try not to worry.'

With Sami happily holding her hand as she rode in the wheelchair—Zafir manoeuvring her and Rashid dutifully following behind at a suitably discreet distance, but still within earshot—Darcy started to relax a little.

The clinician's idea about going to the park had been a good one. There was nothing like a dose of fresh air, the sight and scent of recently rained-on grass and a plethora of English oak trees to help raise the spirits, she thought. Add to that her beautiful little son, skipping cheerfully alongside her, and his equally beautiful, often brooding father wheeling her, in those precious few hours before their immediate future was decided on she could hardly have wished for more...

They made their way towards the wide glinting lake in the afternoon sunshine, and Sami rushed ahead when he spied the small flotilla of ducks converging at the waterside.

'Mummy, there are *loads* of ducks here!' he called out excitedly.

Zafir shouted back. 'Don't get too near to the water, Sami. Wait for me and your mother.'

'All right... But I only want to talk to them, Your Highness.'

In response, Zafir threw his head back and laughed heartily. The sound raised Darcy's flesh to goosebumps, it was so joyful.

She twisted in her chair to look up at him. 'What's so funny?'

'He is so polite and well mannered...a real credit to you. Who told him to call me *Your Highness*? Did you?'

Returning his smile, she dimpled. 'No. I expect it was my mum—either that or he heard her refer to you as that.'

'Like I said—he is a credit to you, Darcy.'

For a long moment she allowed herself to bathe in the undeniable warmth of his lingering glance, and she almost forgot that there had ever been any disagreement between them. But even then she knew not to hope for too much. So many things were still unsettled.

Just as they reached the lakeside, and saw Sami happily chattering to the ducks, they noticed a fit and spry elderly couple with tans like mahogany moving purposefully towards them.

The woman called out. 'Is that your little boy? I'm guessing he must be. You can see where he inherits his good looks. He's a real mixture of you both, if you don't mind my saying? By the way, that's a magnificent costume you're wearing, sir. Are you in the theatre?' she asked curiously, staring at Zafir.

After a wry glance towards Darcy first, he looked back and answered, 'I fear you have found me out. I should have changed when rehearsals ended, but my son was eager to feed the ducks'

'Oh, my—do you mind if I get a picture of you?'

Fully expecting her companion instantly to say no, Darcy was amazed when Zafir agreed.

'Why don't you take one of all of us?' he suggested, standing next to her with his hand resting possessively on her shoulder and at the same time calling out to Sami to come and join them.

One photo had turned into three by the time the American couple said their effusive goodbyes and departed, by which time Sami declared that he was hungry.

'Then we should go to the café and have a sandwich. We can save some bread to feed the ducks,' Zafir suggested.

'Can we have cake too?'

'But of course.'

'Cool.' With a delighted grin the little boy ran to Zafir's side and slipped his hand into his as if it was the most natural thing in the world for him to do... In fact, as if he had been doing it all his life...

CHAPTER FIVE

SAMI FELL ASLEEP in the car and, with her arm protectively tucked around him, so did Darcy. An undeniable sense of 'rightness' filled Zafir as he observed the pair, and the more he looked the stronger the feeling grew.

Other than the very first time he'd set eyes on his stunning blue-eyed secretary, he'd never had such a powerful sense of something significant happening—something that he couldn't control. Something that might possibly change his life...

He had always been restless by nature, too hungry to settle for what he deemed the 'ordinary' aspirations of others. But coming from royal lineage meant that somewhere along the line it was essential that he marry and have children. It had been playing on his mind for quite some time now, and his mother regularly got in touch to remind him about it and his agreement to Farrida. But she was the *last* woman he wanted to think about now...

There was still a fire in him to try and make a positive difference to those less fortunate, and he would continue to do so in whatever way he could, but having a loving relationship and the joy of a family of his own had suddenly become the most important thing of all. Was it seeing Darcy again that had made the idea seem more urgent?

He had never forgotten their love affair, and nor had he got over it… That period in his life had been an incredible time out of time, and for a while he had been joyously lost in his feelings for her. If she *had* betrayed him with his brother, as he'd thought, he wouldn't be able to forgive her easily. Yet he couldn't deny that he was desperate to know if her son *was* his.

The time when he'd receive the test results from the clinic couldn't come quickly enough.

Moving suddenly, Darcy yawned and sat up. A few strands of silky blonde hair had worked loose from her ponytail, and as the sunlight zeroed in on them through the window beside her they seemed to crackle with electricity.

'Are we nearly home?'

For a moment those matchless blue eyes that were highlighted by dark gold lashes stopped him in his tracks. It was like glancing into the most extraordinarily still mountain lake. The bewitching appeal that had hypnotised him from the very first hadn't decreased in the slightest. In fact it had become even more mesmerising.

Snapping out of the near trance he'd fallen into, he sucked in a breath to compose himself. 'We are just approaching your house…look.'

'What a relief.'

'You must be tired. Let me help you.'

'It would help me more if you could carry Sami.'

'Gladly.'

When they reached the living room it was to find

Darcy's mother waiting. When she saw Zafir her smile was awkwardly deferential, but she immediately lifted the still drowsy Sami from out of his arms.

'He's probably had a bit too much excitement for one day, Your Highness. Darcy told me you were heading off to the park when she rang. I'll take him up to his room and read to him for a while. If he falls asleep I'll come back down and make you both a nice cup of tea.'

The couple were silent as Patricia disappeared upstairs, but it wasn't by any means an *easy* silence. The two of them were both behaving as though they were wary of saying or doing the wrong thing. The situation was a veritable powder keg that might blow up in their faces at any time, and they both knew it...

Chewing down on the inside of her cheek, Darcy gingerly lowered herself onto the couch. She was grateful when her companion immediately stepped forward to relieve her of the crutches and lean them against a chair, but she *wasn't* grateful that the tantalising scent of his cologne too easily had the power to scramble her brain. Plus, her injured ankle had developed the same nagging ache as a persistent sore tooth, and she couldn't suppress her irritation. Add to that the stress of going for a paternity test to prove to her son's father that he *was* the one responsible for siring him—surely it would be one stress too many in *anyone's* book?

'You don't have to stay for a cup of tea,' she declared suddenly. 'Let's not pretend this is some kind of fond reunion, when we both know it's anything *but*. My mum was just being polite.'

'And clearly you don't feel the same need? To be

polite, I mean?' He crossed his arms over his chest, his black eyes glinting disapprovingly.

'I can be as polite as the next person. But that doesn't mean I have to act pleased that you're here. If I hadn't had that fall at your house we wouldn't even be having this conversation. In all this time you've never bothered to find out what happened to me. You sacked me from a job I loved and probably didn't lose an ounce of sleep wondering how I would manage to survive. And I don't suppose it ever crossed your mind that you might have left me pregnant?'

At last. To say what was true was like puncturing a painful cyst that had troubled her for too long. Although upsetting, she was glad of the release of expressing her pent-up emotion. Even more so because she'd been certain that she'd never get the chance...

The expression on Zafir's handsome, strong-boned face was stunned. There was a visible tremor in his hand when he lifted it to push back a swathe of rich dark hair.

'As we are on the subject, did it ever cross *your* mind how I must have felt when I found you in the arms of my brother?'

White-hot rage such as she'd never felt before erupted inside Darcy. 'As I told you at the time—and again the other day—it was a set-up! If you'd had any *real* feeling for me you would have seen that. Xavier had been plaguing me for weeks. When you came into the office, just as he grabbed me and kissed me, I knew by the look in your eyes that you hadn't seen the triumphant smirk on his face. You wouldn't even give me the chance to put my side of the story.

Instead you condemned me. It was as though what we had shared meant *nothing* to you.'

The interminable silence that ensued made Darcy feel as if she was walking barefoot on broken glass... Already she felt as if she was inwardly bleeding.

When it came, Zafir's reply was surprisingly frank.

'If what you say is indeed true, then I have undoubtedly paid the price for my actions. Not only did I not know that I might have fathered a child, but I might have hurt his mother beyond measure... a woman I'd come to care for and respect...'

He looked to be having trouble continuing for a moment, and Darcy caught her breath.

'But all this is still supposition. Can you not see that I *had* to take my brother's word over yours? It would not have gone down well with my family if they'd discovered he was lying. Our good reputation is the cornerstone of our rule and it would have near destroyed them. Remember I saw you both with my own eyes, kissing passionately. What else could I think other than you'd discovered you preferred him to me?'

'How can you even *suggest* such a thing? You ask me what it would have done to your family if they'd learned that Xavier wasn't the blue-eyed boy they thought he was...that he'd lied to protect himself and implicated me...but what about the cost *I* paid for being gullible enough to believe that you loved me, Zafir?'

He definitely flushed a little beneath his smooth tanned skin. 'I know it may not seem to you that I value the truth right now, Darcy, but I hope to change that opinion. If it is proved that I have indeed wronged you, then I give you my word that I will do everything I can to put things right...no matter what the personal cost.'

'And you will tell your family the real story? That I was having a relationship with you? That you were confident up until that incident that I would never cheat on you? I told you from the start that I wouldn't consider being intimate with you if my feelings weren't strong. Is it likely I'd go after your *brother*? Anyway, it was cruel of him to not only ensure I lost my job, but to paint such a horrible picture of me...a picture that made it look like I had no morals at all.'

Zafir's lips tightened and his expression was pained. 'I very much regret it if he did that. I will talk to him again about what happened and remind him of what he told me at the time. Then I will give him the chance to think over the accusations he made and be absolutely sure he's telling me the truth. Thankfully he is married now, and appears to be happy. I only pray his good fortune will help guide him to do what is right.'

'And if it doesn't?'

'Then it will be up to me to decide what to do.'

Now Zafir not only looked pained, but weary too.

Darcy had a sudden insight into what a burden it must be to be the head of such a family as his, no matter how admired or influential they were. He had to utilise his wisdom in dealing with many differing personalities, glean what was truly going on in their disputes and act accordingly. And it didn't prevent the individual members of that family from acting purely out of self-interest if they so chose.

She'd discovered long ago that not everyone had a conscience telling them to do what was right...

'By the way, can I verify that you don't have a relationship with anyone right now?'

His examining glance honed in on her like a searchlight.

'I thought I told you that before? No, I don't.'

'That will make things a lot easier.'

'What do you mean? Aren't you engaged? Or did you forget?'

'As far as that's concerned, I will tell you my plans when I have the results of the test. But be assured I will do what is right.'

Darcy chewed down on her lip. 'Right by *whom*, exactly?'

'That's enough.' He couldn't hide his mounting irritation. 'I will talk to you later, when I hear from the clinic. Right now I need to spend some time alone, and that being the case I think it's time I left. Ring me if you need anything, but your top priority should be to rest and recover.'

Just like that he was gone.

The sound of the door closing was like the sound of a portcullis slamming down on her heart. Did he still harbour the belief that she was lying? His brother had sounded so convincing that day—using every trick in the book to make Zafir believe he was sincere, mercilessly using their family relationship to make him doubt his own judgement.

Leaning back against the couch cushions, Darcy shut her eyes tight and tried to jettison the memory of that terrible day from her mind. She'd felt so alone... alone and worthless. If that was the result of her lover not standing up for her, choosing to believe his brother's version of events over hers, then she'd sooner stay single for the rest of her life than risk a similar demoralising situation. But she couldn't stem her deep regret that she and Zafir hadn't been able to put things right and save themselves the unnecessary heartache that had followed...

When the phone rang that evening, just after ten, Zafir all but jumped to snatch up the receiver and answer it. Anyone who had seen him just then would hardly have described him as being cool, calm and collected.

Having abandoned his usual formal attire for a more casual black tee shirt and jeans, he'd been lying on the couch, trying to give his restless attention to a book on the history of the pharaohs and knowing it was utterly pointless. All he'd been able to think about—all he'd *wanted* to think about—was Darcy and the golden-haired child who might turn out to be *his*...

'Am I speaking to His Highness Sheikh Zafir el-Kalil?' enquired a very circumspect English voice.

'That is correct.'

'Well, sir, I am contacting you about the paternity test you had at the clinic this morning. I now have the results for you.'

'Well?' Zafir snapped, feeling sweat break out on his brow and his heart clamouring even as he unflinchingly infused his tone with authority.

'The test proves that the DNA of the child matches yours, Your Highness. You are indeed the male parent of Master Sami Carrick.'

'Allah Be Praised! The boy is mine!'

Instantly possessive, he had no reservations in displaying his joy and gratification at the news.

I have a son... I have a son...

His heart had never hammered so hard. But he was already making plans as to what he should do first. As well as being portentous, the knowledge that he was a parent was the most incredible thing that had ever happened to him. But there was also a less than desirable aspect to the news. It brought home to him the fact that in effect he had mercilessly abandoned the mother of his child when she'd undoubtedly needed him the most.

That thought alone was like a sharpened scimitar slicing through his gut, and the impact on him was beyond estimation...

'Is there anything else I can do for you, sir?' the clinician enquired.

Staring round at the lavish but tasteful furniture in the elegant room that befitted his status, Zafir couldn't think very much beyond the incredible revelation he'd just heard.

Dazedly he shook his head. 'No. There is nothing else.'

'In that case I'll put the information in an envelope and have it despatched to you by courier just as soon as I can.'

'Tonight would be good.'

'I will aim to do just that, Your Highness.'

The Sheikh's sleek car drew up in front of her house and stopped. The property next door, along with several others in the sedate little cul-de-sac, didn't sug-

gest much activity—either inside or out. Many of the
lights were already extinguished—probably due to
it being Sunday and tomorrow the start of the working week.

Its leather-coated driver didn't get out for a full
five minutes. His Highness the Sheikh was thinking hard.

He was wondering about the best approach to
achieve the result he needed without any argument.
If he'd been back in Zachariah there was no question he would have achieved it without dissent. But
his royal status hardly held much sway with Darcy,
he knew. She was an independent woman, as well as
a British citizen, and given that she had given birth
in this country she would have certain inalienable
rights that he couldn't ignore.

Breathing out a frustrated curse, he pushed back
his hair. Tonight he'd deliberately elected to leave
Rashid back at the house and drive himself because
he needed some privacy. His freedom hadn't been
gained without a few strong words from the bodyguard, though, and the assurance that if anything
untoward happened he wouldn't be blamed.

At last, deciding to go with his instincts rather than
waste any more time devising a plan, Zafir left the
vehicle, strode up the pathway and rang the doorbell.

He was very glad that it chimed softly. It was late.
If Darcy had gone to bed, he hoped she was still
resting on the couch rather than having made the attempt to go upstairs to the bedroom. At least then she
wouldn't have to struggle too far to get to the door.

Wearing lilac-coloured pyjamas and a matching
robe, the woman who dominated his thoughts above

all others opened the door. The blue eyes that were usually so brilliant were visibly drowsy, and her corn-coloured hair curled in mussed gold coils around her shoulders. She was leaning on a single crutch in order to balance and not put her weight down on her injured ankle.

Before he uttered a word, Zafir scooped her up into his arms and kicked the door shut with the heel of his boot. Still not speaking, he headed straight for the living room. By the dimmed glow of a single lamp he saw that the couch was covered with a rumpled duvet, and the coffee table held a half-eaten sandwich on a plate and what looked to be a congealed mug of tea.

His brow crumpled. 'Was this all you had for your supper?'

'Hello to you too, Your Highness... Didn't you have anything better to do tonight other than to come here, examine my food and annoy me?'

'You would try the patience of a saint, Darcy.'

His tone exasperated, he set her down as carefully as his temper would allow on the couch. Not only would the woman try the patience of a saint, but the feeling of her curvaceous body in his arms and the naturally seductive heat she exuded was apt to make him lose all desire for conversation instantly and want to communicate in a way that would leave her in no doubt as to his feelings.

Did a man ever forget the one woman who had made his breath quicken and his blood surge the moment he had laid eyes on her?

'Presumably you've had the results from the clinic?' she murmured.

'Yes, I have.' Crossing to a plain cream armchair,

Zafir flicked open the single button on his jacket and settled back in the chair. 'It's just as you said all along…I am Sami's father.'

Bringing her knees up to her chest, Darcy wrapped her arms round them and sighed softly. 'Now you know for sure I wasn't lying.'

The look she gave him was hardly accusing. But it was so nakedly direct that it was like an arrow aimed straight at his heart—an arrow that once it had hit its target broke and embedded its shards in his chest. That soulful, wounded glance would be with him for ever.

Once again, an excoriating sorrow filled him. He had abandoned her. And not just her, but the boy he now knew was his legitimate son and heir…

CHAPTER SIX

Leaning forward in his seat, Zafir rested his hands on his knees. 'In light of this revelation, you do realise that your life and Sami's will have to undergo some quite radical changes?'

'What do you mean? Are you going to take me to court and sue for custody? Because if you do—if you *dare* even try—I'll...'

'You'll *what*, Darcy?'

Already knowing he would have a fight on his hands if he made any kind of claim on the boy, Zafir also knew that when it came down to it *he'd* have the upper hand. Because of his wealth and status he'd have access to some of the best legal minds in the world to represent him in any dispute. Yet separating the child from his mother had never been a consideration. Seeing Darcy again, and discovering that in spite of the disturbing events that had parted them he was still powerfully attracted to her, had put him in the most agonising quandary. Even more so because during the years they'd been apart she had given birth to his son.

Like a deflated balloon, she sank back against the cushions. She carefully straightened her legs, and he saw her wince as though in pain.

'Don't make me descend into fighting you, Zafir. Don't you think I've been through enough? I can understand that you'll want to get to know Sami, and I'll tell him that you're his father, but what I *won't* do is to let you dictate where he should live or how he's raised. His happiness means everything to me, and despite what you and your family might think of me I *know* I'm a good mother.'

In the edgy silence that followed Zafir fought the strongest urge to go to her and take her in his arms. She seemed particularly fragile tonight, as if the momentous events of the past few days had finally sunk in and shaken her defences. But he decided not to risk worsening their already tense relationship by wading in and making demands straight away. Instead he would try and use tact and diplomacy, and slowly help her come to see that his intention was to help *improve* their lives, not make them harder.

'I don't doubt that you're a good mother. And I can already see how much Sami means to you. You do not have to prove anything to me on that score. And as for my family—they will go along with whatever I decide. Given that I will be informing them I now have a son, there will be much cause for celebration. In fact the whole kingdom will be celebrating.'

'What about your engagement? Do you think your fiancée will be joining in the celebrations?'

It was hard to keep the jealousy from her tone. How on earth was she going to have future dealings with him and pretend that she was well and truly *over* him? Even though she didn't want to admit it, her emotions around him were still raw, and liable to splinter and shatter if he expected her feelings to have deadened in the time they'd been apart. Had *his*?

But his next words truly astonished her.

'I have already decided to bring the engagement to an end. In any case, like I told you, it was never a love match. Farrida will be generously compensated for any disappointment she may have, but she knows how important it is for me to have an heir. You need not give the matter a second thought.'

'Do you really believe that, Zafir?' Darcy's blue eyes flashed. 'As far as your people are concerned, I'm a woman who's not to be trusted, remember? The woman you fired because you thought I was cheating on you with your brother. Do you think they'll accept me and my son after such a story? It must have done the rounds by now. I don't doubt they'll think you've lost your mind to break off your engagement and let me back into your life.'

'If anyone expresses any doubt whatsoever in my decisions about my personal life then I will make sure to put them right when I return. But in the meantime it won't help our situation if you and I continue to bring up past disappointments and use them as weapons to cut each other down. Do you honestly think it will help Sami learn to accept me as his father if he sees me as some kind of bully who just tells his mother what to do and seems not to care about her feelings?'

'I don't want him to think that…of course I don't. But the truth is I have no idea *what* you feel about me. Going on past experience, I would say that you cared more about everyone else's feelings than mine.'

'Then you would be wrong.'

'You think? Then why didn't you believe me when

I told you I wasn't involved with Xavier? That he had in fact been harassing me?'

Zafir owned to feeling more than just a little uneasy. His brother's reputation hadn't been the only thing called into question. He recalled that at the time leading up to the day when he'd found Darcy compromised there had been rumours of secret assignations between the pair flying round the office, and they had been substantiated by one of the senior secretaries.

Jane Maddox had been a thirty-something singleton who'd liked to take some of the younger secretaries under her wing. But now Zafir remembered that she'd had a soft spot for his brother, and a tendency to be jealous of any woman younger or prettier than her who might have a chance with him. Being quite a plain woman herself, she'd been particularly jealous of Darcy's beauty. Had she sought to ingratiate herself with Xavier by supporting the lie that the blonde had come on to him?

Many times over the years Zafir had wondered painfully if he'd rashly jumped to the wrong conclusions. If he had, he now knew that it had cost him dear.

'We've been over this. You *know* why,' he answered passionately. 'What was I *supposed* to think when I saw you wrapped in his arms that day? Have you *any* idea what that did to me? It made me go a little crazy. I was jealous, hurt, and mad as hell. There was no time to think rationally about anything.'

'And the relationship we'd had wasn't strong enough for you to trust me?'

'I didn't say that. It's *because* I trusted you implicitly that I was devastated by what looked to be your betrayal.'

'Maybe you should have looked into things a little deeper rather than just accepting what you saw on the surface as being the truth?'

Darcy hunched her shoulders and the pain in her eyes was a fresh wound that ate into his soul.

Breathing out again slowly, she went on, 'I know it's not easy for either of us to forget the past and put it behind us, to forgive and forget and move on. But I too was devastated when you wouldn't listen to the truth. Back then I thought I knew who you were, and there were so many things about you that I admired— particularly your loyalty to family and friends and the way you always tried to help people in need. I thought you were pretty special—and not just because you came from royalty. I didn't care about that. It was the *person* I was interested in, not the trappings. When I first met you I thought you were charming, kind and considerate—unlike any other man I'd met before. I allowed myself to be *seduced* by that man. In short, I grew to trust you, Zafir, and I thought you felt the same way about me. However, I've long since learned that I made the most colossal mistake.'

She was twisting her hands together, and her candid gaze was sorrowful.

The desolate words dried his mouth and made his heart beat too fast for him to think straight. Suddenly the impulse to try and change her mind about him, to make her remember the man she'd once fallen in love with, was overwhelming. It was like a forceful current that threatened to drown him if he didn't act to save himself.

So he went to her, and with gentle but firm hands lifted her up onto her feet. For a long moment he stared into the incandescent blue eyes that usually sparkled like crystal. But tonight...tonight he saw they were bathed in tears...

Just before his lips touched hers, he murmured huskily, 'You didn't make a mistake, *habibi*...perhaps it just wasn't the right time for us?'

Then his mouth slowly and deliberately took hers as his hands held her steady and his senses were suffused by the intoxicating delight that only she could bring. How had he lived so long without it? Zafir longed to touch her body again as he used to, to explore those incredible curves without restraint, and he was frustrated that he couldn't because they weren't alone in the house.

But as the pleasure built inexorably inside him Darcy moaned low in her throat and began to drive her fingers through his hair. There was a hint of wildness, almost of *desperation* in her touch, and he remembered how he'd loved that about her—the way she didn't try to constrain her feelings when they were being intimate. It told him just what he needed to know...that she'd missed the fire and passion they'd once ignited in each other as much as he had, and couldn't help but set a match to it again.

Now the sublime taste of her lips and her silken tongue were arousing Zafir almost to the point of pain. Because the sensations were so intense it was hard to resist her. Hard to not want more, *much* more than just this tempting embrace. But, regrettably, he knew he was going to have to bring their heated ex-

change to an end. Leave it any[...]
be near impossible to turn back.[...]

Garnering his resolve, he re[...]
mouth away. Staring back at her,[...]
breathing hard. Her face was as flu[...]
as a Millais portrait and once again[...]
sparkled like sunlit pools.

'Regrettably, this is not the time or t.. place for
this,' he said 'Your mother and our son are sleeping
upstairs and you need to rest that ankle. Sit down…
I have something else to say to you before I go.'

Without protest, Darcy let him help her. But when
he dropped down beside her on the crumpled duvet
he sensed her wariness had returned.

'One of the things I intend to do before I take you
home to meet my family is to marry you.' His emotions were taut as a high-wire as he said this, but he
forced them back and continued, 'It is a necessary
formality so that Sami can take my name and legally
have my protection. When we get back to Zachariah
we will do things properly and have an official ceremony.'

A doubtful frown crinkled her silkily smooth
brow. 'Did I hear you right? Was that meant to be
some kind of proposal?'

Zafir's lips twisted wryly. 'I admit it was hardly
romantic. But sometimes necessity has to come first.
Then later…with time and desire…a man can make
up for the deficit and display his true affection.'

'Is that one of your country's philosophies?'

Making his hand into a light fist, he stroked down
her delectably soft cheek with his knuckles. Her skin
had the same exquisite texture as an infant's.

...pping up her chin he answered, 'No. I am just expressing that I do not want you to feel short-changed in any way. That I am mindful of what a new bride might understandably expect from her husband.'

Drawing back, Darcy shakily touched her palm to her hair. 'How can I feel short-changed when a proposal is the last—the very *last* thing I want from you?'

'Foolishly, I did not consider the possibility that I'd left you pregnant when we parted, and I confess to being ashamed about that. And know this: it will always haunt me that I did not, because you had to raise our son on your own. I want to make amends. When I learned about him, did you never consider that I might want to meet my responsibilities and marry you?'

'There was a time when I wanted nothing *more* than to be your wife, Zafir. But I don't want to marry you just because you feel you should assume your parental responsibilities. We've been apart for a long time, and many things have changed.'

'That sounds suspiciously like you might want to marry someone else...' After the stratospheric highs of just a moment ago, when he'd kissed her, he came crashing back down to earth—not unlike a brick or a stone that had been dropped from a great height.

'Of course I don't. I'm not even seeing anyone.'

'Then why create obstacles that aren't there?' Zafir knew his eyes must be radiating his confusion and, to be frank, his growing impatience.

'The fact that neither of us trusts each other is a pretty big obstacle, wouldn't you say? It's not something that's easily going to be overcome by a hasty marriage.'

'I have already told you that time and desire will help pave the way to true affection between us. But, more importantly, we need to show our joint commitment to our son. As far as I'm concerned, the sooner we marry the better. I'm not going to be relegated to becoming a part-time father, as seems to be the trend these days in the West, just to suit *you*. The boy is my son and heir and you should not forget that.'

Getting to his feet, he turned round to view her.

'I'm going to leave you now, so you can get some sleep. But tomorrow we will meet for lunch and start the process of putting some plans into place. I'll send a car for you at one o'clock.'

With a glance that he'd resolved would keep a guard on his innermost feelings, Zafir walked to the door and left her alone.

On her return from doing the school run with Sami, Patricia Carrick took off her raincoat and, as was her habit, meticulously hung it on the coat stand. Then she went into the living room to find Darcy.

She wasn't at all surprised to find that her daughter had vacated the sofa, where she'd spent the past couple of nights, but was more than a little annoyed that she had done so. She was supposed to be resting that ankle. But even as a child Darcy hadn't taken to being told what to do, even if it had been for her benefit. In truth, the only person whose advice she had ever really listened to was her father...

Having heard the front door slam shut, Darcy called out, 'I'm in the kitchen, Mum.'

In Patricia's absence she'd washed and dressed and, using her walking cane, had carefully limped into the kitchen to put the kettle on.

'Cup of tea?' she offered.

Standing in the doorway, her mother folded her arms and shook her head in disapproval. 'Do you really think it's a good idea to be pouring out a kettle of hot water in your condition?'

'I've made English Breakfast. I know it's your favourite.'

'Never mind that—did you hear what I said?'

Leaning against the worktop, the younger woman sighed and pushed back the golden tresses that were still spread about her shoulders because she hadn't tied it back yet.

'Yes, I did. You're worried about me pouring hot water from the kettle when I'm on my own having had an accident. For goodness' sake, I'm not a child. I *know* I have to be careful. If I was on my own and didn't have you around to help I'd have to manage.'

'Which brings me to the next thing I want to talk to you about…I want you to tell me the truth about your relationship with the Sheikh. That bank you used to work for in the city…didn't the owners come from a little-known country in the Middle East?'

Feeling discomfited that her mother should mention that right now, Darcy attempted a non-committal shrug. But, having never revealed the identity of her son's father in case of possibly compromising him, she now feared the older woman was fast closing in on the truth.

'What's that got to do with anything?'

'There's something that went on between the two

of you in the past, isn't there? I could sense it as soon as I met him. Why on earth would someone as important as he is bring my daughter home from the hospital if he didn't have some kind of vested interest?'

'I worked for him once…that's all.'

'Give me *some* credit, love.' Her mother crossed the floor to draw Darcy's hand into hers. 'Do you think I'm too old to remember what sexual chemistry is like? The air fairly crackles when the two of you are together.'

She was cornered as surely as a fox in a trap…

Chewing down on her lip, Darcy knew she could no longer hide the truth. Even though she'd been even more driven to find Zafir and tell him about Sami when she'd learned he was engaged, she'd lived with the secret for so long without telling anybody that it was going to be hard on her to give up her anonymity. She had never sought fame or fortune, and now it seemed she was going to achieve both…

Last night Zafir had sworn that he was going to marry her, also that they were going to return to his country so he could proclaim Sami his son and heir. An ordinary, simple life would no longer be hers.

There would be no more having to make ends meet on just her own money and her mother's small wage, no more struggling to pay the bills. Whilst some might say that was a *good* thing, she wondered how she could possibly make a marriage work with someone who'd let her down as devastatingly as Zafir had done. Not only that, but with someone who had abandoned her without even giving her a chance to air *her* side of the story.

'Presumably you have told him that Sami is his son?'

'Yes…I've told him.'

'So what does he aim to do about it? I imagine that because he is who he is, his code of honour will be strong…that he will want to do what's right for you and his son?'

Turning away, Darcy reached for the canary-yellow teapot she'd left on the worktop and began to fill two matching mugs. She knew her mother was impatient for her answer but she deliberately didn't hurry to give it.

'Can you put the mugs on a tray and carry it into the living room for me?'

Patricia, her still slim figure attired smartly in a fitted navy skirt and an unfussy white blouse, was exasperated. 'Answer my question… What does the Sheikh intend to do about it?'

Unable to disguise her uncertainty, Darcy sucked in a breath and said quietly, 'He told me that he intends to marry me and make Sami his heir.'

'I knew he was an honourable man the moment I set eyes on him. Now, let's go and have that cup of tea, shall we?'

Much later on that night—in fact in the early hours of the morning—Zafir let the telephone receiver clatter noisily back onto its rest and scraped his hands wearily through his hair.

Making his way into the kitchen, he poured another drink from the coffee pot that his housekeeper always made sure to keep replenished, and uncharacteristically added a couple of sugars. He was in dire need of a caffeine and sugar hit after his testing exchange with Farrida.

As he had guessed, she hadn't taken the news of his cancelling their engagement quietly. She'd expressed the gamut of emotions—from noisy tears and pleas for him to see sense to accusations of him being hypnotised by this woman, who must clearly be holding him to ransom because she'd borne his child.

In the end Zafir had had to exert his authority and tell her once and for all that their engagement was at an end and that he fully intended to marry his child's mother. That Farrida should learn to accept the fact and that her stepping down from their arrangement would be amply compensated. She would retain her lauded reputation as one of the country's most beautiful and accomplished women and be free to marry another distinguished man of her choice.

A short while after finishing his call, the relief he felt at jumping that particularly testing hurdle was off the scale. It meant that he was now entirely free to marry Darcy without anything standing in his way—because more and more it was dawning on him that she was the one woman in the world he'd always known he was meant to be with.

Sitting in the lobby of one of London's most exclusive hotels, Zafir looked every inch a royal prince. Attired in his traditional dark robes and long leather boots, with his unbound ebony hair gleaming whenever it caught the light, he cut an impressive figure.

Whilst he didn't particularly *want* to announce his status to all and sundry, he saw no reason to hide it. And yet his nature was complex. His father had always said he was a contradiction. One minute he enjoyed the preferential treatment accorded to him by his status, and the next he almost wanted to deny it and disappear into the shadows.

Now, waiting for Rashid to arrive with Darcy, he couldn't help but feel on tenterhooks. When he'd told her that he intended for them to marry and then officially announce Sami as his heir she had seemed anything *but* pleased. That disturbed him. Could she not see at the very least that there were untold benefits for her in becoming his wife? For one thing she wouldn't have to struggle any more, and both she and their son would be supported, cherished and adored by his people for the rest of their lives, not wanting for anything.

But there was one fear in this rosy vision of their future together that Zafir could not easily dissipate. And that was that Darcy would never find it in her heart to forgive him for choosing to believe his brother over her...

'Ms Carrick is here, Your Highness.'

Suddenly Rashid was there in front of him, his eye-catching companion supported by her walking aids beside him.

'Darcy,' he acknowledged, not hesitating to touch his lips to the side of her cheek. The feeling of her smooth skin and the bewitching imprint of her lovely perfume would stay with him long after she'd gone from him, he mused. 'It is good to see you.'

'You too,' she murmured.

Addressing his guard, Zafir questioned, 'You had a good journey, I trust?'

'Yes, Your Highness. We did not have any problems.'

'Good.'

As Zafir glanced around him he wasn't surprised to note that many of the hotel's visitors and residents gathered in the glamorous lobby were keenly observing their little group. And they were mostly paying attention to Darcy, he saw. Not that he could blame them. Her glorious sunny hair was caught up on top of her head in a very feminine topknot, her make-up was classy and understated, and she was wearing a long jacquard patterned dress with a cinched waistband and a black velvet coat open at the front.

Her beauty was *beyond* stunning. Was it any wonder he was so proud and pleased at the mere sight of her?

Making a quick scan of her flushed features, he immediately checked to see if she wouldn't be better off in the wheelchair. Knowing how stubborn she could be, he didn't want her to risk making her injury worse by insisting on standing when she needn't.

'How are you feeling today?'

'Much better after a decent night's sleep, I'm pleased to say.'

'You are still occupying the downstairs sofa?'

Colouring, she glanced briefly across her shoulder. In case anyone was listening, Zafir thought.

'I hope to change that arrangement tonight and go back to my bed.'

'You think you can manage the stairs?'

'I won't always have you around to carry me, so I had better get used to trying to manage... *Your Highness*.'

She had responded giving him a look that told him she'd crawl if she had to, rather than accept any more help from him. Whilst he was amused, he was also

irritated that she seemed not to remember his assertion last night, when he'd unequivocally told her that
he intended to marry her.

'Anyway…we need to get on with our business.
I've arranged for us to have some coffee in my suite
so we might talk in private. Rashid, you may accompany us and do the usual checks.'

'Of course, Highness.'

Gesturing that Darcy should precede him, Zafir
waited until she was ready and confidently in control of her crutches, then led her towards the elevator.

CHAPTER SEVEN

OF COURSE DARCY had experienced the sensation of having butterflies in the tummy before, but never butterflies that felt as if they were *drunk*. But that was just what it felt like as she travelled up to the topmost floor in the elevator with Zafir and his bodyguard.

Their meeting was going to take place in his private suite, he told her. It was a facility he used when he worked late at the bank or needed a private meeting. It would be the first time they'd been properly alone together since contact had been renewed. Naturally she was concerned about how things would go. As far as his desire for marriage went, would he insist on a wedding? Or would he be more reasonable and agree to some kind of compromise? Whilst she didn't doubt that he would be a good father, she was far from certain that he would make an equally good husband...

'Here we are.'

Her striking companion's enigmatic gaze surveyed her thoughtfully as, in keeping with royal protocol, he waited for Rashid to open the door to the suite. He gave her no clue as to what he might be thinking.

The bodyguard went in first to make a quick and

efficient reconnaissance. It was another reminder of Zafir's importance that his security was paramount. But when the inspection was over he clearly didn't expect his guard to linger. Instead Zafir instructed him to go and get some lunch and said that he would contact him when they were ready to leave.

'Thank you, Your Highness.' Rashid included Darcy in a respectful, yet cordial little bow and once again she sensed herself warming to the man.

'Darcy?'

With a flourish, Zafir indicated that she should go in before him, and he waited patiently as she complied. The wildly fluttering butterflies in her belly didn't grow any calmer as they entered the suite's sumptuous high-ceilinged sitting room. There were three other doors leading off the area, she saw, and she assumed these must lead to the bedroom and bathroom and perhaps a study? And, if this first room was any indication, presumably they would all reflect the same high level of comfort and good taste.

Furnished with gold-coloured sofas, matching armchairs, stunning framed art that had to be the real thing, and a beautiful Murano glass chandelier, the sitting room was exquisite. On the polished cedar-wood surface of an elegant chiffonier was positioned an elegant crystal vase filled with an abundance of scented cream roses. Their perfume all but drenched the air.

Silently acknowledging the congeniality of her surroundings, Darcy consciously steadied her breath to take it all in. Yet what dominated her thoughts above everything else was the fact that she was here *alone* with Zafir.

Owning to feeling nervous, she distracted herself by glancing at the view outside the windows. The soundproof glass rendered the noise of the busy traffic muted and agreeable, and through it she glimpsed the endless green lawns of Hyde Park and the waters of the Serpentine, glinting in the afternoon sunshine. It was clear to her that the guests who occupied the hotel were from a highly privileged world of money and class. Such a view was not open to everyone.

The luxurious ambience inside and out was second to none—this exquisite accommodation was accessed predominantly by the rich and famous. It was already plain that no stone had been left unturned in providing everything a guest might want. And that included a dedicated staff, ready and willing to do their bidding at the drop of a hat.

It was a taste of the elite lifestyle she was contemplating marrying into, Darcy realised, and for a dizzying moment her anxiety increased. How would she adapt to such privileged circumstances if she became Zafir's wife?

Financially, the past few years had been unquestionably hard, and she often didn't sleep at night because she was worrying about how she was going to meet her bills. To have that worry taken away in practically one fell swoop was tantamount to a genie suddenly appearing and granting her her most longed-for wish.

Yet she already knew that having money didn't solve everything. For instance it couldn't ease the devastating emotion that followed the death of a loved one…or the catastrophic end of a relationship with a

lover who had become your sun, moon and stars…
both of which she'd experienced personally.

One thing was eminently clear—some proper time
for reflection was needed before she made any firm
decisions.

Moving away from her companion with the help
of her walking aids, she gingerly made her way over
to an armchair. Deliberately avoiding the inviting
gold-coloured sofas, because the sinful sumptuous-
ness they presented looked as if it might swallow her
whole if she sat in one, Darcy got comfortable in the
single chair.

There was always a chance that Zafir might decide to join her if she chose the sofa. Right then such
a possibility should be avoided at all costs, she decided, because every time he came near her it was like
being drugged or put under a spell. The dangerous
attraction she'd once had for him had not, it seemed,
diminished. In fact it was just as raw and magnetic
as it had ever been…

'I've arranged for us to have some coffee and sand-
wiches,' he announced. 'They should be here soon.
Ah…'

There was a sudden knock at the door just as he
was speaking, and when he opened it an immaculately attired butler entered carrying a silver tray. At
Zafir's behest he proceeded to lay out the tray's contents elegantly on the room's pristine Burr wood coffee table, and in doing so turned the action into a
near art form.

Cordially thanked and tipped, he discreetly left.

Dropping down onto a sofa, her companion remarked, 'I know I suggested lunch, but I've changed

my mind. I've decided we should go out for dinner tonight instead. I also think we might take Sami with us.'

Coming out of the blue like that, the suggestion took her aback, and Darcy had immediate reservations. Stroking her hand across her knee under the warm jacquard dress, she replied, 'That wouldn't be a good idea. He's got school tomorrow, and he'll be cranky and tired if he stays up late.'

His lips pursed for a moment, and she saw a muscle flinch at the side of his carved bronzed cheekbone. She didn't suppose he was denied anything very often.

'What can I do but bow to your greater experience as a parent?' he remarked stiffly. 'But, just the same, I won't *always* be so willing to exclude our son from our engagements. He will have to get accustomed to a whole new way of life when we get to Zachariah, and you will soon learn that we do not keep the same hours as you do here. We often eat late.'

'If that's the case, what about his schooling?'

He stared at her as though the question was inconsequential. 'He will, of course, be privately tutored.'

'I take it by that comment you've already assumed we're going back with you?'

There was a flash of gilded flame in his eyes. 'I am fast growing tired of your stubborn resistance. It was my honest intention to be more amenable to your desires, Darcy, but I find I am running out of patience. Once and for all—we are going to be married and we will return home to my country as soon as possible. My plan is that we will spend three months of the year there and divide the rest of our time between London and the States…taking time out in which to have our vacations. Now, let's have some coffee—after which I have some papers for you to sign. Then we will get down to discussing arrangements.'

'What are the papers?'

'One of them is your agreement to marry me. The other is documentation concerning your personal details. You have brought your passport and birth certificate for verification, as I asked?'

Shifting a little in her seat, Darcy's first instinct was to counter this statement with a stubborn reply that would let him know she still had her doubts about the matter, but something told her it wouldn't make any difference…not when he had already firmly decided on what was going to happen.

She would need some time to work out how best to fight her corner, always keeping firmly in mind the needs of her son. They were paramount.

Through tight lips, she answered, 'Yes, I have.' Removing the suede cross-body bag she was wearing, she laid it down on the couch. 'But I'm still not sure that marrying you is the right thing to do. Have you talked to Farrida yet about calling off your engagement?'

'I have. The arrangement is no more, so there is no need for you to worry.'

'And she accepted your change of mind? I imagine that was pretty hard for her to hear.'

'In my country arranged marriages for dynastic purposes are quite usual. They are not complicated by feelings. Farrida accepted the change in my plans with the good grace of the high-born lady that she is.'

The look he gave Darcy was decidedly cool. It

conveyed the fact that his mind was definitely made up so no further discussion about it was necessary.

'I see.'

'We are discussing plans for *our* marriage and our return to my country,' he reminded her. 'There is no question that it is right. My son has been too long without the support of his father and your becoming my wife will mean that you no longer have to live a hand-to-mouth existence, unable to provide all the things he needs, the things that are his right as my heir. I think it's time we had that coffee…don't you?'

'I'd prefer tea, if it's all the same to you.'

'Of course—I should have known by now that you don't conform to anything you don't like, Darcy so I ordered some tea as well.' Deftly arranging the cups and saucers on the table as though he wasn't fazed by the domestic task, he teased her. 'Shall I do the honours and pour?'

'I won't say no.'

His big hand fastened incongruously around the delicate porcelain handle of the teapot, and Zafir's silken black eyes glinted with more than just a little provocation. 'How interesting… Tell me, what *do* you say no to?'

Immediately growing warm, she unconsciously smoothed back a curling lock of flaxen hair that had drifted against her cheekbone. If the man had sought to unsettle her with his dangerously suggestive comment then he had succeeded.

'A girl could die of thirst waiting for you to pour that tea, you know.'

Returning the pot to the table, he got slowly to his feet. His dark robes fell back into position with a graceful fluidity that put her in mind of a gently flowing river.

'Are you really so thirsty that you couldn't wait for a few more minutes for that thirst to be satisfied?' he questioned.

Unable to find her voice right then, Darcy gulped. Her breasts were already hot and heavy with desire, and her tightened nipples were tingling fiercely inside a dress that increasingly made her feel as if she was in a steam room. And yet she was intimately aware that the temperature of her body wasn't anything to do with what she was wearing but *everything* to do with the sinfully handsome man who stood in front of her.

She recalled that he'd once told her that his heritage was an ancient one, much revered by historical scholars. How could anyone doubt the provenance of such ancestry? One only had to glance at Zafir's mesmerising visage to be transported into another world… The proud forehead, the carved cheekbones and flowing black hair…all easily brought to mind a culture that was laden with majesty and mystery.

Even so, the people of his tribe had once trekked through the desert on blisteringly hot days searching for watering holes, had spent long, cold nights under a star-filled sky in temperatures probably as bitter as those in the North Pole. Resilience and faith must have been bred into his ancestors' bones for them to have survived such extremes of climate and still make a good life for themselves and their families.

As though intrigued by her silent musing, Zafir gave her a long, slow smile. It was then that Darcy saw his expression was indisputably *hungry*, and she sensed herself succumbing to the unspoken invitation in his eyes as though caught in a sensual undertow she didn't have a prayer of resisting…

'Rather than pour you a cup of tea, I have another suggestion.'

'Oh?'

'Would you not prefer me to make love to you?'

She gasped. 'You shouldn't say such things to me. You—you *know* you shouldn't.'

'Why not?'

He planted himself mere inches from where she sat, so close that his heat mingled irresistibly with the now familiar seductive scent of agar and drifted down to her.

'Would you rather I pretend to be coy, like an inexperienced schoolboy, rather than be a man who intimately knows what he desires and is not afraid to declare it?'

'Doesn't the kind of desire you're alluding to need to be reciprocated?'

'Are you telling me you don't want me, Darcy?'

She felt suddenly quite faint. The things that his deep bass voice alone could do, never mind his looks… Where on earth was she supposed to go with such a question?

'All I'm saying is that I—I need to be sensible, and you're making it impossible for me.'

'Once…not so very long ago…you were my woman. Now we have a child together. That confirms you are *still* my woman.'

'I am no such thing. And nor am I some chattel to do with exactly as you want just because you think it's some inalienable right you have.'

'Is that really how you view me? As someone who

wouldn't even *consider* another person's rights if they happened to conflict with my own? That is a shame. But, that aside, if you're saying that you no longer have any feelings for me other than hatred, then I have to remind you that I am still the father of your son and I fully intend to claim my paternal rights— with or *without* your approval, because my people need an heir.'

Although Darcy's heart was racing, her voice was calm when she replied, 'I don't hate you. I never did—despite what happened. But my child's well-being and future are not up for being bartered with.'

'It is not my intention to barter.'

A maddening smile touched the corner of his lips, as if he already knew he held the trump card.

In response, a wave of exasperation bubbled up inside her and suddenly burst free. 'Look…you had your chance with me once, Zafir, but you threw it away. Yes—threw it away as though it was nothing. My trust was destroyed when you did that. It was smashed into the dust. If you think it can be so easily reinstated by giving in to plain *lust* then I have to tell you in no uncertain terms that it can't.'

The look she saw in his eyes just then mesmerised her. She suddenly knew that he wasn't going to respond as she'd thought.

'My desire for you is not born out of plain *lust*, Darcy. I still have feelings for you, despite any ill-advised actions I may have taken in the past. And now a child—*our* child—has been brought into the equation. That alone changes everything. Can we not make our peace…at least for *his* sake?'

An audible groan escaped her. She sensed the last

vestiges of her resistance melt helplessly away, and knew she was fighting a losing battle to stay strong. 'I would do anything for Sami.'

'You may not know it yet, but so would I.'

Knowing he meant it, Darcy felt her aroused senses wanting to dance to a whole different tune from the one she'd intended. Unprotestingly, she succumbed to the compulsion.

As if already aware of her decision, Zafir carefully guided her up onto her feet. His big hands circled her waist, and she was glad it had remained so slender after her pregnancy.

'What else do I have to do to make you know how much I want you?' he asked huskily. 'And not just purely to satisfy my craving for your body. There are many reasons why I desire you. Although it's a long time since we were together like this, the memory has never left me. Did you think it would?'

Warring with the urge to lay her hand against his bronzed cheek, she knew her voice was a tremulous whisper as she said softly, 'You don't play fair, you know... But then...you never did.'

'I think our refreshments can wait.'

Without warning, he lifted her high into his arms against a chest that anyone could see was magnificent. And she could personally attest to the fact that it had muscles like steel and skin as sensuously smooth as satin. The smile he gave her was unashamedly knowing and sexy, and it spoke of things that only lovers had shared.

In the past there had been many times when he'd buckled her knees with such a look. What woman could resist such hot temptation for long? No matter how stoic her vow, she wouldn't be human if she refused him—and Darcy had never forgotten the time she'd spent in his arms. She hadn't been able to resist him then and neither could she do so now.

'We have a lot of time to make up for.'

Zafir headed purposefully towards the bedroom and forced the chic double doors open with the toe of his boot. As soon as they'd entered the room he carried her across to the canopied bed...

Removing his boots, and helping Darcy dispose of her leather flats, Zafir lay down with her on the bed. For long minutes they clung together on top of the counterpane, just staring at each other. The only sound they heard in those timeless few moments was the slow in and out of each other's breath.

But then he lowered his head and started to kiss her.

It was akin to pouring petrol on a fire.

Those initial experimental kisses quickly turned into a conflagration of desire and passion as they eagerly started to rediscover each other. When they stopped for a while, to draw breath, Darcy threaded her fingers through his hair.

'It still feels like silk. What made you decide to grow it?'

Smiling down into her eyes, he chuckled. 'It is a family tradition, I guess. Do you like it?'

She dimpled. 'I do. I like it very much.'

'I will have to tie it back for a while.'

'Why?'

He was already reaching into his tunic to produce the black velvet ribbon he carried should this need arise. Right now Zafir wanted nothing to impede his view of his lover.

'I want to see you...in fact I want to see *all* of you.'

Deftly securing the ribbon around the ponytail he'd fashioned, he never once withdrew his gaze from Darcy.

Like a trained musician who never forgot how to play the notes his very soul was imbued with, he began carefully to peel the clothes from her slim yet curvaceous body. His sense of awed reverence as he did so took his breath away. She was just as beautiful and perfectly formed as he remembered—and her scent and her skin were casting a spell on him that made him fiercely glad to be alive.

During the years they'd been apart he'd often dreamed of her. And, vivid as those dreams had been, they had more often than not *tortured* him. What good were dreams when they only served to remind him of what he had lost? But even those enticing images of Darcy his mind had so helpfully conjured up couldn't hope to come near to the reality of having her here with him in the flesh.

After giving in to his voracious need to divest her of her clothes, Zafir briefly stood up to draw the sumptuous voile hangings of the canopy around them. The delicate but effective shield immediately helped reduce the daylight that streamed in through the windows and he started to remove his robes.

Just before he leant towards her his hypnotised glance drank in the sight of her perfectly pale rounded breasts and he saw that her delicate pink nipples were already puckering...just as if they waited for his touch. Although he ached to take them into his mouth and suckle he wanted to touch his mouth to hers again first.

His glance holding hers, he savoured her pert, plump lips as though they were an opening to nothing less than the nectar of the gods. And they *were,* he acknowledged as his tongue swept the hot satin interior and feverishly duelled with hers. Each hungry kiss stoked a fire inside him that had never burned so hot with any other woman but *her,* and the near pain in his groin when he didn't immediately take her was testimony to his voracity and need.

Suddenly aware that her hands were pushing against his chest she freed her lips from his.

'Have you *any* idea what you're doing to me?'

'I hope I'm turning you on, angel.'

'You are, Zafir. But there's something I want to tell you—something I should have told you a long time ago.'

His body stilled. 'What is it? What didn't you tell me before, Darcy?'

She knew she was trembling. She was unable to help herself. *Would he believe her?* She had been so eager for him that night, and she had let her feelings dictate her actions, telling herself that everything would be all right.

'The first time we made love at the hotel…on our special night out…do you remember?'

The corners of his lips lifted in a knowing smile. 'Of course I remember. My heart gallops even now at the memory.'

Her throat tightened. 'Well…you didn't seem

to mind my lack of experience, which I was sure I couldn't help but show, and I thought perhaps it didn't matter because you didn't mention it… But I was a *virgin*, Zafir. You are the first and only lover I have ever had.'

His face visibly drained of colour. 'If that is true… I *should* have noticed. But you only expressed pleasure, not pain. Did I hurt you that first time?'

She wrapped her hand around his. 'There was initial soreness, but after that everything fell beautifully into place and I just thought it *wonderful*.'

'But why didn't you *tell* me? How can you not know that it is the greatest gift a woman can give to a man?'

'I suppose I feared that it didn't count for much these days if a woman wanted to save herself for… for someone she cared for.' Darcy wouldn't say *loved*. That was one step too far right now, and she'd already risked too much. 'I thought that most men wanted somebody experienced.'

'You're crazy…where did you learn that?'

'Most women I talked to seemed to think of being experienced as an asset. I never went along with that.' She knew she blushed. 'I guess I've always been a bit of a romantic.'

'I'm glad that you are.'

He swept back her hair from her forehead and planted a kiss there. His velvet eyes seemed suddenly to darken with desire.

'Do you still want me?'

'I do…I want you *now*, Zafir.'

'I want you, too.'

'Then don't make me wait any longer.'

* * *

He saw with satisfaction the indubitable hunger in her eyes.

'I won't leave you waiting for long, my angel,' he promised, 'but I need to use protection. I have it here, in the pocket of my robes.'

As he turned to collect the garment he'd left on the bed Darcy stayed his hand. Her smile was unsure and shy again, he saw.

'I'm—I'm on the pill now, so it won't be necessary.'

Zafir's heart thumped hard, in spite of the fact she'd already told him she wasn't seeing anyone else. Now he'd learned that she'd been a virgin when they'd first made love, he hated the thought that she might have had another man in her bed after their split...

'I had to protect myself after—after what happened before,' she explained.

'But you *wanted* Sami? You wanted to have our baby?'

Widening the azure-blue eyes that contained the mesmerising hues of both sea and sky, she answered, '*Always*. He is everything to me...you *have* to know that.'

'There is no doubt in my mind, *habibi*. I only have to look at the two of you together to be assured.'

Without comment, she wound her slender arms possessively around his neck and pulled him fervently down to her.

Zafir needed no further bidding. Pressing her deep into the bed, he felt his blood pumping hard in anticipation of making her his again. Sliding his hands beneath the tender silk of her bottom, he nonetheless took his time in guiding her slim legs round his middle, so as not to jolt her ankle.

But quickly the molten desire that was building inexorably inside him took command, and he didn't hesitate to ease deep inside her. He thought he might have offered up a prayer of thanks at the moment of contact, but he couldn't be sure. All he knew was that it was an altogether dizzying as well as supremely satisfying experience to be so intimately acquainted with her again.

No other woman could make him feel the way Darcy did. And knowing that she'd had his child after he'd so foolishly and painfully rejected her, discovering she'd been a virgin that first time, made the undoubted bond they'd once forged even more meaningful now...

His glance hungrily sought hers as he raised himself to look down at her. Guided by a force that was as ancient as time itself he started to move more rhythmically inside her, registering with pleasure her softly quivering lips as she moaned low. Claiming them in a hot, hard kiss, he lifted her arms high above her head as he plunged deeper. His action quickly elicited the reaction he'd hoped for. Raising herself up to meet him, her body suddenly contracted.

'Oh, Zafir,' she moaned ardently, her satin-soft thighs gripping him hard.

Glancing down at her, he saw she had tears in her eyes as she irresistibly came apart in his arms...

CHAPTER EIGHT

ZAFIR WAS INDEED a man of contradictions, Darcy thought as she lay wrapped in his arms, her hand idly resting against the curling dark hair on his impressive chest. Not only was he a hot and passionate lover, he was also a touchingly considerate one. Twice he had deliberately delayed the culmination of his own pleasure until she had reached hers, and now after the second time he lay down beside her, gave her a wry smile and teased her.

'Either I'm seriously out of practice or your sexual drought has rendered you insatiable, my love. I am all but worn out.'

'Are you saying that you can't keep up with me?' she responded, at the same time registering with delight that he'd called her his *love*.

'I trust that is a joke?'

Darcy grinned. 'Do you really think I'd have the *nerve*, as a subordinate, to call your sexual prowess into question, Your Highness? I wouldn't dare! I'm sure people have been thrown into dismal dark dungeons for less.'

'You'll pay for that disrespectful remark, you little minx.'

Turning and fastening his hands round her waist, he effortlessly hauled her on top of him with a fierce look. It wasn't even remotely threatening, yet never had he looked more like a warrior than he did right then. His dark hair was still tied behind his head with the black ribbon, and the style drew immediate attention to his iron jaw and hollowed cheekbones as his smouldering dark gaze mercilessly took her prisoner.

Eagerly possessive and desirous, she felt as limp as a rag doll when she gazed back at him. Perhaps he was right. Perhaps she *was* insatiable…at least as far as he was concerned.

'I vow that I will make it my life's work to keep you pleasured until the end of our days, my Queen,' he taunted her.

'That's all well and good, but I'm hardly a *queen*.'

'Not yet…at least not officially…but you soon will be. In my country I am King, and naturally the woman I marry becomes Queen.'

'If that's intended to reassure me, it *doesn't*. To be frank, it makes me want to run away and hide.'

Zafir's breath momentarily grew still. 'Are you serious? Why would you want to do such a thing?'

'Because I've always lived a fairly quiet life, and now it seems I'm going to be thrust into the limelight.'

'You will grow into the role, my sweet—as those of us born onto this path *have* to. But, remember, I will always be there by your side to help you.'

Overcome by the declaration, Darcy made to move away. But her lover dropped his hands firmly onto her slender thighs and held her fast. Her blood instantly slowed and then pumped sluggishly with the heat of molten lava as it became evident he was already aroused.

'Don't go away. All I want to do is to make you feel good. Have you forgotten how it used to be between us? What finally drove us into bed?'

'I remember. And I don't deny the old attraction between us is still there. But it doesn't mean that we can make things right again so easily.'

'If I have caused you pain at *any* time then I sincerely regret it. But we have a son now, and I want to try and make amends for the wrongs of the past. Can you not see that my intentions are sincere?'

Wanting desperately to believe him, Darcy was still wary of letting down her guard. The proof of the pudding was in the eating. She prayed Zafir's declaration was genuine but, glancing at him right then, she found herself helplessly captured by the sight of his rippling smooth muscles and powerfully built shoulders.

She knew already how hard it was to resist him. Seeing the shamelessly inviting look in his slumberous ebony eyes, she felt her breath catch. It would be oh, so easy to give in to the temptations of the flesh and discount all that had gone before in the hope that, given time, her trust would be repaired. Then again, would she be a fool for giving in so easily and then, a little bit further on down the line, come to regret it?

'You do not answer, and that perturbs me.'

'It's just that good intentions aren't always fulfilled…no matter how strong the desire.'

'I think all this talk is complicating what should be very simple. All we need to ask right now is *do* we desire each other or *don't* we? I know what my answer is.'

Zafir cupped her face and immediately brought her mouth down to his. His hands were large and warm next to her skin, and oddly protective. The kiss quickly became languorous and deep, with Zafir's hot, silken tongue hungrily sweeping the soft satin textures inside her mouth and seductively duelling with hers. A charge of demanding sexual need swept through her.

'Your breasts are like velvet ivory...the touch and the texture of your skin exquisite. Can you remember how it felt when I touched you there?' he whispered against her neck.

Stunning her, he filled his hands and captured her nipples between his fingertips. His lascivious glance unflinching, he shamelessly added some pressure and pinched hard...

She nearly shot through the roof at the dizzying sensation of pain mingled with pleasure. Then he took one nipple into his mouth and suckled. Throwing back her head, Darcy whimpered. Her hair had already been coming adrift from the tortoiseshell clip, and now the golden strands loosened even more.

Zafir's hungrily searching hands began to explore the rest of her...he was running his hands freely over her body. In the meantime her hair brushed against the nipples he had so erotically inflamed and she couldn't suppress a feverish groan. Against the tenderness of her flesh the strands felt more like knives rather than something so innocuous...

'I never *could* get enough of you,' he confessed huskily.

Leaning towards him to fully receive his kiss again, all she could manage in reply was a murmured, 'Mmm...'

In less than a heartbeat, he thrust inside her. He was hard, hot, and everything she could have wished for, and straight away their bodies fell into a sensual rhythm.

Feeling dazed with relief at having this basic but very necessary human need fulfilled, she realised how much she'd missed the carnal satisfaction this man could deliver. She was thrilled by the touch of his mouth against hers, and his avid response told her he felt the same. No matter how much time had passed since they'd first become lovers, it seemed their physical desires remained perfectly in tandem. And with intimacy came the knowledge that she was somehow able to set aside the devastation and heartache she'd endured and focus her attention purely on the present.

It was a welcome revelation. The truth was that all she'd ever wanted from Zafir was his *love*...passionate, devoted and undying. Anything less would just not be good enough.

Darcy had the distinct sense that time had slowed down, and now it was stopping altogether as she was in Zafir's arms. All she was aware of was *him*. One caress flowed into another like a seamless symphony, as though they had never forgotten which note came next. She didn't want his amorous attentions to end. Together they were creating a magical world of their own, where no one could intrude or make demands, and she revelled in the freedom of that.

When the urgency of their lovemaking came to a wholly gratifying end they lay back together on the cool sheets beneath the counterpane. Her satisfying sense of fulfilment thankfully didn't disperse quickly. Instead of feeling almost numb to the idea of experiencing intimacy again, Darcy wondered how she had managed so long *without* it. Yet again the man at her side had awakened feelings in her she'd been sure she'd buried long ago. The notion that they'd been revived and might possibly remain in that state for many years to come couldn't help but tantalise her.

With a sigh, Zafir turned towards her. Lifting his hand, he let his artistic fingers explore her face with fascination. They put her in mind of a master sculptor, so enamoured of his craft that he wanted to imprint the shape and texture of the features he studied on his memory for always.

The very notion that he should want to do such a thing made Darcy's heart race. For such a masculine man his touch was remarkably gentle, and what woman *wouldn't* revel in the carnal feelings it instigated?

But all of a sudden he looked perturbed.

'You tell me there has been no one in your life since me...' He frowned. 'But during all these years have you not missed having a man to hold you and make love to you? Knowing how passionate you are, I cannot believe you have never longed for that.'

In truth, she had forgotten how frank Zafir could be sometimes. Now she recalled how he always cut to the chase rather than beating around the bush.

Her cheeks flaring with heat, she replied, 'Occasionally I've missed not having someone to hold me—yes, of course I have. The single life gets lonely sometimes. But I've not wanted another relationship since I had Sami. I certainly haven't missed the physical side of things so much that I would risk bringing a stranger into my son's life.'

'It pleases me to hear that. Your devotion to our son is commendable. It reaffirms that my decision to marry you is the right one.'

'And you, Zafir?'

Focusing her attention on him so she wouldn't misread his expression, Darcy tucked some drifting tendrils of hair around her ear. In the throes of their lovemaking her disarrayed hair had fallen down past her shoulders.

'Have you had many other women in your life since me?'

She almost held her breath.

'I suppose it is only fair that you should ask me that.'

Reaching behind him, he arranged his pillows behind his back and sat up.

His powerful shoulders tensing, he glanced round at her. 'I don't deny that in my position I have many opportunities to meet beautiful and well-connected women. But that doesn't mean I want to sleep with them all. And if all I wanted was to be with someone suitable who met with the dictates of my family do you not think I would have gone ahead and married Farrida?'

Now she sat up too. Tugging the counterpane a little further to cover her breasts, she drew up her knees. 'It's just that you're a very attractive and virile man, and I can't see you willingly going without—without sexual attention for very long.'

His answer was part grimace and part smile.

'You're right, of course. But it goes against my personal code to be promiscuous, so when I first returned to Zachariah after our relationship ended I took a mistress. We entered into what you might call a business arrangement, in so far as there were no feelings involved. But it wasn't long before we parted. The whole thing felt indescribably empty to me. That was when I resolved to get on with my life and put my energies into running the business.'

Her mouth drying at this latest revelation, Darcy listened intently. But her heart still clamoured painfully at the thought of him being with other women.

She forced herself to ask, 'So, because it felt so empty, you decided it was a better option to marry Farrida? At least you know her family. When did you meet up with her again?'

'We bumped into each other at a function in New York. She reminded me of our families' hopes that we would marry if we hadn't met anyone else by the time we reached thirty.' He shrugged. 'Well, I was thirty-six and she was thirty-five. She'd had a couple of relationships that hadn't worked out and she told me she was getting "broody".'

He flushed a little under his skin at the phrase.

'It was most unlike her. She's never been one for sentiment. Time was running out, she said. And, knowing that I was still single and needed an heir, she thought it the ideal solution that we get together.'

'So you agreed that you would get engaged?'

Zafir's expression was rueful, but frank. 'I did. As I've already indicated, the agreement was a purely pragmatic one.'

'And then *I* turned up again.'

'I can only thank the powers that be that you did... especially when I found out that I already have the heir that I longed for.' He affectionately drew his fingers down her cheekbone.

'But I'm neither suitable nor well-connected, Zafir... What if your family don't approve of us marrying? What if they suggest you make me your mistress instead?'

His hand lowered to cup her chin and his dark eyes were unflinchingly possessive. 'You are most definitely going to be my wife, Darcy...*not* my mistress.'

'And that's really what you want, is it?'

His eyes narrowed. 'Do you honestly need to ask me that? Haven't I already made my feelings more than clear?'

She shrugged a shoulder. 'I'd like to think that everything you've told me is true, but after what happened last time I'm understandably wary.'

'Are you saying that you will never trust me again?'

'No. That's not what I'm saying. But it's going to take me some time.'

'I cannot say I like that...but I understand. So I will ask you again—do you agree to marry me?'

'Yes, I do.' The slight smile she gave him was fleeting. 'Seeing as you *are* my son's father, and that you intend to honour your responsibilities as far as he's concerned, I know it makes sense.'

Zafir's own smile was wry. 'Indeed... But you could also endeavour to look a little happier about the prospect. Our son's life *and* yours are definitely going to change for the better.'

'I'm sure time will tell,' Darcy murmured.

Reaching down to where Zafir had discarded her clothes, she matter-of-factly pulled her dress over her head, balled up her underwear in her hand and wriggled to the end of the bed. Once there, she moved the voile hangings to one side and, testing her ankle, gingerly stood up.

'Where are you going?' he demanded, his tone sounding irritable.

'I'd like to have a bath… It's easier than negotiating a shower.'

'Of course.' His expression visibly relaxed.

'Can you help me to set things up?'

'I will do more than that. I'll accompany you and make sure you have everything you need. You're going to need my help, getting in and out of the bath.'

Knowing that she wasn't exactly in a position to refuse, she reluctantly nodded. 'You won't have to do this for much longer, you know. When my ankle is better I'll—'

'I know it's your nature to want to be independent, Darcy, but sometimes…'

Joining her, he firmly turned her towards him and she gasped. He was shamelessly naked—hadn't even paused to grab a sheet to wrap around him.

As his warm breath gently fanned her face he smiled. 'Sometimes it doesn't hurt to accept help… yes?'

The next day Zafir went in to his plush office at the bank. Having grabbed some coffee on the way, he sat down at his desk and buzzed Jane Maddox, one of the senior secretaries, to come in. Studying her over the steaming cup as she entered, he straightaway noted that her perfume was a little on the over-powering side.

You could tell a lot about a woman by the perfume she wore, he mused. It certainly didn't make him warm to the brunette, even though he'd never found fault in her work. But, more importantly, today he wanted answers to questions that were long overdue.

'Sit down,' he instructed, indicating the leather chair opposite him at the desk.

'I trust all is well, your Highness?'

Intent on keeping the secretary on edge, he took his time responding. When he did reply, his tone was deliberately aloof. 'That rather depends on your answers to my questions, Ms Maddox.'

Her thin, rather drawn face couldn't hide her disquiet. 'May I know the topic of these questions, sir?'

'You may.'

He bit back the fury that had been simmering inside him since he'd heard that Darcy had tried to contact him many times, to no avail. This woman was in charge of his administration, and if anyone knew what had happened to all Darcy's messages it was her.

He let the woman have the full force of his gaze. 'The topic, Ms Maddox, is Darcy Carrick…'

They were about to be married.

They were having a simple, dignified ceremony at one of London's most famous register offices and their two witnesses were Rashid and Darcy's mother, Patricia, who diligently held their son's hand.

As the male celebrant began to lead them through their vows Zafir had had a sense of everything being quite surreal. He'd been crazy about the woman at his side from the very first moment he'd set eyes on her, and knew that his decision to marry her couldn't be more right. But the fact that they'd originally separated due to what was beginning to look like the most terrible misunderstanding on his part didn't sit well with him.

It didn't sit well at all.

Especially now Jane Maddox had admitted that she'd made the decision not to pass on any messages from Darcy because she hadn't wanted to upset him all over again. In her opinion, she'd done him a favour.

'How dare you make such a judgement on my behalf?' he'd demanded coldly. 'Just who do you think you are?'

Zafir was by no means a violent man, but he didn't know how he hadn't immediately throttled her. Instead, he'd had great satisfaction in telling her to collect her things and leave the building, never to set foot in it again.

With a heartfelt sigh he glanced at Darcy and again was taken aback by her beauty. Not only did she resemble the mythical Aphrodite, goddess of beauty, love and sexual rapture, but she had a beautiful heart too. She hadn't hesitated to raise their son on her own when she'd been abandoned by him and that told him a lot. Now Zafir aimed to make it up to her in whatever way he could.

It grieved him deeply that he'd unknowingly turned his back on her when she'd been pregnant with his child. But how could he even have suspected that was the case? How did a man even *begin* to come to terms with such a thing? He wished that his father still lived. He was the only person who could have helped him with his sage advice...

When the time came for him to repeat his vows he nearly missed his cue because he was so lost in the tumult of his feelings. He'd missed not having intimate relations with Darcy in the days leading up to the wedding, but she'd explained that she needed some time on her own with Sami.

Zafir hadn't been able to argue with her when she'd told him that she wanted to introduce him to the idea of her getting married sensitively, and also to inform both his school and her employers that they would shortly be leaving to start a new life abroad.

In light of that, Zafir had agreed to abstain from any intimacy until they were married. He was already feeling the strain.

He'd worked hard to bring the ceremony forward, but it had still been several days before he'd been able to make it happen. In the interim, he had utilised his time wisely. First of all he had rung his mother, to give her the news. Admittedly she had been upset when he'd broken off his engagement to Farrida, but she had been overjoyed when she'd learned he had a son and heir.

Even though she didn't know the woman who was the mother of his child, she had agreed that it was the right thing to do to marry her. She knew he wouldn't have made such a decision if he didn't care for her. Understandably, she still had a lot of questions, but Zafir assured her that they would all be answered to her satisfaction on his return. He'd also told her that his new family would need some time to adapt to their new situation, and to their royal status, and had asked her not to advertise the fact that he was coming home with them straight away.

They would all need a little privacy for a while... at least until the official wedding took place.

His second phone call had been to his brother. He had told him they needed to have a serious talk, and Xavier had responded with an unusual equanimity in his voice.

'I will very much look forward to that, my brother. I, too, have some important things I need to tell you.'

He had sounded almost *eager* at the prospect, and it had made Zafir wonder at the reason for this new affability.

For today's ceremony Zafir had relinquished his traditional garb for a tailored tuxedo, and Darcy wore a simply cut classic cream suit trimmed with lace that her mother had bought her. He was glad that he hadn't insisted that he buy her a dress, because it seemed important to both women that they'd had their way. Darcy had her golden hair styled in an elegant chignon, with a delicate crystal and seed pearl headband to complete the stunning look.

In Zafir's eyes, she had never looked more like a princess than right at this moment. He was excited at the prospect of introducing his new bride to his people when they had their official wedding in Zachariah, and was already considering making the day a public holiday in honour of the occasion. But, more important to him than that, he could hardly wait to introduce his son and heir.

He was truly looking forward to getting to know his little boy. One day Sami was going to be a ruler they would all be proud of.

CHAPTER NINE

SITTING BESIDE HER son in the plush leather seats of a private jet, Darcy felt like pinching herself to make sure she wasn't dreaming. Once upon a time, when her love for Zafir had been new and fresh, she'd often fantasised about them being together for good. However, in her private moments, before everything had gone so wrong, she'd also known that realistically it wasn't likely to happen.

How could it? He was an important person in the world while she…well, she was a million miles away from inhabiting such an elevated sphere as he did.

It had been more than painful to contemplate a life without him…akin to being flayed alive… And then had come another twist in the tale and fate had given her Sami. Once again, her world had been utterly shaken.

And when she'd finally set eyes on Zafir again, after so long trying to contact him, having plunged from the wall of his house in her urgency to see him, their bittersweet reunion had left her reeling. Even now Darcy was still struggling to come to terms with the way events had transpired. Not least, she thought, contemplating the diamond-encrusted gold wedding band on her finger, the fact that she and her illustrious ex-boss were now married and heading out to his home in Zachariah.

'I like this plane, Mummy. It's cool.'

'What?' Lost in thought, she flushed when she realised that both her son and his father were studying her intently. 'Yes, it is, darling. Aren't we lucky to get to travel like this? Not everyone is so fortunate.'

Falling silent for a moment, the tousle-haired little boy turned his gaze on Zafir. 'Do you really live in the desert?'

Having forgone the traditional robes he usually wore, her husband was wearing dark jeans that emphasised his taut-muscled thighs teamed with an ebony-coloured cashmere sweater. Whatever he wore, the man always looked effortlessly classy. She supposed it must be in the blood.

Leaning forward with a conspiratorial smile, he replied, 'I do, indeed... My family and I have our own kingdom.'

'What's that?' Sami's big brown eyes were on stalks.

'It's our own private country.'

'Are there any dragons there?'

His father chuckled. 'I'm sorry to say we don't have any dragons. The main creatures we have are camels and horses. But nevertheless it is still a magical place, my son.'

The fact that Zafir so often referred to Sami as his son when speaking to him made her insides somersault. The little boy had very quickly taken to the idea that the Sheikh was his father, and she found it touching that he'd accepted him so readily. At least Darcy didn't have any worries on *that* score.

'He has a very creative imagination,' her husband remarked, and his twinkling glance at her made her feel as if she was being massaged with some heavenly warm oil. 'It clearly must come from his mother.'

'Oh, I don't know—I'd say his father is no slouch in that department either.'

'What's a slouch, Mummy?' Sami asked, yawning.

She bit her lip at the amused, knowing gleam in the Arabian's eyes.

That first time they'd made love he'd introduced her to the art like a connoisseur. He had ensured his every touch was exquisite and meaningful on the magical road to her fulfilment, even though he'd been as passionately hungry as she was. He might not have known at the time that she was a virgin, but he'd treated her like one.

He was by no means a selfish lover. Many times that night he'd conveyed by both word *and* deed that it wasn't something he ever took lightly...that it was important to him that his lover was at the very least treated like a princess.

Darcy had never forgotten that night. She couldn't help anticipating that her wedding night would be equally unforgettable...

As though reading her mind, Zafir asked lazily, 'Are you tired? It's been quite a week for you, what with one thing and another. No doubt you must be looking forward to going to bed?'

Knowing the hot colour in her face must easily betray her, she said quickly, 'I'm not tired, but I know who *is*.'

She could already sense the way her son's warm weight was slumping in her arms and she was glad for him. It would make the transition to this new country a little easier for them both if he got some sleep.

They arrived in the balmy temperatures of early evening. The warm air was laden with the exotic and mysterious perfumes of the desert, and anyone who wasn't a local would only have to shut their eyes and breathe it in to know they must be in an ancient landscape—a land where magic and mystery still predominated.

Those attributes were undoubted blessings, in Zafir's eyes. They were equally as powerful as its history, he believed.

On the plane he had given Darcy the news that his mother was sending a royal escort to meet them, and he hoped that she wouldn't feel overwhelmed by a procedure that for him and his family was commonplace. This was one of the privileges she would have to get used to, he'd told her.

But he'd instructed his retainers that their arrival home shouldn't be made known to the public immediately, as his family had some major readjustments to make first. This was a new situation for all of them, and they would all have to learn to adapt.

As Zafir guided Sami down the steps of the plane, then returned to assist his wife, he immediately sensed her anxiety. Although the white stretch limousine that stood waiting on the Tarmac would be impressive by anyone's standards, no doubt it might be daunting to anybody not used to experiencing such an elite way of travelling. It would be further confirmation to Darcy that her life really *had* begun to change for the better.

The chauffeur had already opened the car doors, Zafir saw, and now the dependable Rashid—who'd been sitting at the back of the plane to give him and his family some privacy—dutifully joined him.

'I will see to the luggage, Your Highness.'

'Thank you, Rashid.'

Having undertaken the task, his loyal retainer transported the baggage out of the plane and, with the chauffeur's assistance, deposited them in the boot.

Once inside the vehicle, the small family sat to-gether—that was until Sami asked if he could sit on one of the seats that hugged the sides, in order to look out of the windows. Although tinted on the outside, from the inside everything was seen just as though the panes were clear glass.

'You may sit wherever you want, Sami. I can sit next to you, if you like, then if you have any ques-tions about what you see, you can ask me,' his father told him.

'Will we see some pyramids?'

Zafir's lips curved in amusement. He was already enchanted by his son. 'No. We don't have them in this country. But we do have other spectacular sights to see. This is a land as old as time itself, and its history is remarkable.' As he said this, the great pride in his voice was unmistakable.

As they progressed towards his desert home, very soon leaving the main city behind, Zafir expelled a relieved sigh. In truth, he was glad to be getting away from the rest of humanity for a while—glad to be pulling up the drawbridge and just being with his family. Marrying Darcy and becoming acquainted with his son had made him realise that this was what he had *always* longed for...to have a family of his own.

But it was *Darcy's* presence that preoccupied him the most. After so long apart, he liked to think he was starting to get to know her again. Yet she never failed to surprise him. It was her beauty that had first attracted him, but she was so much more than that. He'd since discovered that she was fiercely loyal to those she loved, was hard-working, funny, and quite often contrary. There would never be a dull moment when they were together and he'd be a fool to take her for granted.

She was extraordinarily intuitive about what to wear too. Today, in deference to meeting his mother, she was wearing a very graceful mocha-coloured maxi-dress with a slim white jacket. Her pretty hair had been fashioned into plaits that she'd styled into a corona and fastened with an elegant gold clip that he'd bought her. She looked young and ravishing— just like a fairytale princess about to enter a palace that might have been created just for her.

'How are you holding up?'

When she turned her shimmering blue gaze towards him his insides rolled over, just as though he'd plunged to the earth from the greatest of heights. He couldn't envisage a time when he would ever tire of looking into their silken depths. She was like an angel who rendered him spellbound.

'I'm fine.'

There was the briefest glimpse of that guarded smile he sometimes saw, and Zafir wondered if she would ever look at him with complete trust in her eyes, as she had done in the early days when they'd first been together. He swallowed hard at the thought that she might not.

'And your ankle…the injury is not bothering you so much today?'

'No. It's definitely on the mend, thank goodness. How about you? How are *you* feeling? I know how important today must be for you.'

Taken aback by her thoughtfulness, he couldn't deny his pleasure and his answering smile was wide and freely given.

'I'm good. Why wouldn't I be, when I am about to introduce my wife and son to my mother for the very first time? I'm as excited at the prospect as I know she is.'

Darcy's first sight of the palace was one she would never forget. From a distance it looked like an ice castle, rising out of the earth, its crystalline perfection so exquisite it was breathtaking. But they weren't in the Arctic, she reminded herself, they were in the *desert*. And the stunning building in front of her wasn't fashioned out of ice, but out of the purest white marble.

The magical effect it conveyed was heightened by the setting sun, its rose-gold rays bathing the construction in an ethereal light.

On either side of them, as they drew nearer, she saw two spectacular marble fountains whose graceful jets seemed to reach up towards the heavens before plunging back down to earth again. The sound of rushing water was surprisingly soothing, and effort-lessly created an oasis of contemplative calm.

She thought she would like to sit by them on her own one day, and reflect on the amazing chain of events that had brought her here. But for now, with her arm linked in the crook of Zafir's, she was content to let him guide her and Sami down the ornate mosaic-tiled walkway that led to the main entrance of the building.

She was still using a walking cane to lean on, but knew that soon, thankfully, she would need it less and less. Her ankle was indubitably healing. As for Sami—he walked alongside his father with his usual boyish spring in his step, agog at all the splendour around him and for the moment rendered speech-less by it.

There were two uniformed guards standing to attention by a pair of tall, intricately decorated twin doors that stood beneath an impressive arched stone doorway. On seeing Zafir, they immediately bowed. Acknowledging them with a smile, he seemed genuinely pleased to see them, asking them both about their health and their families.

Seemingly satisfied with their response, he remarked that he was pleased that all was well with them. But when all was said and done he was still the King of the realm and he was soon indicating that he needed to move on.

He told Darcy that he was taking her to meet his mother…the woman their people still referred to as the Queen.

Although she was understandably nervous at meeting the Dowager Queen Soraya el-Kalil there was also a fair amount of excitement pulsating through her veins. What would she be like and would she really welcome a commoner as her new daughter-in-law?

Well, it was too late now because the deed was done. She and her son, the King, were already married.

They had to negotiate a large expanse of marble corridor before being led by a retainer to the private suite of rooms designated to the ruling Sheikh's mother. Straight away they were shown into the sitting room.

The first thing that surprised Darcy was how homely it was. Although there were some mouthwateringly beautiful pieces of furniture, and sumptuous Arabian furnishings, they weren't overly ostentatious, and she was further reassured by the array of family photographs that resided on practically every surface. She itched to examine them more closely, certain that there must be some of Zafir as a boy.

But just then a woman who couldn't be anything *but* a queen gracefully appeared through an inner arched doorway and stopped all her thoughts in their tracks.

She was robed in ivory silk, and her hair was as black as a raven's wing with a stunning silver streak at the front, made more evident by a regal chignon. Her face was truly beautiful. She had winged dark brows and incredibly glossy ebony eyes and the smile she directed at them all was unstinting in its welcome.

Darcy owned to feeling relieved.

'My son… It is so good to see you!' Affectionately placing her hands against Zafir's cheeks, she stood on tiptoe and kissed him. 'I trust you had a good journey?'

'We did, indeed. Everything went according to plan, as I had hoped.'

'That is good. And now we get to the important part... You must introduce me to your wife, and also to my long-awaited grandson.'

'Mother... I'd like you to meet my wife, Darcy.'

'Oh, my goodness let me look at you, my dear.'

Her new mother-in-law carefully took her free hand in hers and held it. Darcy was surprised at the strength in her grip. She was not holding back on thoroughly examining the newest member of her family, but she never once lost her generous smile as she did so.

'Zafir has told me that you resemble a fairy princess, but I confess I thought that must be love talking. I see now that he was right. You are absolutely exquisite, my daughter.'

For a moment the younger woman didn't know what to say. The Dowager Queen really believed that Zafir *loved* her? How long before she realised that wasn't the case—that he'd only married her because he wanted to claim his son and heir?

'You are very kind, your Highness.'

'I only speak the truth. I also thank you for raising my grandson on your own until you reunited with his father. It must have been very hard to manage work and child-rearing under such circumstances?'

Flushing, Darcy responded. 'My mother was a great help to me, and I've always done the very best I could by Sami...after all, he's the light of my life.'

'Bless you for that, my child. Talking of which—it is time I met a certain young man.'

Sami was shuffling from foot to foot, as though his energy couldn't be contained. That told her he was excited. But he stilled when his new grandmother approached. She greeted him with the same enthusiasm with which she'd greeted his father, only this time she leant down so that she was nearer his level.

'I am so pleased to meet you, little one. I am the mother of your father, the King. That makes me your grandmother.'

'I already have one of those. Her name is Patricia. What's *your* name?'

Soraya affectionately kissed the top of his head and said fondly, 'You may call me Nannaa. That is the usual name for my role in this country.'

'Cool...then I'll have a nanny and a *nannaa*. I hope I won't muddle them up.'

'I doubt that you will, my son. You are far too clever for that.'

Crouching down beside him, Zafir dropped his arm round the diminutive waist and gave him a squeeze. Darcy felt an inward glow of pride as she watched the pair. She was even more gratified when she sensed that Sami was happy with the new arrangements. He might even *welcome* them.

She made a mental note to talk to him about his feelings later.

Soraya had straightened, and her interested glance encompassed them all. 'Tell me, what do you want to do about eating? Are you ready for something now or would you like to rest a little before supper? If Sami is hungry—which I have no doubt he *is*—I will order some food to be brought here, and I can get to know him a little while the two of you go to your rooms and rest a while.'

Zafir's charismatic dark gaze turned immediately to his wife. 'Would you like to do that? It will give my mother the chance to talk to Sami on her own and you can have some private time to recover from the journey.'

'If that's what Sami wants…'

'I do, Mummy—and I'm very, *very* hungry!'

'That's settled, then.'

Darcy stole a fond kiss from her son before they left him. Whilst she welcomed the prospect to rest and recover from the long journey, she couldn't deny the sense of elation she felt at knowing that she and Zafir would be spending some precious time alone.

The last time they had been intimate had been on their wedding night. After that they'd had to stay in London for a few days before they left, in order for him to finish some important work at the bank. He would be working late most nights and starting early, he'd told her.

Not being with him had been hard to bear. His closeness hadn't just become important to her, it was fast becoming *essential*. But for now she wouldn't let the thought scare her as it usually did. She would just have to learn to trust that he wanted this closeness as much as she did.

Zafir owned to a huge sense of relief. Things had gone better than he'd hoped. His mother had already fallen for her grandson, and she had embraced Darcy with admiring eyes and a full heart.

Now, all his senses tightened with anticipation as he showed his wife into his personal suite at the palace. It was spacious and cool at the same time, as well as undeniably grand. But as he closed the doors he frowned when he saw the thin sheen of sweat that had broken out on her brow.

'I think you need this rest more than you know,' he said, concerned. 'I am sorry if I presumed too soon that you were back to full health.'

In answer, her determined glance told him she was already garnering her strength *and* her defences. But her plump lower lip quivered and the action betrayed the vulnerability she fought so hard to hide.

'You haven't presumed anything. I really am stronger than I look and I recover quickly,' she insisted.

Zafir knew it was time to employ some tact. 'That may be so, but I still think you should go and lie down. It will give me a chance to unpack and change out of these clothes. I can find something more suitable for you to wear too.'

Placing his hand beneath her elbow, he gently steered her towards the bedroom.

'When you wake, we can discuss things some more.'

It didn't take long for Zafir to deduce that his wife had succumbed to a naturally deep sleep. Before she'd lain down on the canopied double bed she'd let him remove her shoes and had given him her jacket to hang up. He'd stolen a brief, necessarily restrained kiss from her lips then draped a light merino shawl over her. Her eyelids had closed straight away.

Whilst he couldn't deny he was disappointed that

he couldn't join her, to express just how much he'd missed her these last few nights, he decided he would take the opportunity to ring his brother Xavier and ask him if they could meet up for their long overdue confidential chat.

CHAPTER TEN

DARCY SCREWED UP her eyes, then blinked to focus her attention. When she saw where she was—lying on a grand canopied bed the size of a small living room, no less—her heart sped like one of those intercity trains to King's Cross.

Where was her husband?

Did he think it rude of her to abandon him and their son so quickly? Had she already risked his good regard by behaving like this? They must both be as tired as she was after their long journey. The ebb and flow of emotional turmoil would surely drain *anyone*.

Then she remembered an incident that made her stomach lurch guiltily. Zafir had kissed her just before she'd fallen asleep. If she'd given him the slightest encouragement, shown him that she welcomed that brief brush of the lips, then he undoubtedly would have joined her and not been in such a hurry to disappear. But in truth an overwhelming weariness had seized her, as if all the events of the past few weeks had finally caught up with her, and she'd begged for respite.

Rousing herself, Darcy got to her feet. She turned

on the embossed gold lamp beside her and light illuminated the now nearly darkened room.

Grateful to find that her husband had thoughtfully left out for her the flat open-toed sandals she'd packed, she silently thanked him. Tucking her feet into the cool leather shoes, she patted her hair, glanced briefly into a nearby mirror to check her appearance, then pinched her pale cheeks to restore some much needed colour. Finally she collected a shawl and her walking cane and limped across to the door.

The first thing she would do, she decided, was to go and check up on Sami. She prayed that by now he would be seeing the whole episode as one big adventure and not be too upset by events. And as soon as she was able she would send a message to her mum, to assure her of their safe arrival.

Stretching out her hand to fasten it round the brass door handle, she felt it open as if by magic. It was Zafir.

He was dressed in cool white cotton pants and a baggy shirt. He'd left his long hair loose and wore a beaded pendant round his neck and a couple of interesting bracelets on his wrists. One was fashioned out of some eye-catching gold coins and the other was made from twisted strands of softened black and copper leather.

In spite of not wearing his traditional robes, he still looked magnificent. As their gazes met and clung Darcy was glad of her walking cane to help steady her.

'You're a sight for sore eyes,' she teased him tentatively, unsurprised at the quiver in her voice.

'It's good to be able to dress casually from time to time. Where were you headed off to?'

Entering, he closed the door behind him. Without asking, he linked his arm in hers and led her back into the room. Immediately she sensed hot colour seeping into her face. It was becoming something of a trademark for her, she was sure.

'I wanted to check up on Sami. I didn't mean to fall asleep for so long. Has he had something to eat yet, do you know? He must be hungry. Goodness only knows what kind of mother you must think me...'

The expression on his face melted her to her core. His black eyes crinkled sexily and the dimples in his bronzed cheeks were out in force. Once again she regretted not inviting him to join her earlier.

'You are like the Madonna herself, my angel... pure, selfless and devoted to her son. I feel blessed to have found you again.'

'You definitely know how to melt a girl's heart, Your Highness!' She grinned, feeling more elated and sure of herself than she'd ever felt before.

'If all it takes is just a smile and telling you how important you are to me to elicit such a response, then I truly am blessed, Darcy.'

Carefully examining him, she lightly caught hold of his hand and enquired, 'So what have you been doing with yourself while I was sleeping?'

'I was making sure Sami was all right, of course, but it seems that my mother has already assigned herself his chief protector. She has fed and watered him and presently he is fast asleep in his new bedroom, with the Queen herself keeping a close eye on him should he need anything.'

Darcy frowned and again felt guilty. 'She doesn't have to do that. He's really asleep? He almost never does that so easily. I know he napped for a little while on the plane...it must be because he's out of his routine.'

Zafir nodded. 'He is probably much more accepting and relaxed about the situation than we realise. He's a four-year-old boy, remember, who has suddenly found himself in the equivalent of Wonderland.'

'You're right. I suppose I worry too much. But, that aside, what else were you doing after you left me asleep?'

Tucking a swathe of luxuriant hair behind his ear, he answered, 'I was arranging a meeting with my brother, Xavier, for tomorrow. We haven't met up for quite some time, I'm sorry to say.'

'Do you want to tell me why?'

'I think you can probably guess.'

'You mean because you weren't entirely convinced that we weren't having an affair? Do you now think you might have made a mistake and it's made you rethink your actions?'

Turning over her slim palm to examine it, he commented huskily, 'That and the fact that I met up with one of the bank's head secretaries, Jane Maddox, before we left—do you remember her?'

Darcy nodded. 'Of course I do. She never liked me from day one.'

'That's because she's a bitter, jealous woman—as I found out. She deliberately didn't tell me about your messages. No doubt she told her cohorts to do the same. If she could do that, then what's to stop her from lying about you having an affair with my brother? Anyway, I got rid of her. And when Xavier and I meet tomorrow I will know for sure.'

'You mean you sacked her?'

'That's the prerogative of being CEO.'

'So you'll ask Xavier again what really happened and find out if he lied to you after all?'

'Let us not worry about that right now. I have already made my pledge to you, Darcy, and that will not change. My son and I have been brought together at last and that means everything to me.'

'I see.'

'Don't look so sad. Everything will turn out well, I am sure. In the meantime, my mother wanted me to tell you how excited she is about the wedding and that—with your approval, of course—she will be organising it.'

'That's...that's very good of her. Do you know when it will be?'

He sighed. 'We're hoping for the beginning of next week. That will give me the opportunity to declare the day as a public holiday. Do you think your mother would like to fly out and join us? I know she was at the ceremony in London, and professed not to mind missing this one if she had to, but perhaps she was just being polite. I can easily arrange her travel, if you like?'

'I'm going to ring her soon. I can ask her about it then. What about what Sami and I are going to wear? Does *our* apparel have to be traditional?'

'As it will be a royal wedding—of course. Are you hungry?'

'What...?'

When he looked at her with that carnal hungry

gaze of his, as if he could eat *her* for dinner, Darcy could barely think straight, let alone answer with an uncomplicated yes or no.

The handsome Sheikh moved in even closer and tenderly tipped up her chin. 'I asked if you were hungry. We will have to go in to supper shortly, and I need to know if you require anything in particular?'

Moistening her lips, she turned her startled blue eyes fully on his face. 'I'll have whatever everyone else is having. I don't have any preferences.'

That made him chuckle. 'My, my... When did you start to become so easy to please?'

She pouted. 'That doesn't make me a pushover, if that's what you think. I just want to make life easier for people.'

'What about making it easier for *you*? I have another question. Do you want to take a bath and freshen up before we go to eat?'

'That would be great—if I have time?'

'You can take as long as you like. I know that a lady doesn't appreciate being hurried.'

'Good. Then can you show me where my things are and I'll go and do just that.'

The Sheikh and his brother Xavier met at the official Offices of the Monarch in Zafir's private quarters.

In Zafir's opinion, his younger sibling seemed noticeably happier, and he was well dressed in a tailored suit with his dark hair grown a little longer than usual. Yet when he sat down in a colourful Rococo chair, with attractive motifs and intricate scrollwork, and Zafir indicated that he wanted to discuss certain significant events from the past, he grew distinctly uneasy.

'There is something in particular that I'd like to know. Did you lie to me that day about what you and Darcy were doing when I found you both in my office? Had you tried to force yourself on her? If you had, and did so to make me think you were having an affair, what on earth possessed you? Did you perhaps think I needed taking down a peg or two? Have you *any* idea of the torturous outcome of your cruel thoughtless behaviour?'

Flushing guiltily, his brother was immediately contrite. 'I didn't deliberately set out to make you suffer, Zafir...'

His opening words caused Zafir's stomach to plunge painfully.

'My actions were the consequences of my being greedy and immature. What happened has been a heavy burden on me for such a long time. I am very glad to have the chance to clear the air and set things straight.'

Shifting in his seat, Xavier wiped a hand across his perspiring youthful brow.

'Your secretary—Darcy—was the most beautiful woman I had ever seen. When she didn't respond to my attentions favourably, it wounded my ego. I took it as a personal insult. Who did she think she was, refusing the interest of the Sheikh of Zachariah's brother himself? Knowing that you'd made her your personal assistant, I was eaten up with jealousy and a red mist came over me. How *dared* she turn her back on me?

'Like the vain, insecure boy I was, I decided to pay her back by making it seem as though *she* was the one chasing *me*. I kept my eye on the door and arranged it so that you'd find the two of us in a compromising position. I gave her no opportunity to defend herself. So, yes, I *did* force myself on her. I didn't hurt her, but the thing is…I know my behaviour was despicable.'

'Do you think I don't know that? I was truly ashamed of what I had done when you fired her. I never wanted you or our family to think badly of me, but I was honestly glad when you eventually gave me my marching orders and sent me home. It gave me a much-needed opportunity to come to my senses.'

Taking a deep breath in, Xavier slowly released it.

'Can you ever find it in your heart to forgive me? I'm a different person now. I like to think a *better* one. I would never do such a thing again in a million years. You know that I am married now, with a beautiful little daughter. I am absolutely dedicated to my wife and family and I live in fear that something untoward might disrupt that happiness. I cannot put it more clearly. But my life is in your hands, my brother. Our mother tells me that you are getting married yourself, and that your fiancée is from England. May I know her name?'

Zafir didn't immediately answer. Xavier's glossily dark hair flopped onto his brow and he impatiently pushed it back again.

Twisting his hands together in his lap, Zafir straightened his formidable shoulders. A spasm of sorrow flashed across his brooding dark gaze.

'I think you already know her name. It is Darcy… the girl I fired because of you.'

The younger man was visibly shocked. 'You are serious?'

Zafir's daunting black eyes stared back at him. 'I would not joke about such an important matter. I have a son by her. She was pregnant when I fired her—and, trust me…no one in the world could be as sorry as I am about that. Not just that she had my child, un-supported by me…that's bad enough. But because I acted so abominably.'

'May Allah forgive me… This is nothing less than a nightmare.'

Pushing restlessly to his feet, Zafir moved his head from side to side. 'It would be for me too, if I hadn't had the presence of mind to marry her in London, before we came home. Having the big heart that she has, Darcy decided not to keep me from my son and confessed all to me. But it still makes me ashamed that I made her suffer so needlessly and for so long.'

'I can hardly believe that you have a *son* by this woman!'

'His name is Sami.'

'And…and you've *married* her? Does that mean that you still have feelings for her?'

Impatience flashed in Zafir's eyes. 'What do *you* think, Xavier? Of *course* I have feelings for her. I—Never mind that. Darcy should be the one to hear first how I feel. I'd strongly advise you not to speak of this with anyone but me.'

The younger man also got to his feet, swallow-ing hard. His tone was gravely serious when he ad-mitted, 'I have done you a great wrong, My King. If you banished me from the kingdom for the rest of my life I could not blame you. Your wife must truly despise me.'

'I do not think she has it in her to despise *anyone*.

Her forgiveness seems to know no bounds—even though it is probably to her detriment, I'm sad to say.'

'And… What about you? Can *you* ever forgive me for what I did?'

Expelling a long sigh, Zafir grimaced. 'I have thought about this for a long time. Following Darcy's example, I feel I should at least *try*. It is no excuse, but you were young—and very, very foolish. But, as my wife has also said, I want you to know that I am no pushover. If you attack me, verbally or otherwise, I will defend myself in whatever way I deem necessary. Call me a fool, but I am giving you one more chance to help make things right. From now on I want no more lies or deceit. If you transgress this edict *one inch*, be sure that I will cut you out of my life for good.'

Duly chastised, Xavier moved across to him and unhesitatingly hugged him hard. 'I am truly grateful for this chance. I will not disappoint you by word or deed again—I swear. From now on you will hear only praise from my lips.'

With a wry grin, Zafir set him apart a little then laid his hands firmly on his shoulders. 'I like to think I'm not so egotistical as to expect *praise* from those I love. But a little respect never goes amiss…'

Last night's lovemaking had left her tingling all over. Zafir had been so tender and thoughtful, but still breathtakingly passionate.

In the early light of what promised to be another flawless sunlit day, with her spirits raised and her heart filled with hope more than ever before, Darcy washed and dressed.

Zafir had already left for his meeting with his brother, and she eagerly went to find Sami and her mother-in-law. She tried not to think too much about what would transpire between the two brothers and determinedly hoped that things would go well.

The two women and Sami enjoyed a healthy, nutritional breakfast and chatted easily. The bond that was already forming between the young boy and the gracious matriarch was becoming more and more evident.

Around midday, when Zafir still hadn't returned, Darcy found herself restlessly walking through the beautiful palace gardens with her companions. Idly chatting about this and that, Sami and the Dowager Queen seemed almost to forget she was there.

As soon as she was able to, without seeming rude, she slipped away to sit on a charming bench in front of the cascading fountains. At first she fell into something of a dream. Then she mentally shook herself. All she really wanted to think about was her husband. It was as though her feelings for him knew no bounds.

Their heady lovemaking last night had left her feeling especially womanly and satisfied, and she wondered how soon it would be before they repeated the exercise. Doubt and apprehension had finally dispersed, leaving her with a real sense of well-being and happiness. Zafir hadn't yet told her that he loved her, but sometimes loving intentions could be just as powerful as words...such as when he had so gently and carefully helped her to bathe, treating her as though he wanted nothing more than to meet her every need...

* * *

Darcy was wearing the eye-catching yellow kaftan his mother had gifted her with, plus a gracious silk cowl edged with gold, to protect her pale skin from the sun, and when he at last found her Zafir thought she looked utterly adorable. His heart soared at the sight of her and he knew then that he wanted to make her feel the most treasured and happy woman on earth.

Any previous hesitation he might have had, fearing her feelings might not be as strong as his, had all but disappeared—like the foreboding black clouds that heralded an oncoming storm. Following his discussion with Xavier that morning, his brother's frank testimony had helped Zafir make his peace and remember everything that was good and meaningful in his life.

Stealing silently up behind his wife, where she sat on the elegant white bench, he gently lifted the silken cowl that nestled against her shoulder and planted a tender kiss at the side of her neck. Breathing in her exquisite personal scent, he found himself longing to demonstrate his feelings more freely…

'Mmm…that was delicious.'

'You're back.'

Her mouth curved softly with pleasure and when he moved round in front of her Darcy was fiercely glad that he had come. It seemed that not a single moment went by without her feeling impatient with desire to have him close again.

As if attuned to her every need, he carefully sat down beside her. Falling easily into the richly dark gaze that reminded her of molasses, she played with his long hair and trailed her fingertips down his cheek.

'So...how did the meeting with Xavier go? Did he tell you the truth about what happened that day?'

Appearing more serious than usual, her husband nodded assent. 'Yes...he did. What can I say? I was appalled to learn I had been so gullible, so easily taken in. Whatever I may do for you and Sami in the future, it will never be enough to make up for my dangerously foolish behaviour. I let my love for my little brother make me blind to the truth, even though in my heart I suspected he might be lying. Can you forgive me for making you suffer so?'

'You didn't do it on purpose, Zafir.' She softly touched her palm to his bristled cheek. 'I don't think either of us expected our feelings to grow as strongly as they did, and maybe the power of those feelings blinded us to what was going on around us...'

'You unselfishly include yourself in that scenario when you have no need to.' Her husband frowned. 'Where did you learn such selflessness?'

Lifting her elegant shoulders in a shrug, Darcy mused, 'I suppose if I *have* learned such an attribute it must have come from my late father.'

'If I'd ever had the good fortune to meet the man, I know I would have admired him immensely.'

'And he you, Zafir. He wasn't impressed by wealth or position, but he knew a truly *good* man when he met one. What about your own father? You told me you cared for him very much?'

Sighing, he slid his hand over hers and held it fast. 'He was my rock and my mentor as well as my father and King. He lived his life by demonstrating strong values and a code of ethics that our people still try and adhere to. They didn't just admire him—they wanted to reflect those values in their own lives and show the rest of the world that it was possible to live in harmony.'

'And did he achieve that?'

His answering smile was gentle. 'I like to think he came close. There will always be wars and dissension the world over, but he didn't let that stop him from trying to be a peacemaker. I am far more argumentative, and I give way to anger much more easily than he did.'

'But I bet he saw qualities in you that he was immensely proud of and loved you nonetheless?'

Chuckling, Zafir leant forward and affectionately kissed her on the mouth. 'You must know by now that I've always been impressed by you, Darcy. Not just for your beauty and grace, but for who you *are*... From the moment I met you, when you became my assistant, throughout our affair, and even after I stupidly told you to go, I always knew I would never find another woman like you.'

'You shouldn't tell me things like that... It might give me a big head, thinking that I could turn the head of a *king*.'

'What? You mean the knowledge could possibly lead you to becoming *unbearable*?'

'Not a chance, Zafir. I only want you to feel that you've made the right choice in choosing me to be your wife. If I know that, then I'll be as docile and sweet as you could wish.'

'Never!' He laughed. 'If you became like that then you wouldn't be the feisty and sexy woman I fell for.'

Her expression caught somewhere between hope and delight, she flung her slim arms round his neck and rained down avid kisses on his face.

'I'm glad that you like me just as I am and don't want me to change. In turn, I want *you* to know that I absolutely adore you and our son. If I can live with both of you for as long as for ever, then I'll think my-self blessed beyond measure.'

'I echo that statement entirely, My Queen. Now, do you think we might slip back to our suite for a while? Sami is probably quite happy to spend some extra time with his grandmother, and we won't even be missed.'

'Did anyone ever tell you that you're a very *bad* influence?'

She squealed when he lifted her high into his arms for answer, and unhesitatingly carried her across to the mosaic walkway that led to his rooms.

On the way his guards caught sight of the couple, and whispered what she hoped was something com-plimentary, even envious, beneath their breath.

She smiled like a cat that had got the cream…

CHAPTER ELEVEN

'Mummy, are you smiling because Daddy makes you happy?'

In the large stylish chamber where Zafir had allocated her a beautiful desk to write letters and answer correspondence, Darcy sighed contentedly and reached down to her small son to lift him onto her lap. He was a warm bundle of flesh, bone and sheer deliciousness, she thought affectionately as she pressed her lips to the back of his neck.

She loved him beyond distraction.

'Yes, your daddy makes me happy,' she told him, 'and so do you. I adore both of you, more than words can say. But there will always be a very special place in my heart just for you, Sami.'

The curly-headed little boy grinned, showing his teeth. 'I like it when you talk to me like that...all lovey-dovey.'

Ruffling his hair, she laughed. 'You're just a great big softie.'

'What's a ring-bearer, Mum? That's what I'm going to be at the wedding, isn't it?'

The mention of the wedding was guaranteed to

give Darcy the jitters. She could hardly believe that the big day had nearly dawned.

For the past few days preparations involving her wedding dress, correct royal etiquette, trying on the exquisite jewellery that was traditionally passed on to the Sheikh's bride, as well as perusing the guest list had consumed her. Whilst she didn't know most of the invitees, her mother-in-law had assured her that she'd invited not only the most prominent people, but many ordinary citizens as well and that there was nothing for her to worry about. She would be there to steer her right.

That was easy for *her* to say. The glamorous Dowager Queen came from a highly privileged world, whilst her new daughter-in-law *didn't*. But Darcy was determined to keep her feet firmly on the ground and take things in her stride.

As for Zafir—he had been just as preoccupied. Probably even more so. What with the preparations for the wedding, and visiting as many of the disadvantaged and sick as he was able to in the lead-up to making his official vows, he was also keeping himself apprised of what was going on with his businesses in London and New York.

When Darcy had asked if she could help, by going with him on his visits, he'd told her that it was traditional that the new bride shouldn't be seen by the public until the wedding. Frustrated, she was consoled by the fact that tomorrow night would be their official wedding night, and their guests could hardly complain if the bride and groom absented themselves early to go to their rooms.

'A ring-bearer is the person who carries the wedding rings for the bride and groom. We call them page boys in England, but I think that ring-bearer sounds magical. It's like a name out of one of those fantasy stories you so love. In any case, I think you'll look fabulous in your new clothes.'

'You *would* say that, Mum.'

'Your dad would say that too...and Nannaa Soraya and Nanny Patricia.'

Satisfied, if a little embarrassed by all the attention he was suddenly receiving, Sami jumped off his mother's lap and ran to the door. He called out, 'I'm going to play football with Rashid. I'll be in the big garden.'

Giving her son a reluctant wave, she called back, 'Well, be good...and also be *careful*. I don't want you hurting yourself before the wedding.'

'I will!' he yelled.

'Was it your idea or your mother's to have this little soirée before the wedding?'

Giving the exquisite blonde he'd already married back in London a knowingly indulgent smile, Sheikh Zafir el-Kalil of Zachariah found himself still warring with the possessive urge to steal her away and take her somewhere where they could be alone.

Gently steering her into a closeted corner of the vast communal living room that already teemed with people, he dropped his hand to her slender waist in the charming lapis lazuli dress she wore, noting that it perfectly highlighted the shade of her vivid blue eyes.

'It was my mother's idea and I didn't want to deny her. She's waited a long time for me to get married *and* to sire an heir. Celebrating her heart's desire is the least I could do, and in my opinion a small party won't hurt.'

'And you don't mind all the other things you have to do besides be the star attraction at the wedding?'

'I won't be that on my own. Everyone wants to see *you* too, Darcy.' The black eyes strayed meaningfully over her features. 'But I don't deny it's my role to be seen and ensure that my people are happy.'

She grimaced a little. 'That must be quite a hard expectation to fulfil. I meant to make sure that everyone else's needs are met and yet still have time to enjoy the celebrations yourself?'

'My father taught me from a young age that my position was above all a privilege, and that first and foremost I should help to take care of our people not just by visiting those in difficulty when I could, but by demonstrating good values and morals. He told me that would be a big part of my remit as the country's royal heir, then their King.'

'You're looking very serious all of a sudden. Do you think you've been trying to do a bit too much?'

For answer, Zafir pulled Darcy into his arms, right then uncaring as to who might be looking at them, and reassured that no one would interrupt.

'It's a serious undertaking, being the country's Royal Head of State, but it definitely has its compensations.'

Helpless to do anything else but happily agree, she tenderly laid her hand against his cheek. 'Oh...? And what are those?'

'Wait until we're alone in our rooms and I'll show you.'

* * *

It had been a long day and a tiring one, threaded through with a whole gamut of emotions and perhaps a bit too much champagne... God only knew how she would fare tomorrow, Darcy thought as a perfectly attired manservant suddenly appeared and handed Zafir a note.

They were standing together in one of the more intimate gardens, where all kinds of exotic aromas pervaded the air. As for their well-heeled guests—the majority of them had already left to make their journeys home.

Before she went to bed, Darcy decided, she would look in on Sami and give him a kiss, even though he was likely fast asleep. But right now the dazzlingly bright full moon was working its magic and it tempted her to stay a little longer and contemplate her extraordinary good fortune.

'Thank you, Amir. I will see to it.'

As he turned his attention back to his wife it was clear that Zafir was perturbed by the note's contents.

Tucking a loose coil of buttery gold hair behind her ear, Darcy frowned. 'Is it anything to be concerned about...the note, I mean?'

Smoothly depositing the missive into an inside pocket, Zafir patted down his silken robes. 'It's just an old friend—a business associate, really. He only wants to say a quick hello and wish me well. Go back to our rooms and I'll join you there.'

His matter-of-fact tone was obviously meant to reassure her. But, no longer as enchanted by the silvery orb that spectacularly lit up the inky dark sky, Darcy was disappointed that she couldn't wax lyrical about it with her husband.

Her spirits somewhat dampened, she automatically turned her cheek towards him to accept his kiss and answered, 'Okay. I'll see you later, then.'

Evidently reluctant to leave, he remarked, 'It will be *sooner* rather than later, my angel. That's a promise.'

Yet her heart was filled with unease as she watched him walk away and very soon lost sight of him. His tall, broad-shouldered figure had quickly been swallowed up by the darkening shadows. Hugging her arms over her chest, she made herself stay a bit longer, to breathe in the scented air and contemplate what their future together might bring.

Since he'd received that note, she suddenly found she didn't feel so optimistic any more... He'd been worryingly reticent to talk to her about it.

Breaking into her reflections, the sound of a sultry female voice reached her. It might have come from anywhere. Beyond the flickering lanterns that had guided their way along with the brightness of the moon it was still dark. But it was what the woman was saying that rendered Darcy rigid as a statue.

'I *had* to see you alone, Zafir. I wanted to tell you that I made the most terrible mistake when I agreed to let you go. Our relationship meant so much more to me than I let on. It was never just a convenient arrangement, as you thought. I've been in love with you all along, my darling.'

'*What?*'

'Yes, I'm in love with you...can't you tell? You know I would never have come here if I didn't think there was a chance you might feel the same way too. Can anything be done to bring this marriage of yours to a quick end, so that we can be together as our families always hoped we would?'

The man's reply was low and gruff. 'You stun me, Farrida. You say that you *love* me?'

Darcy had no desire to wait and hear any more. It was as though she were a fragile sheaf of corn being pummelled by the wind.

Still limping, she fled as fast as she was able, not knowing where she was heading. Her only certainty was that she had to get away. The urge to escape, to move as quickly as she could away from the scene and gather her wits, had never been so strong...

Breathless and tired, she finally stopped trying to run. Aside from the nagging ache in her ankle, it would be easy to get lost in the vast acreage of the gardens. Even in her haste to get away she'd had the sense to note a couple of helpful landmarks. But it was only when she dropped to the ground behind some high hedges to rest that the full impact of what she'd just heard sank in...

Had Zafir ever really cared for her at all? Had he fooled her into thinking he did just because he wanted to be close to his son? Did he plan to take him away from her?

Darcy didn't realise she was crying until the tears started to gather under her chin and trickle down onto her gown. If this was heartbreak then she knew it intimately. She knew despair too, but she wouldn't let either of them break her, she decided. She might not have the wealth and powerful connections of Farrida, and she had not been Zafir's childhood friend, but she wouldn't give up her child—no matter what they threatened or did. She would rise up and fight for what was right, despite it all.

Somehow, amidst the torrent of violent emotion that deluged her, a sense of calmness and purpose found its way into her blood. The impulse was stronger than she thought, and it quelled the urge to escape. It was hard to believe that she'd started to think clearly again, but she had.

Could a man *really* pretend to be so enamoured of her and treat her as if she was the brightest star in his galaxy if he was in love with someone else? It didn't seem feasible. No, whatever happened she would fight for her man—he was the love of her life and the father of her child.

Farrida might have decided at the eleventh hour that she loved Zafir, but one thing was for sure: Darcy loved him more...

Being summoned by Farrida to his private gardens in order to hear her tell him that she'd always loved him and then demand that he should bring his marriage with Darcy to an end so that they could be together was more than a bolt out of the blue—it was the epitome of the woman's arrogance!

All it had done was remind Zafir of how spoilt she was. She couldn't bear not to have anything she wanted handed to her on a plate just because she *wanted* it...

Zafir decided that he'd had a lucky escape.

Having put her in the picture and told her that meeting Darcy was the best thing that had ever happened to him, and that she was already his wife, he had almost felt sorry for the woman when she'd burst into tears, sobbing that he'd betrayed her, and then hurried off in search of her driver to take her home.

The unfortunate episode had made him even more anxious to return to wife. She'd wanted to share her charming reflections with him in the moonlight and he'd abandoned her to talk to Farrida. Now all he wanted to do was go to her and take her in his arms again...

When he returned to their rooms to find that Darcy wasn't there he was immediately concerned. His mother and Sami had long gone to bed, so he presumed she wasn't with them. Straight away he checked with some of his retainers and asked if they'd seen her. When they answered that they hadn't, Zafir really started to worry. At last, when one of the attendants clearing away after the party said that he'd seen her hurrying off down a path that forked into two separate gardens, his heart hammered hard.

What on earth was she playing at?

Not even pausing to take someone with him to help search, he headed off into the dim undergrowth, confident that he knew the grounds intimately enough to search alone.

But after a good hour had passed, with neither sight nor sound of her, he knew he should return and have the palace thoroughly searched. But first he would go back to their rooms and hope against hope that Darcy had somehow found her way back...

Relieved to have found her way out of the gardens, Darcy returned to their luxurious suite, undressed and donned a powder blue silk nightgown and robe. Then, in the dim lighting that discreetly lit the hallway, she carefully made her way to her son's bedroom.

Initially she'd given her mum the option of sharing her grandson's room when she'd arrived for the wedding, but the older woman had declined because Sami had told her that he wanted to be a big boy now and not a baby.

Zafir had allocated his mother-in-law a sumptuous suite down the hall, full of every luxury and feminine requirement she could wish for, and had stated that he was pleased to know his son wanted his own space—it meant that he was growing up.

The comment hadn't exactly reassured Darcy... She didn't want her little boy to grow up too soon.

Finding Sami asleep in a bed that was one size up from a traditional single, she saw that he had kicked off the sumptuous counterpane and was sleeping on his front with his arms spread over the pillow. His hair was a tangle of curls and he might easily be mistaken for a girl. But she knew that when he sat up, the curls would fall naturally into place, and that the firm cleft in his chin and his already decisive jaw—so like his father's—would definitely declare him to be a boy.

Knowing her worries would feel eased if she was at his side she removed her robe and carefully sat down on the bed. Pulling back the covers, she snuggled up next to him. It was a comfort just to smell his scent and give him a cuddle.

In a few short seconds Darcy sensed her eyes start to drift closed. Another moment passed and sleep reached out to embrace her.

Just before she succumbed, a hauntingly handsome face floated into her mind. It was Zafir's.

'Why did you have to go to her?' She moaned softly. 'Aren't I enough for you?'

Remembering her resolve, she determinedly pushed away the idea of his falling for the sultry Farrida's declaration of love and reminded herself of all the things *she* had that the other woman didn't...especially the beautiful son that their loving had made...

Zafir was shocked and distressed when he found that Darcy still hadn't returned to their rooms. Sweat was trickling freely down his neck under the heavy fall of his hair. Even the long loose tunic he wore beneath his robe felt oppressive.

'She should be in bed,' he said out loud, his heart hammering wildly beneath his ribs. 'Where *is* she?'

Adding to his irritation, he was still furious that his ex-fiancée had taken it upon herself to put in an appearance on the night before his wedding. He'd told her never to try and see him again—at least not in private—and that she categorically would not be welcome.

There was only *one* woman who mattered to him above all others and that was Darcy. He would shout out his feelings about her from the rooftops if he had to, and tell *everyone*...

As if a light had suddenly dawned, Zafir knew *exactly* where to find his wife.

Shrugging off his robes, he dressed in jeans and a tee shirt and headed down the corridor to his son's room. Before he entered he shoved his hands through his hair and briefly took stock of events. Then he gently opened the door.

Even at a distance he saw the golden sheen of

Darcy's hair as it spilled down over her shoulder. He also saw Sami's abundant curls. It still gave him a thrill to know that this beautiful little boy was his, and would one day reign over this kingdom as his ancestors had proudly done before him.

Crossing the room to the bed, he bent over his wife to gently wake her. Her skin radiated warmth and softness even before he touched it, and it made him want to slip in beside her. But, knowing he wouldn't be satisfied with that alone, he whispered her name against her ear, then brushed his lips against her cheek.

'Darcy? Where did you get to? Let me take you back to our bed. I didn't mean to be away from you for so long.'

Her big blue eyes opened and stared. 'You're back? Don't worry about helping me to our bed. I'm happy to stay right where I am…really, I am.'

'But I'm *not*. I'm taking you back where you belong.'

Giving her little chance to refuse, Zafir reached towards her, peeled back the covers and lifted her out of the bed to hold her firmly against his chest. Then he stooped down to rearrange the covers more securely round Sami.

Murmuring, 'Let's go,' he turned and carried her out of the room.

Carefully kicking the door shut with the heel of his boot, he wordlessly transported his precious cargo to their bedroom. When they got there, unable to help himself, he let his hands linger as he carefully laid her down on the bed.

'Why didn't you wait for me here? I came back to

find you gone. A member of my staff told me he saw you hurrying out to one of the gardens. What happened? Why did you run away?'

Sitting up, Darcy leant back against the plethora of plumped-up silk pillows and folded her arms. It didn't take a genius to work out that she was cross.

'I didn't wait for you in our rooms because I knew you were talking to your ex-fiancée.'

The colour drained from Zafir's face and his answering sigh was audible.

'You heard us? I didn't seek her out, if that's what you think. She showed up unannounced and said she wanted to talk to me. I didn't even know she was here until I received her note.'

Darcy sucked in her cheeks 'So what kind of *business* did you do together? That's what you said, wasn't it? That it was from a business associate? Or need I ask?'

Impatient and rattled, he dropped down beside her on the bed. 'We didn't do *any* business together. I broke off my engagement with her when we were in London. You *know* that. She clearly didn't take it well, and when she knew I was back in Zachariah she followed me here. Am I going to be punished by you for the rest of my life for having had a brief engagement to her?'

'She told you that she loved you.'

'You heard her say that?'

Darcy nodded. 'I did.'

'And did you hear me tell her that I was stunned by the confession? I never showed her by word or deed at any point that I reciprocated the feeling, and I certainly wasn't going to indulge her little fantasy and call off our wedding. The truth is that even if I didn't know already she has such an unattractive trait, this has only served to prove to me again how arrogant she is.'

'She sounded upset.'

'Forget about Farrida. It's you that means everything to me—you and *only* you. I went crazy when I thought you might have run away.'

The expression on his face truly mirrored his fear and despair, and it echoed Darcy's feelings when he'd told her to go...that he never wanted to see her again. He'd been torn then between loyalty to his brother and an unknown future with a woman who, although she was his lover, had not yet taught him that she would never lie to him.

It had been a testing time for them both. She certainly didn't want to hold any more blame in her heart towards him.

'Why would I run away from you, Zafir? My home is here, with you and Sami. I'd be a fool to run away from my heart's desire. Besides...I'm tired of running. No matter what transpires, I intend to be here for you, through the dark times as well as the good. Isn't that what we promised each other when we got married?'

Zafir was visibly moved by her heartfelt words. 'I hardly feel worthy of receiving such devotion...not when I've visited so much sorrow on you,' he confessed. 'I wish I could rewrite the past and make everything as it was when we first met. Life seemed so full of promise then. Yet now, having declared how you feel about me, you need never fear I will ever take it for granted. Knowing you has changed everything for me. It was only when we first made love that I realised my heart wasn't impenetrable after all.'

Without hesitation, Darcy gently wrapped her arms round his strongly corded neck and smiled into the ebony eyes that she loved beyond measuring. Tenderly, she asked, 'Are you saying that I broke down those impenetrable walls that very first time?'

'What do *you* think?'

'I think that love is like a miracle. And that no matter what happens it can't ever entertain the idea of punishment. But I've learned that it can and *does* involve forgiveness. We've both been hurt, but we've been given the chance to right the wrongs of the past. We shouldn't throw it away. Instead we should bravely face our future together and live the very best life we can. Don't you agree?'

'And you can really find it in your heart to forgive me?'

'Unreservedly I can—and *do*.'

Before he bent his head to kiss her Zafir honestly thought himself blessed amongst men to be given this second chance at happiness when he'd been so close to ruining everything. But his wife was a forgiving soul unlike any other, and when their lips met the blood in his veins throbbed like the most wondrous life-giving elixir, making him willing to live any number of lifetimes—rich or poor—if he could live them with her by his side as his wife and soul-mate...

CHAPTER TWELVE

THE DAY OF the wedding dawned especially fine and clear and the expectant buzz in the air was almost tangible. Her mother-in-law told her that all the omens were good ones, and Darcy smiled and hugged her. Throughout her dressing for the ceremony, in the silk and voile gown and delicately beautiful headdress that had been made for her, the excitement and pleasure she experienced was beyond anything remotely imaginable...

The folk around her seemed to feel the magic too. Smiles and good wishes abounded, and for the first time in her life she sensed that she could rest in the knowledge that she was honestly loved and admired. And it was all because of the incredibly handsome and generous-hearted Sheikh she had already married.

Even on this, their royal wedding day, Zafir was still accepting the kind wishes and prayers of those in the kingdom less fortunate than others, and the palace doors had been opened not just to the well-heeled guests who had travelled from afar but to the local population, who wanted to pay their respects and who undoubtedly thought themselves blessed under his rule.

When it came to the wedding itself the bride's vivid blue eyes moistened at the beauty of the ceremony, and at the reverent and uplifting sacred text that was spoken over them. When she looked at her groom—resplendent in his magnificent robes on a day that meant so much to both of them—and intoned the words that told the world she was unreservedly becoming his wife and helpmeet, she meant it with all her heart.

Then came the moment when Zafir declared that he would be her husband, father of her children, soulmate and ever-present consolation, and she sucked in her breath when she saw that his silken ebony eyes were damp with tears.

At the closing instruction from the celebrant that he could now kiss his bride Darcy walked into his arms and met his kiss as though experiencing the touch of his lips for the very first time. As for her husband—he was in no hurry to shorten the gesture. He deliberately took his time, and the crowd around them gave a cheer that raised the rafters.

The feeling of his mouth against hers was more wondrous than ever, and she couldn't help but find herself excitedly speculating as to how many more children they would have together. They would be the children of a wonderful dynasty. And their darling little brother Sami had already cemented their parents' undying love for each other by helping to bring them back together when they had believed all was lost...

It was after midnight when they left to travel to the secret location that Zafir had arranged for their wedding night.

Darcy had been unbelievably fêted and spoiled, before *and* after the magnificent ceremony, and still the surprises showed no sign of relenting. But when they arrived at their destination, after travelling there on horseback—on a pure black stallion that Zafir owned, she in front and he behind, holding the reins—she was enchanted by the magical sight that met her eyes. The generously-sized Bedouin tent that nestled under the stars between palm trees and golden desert sands took her breath away.

'Am I dreaming?' she murmured as Zafir tenderly helped her down from the saddle, his dark eyes glinting like the most desired jewels in the kingdom.

'If you are, then I thank Allah I'm in the same dream.' He smiled.

The tent's interior brought even more enchantment. With its saffron-coloured satin walls, gold lanterns and beaded chandeliers, it was straight out of a fairytale. The scent of agar along with the alluring aroma of seductive herbs and spices hung in the air, and as Darcy breathed in the atmosphere her gaze strayed helplessly to the vast canopied bed in front of them. It was draped with gold damask and turquoise and arrayed with matching pillows, and never had a bed looked more inviting…

As Zafir moved to stand behind her, his big hands resting on her shoulders, she automatically leant back against his chest and sensed herself melt.

'Are we…? Should we?'

'Get into bed?' he finished, his voice smokier and more seductive than she'd ever heard it before. 'Of course.'

He carried her there, planting hot kisses on the side of her face and neck as he went. Even as she tried to

kiss him back he dropped her unceremoniously onto
the bed, peeled off his boots and lay down beside her.
He was both heavy and strong, and she revelled in the
realisation that he was about to make her his again.

The urgency she was feeling made her throw cau-
tion to the wind. But even as Darcy tore at his clothes
Zafir matched her by stripping her of hers, and in a
few short moments he had plunged inside her, fill-
ing her with his heat and silken hardness like never
before, his bunched biceps helping to support him,
his long hair brushing tantalisingly against her skin.

'Look at me...' he breathed, and there was a note
of command in his voice as his mesmerising gaze
hungrily possessed her.

His body and mind were in total tandem, leaving
her in no doubt that he wanted her above all others—
not just for now, but for ever...

It was then that he started to move inside her more
slowly, urging her to wrap her legs round his torso,
and the undeniable sense that he was taking her close
to the edge before she tumbled headlong over the
precipice gripped her wantonly.

When the moment of surrender finally came Darcy
was hypnotised by the depth of feeling and emotion
that deluged her. As her hips bucked against his her
eyes were drowned in tears.

'I love you...' she breathed. 'I've *always* loved
you.'

In answer, he kissed her hard, and his body started
to move more urgently. When he'd joined her at the
other side of the precipice he dropped his head onto
her chest until he could breathe more evenly again.

When he could, he lifted himself up and smiled deeply into her eyes.

'I have always loved you too, My Queen. How could you even imagine I could love anyone else *but* you?'

'I've waited long enough for you to tell me!' she teased.

Zafir sighed and gently smoothed back her hair. 'My love for you has always been there in my eyes for you to see… But perhaps I should have been brave enough to tell you in words sooner rather than just show you how I felt?'

'You can tell me and show me as often as you like now that your secret is out.'

Darcy gave him a nudge and he accommodatingly rolled over onto his side. She quickly laid her arm over his chest and snuggled close.

'If I ever make the mistake of not telling you enough how much I love you I want you to remind me…frequently and *often*. Will you do that for me, my angel?'

'Yes, My King. That's the one thing I can honestly guarantee.'

EPILOGUE

One year later...

STILL DRESSED IN her simple white cotton nightgown,
with the matching robe untied and her golden hair
freely spilling down over her shoulders, she went
barefoot in a joyful skipping motion along the myr-
iad marble corridors in search of her husband.

He hadn't been back long from his business trip
to the States, and because he'd returned in the early
hours Darcy hadn't yet had the chance to speak to
him. Unbelievably she'd slept through his arrival and,
unselfishly, Zafir had let her sleep on undisturbed.
But as soon as she'd opened her eyes she'd remembered that he was chairing an important meeting in
the opulent stateroom with his board members early
this morning, and decided she wouldn't let any more
time go by without seeing him.

To do so would be akin to being deprived of the
capacity to breathe...

Meeting or no meeting—she would go to him and
let him know in no uncertain terms just how much
she had missed him.

A smartly dressed manservant in royal livery was

guarding the double doors of the boardroom. When she told him that she wanted to speak to her husband the Sheikh, Darcy was surprised to be confronted by Rashid instead. The smile on his generous round face was warmly welcoming, as if Darcy were a trusted member of *his* family too, but she couldn't help but be disappointed that he wasn't Zafir.

Her bones *ached* to hold him. Two weeks was a long time to be apart from the man she loved.

'His Highness told me he wasn't to be disturbed, your Highness. It is an important meeting, but it should come to an end in about an hour. Perhaps you would like to return to your rooms and dress before you meet with him?'

He lifted a kindly eyebrow at Darcy's semi-dressed state, in her nightgown and peignoir, as if he were a fond father who sought to remind her of the correct etiquette...

'I can arrange for a cup of tea and some crumpets to be made for you and have them taken out to the terrace, if you'd like?'

Disappointed at having her wishes diverted, the newest member of the royal family suddenly realised how inappropriate her clothing was. Reaching for the tie belt of her peignoir, Darcy pulled it tight and protectively folded her arms across her chest. Then she blew out an impatient breath and a long buttery ringlet drifted down onto her brow. She shoved it away.

'I know you mean well, Rashid, but food and drink is the *last* thing I can think about right now. If you knew how desperate I was to see my husband you would surely grant me a few short minutes with him…I promise I won't keep him much longer than that.'

Darcy detected the exact moment when the man's expression softened helplessly.

'You could persuade a rose to grow in the most barren part of the desert with a look like that, Your Highness,' he commented. 'Very well—I will see what I can do'

'Thank you. You're a treasure.'

Impatiently heading towards the closed doors of the stateroom, leaving behind his curious board members at the grand polished table, Zafir sensed his heartbeat accelerate uncomfortably. Rashid had told him that Her Highness needed to see him urgently, and that he presumed it must be important because she wasn't dressed yet.

Frowning, he immediately thought something must be wrong.

When he flung the doors wide and saw Darcy, pacing up and down, looking utterly adorable and sexy in a nightdress and peignoir that were almost sheer and that clung to her curves like the personification of temptation itself his heart raced even harder.

What was the woman trying to do to him? Surely she knew by now that two weeks without intimacy… hell, even *one night*—tested him to the very limits of his endurance? The only reason he hadn't immediately pulled her into his arms and made love to her last night, on his arrival back home, was that she'd looked so peaceful sleeping.

More importantly, she needed all the rest she could

get right now, due to her condition. Zafir didn't want her to endanger the new baby...

When he spoke, his tone was more admonishing than he'd intended it to be. 'Darcy. What do you mean by parading in front of my retainers like that and putting them in an impossibly compromising position?'

'What are you talking about?'

Moving in closer and catching her firmly by the arms, he swept his simmering black eyes over her figure in a mixture of anger and frustration. 'Have you *no* sense of propriety, appearing like that in front of my men? Why didn't you think to dress properly first?'

'Why didn't I think to...to dress *properly* first?' she echoed.

Her teeth momentarily clamped down on her plump lower lip. In fact she looked as if she might even cry...

'I didn't think because I was in a hurry to see you. I didn't think about much else beyond that. Now I wish I'd been more—more *sensible*. God forbid if I've offended you.'

Wrenching one arm free from his grip, she looked as if she intended to get as far away from him as possible.

As if a rock had been dropped on his head from a great height Zafir flinched, then hauled her urgently into his arms.

'I merely wanted to bring it to your attention that you open yourself to all kinds of unhelpful speculation, appearing like that,' he breathed.

Somehow he found the smile that he'd wanted to greet her with.

'You're far too beautiful for any man to be confronted with first thing in the morning...and the last thing I want is for my servants to be lusting after you.'

The frown between Darcy's brows immediately disappeared, and he urged her even closer to his chest. Her scent was intoxicating...more intoxicating than honeysuckle-drenched air after a rainstorm. Zafir was already having trouble retaining his equilibrium.

'I want to kiss you. I want to kiss you properly and thoroughly. But I dare not do so right now. My board members will be alarmed if I don't return soon. Have you any idea just how much I've missed you?' He ran his hands gently down over her belly. 'You and the beautiful bump that will tell the world you're having my child.'

'*Second* child, don't you mean?'

'I've been wondering if this time it will be a girl...'

His remark clearly delighted her, and his wife dimpled. 'That's what I wanted to tell you. The doctor who'll be looking after me at the hospital rang to ask if I wanted to know the baby's sex.'

Zafir couldn't deny that he'd been delighted when his wife had agreed to have the baby born in Zachariah. It was the icing on the cake after all they'd been through.

He couldn't resist stealing a kiss from the side of her delectable mouth. Any more than that and he would be well and truly lost—certainly not fit to make any decisions at the board meeting.

'And what did you tell him?'

'I told him that it had to be a joint decision made with my husband.'

'I would not protest if you wanted to know.'

'I know that.'

Now it was her turn to steal a kiss. And as soon as her lips touched his Zafir groaned. His whole body irresistibly became more alive under her attentions.

'But would *you* like to find out…if it's a boy or a girl, I mean?'

Pausing to lift a swathe of coal-black hair from behind his nape, he smiled. 'My only preference is for the child to be healthy and for you to have a pregnancy that is as stress-free as possible.'

'Then I think it's probably best if we *don't* find out. We'll just have a lovely surprise when the baby is born.'

'I agree. Now, I want you to turn right around and return to our rooms. And if you decide to go back to bed and wait for my meeting to finish then I assure you that it will be finished sooner rather than later, my sweet.'

Another kiss was eagerly stolen. And, considering the circumstances, this time it lasted a little longer than perhaps was altogether wise…

* * * * *

*If you enjoyed this story, take a look at these
other great reads by Maggie Cox...*
REQUIRED TO WEAR THE TYCOON'S RING
A TASTE OF SIN
Available now!

And why not explore these other
SECRET HEIRS OF BILLIONAIRES
themed stories?
THE DESERT KING'S SECRET HEIR
by Annie West
DEMETRIOU DEMANDS HIS CHILD
by Kate Hewitt
THE SECRET TO MARRYING MARCHESI
by Amanda Cinelli
Available now!

MILLS & BOON®

EXCLUSIVE EXTRACT

Raul Di Savo desires more than Lydia Hayward's
body—his seduction will stop his rival buying her!
Raul's expert touch awakens Lydia to irresistible
pleasure, but his game of revenge forces
Lydia to leave... until an unexpected
consequence binds them forever!

Read on for a sneak preview of
THE INNOCENT'S SECRET BABY

Somehow Lydia was back against the wall with Raul's
hands either side of her head.

She put her hands up to his chest and felt him solid
beneath her palms and she just felt him there a moment
and then looked up to his eyes.

His mouth moved in close and as it did she stared
right into his eyes.

She could feel heat hover between their mouths in a
slow tease before they first met.

Then they met.

And all that had been missing was suddenly there.

Yet, the gentle pressure his mouth exerted, though
blissful, caused a mire of sensations until the gentleness
of his kiss was no longer enough.

A slight inhale, a hitch in her breath and her lips
parted, just a little, and he slipped his tongue in.

The moan she made went straight to his groin.

At first taste she was his and he knew it for her hands

moved to the back of his head and he kissed her as hard back as her fingers demanded.

More so even.

His tongue was wicked and her fingers tightened in his thick hair and she could feel the wall cold and hard against her shoulders.

It was the middle of Rome just after six and even down a side street there was no real hiding from the crowds.

Lydia didn't care.

He slid one arm around her waist to move her body away from the wall and closer into his, so that her head could fall backwards.

If there was a bed, she would be on it.

If there was a room they would close the door.

Yet there wasn't and so he halted them, but only their lips.

Their bodies were heated and close and he looked her right in the eye. His mouth was wet from hers and his hair a little messed from her fingers.

Don't miss
THE INNOCENT'S SECRET BABY,
By Carol Marinelli

Available March 2017
www.millsandboon.co.uk

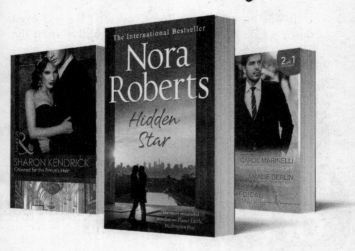